W9-BWL-569

MAD RIVER ROAD

Also by Joy Fielding

Puppet
Lost
Whispers and Lies
Grand Avenue
The First Time
Missing Pieces
Don't Cry Now
Tell Me No Secrets
See Jane Run
Good Intentions
The Deep End
Life Penalty
The Other Woman
Kiss Mommy Goodbye
Trance
The Transformation
The Best of Friends

MAD RIVER ROAD

JOY FIELDING

ATRIA BOOKS
New York London Toronto Sydney

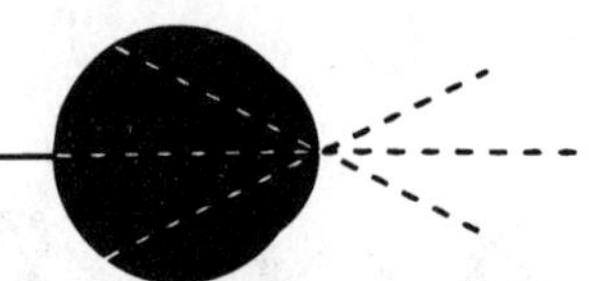

This Large Print Book carries the Seal of Approval of N.A.V.H.

ATRIA BOOKS
1230 Avenue of the Americas
New York, NY 10020

ISBN-13: 978-0-7432-8467-7
ISBN-10: 0-7432-8467-4

This Atria Books large-print hardcover edition February 2006

10 9 8 7 6 5 4 3 2 1

Manufactured in the United States of America

For information regarding special discounts for bulk purchases, please contact Simon & Schuster Special Sales at 1-800-456-6798 or business@simonandschuster.com

To Novella

ACKNOWLEDGMENTS

People always ask how I choose my titles. I answer that each book is different. Sometimes the title is the easiest part—it just pops into your head, and you construct a book around it. Example: **The Deep End.** Sometimes the title comes to you during the course of writing the novel. A phrase or an expression, sometimes just a word—it rises out of the book itself and demands to be placed front and center. Example: **See Jane Run.** Sometimes it's pure agony—I've finished the book and still don't have a clue what to call it. Example: **Don't Cry Now.** Sometimes it's a tough choice among a number of alternatives. Example: **Grand Avenue.** Happily, **Mad River Road** fell into the first category.

I was on a book tour—please don't ask which book—and my travels brought me to Ohio, specifically Cincinnati and Dayton. While there, I saw a sign indicating a street named Mad River Road, and I thought immediately, What a great title for a book! I filed it away in the back of my brain and hoped one day to be able to use it. Several years—and books—later, the idea appeared. I have to confess, I've never actually visited the real Mad River Road, and I have no idea whether the street and houses I constructed bear any resemblance to the real thing. I just loved the name. I hope you'll love the book and forgive me for the liberties I've taken.

I'd also like to acknowledge the following people for their continued help and support—Owen Laster, Larry Mirkin, Beverley Slopen, Emily Bestler, Sarah Branham, Jodi Lipper, Judith Curr, Louise Burke, Maya Mavjee, John Neale, Stephanie Gowan, Susanna Schell, Alicia Gordon, and all the other terrific people at the William Morris Agency, Atria Books in New York, and Doubleday, Canada. As well, I'd like to take a moment to thank my various publishers and translators around the world. I am so grateful for all your enthusiasm and hard work. A special thank-you to the team at Goldmann in Germany—Klaus, Giorg, Claudia, and Helga—for arranging that wonderful tour of Germany last fall, as well as a special hello to Veronika, whom I miss very much.

Heartfelt gratitude to Corinne Assayag, who designed and oversees my website. And to the many readers who e-mail me to tell me they love my books—and even the few who say they don't. While I'd love to make everybody happy every time out, it's impossible. Reading is such a personal, subjective thing. I can only aspire to do the best I can on each book and hopefully to improve a little as time goes on.

Thanks also to Carol Kripke for her insights into why certain people act the way they do. Such insights proved very helpful in creating several of the characters who spend time on Mad River Road.

A big hug to my gorgeous daughters, Shannon and Annie, who continue to be a source of inspiration and pride. And to my husband, Warren, who insists on doing all the driving—he claims he's more relaxed when he drives than when I do—on our trips back and forth to Florida each year. He serves as both chauffeur and tour guide on our trips up and down I-75, and I want to thank him publicly for his efforts, his good humor, and his stamina.

PROLOGUE

Three o'clock in the morning. His favorite time of day. The sky was dark, the streets deserted. Most people were asleep. Like the woman in the bedroom down the hall. He wondered if she was dreaming and smiled at the realization that her nightmare was just about to begin.

He laughed, careful not to make a sound. No point waking her up before he'd decided the best way to proceed. He imagined her stirring, sitting up in bed, and watching him approach, shaking her head in a familiar mixture of amusement and disdain. He could hear the scorn in that gravelly, low-pitched voice of hers. Just like you, she would say, to go off half-cocked, to rush into something without a clear plan.

Except he did have a plan, he thought, stretching his arms above his head and taking a moment to admire the leanness of his torso, the hardness of his biceps beneath his short-sleeved, black T-shirt. He'd always taken great pains with his appearance, and now, at thirty-two, he was in better shape than he'd ever been. Prison will do that for you, he thought, and laughed his silent laugh again.

He heard a sharp noise and looked toward the open window, saw a giant palm frond slapping against the top half of the pane. An escalating wind was whipping the delicate white sheers in several different directions at once, so that they looked more like streamers than curtains, and he interpreted their frenzied motion as a sign of support, as if they were cheering him on. The Weather Channel had promised a major downpour would hit the greater Miami area by dawn. Seventy percent chance of severe thunderstorms, the pretty blond announcer had warned, although what did she know? She just read whatever was on the cue cards in front of her, and those stupid forecasts were wrong at least half the time. Not that it made any difference. She'd be back tomorrow with more unreliable predictions. Nobody was ever held accountable. He cocked his gloved fingers into the shape of a gun, pulled an imaginary trigger.

Tonight someone would be.

His sneakered feet cut across the light hardwood floor of the living room in three quick strides, his hip knocking against the sharp corner of a tall wing chair he'd forgotten was there. He swore under his breath—a rush of colorful invectives he'd picked up from a former cell mate at Raiford—as he lowered the window to a close. The gentle hum of the air-conditioning unit immediately replaced the tortured howling of the wind. He'd made it inside just in time, thanks to an agreeable side window that had proved as easy to manipulate as he'd always suspected. She really should have installed a burglar alarm system by now. A woman alone. How many times had he told her how easy it would be for someone to jimmy that window open? Oh, well. Can't say I didn't warn you, he thought, remembering the times they'd sat sipping wine or, in his case, guzzling beer, at her dining room table. But even in those early days, when she was still being cautiously optimistic, she couldn't help but let him know that his presence in her home was more tolerated than welcomed. And when she looked at him, if she deigned to look at him at all, her nose would twitch, a slight, involuntary reflex, as if she'd just caught a whiff of something unpleasant.

As if she was in any position to look down that pretty little upturned nose at anyone, he thought now, his eyes growing comfortable with the darkness, so that he was able to trace the outlines of the small sectional sofa and glass coffee table that occupied the center of the room. You had to hand it to her—she'd done a nice job with the place. What was it everybody always said about her? She had flair. Yeah, that was it. Flair. If only she'd been able to cook worth a damn, he scoffed, remembering those awful vegetarian concoctions she'd tried to pass off as dinner. Hell, even prison food was better than that god-awful crap. No wonder she'd never been able to find herself a man.

Not that he didn't have his suspicions about that either.

He walked into the tiny dining area adjoining the living room, ran the palms of his hands across the tops of several of the high-backed, fabric-covered chairs grouped around the oval glass table. Lots of glass in this place, he noted with a smile, flexing his fingers inside his tight latex gloves. He wasn't about to leave behind any telltale prints.

Who said he was always going off half-cocked? Who said he didn't have a plan?

He glanced toward the kitchen on his right and thought of checking out the fridge, maybe even grabbing a beer, if she still kept any around. Probably didn't, now that he was no longer a regular visitor. He'd been the only one of their crowd who ever drank the stuff. The others clung stubbornly to their Chardonnay or Merlot, or whatever the hell garbage it was they insisted on drinking. It all tasted the same to him—vaguely vinegarish and metallic. It always gave him a headache. Or maybe it was the company that had given him the headaches. He shrugged, remembering the hooded looks they'd shot one another when they thought he wasn't looking. He's just a passing fancy, those looks said. Amusing in small doses. Full of facile charm. Grin and bear him. He won't be around long enough for it to matter.

Except he was.

And it did.

And now I'm back, he thought, a cruel smirk tugging at the corners of his full lips.

A wayward strand of long brown hair fell across his forehead and into his left eye. He pushed it impatiently aside, tucking it behind his ear, and headed down the narrow hallway toward the bedroom at the back of the tidy bungalow. He passed the closet-size room where she practiced her yoga and meditation, catching a whiff of leftover incense that emanated from the walls like a fresh coat of paint. His smirk widened. For someone who worked so hard to stay calm, she was surprisingly high-strung, always ready to argue some obscure point, to take offense where none was intended, to jump down his throat at the slightest provocation. Not that he hadn't enjoyed provoking her.

Her bedroom door was open, and from the hallway, he could make out the shape of her narrow hip beneath the thin white cotton blanket. He wondered if she was naked underneath that blanket, and what he might do if she was. Not that he was at all interested in her that way. She was a little too toned, a little too brittle for his tastes, as if, with the slightest degree of pressure, she might break apart in his hands. He liked his women softer, meatier, more vulnerable. He liked something you could grab onto, something you could dig your teeth into. Still, if she was naked . . .

She wasn't. He could see the blue-and-white cotton stripes of her pajama top as soon as he stepped inside the room. Wouldn't you just know she'd be wearing men's pajamas? he thought. Shouldn't be surprised. She'd always dressed more like a guy than a girl. **Woman,** he heard her correct as he approached the queen-size bed. Fit for a queen, he thought, staring down at her. Except that she didn't look so queenly now, curled into a semifetal position on her left side, her normally tanned skin pale with sleep, chin-length dark hair plastered across the side of her right cheek, and straying into her partially opened mouth.

If only she'd learned to keep that big mouth shut.

Maybe he'd be visiting someone else tonight.

Or maybe he wouldn't have had to visit anyone at all.

The last year might never have happened.

Except, of course, it had happened, he thought, clenching and unclenching his fists at his sides. And it had happened largely because old Gracie here couldn't keep her stupid thoughts and opinions to herself. She was the instigator, the agitator, the one who'd turned everyone against him. Everything that happened had been her fault. It was only fitting that tonight she be the one to make things right again.

He looked toward the window on the other side of the bedroom, saw the sliver of moon winking at him from between the slats of the white California shutters. Outside, the wind was painting the night with a surreal brush, combining disparate colors and surfaces; inside all was still and serene. He wondered for an instant whether he should leave without disturbing her. Probably he could find what he was looking for without having to wake her. Most likely the information he sought was secreted in one of the side drawers of the antique oak desk that was squeezed into the corner between the window and the dresser. Or maybe it was stored safely inside her laptop computer. Either way, he knew everything he wanted was within easy grasp. All he had to do was reach out and take it, then disappear into the night without anyone being the wiser.

But what fun would there be in that?

He slipped his right hand inside the pocket of his jeans, felt the hardness of the knife's handle against his fingers. For now the blade was tucked safely inside its wood casing. He'd release it when the time was right. But first, there was much to do. Might as well get this show on the road, he decided, lowering himself gingerly to the bed, his hip grazing hers as the mattress slumped to accommodate him. Instinctively, her body rotated slightly to the left, her head lolling toward him. "Hey, Gracie," he cooed, his voice as soft as fur. "Time to wake up, Gracie-girl."

A low groan escaped her throat, but she didn't move.

"Gracie," he said again, louder this time.

"Mmn," she mumbled, her eyes remaining stubbornly closed.

She knows I'm here, he thought. She's just playing with me. "Gracie," he barked.

Her eyes shot open.

And then everything seemed to happen at once. She was awake and screaming as she struggled to sit up, the horrible catlike wail assaulting his ears, then racing wildly around the room. Instinctively, his hand reached out to silence her, his fingers wrapping tightly around her neck, her screams turning to whimpers beneath the growing pressure on her larynx. She gasped for air as he lifted her effortlessly with one arm and pinned her to the wall behind the bed.

"Shut up," he ordered as her toes struggled to maintain contact with the bed, her hands scratching at his gloves in a fruitless effort to free herself from his stubborn grasp. "Are you going to shut up?"

Her eyes widened.

"What was that?"

He felt her trying to croak out a response, but all she could manage was a ruptured cry.

"I'll take that as a yes," he said, slowly releasing his grip, and watching her slide down the wall and back onto her pillow. He chuckled as she collapsed in a crumpled heap, struggling to gulp air back into her lungs. The top of her pajamas had ridden halfway up her back, and he could make out the individual vertebrae of her spine. It would be so easy to just snap that spine in two, he thought, savoring the image as he reached over to grab a handful of her hair, then yanking her head around so that she had no choice but to look at him. "Hello, Gracie," he said, watching for the disdainful twitch of her nose. "What's the matter? Did I wake you in the middle of a good dream?"

She said nothing, simply stared at him through eyes clouded with fear and disbelief.

"Surprised to see me, are you?"

Her eyes darted toward the bedroom door.

"I think I'd get that thought right out of my head," he said calmly. "Unless, of course, you want to make me really angry." He paused. "You remember what I'm like when I'm really angry. Don't you, Gracie?"

She lowered her eyes.

"Look at me." Again he tugged at her hair, so that her head was stretched back against the top of her spine and her Adam's apple pushed against her throat like a fist.

"What do you want?" Her voice emerged as a hoarse whisper.

His response was to pull even harder on her hair. "Did I say you could speak? Did I?"

She tried shaking her head, but his grip on her hair was too tight.

"I'll take that as a no." He let go of her hair and her head fell to her chest, as if she'd been guillotined. She was crying now, which surprised him. He hadn't expected tears. At least not yet. "So, how's everything been?" he asked, as if this was the most normal of questions. "You can answer," he said when she failed to respond.

"I don't know what you want me to say," she said after a long pause.

"I asked you how everything's been," he repeated. "You gotta know the answer to that one."

"Everything's been fine."

"Yeah? How so?"

"Please. I can't. . . ."

"Sure you can. It's called conversation, Gracie. It goes something like this: I say something and then you say something. If I ask you a question, you answer it. If you don't answer it to my satisfaction, well, then, I'm going to have to hurt you."

An involuntary cry escaped her throat.

"So, my first question to you was 'How's everything been?' and I believe your answer was a rather unimaginative 'Fine,' and then I said, 'How so?' And now, it's your turn." He lowered himself to the bed, leaned in toward her. "Dazzle me." She was staring at him, as if he'd taken complete leave of his senses. He'd seen that look many times before. It never failed to make him angry.

"I don't know what to say."

He detected a hint of defiance creeping into the corners of her voice but decided to ignore it for the time being. "Well, okay. Let's start with work. How's that going?"

"It's okay."

"Just okay? I thought you loved teaching."

"I'm on a sabbatical this year."

"A sabbatical? No kidding. Bet you think I don't know what that means."

"I never thought you were stupid, Ralph."

"No? Could have fooled me."

"What are you doing here?"

He smiled, then slapped her with such force

she fell back against her pillow. "Did I say it was your turn to ask questions? No, I don't believe I did. Sit up," he shouted as she buried her face in her hands. "Did you hear me? Don't make me tell you again, Gracie."

She pushed herself back into a sitting position, her fingers trembling in front of her now red cheek, any trace of her earlier defiance erased by the palm of his hand.

"Oh, and don't call me Ralph. Never did like that name. I changed it as soon as I got out of prison."

"They let you out?" she muttered, then winced and pulled back, as if trying to shield herself from further blows.

"Had to. Can't begin to tell you how many of my rights it turns out had been violated." He smiled, remembering. "My lawyer called what happened to me a real travesty of justice, and those judges he appealed to, well, they had no choice but to agree with him. Now, where were we? Oh, yeah. Your sabbatical. That's pretty boring. I guess I don't need to hear any more about that. What about your love life?"

She shook her head.

"What does that mean? You don't have a love life, or you don't want to tell me about it?"

"There's nothing to tell."

"You're not seeing anyone?"

"No."

"Now, why doesn't that surprise me?"

She said nothing, glanced toward the window.

"Storm's coming," he said. "Nobody else is though." He smiled the boyish grin he used to practice for hours in front of the mirror, the one that had always been guaranteed to get him into the pants of any girl he wanted. No matter how much they protested, they just couldn't resist that smile for very long. Of course Gracie had always been impervious to his charms. He'd smile at her, and she'd just stare right through him, as if he didn't even exist. "When was the last time you got laid, Gracie-girl?"

Immediately, her body tensed, recoiled.

"I mean, you're a reasonably attractive

woman. And you're young. Although you're not getting any younger, are you? How old are you anyway, Gracie-girl?"

"Thirty-three."

"Is that right? You're older than me? I never knew that." He shook his head in mock wonderment. "Bet there's lots about you I don't know." He reached over, unbuttoned the top button of her pajamas.

"Don't," she said without moving.

He opened the second button. "Don't what?" Not even a **please,** he thought. Typical.

"You don't want to do this."

"What's the matter, Gracie? Don't think I'm good enough for you?" He ripped off the remaining buttons with an almost effortless tug, then pulled her toward him by both halves of her collar. "You know what I think, Gracie? I think you don't think any man is good enough for you. I think I need to show you the error of your ways."

"No, look, this is crazy. You'll go back to jail. You don't want that. You've been given a second chance. You're a free man. Why would you want to jeopardize that?"

"I don't know. Maybe because you look so darn cute in those little dyke pajamas."

"Please. It's not too late. You can still walk out of here. . . ."

"Or maybe because if it hadn't been for you, I wouldn't have spent the last twelve months of my life in jail."

"You can't blame me for what happened. . . ."

"Why can't I?"

"Because I had nothing to do with it."

"Really? You didn't poison anyone's mind against me?"

"I didn't have to."

"No, you didn't **have** to. You just couldn't help yourself, could you? And look what happened. I lost everything. My job. My family. My freedom."

"And you had nothing to do with any of that," she stated bitterly, that pesky note of defiance once again creeping into her voice.

"Oh, I'm not saying I'm altogether blameless. I have a temper. I'll admit that. Sometimes it can get a little out of hand."

"You beat her, Ralph. Day in, day out. Every time I saw her, she was covered in fresh bruises."

"She was clumsy. I can't help that she was always walking into things."

Gracie shook her head.

"Where is she?"

"What?"

"As soon as I got out, I headed straight for home. And what do I find? A couple of queers have set up housekeeping in my apartment. That's what I find. And when I ask them what happened to the former tenant, they blink their mascara-covered eyes and tell me they have **absolutely** no idea. **Absolutely** no idea," he repeated, his voice lifting a full octave on the word. "That's how this skinny faggot says it, like he's the queen of fucking England. I almost popped him one right then and there." He tightened his grip on her collar with one hand, retrieved the knife from his pocket with the other, used his thumb to snap the switchblade into view. "Tell me where she is, Gracie."

She was struggling now, frantically kicking her legs, flailing at him with her arms. "I don't know where she is."

Once again his fingers dug into the flesh of her throat. "Tell me where she is or I swear I'll break your fucking neck."

"She left Miami right after you went to jail."

"Where'd she go?"

"I don't know. She left without telling anyone."

With that he knocked her on her back and straddled her, using the switchblade to cut the drawstring of her pajama bottoms even as his hand tightened its death grip on her neck. "You have to the count of three to tell me where she is. One . . . two . . ."

"Please. Don't do this."

"Three." He pressed the knife against her throat while tugging her pajama bottoms down over her hips.

"No. Please. I'll tell you. I'll tell you."

He smiled, loosened his grip just enough for her to catch her breath, raised the switchblade level with her eyes. "Where is she?"

"She went to California."

"California?"

"To be near her mother."

"No. She wouldn't do that. She knows it'd be the first place I'd think of."

"She moved there three months ago. She thought it was safe after all this time, and she wanted to get as far away from Florida as possible."

"I'm sure that's true." His hand moved to the zipper of his jeans. "Just like I'm sure you're lying."

"I'm not lying."

"Sure you are. And you're lousy at it." He lowered the knife to her cheek, drew a line in her flesh starting just beneath her eye, then dragged it toward her chin.

"No!" She was screaming now, thrashing from side to side, the blood flowing from the cut on her face onto the white of her pillowcase as he positioned himself between her legs. "I'll tell you the truth. I swear, I'll tell you the truth."

"Why would I believe anything you tell me now?"

"Because I can prove it to you."

"Yeah? How?"

"Because I have it written down."

"Where?"

"In my address book."

"Which is where exactly?"

"In my purse."

"I'm starting to lose patience here, Gracie."

"My purse is in the closet. If you let me up, I can get it for you."

"What do you say we get it together?" He pushed himself off her, zipping up his pants as he dragged her off the bed toward the closet. She clutched at the bottoms of her pajamas, trying to hold them up as he pulled open the closet door and quickly scanned its contents. A couple of colorful print blouses, half a dozen pairs of pants, a few expensive-looking jackets, at least ten pairs of shoes, several leather handbags. "Which one?" Already his hand was reaching toward the top shelf.

"The orange one."

With one swipe, he knocked the orange bag to the floor. "Open it." He pushed her to her knees on the white shag rug. Several drops of blood fell from her cheek, staining the orange leather of the purse as she struggled with the clasp. Another drop buried itself into the carpet's soft white pile. "Now hand me the goddamn address book."

Whimpering, Gracie did as she was told.

He opened the book, flipped through the pages until he found the name he was looking for. "So she didn't go to California after all," he said with a smile.

"Please," she cried softly. "You have what you came for."

"What kind of name is that for a street? Mad River Road," he pronounced with an exaggerated flourish.

"Please," she said again. "Just go."

"You want me to go? Is that what you said?"

She nodded.

"You want me to go so you can call your girlfriend as soon as I leave and warn her?"

Now she was shaking her head. "No, I wouldn't do that."

"Of course you wouldn't. Just like you

wouldn't call the police either, would you?"

"I won't call anyone. I swear."

"Really? Why is it I find that so hard to believe?"

"Please . . ."

"I don't think I have any choice here, Gracie. I mean, aside from the fact that I've been looking forward to killing you almost as much as I'm looking forward to killing her, I just don't see where I have any choice. Do you?" He smiled, pulled her roughly to her feet, brought the knife to her throat. "Say good night, Gracie."

"No!" she screamed, flailing at him with all her strength, her elbow catching him in the ribs and knocking the air from his lungs as she squirmed out of his grasp and raced for the hall. She was almost at the front door when the toe of her right foot caught on the bottom of her pajamas and sent her sprawling along the wood floor. Still she didn't stop. She scampered toward the door, screaming at the top of her lungs for someone to hear her and come to her rescue.

He watched in amusement as she reached for the doorknob, knowing he had plenty of time before she'd be able to pull herself to her feet. She certainly was tenacious, he thought, not without admiration. And pretty strong for such a skinny girl. Not to mention a loyal friend. Although when push came to shove, she'd given up her friend rather than submit to his admittedly less-than-romantic overtures. So maybe not such a good friend after all. No, she deserved her fate. She'd asked for it.

Although he had no intention of slitting her throat, he decided, returning the knife to his pocket and reaching for her just as her hand made contact with the brass knob of the front door. No, that would be way too messy, not to mention unnecessarily risky. There'd be blood everywhere, and then everyone would know immediately there'd been foul play. It wouldn't take too long before he was a suspect, especially once they realized he was out of jail, and put two and two together.

She was kicking and scratching at him now,

her green eyes begging him to stop, as once again his fingers tightened around her throat. She was screaming too, although he barely heard her, so caught up was he in the moment. He'd always loved using his hands. It was so personal, so concrete. There was something so satisfying about actually feeling the life slowly drain from someone's body.

He'd drawn a bit of a break with her being on a year's sabbatical. It might be days, even weeks, before anyone reported her missing. Although he knew he couldn't count on that. Gracie had lots of friends, and maybe she was supposed to be having lunch with one of them tomorrow. So he shouldn't get too cocky. The sooner he paid a visit to Mad River Road, the better.

"I thought we'd take a little drive up the coast," he told Gracie as her eyes grew so large they threatened to burst from her head. "I'll just drop you in some swamp along the way, let the alligators have their way with you."

Even after her arms went limp at her sides, even when he knew for certain she was dead, he held on to her neck for another full minute, silently counting off the seconds before opening his fingers one at a time, then smiling with satisfaction as her body collapsed at his feet. He walked into the bedroom and removed the bloody case from its pillow before remaking the bed, careful to leave the room as he had found it. He retrieved her purse from the floor where he had dropped it, pocketed a fistful of cash along with her credit card, and hunted around for her keys. "You don't mind if we use your car, do you?" he asked as he returned to the front door and lifted Gracie's still warm body into his arms. She looked up at him with cold, dead eyes. He smiled. "I'll take that as a no," he said.

CHAPTER ONE

Jamie Kellogg had a plan. The plan was relatively simple. It was to find the nearest respectable-looking bar, find a nice dark corner, where no one could see she'd been crying, and drown her sorrows in a couple of white wine spritzers. Not enough to make her drunk, of course, or even tipsy. She still had the long drive back to Stuart after all. She needed to have her wits about her. Nor could she risk being hungover in the morning. Not with Mrs. Starkey draped around her neck like an albatross.

She looked up and down the almost empty street. The chances were slim to none she'd find a decent bar in this area, although what better place for one than close to a hospital?

She looked back over her shoulder at the low-rise medical building known as Good Samaritan, and grimaced with the memory of the scene that had just played itself out in its intensive care unit. **Don't tell us you're surprised,** she could almost hear her mother and sister whisper in her ear, their voices in perfect harmony with each other, the way they always were, or at least, the way they always used to be, when her mother was alive.

"Of course I was surprised," Jamie muttered without moving her lips. "How was I to know?" A sudden gust of wind carried her question into the warm night air. At least it had finally stopped raining. For the last two days, the entire east coast of Florida had been pummeled by a series of spectacular storms, and some of the streets, including her own, had flooded over. Yes, I know that's what I get for insisting on an apartment overlooking the water, but it's just a little stream, for heaven's sake. It's not like I'm living in some overpriced oceanfront condo, like some younger siblings I could mention. She marched purposefully toward the small parking lot attached to the hospital, all the while continuing her silent dispute with her sister and recently deceased mother. Who would have thought the damn river would overflow?

That's just your problem, her mother began.

You don't think, her sister finished.

"And you don't give me enough credit," Jamie whispered, climbing behind the wheel of her old blue Thunderbird, the only thing she'd walked away with—driven away with?—when her divorce became final last year. She pulled out of the parking lot, hopeful she'd find a suitable establishment before she reached the turnpike.

Luckily her apartment was on the second floor of the three-story building, and so her unit had escaped the water damage suffered by the less fortunate tenants on the floor below. And speaking of water damage, she thought, checking her supposedly waterproof mascara in the car's rearview mirror, gratified to see that her tears had left no lasting trail. Indeed, big brown eyes stared back at her with something approaching serenity. Sun-streaked, shoulder-length hair framed a pretty, oval face that, amazingly, registered none of her inner turmoil. Whose big idea had it been to surprise him anyway? Hadn't he told her repeatedly that he hated surprises?

On impulse, she turned the car left on Dixie and headed south. Yes, it meant she'd have farther to drive later on, but downtown West Palm was only a few blocks away, and she'd undoubtedly find a more welcoming atmosphere in the bars along Clematis than those on Palm Beach Lakes Boulevard. And this way, if she wasn't immediately comfortable with one establishment, she could simply continue on down the street to the next. She wouldn't even have to get back in her car.

A bright red Mercedes was pulling out of a parking space on Datura, and Jamie quickly maneuvered the old blue Thunderbird into its place, careful to align it properly with the curb. She climbed out of the car and fished inside her purse for some change, feeding more than was required into the nearby meter. She wasn't planning on staying very long.

Jamie turned the corner onto Clematis as a young couple, their arms falling intimately across each other's shoulders, their hips seemingly welded together, walked past her, the girl's skinny gold stilettos clicking noisily along the pavement. They stopped at the corner to kiss before crossing against the light. Going home to happily ever after, Jamie thought, watching them disappear into the night. She shook her head. Instead of happily ever after, she'd settle for one night without lies.

The Watering Hole was surprisingly busy for a Wednesday night. Jamie checked her watch. Seven o'clock. Dinnertime. Early May. Why wouldn't the place be busy? It was a popular spot on a trendy street, and even though the so-called season was technically over, there were still plenty of snowbirds around, reluctant to pack their final bags and head north for the summer. Probably that's what she should do, she thought. Just pack up all her belongings and throw them into the backseat of her car. Get the hell out of town. Again.

Who would miss her? Not her family. Her mother had died eight weeks ago; her father and wife number four—unbelievably, he'd married two Joans, one Joanne, and now a former stewardess named Joanna, who at thirty-six was only seven years Jamie's senior—lived somewhere in New Jersey; her sister would be glad to see her go. ("You're worse than my kids," Cynthia said when Jamie had called yesterday to commiserate about all the rain.) Jamie's job as a claims adjuster at an insurance agency was boring and going nowhere, her boss an unpleasant woman who was always in a snit about something. Jamie would have quit months ago if it hadn't been for the fact it was Cynthia's husband, Todd, who'd recommended her for the job in the first place. **What's the matter with you? Can't you ever stick with anything?** she could hear her sister admonish. Followed by, **I should have known. You're such a flake.** To be further followed by, **When are you going to stop**

fooling around and start taking some responsibility? When are you going to go back to law school? To be hammered into the ground with, **Who quits school two credits shy of graduation to marry some jerk she barely knows?** And in case she was still breathing, **You know I'm only saying these things for your own good. It's high time you stepped up to the plate, took control of your life. Are you ever going to be ready?**

Jamie pulled out one of the stools at the long bar and signaled the bartender for a drink. Just wait till Cynthia hears about tonight's little fiasco, she thought, deciding to be bold—opting for a glass of the house Burgundy over her regular white wine spritzer. She peered through the dim light, swallowing the large room in a single glance. It was a long rectangular space that spilled out into a sidewalk patio. A series of banquettes ran along the interior west brick wall, the bar directly opposite, with dozens of tables occupying the center and front sections of the room. The tile floor amplified the noise of the crowd, a crowd that consisted largely of young women much like herself.

Where were all the men? Jamie wondered absently. Aside from a nearby table of forty-somethings who were so caught up in their discussion of redesigning the company logo that they hadn't even looked at her when she squeezed by in her tight, low-rise Juicy jeans and even tighter pink sweater, and a morose-looking man with an overgrown Tom Selleck mustache nursing a drink at the far end of the bar, there were none. At least not yet. Jamie checked her watch again, although only minutes had passed since her last peek. It was probably too early for the men to be out, she realized. Seven o'clock meant that if a man saw a woman he liked, he'd feel obliged to buy her dinner, instead of only a few drinks.

The bartender approached with her wine. "Enjoy."

Jamie took the glass from his hand. She gulped at the wine as if it were air.

"Tough day?"

"My boyfriend's in the hospital," Jamie said,

instantly feeling like a walking cliché. She was confiding in the bartender, for God's sake. How pitiful was that? Except maybe if she told the bartender her sad tale of woe, she wouldn't be tempted to tell her sister, and then maybe the bartender, who was tall and cute and had an interesting scar below his right eye, might ask her to wait around until he finished his shift, and they'd sit by the fountain at the end of the street, and he'd turn out to be sensitive and funny and smart and . . . "I'm sorry. Did you say something?"

"I asked if your boyfriend was sick."

"No. He had an accident at work and needed surgery."

"Really? What kind of accident?"

"He tripped on a piece of carpet on his way to the john and broke his ankle." She laughed. How ridiculous was that!

"Bummer," the bartender said.

Jamie smiled and took a long sip of her drink, waiting until the bartender moved away before looking back up. So much for funny and smart, she was thinking, deciding that no matter how lonely or desperate she got, she would never go out with a grown man who said **bummer.**

She stole a glance at the man with the Tom Selleck mustache, but he was hunched over his drink, protectively. He looked up briefly, caught her gaze, then turned his head away, as if to underline his disinterest. "Mustache looks fake anyway," Jamie muttered, staring into her glass, temporarily mesmerized by her reflection in the deep purple of the wine.

In the next instant, she saw herself walking up the front steps of Good Samaritan Hospital and asking the regal-looking black woman at the reception desk for directions to Tim Rannells's room. "He was scheduled for surgery on his ankle this morning," she informed the woman, tightly clutching the gift she'd brought him, the plastic bag crinkling beneath her fingers.

The woman typed the information into her computer, a worried look flashing across her handsome features. "I'm afraid Mr. Rannells has been moved to intensive care."

"Intensive care? For a broken ankle?"

"That's all the information I have."

The woman directed Jamie to the intensive care ward on the third floor. But the doors to the ward were locked and nobody answered when she pushed the call button, so Jamie spent the next several minutes pacing back and forth in the sterile waiting area, trying to figure out how a healthy, thirty-five-year-old man could enter the hospital for a relatively minor operation and end up in intensive care.

"You might as well sit down," a middle-aged woman with pale white skin, short brown hair, and tired blue eyes said from one of the orange plastic seats lining the bare walls. "I think they're pretty busy in there."

"Have you been waiting long?"

"I'm actually waiting for a friend." She spread the *People* magazine she'd been reading across her lap. "She's inside visiting her daughter who was in a car accident. They're not sure if she's gonna make it."

"That's terrible." Jamie looked around, but there was nothing to see. "My boyfriend was scheduled for surgery this morning," she offered, unprompted. "Somehow he ended up here." She returned to the call button, pushed it several times in rapid succession.

"Yes?" a disembodied voice answered seconds later. "How can I help you?"

"My name is Jamie Kellogg. I'm here to see Tim Rannells," Jamie shouted at the button.

"Are you a relative of Mr. Rannells?"

"You better say yes," the woman advised from her orange plastic chair. "Or they won't let you in."

"I'm his sister," Jamie answered without thinking. Probably because she had her own sister on the brain. Cynthia had been bugging her for weeks about coming over to go through their mother's things.

"Please have a seat for a few minutes," the disembodied voice said before clicking off.

Jamie swiveled back toward the woman in the orange chair. "Thanks for warning me."

"They have these rules," the woman said with a shrug. "I'm Marilyn, by the way."

"Jamie," Jamie said. "I wish someone would

tell me what's going on." She stared at the call button. "You don't think something terrible's happened, do you?" A stupid question, she realized immediately, although that didn't stop her from asking another. "You don't think he could have died, do you?"

"I'm sure someone will be out in a minute," Marilyn said.

"I mean, he just came in for a broken ankle."

"Try to stay calm."

Jamie smiled, although tears were already forming in the corners of her eyes. Her mother was always telling her to stay calm. "My mother was always telling me that," she repeated out loud. "She said I was too impulsive, too quick to react, that I had a tendency to jump to conclusions before I was in possession of all the facts."

"That's quite a mouthful."

"My mother was a judge."

"She certainly sounds judgmental enough."

Jamie sat back in her chair, unsettled by Marilyn's remark. People were forever reminding Jamie what a great woman her mother was. She was surprised by this stranger's unsolicited comment, and by how grateful she felt for it.

"I'm sorry. I hope I didn't offend you."

"You didn't."

The woman turned her attention to the magazine in her lap.

"I have a sister," Jamie continued, unprompted. "She's pretty much what I was supposed to be—a lawyer, married, two kids, you know . . . perfect."

"A perfect pain in the butt, you mean."

Jamie smiled. The more Marilyn talked, the more Jamie liked her. "She's okay. It's just hard sometimes because I'm the big sister. She's supposed to be the one looking up to me, not the other way around."

Jamie waited for Marilyn to say, I'm sure she looks up to you too, which, even if it wasn't true, would have been nice to hear, but the woman said nothing. Suddenly the door to the intensive care unit swung open and an attractive woman wearing black pants, a yellow sweater, and a wide scowl strode into the waiting area. At least two inches taller than Jamie, and older by several years, she was pretty in an aggressive, in-your-face kind of way, her chin-length hair a little too black, her lipstick a little too coral.

"Which one of you is Jamie Kellogg?"

Jamie jumped to her feet. "I'm Jamie."

"You're Tim Rannells's sister?"

Was this Tim's doctor? Jamie wondered, thinking the woman needed to work on her bedside manner. "Half-sister actually," Jamie heard herself say, then bit down on her lip to keep from embellishing further. Hadn't her mother told her that you could always tell when a witness was lying by how many unsolicited details he or she felt compelled to supply?

"Tim doesn't have a sister. Half or otherwise," the woman said, as Jamie felt the color drain from her cheeks. "Who are you?"

"Who are **you**?" Jamie asked in return.

"I'm Eleanor Rannells. Tim's wife."

The words hit Jamie like a giant fist, knocking the wind from her lungs, so that it was all she could do to remain standing.

"I repeat, who the hell are you?"

"I work with your husband," Jamie said quickly, almost gagging on the word. "And this is Marilyn." She pointed to the woman in the plastic orange chair, who immediately dropped her magazine to the floor and jumped to her feet.

"Nice to meet you," Marilyn said, extending her hand.

"You work at Allstate?"

"I'm a claims adjuster," Jamie said. "Marilyn's in payroll."

"Payroll," Marilyn agreed.

"I don't understand. What are you doing here? And why would you say you're Tim's sister?"

"We heard about Tim's accident," Jamie explained. "And we thought we'd drop by and see how he was doing. We bought him a present. It's the new John Grisham."

Eleanor Rannells took the book from Jamie's outstretched hand, tucked it under her arm.

"Apparently the only people allowed into

intensive care are relatives," Marilyn continued, picking up the slack. "So . . ."

"So you became the sister he never had," Eleanor said to Jamie.

As opposed to the wife he does, Jamie thought, wondering if Eleanor was actually buying any of this, or if she was simply too polite to cause a scene. "How is he?"

"He had a bad reaction to the anesthetic. It was touch-and-go for a few minutes there, but it looks like he's out of danger now, although they aren't allowing any visitors."

"Please give him our love," Marilyn said.

"I'll do that." Eleanor patted the novel, which was now securely wedged beneath her arm. "Thanks for the book. Grisham's his favorite. How'd you know?"

"Lucky guess," Jamie said, watching the door of the intensive care ward close behind her boyfriend's wife.

"Are you all right?" Marilyn asked from somewhere beside her.

"He's married."

"Apparently so."

"He's married!"

"Can I get you a glass of water?"

"We've been going out for four months. How could I not know he was married?"

"Trust me," Marilyn said. "It happens to the best of us."

"I'm so stupid!" Jamie wailed.

"You aren't stupid. You just fell for the wrong guy."

"This isn't the first time."

"No, and it probably won't be the last. Don't be so hard on yourself."

"That lying bastard!" Jamie burst into a flood of bitter, angry tears.

"Thatta girl. That's more like it."

"What am I going to do?"

"I'll tell you what you're **not** going to do, and that's waste any more tears on guys like that." Marilyn wiped the tears from Jamie's cheeks with gentle fingers. "You're a sweet and lovely young woman, and you're going to find another guy in no time at all. Now, go home, pour yourself a glass of wine, and climb into a nice, hot bubble bath. You'll feel much better. I promise."

Jamie smiled through her tears.

"And stop crying. You'll ruin your mascara."

"Thanks for coming to my rescue before."

"I enjoyed it. Now, go on. Get out of here."

Jamie began walking toward the bank of elevators, then stopped, turned back. "I hope everything works out with your friend's daughter."

"Thank you."

"I'm sorry, what?" Jamie asked, jumping back into the present tense with the sudden reappearance of the bartender.

"I said the gentleman at the far end of the bar is wondering whether he can buy you a drink."

Really? Jamie thought. He'd barely looked her way when she sat down. And there'd been something vaguely sinister about his posture, as if he was hiding something. The last thing she needed was another man with secrets. But the man with the Tom Selleck mustache had disappeared, and in his place sat a clean-shaven young man with a buzz cut and a crooked smile. He lifted his beer glass into the air in a silent toast.

Jamie pictured Tim Rannells lying in his hospital bed, his wife at his side, reading to him from the gift she'd brought him. Eleanor Rannells was soon joined by Jamie's sister, Cynthia, then by their mother, the three women shaking their heads at Jamie in collective disapproval. **How can you even be considering something so foolhardy?** they demanded in unison.

Jamie shook the women aside with a dramatic toss of her blond hair, downed what was left in her glass in one concerted gulp, then handed her wineglass to the bartender. "Tell him I'm drinking the house red," she said.

CHAPTER TWO

So can I buy you dinner now?"

Jamie laughed, gathering the blanket around her naked breasts and staring at the handsome stranger she'd allowed into her apartment, then into her bed. He had soft, full lips, a small, almost perfect nose, and the bluest eyes she'd ever seen. How'd I get so lucky? she was thinking. She, who was always lurching from one disaster to the next, stumbling from one ill-conceived relationship into another, had somehow stumbled onto the ideal man. In a bar, no less. In a fit of despair and desperation. And not only had he turned out to be even better-looking than he'd first appeared in the bar's dim light, not only did he possess the deliciously sculpted body of a Greek god—she'd almost gasped out loud when he removed his shirt—but he'd proved to be a surprisingly generous and thoughtful lover, as concerned with her pleasure as his own. They'd spent the last several hours in a blur of tireless carnal activity, and her body was literally aching with pleasure, every nerve ending exposed and raw. She felt the pleasant tingling between her legs and brought the blanket to her face to hide a self-satisfied grin. His scent, masculine and clean, immediately filled her nostrils. He was everywhere—on the sheets, her pillow, the tips of her fingers, the creases of her skin. It was a wondrous smell, she decided, leaning back against the headboard and taking a long, deep breath. Everything about the man was wondrous. Even his name. Brad, she repeated silently. Brad Fisher. **Jamie Fisher,** she caught herself thinking. Then, **Whoa girl, don't start that nonsense. This is what always gets you in trouble. Slow down.** "You really want to buy me dinner?"

"I offered earlier," he reminded her.

It was true. After the first round of drinks, he'd actually suggested they have something to eat. She'd turned him down. She had to be at work early the next morning, she'd said, torn between the impulse to flee and the desire to throw herself into his arms.

"Well, at least let me buy you another drink," he'd offered, the second glass of wine appearing, almost magically, at her fingertips.

Jamie glanced at the alarm clock beside the king-size bed that took up most of her small bedroom. The bed was one of her more egregious purchases of late, bought because Tim had told her he required lots of space when he slept. At any rate, that had been his excuse for never spending an entire night at her apartment. But even after she'd surprised him—and hadn't he told her he hated surprises?—by selling the double bed to a tenant down the hall and replacing it with this expensive monstrosity, Tim had still managed to find excuses to leave before midnight: an early morning meeting, a doctor's appointment in Fort Lauderdale, a burgeoning cold. How could she not have been suspicious? What was the matter with her? After everything she'd been through these last few years, was it possible she could still be that naive?

Stupid was more like it.

Of course, her sister had warned her that her bedroom was too small to accommodate such a large bed, and of course, once again, her sister was right. The bed overwhelmed its tiny surroundings, leaving scarcely a foot between it and the walls on either side, rendering it impossible for two people to be mobile at the same time.

"What's the matter?" Brad was asking now.

"Why would you think something is the matter?"

Brad shrugged, brought his finger to the tip of his almost perfect nose. "You just looked so sad all of a sudden."

"I did?"

A crooked grin, leaking innocence and mischief in equal measures, cut across his casually handsome features. "What were you thinking about?"

Jamie fought the urge to disclose everything that was going on inside her head, indeed, to confide every thought she'd had in the last decade. Instead she said, "I was trying to think of a restaurant that might still be serving dinner at this hour."

"How about takeout?"

"Takeout's great."

"Pizza?"

"Absolutely." Amazing how easy life could be, she was thinking as she recited the number for the nearest pizza parlor off by heart. "I don't get out much," she said, feeling her cheeks flush with embarrassment.

Brad stretched across her for the phone that sat next to the alarm clock on the tiny white plastic table, his muscular forearm brushing against the side of her breasts, sending an avalanche of vibrations throughout her body, threatening to bury her alive. She struggled to stay still as he punched in the numbers and placed an order for a large pizza—"Pepperoni and mushrooms all right with you?" he asked as his fingers reached over to caress her breasts beneath the covers. She felt her breath freeze in her lungs. "It'll be here in thirty minutes," he said, returning the phone to the bedside table and leaning back on one elbow.

"Or it's free," he added with that impish grin.

Someone should bottle that grin, she thought.

"So, how are you feeling?" he asked.

"I feel great. You?"

"Never better. Certainly glad I decided to stop in for a drink before heading home."

"And where is home exactly?" Jamie asked, hoping it wasn't too far away, that he wouldn't have to gobble down his pizza and run.

Sorry, but I have an early meeting in the morning, a doctor's appointment in Fort Lauderdale, a burgeoning cold.

"I don't exactly have a home these days," he told her. "I've been living at the Breakers the last couple of weeks."

"You're living at the Breakers?" The Breakers was the most prestigious, and probably the most expensive, of all the luxury hotels in Palm Beach.

"It's only for a little while longer. Till I decide what to do next."

"About what?"

Brad smiled. But the smile had lost its mischief, was older and more circumspect. "How trite will it sound if I say 'my life'?"

"It doesn't sound trite," Jamie protested, although, in truth, it did. At least a little. Certainly her sister would consider such sentiments trite. But then Cynthia would never have picked up the handsome stranger in the first place. She would never have allowed him to buy her a drink, let alone had him follow her back to her apartment, where she'd made love to him on the king-size bed she'd bought to please her married lover. No, Cynthia was much too levelheaded to do anything remotely like that. After all, she'd met Todd in the ninth grade, married him during her junior year at college, and borne him two children by the time she graduated law school.

"You have to be more practical," she'd told Jamie. "If you'd stayed in law school, we'd have our own firm by now."

"The only problem with that is I don't want to be a lawyer."

"You're too much of a romantic—**that's** the problem."

"You're married, aren't you?" Jamie asked Brad, already knowing the answer. Of course Brad Fisher was married. Probably going through a bit of a rough patch. Why else would he be staying at the Breakers? He and his wife had been fighting, and he'd moved out temporarily to give them both a chance to cool down and come to their senses, which he'd undoubtedly do as soon as he finished his pizza.

"Married?" Brad laughed, shook his head. "No. Of course not."

"You're not?"

"Would I be here if I was?"

"I don't know. Would you?"

"I'm staying at the Breakers because the lease on my apartment was up, and I just sold my business, and I'm kind of at a crossroads. . . ."

What kind of crossroads? "What kind of business?" she asked.

"Communications."

It was ironic, Jamie thought, that a word like **communications** could be so ambiguous, it was essentially meaningless. "Could you be a little more specific?"

"Computer programming," he explained. "Plus I designed some software that brought me to the attention of the big guys in Silicon Valley, and they made an exceedingly generous offer to buy me out."

"Which you accepted?"

"Hey, I may be a computer geek, but I'm no fool."

Jamie seriously doubted that either **geek** or **fool** had ever been words used to describe Brad Fisher. Could the man be any more appealing? she wondered, thinking that he was actually getting better by the moment. Not only was he gorgeous, sexy, and a fabulous lover, but he was some genius inventor as well. What's more, he was single, drove a nice car, and was independently wealthy. Or at least wealthy enough to be staying at the Breakers until he decided what he wanted to do with his life. It doesn't get any better than this, Jamie decided. "You'll be horrified to know I'm computer illiterate," she said, in an effort to keep her face from betraying her thoughts. "My computer at work is always freezing up on me. It's such a pain."

"What is it you do?"

"I'm a claims adjuster with Allstate."

He nodded, staring at her through eyes as blue as sapphires.

"Once I lost a whole day's work," she said, trying not to babble, "and my supervisor made me stay late and redo the entire thing. I was there till after midnight."

"It must have been pretty important stuff."

"Nothing that couldn't have waited till morning. But Mrs. Starkey insisted I must have done something wrong, that nobody else in the office ever had a problem with their computers freezing, and that it was my responsibility, and it had to be done, so . . ." She **was** babbling. She had to stop, stop now, before she ruined everything.

"You stayed and got it done."

Jamie took a deep breath, released it slowly. "It was the closest I've come to quitting."

"Sounds like you've come pretty close a few times."

"Only every day."

"You hate it that much?"

"It's just not what I pictured myself doing with my life."

"What is?"

"You won't laugh?"

"Why would I laugh?" he asked.

Jamie released her secret on a sigh. "I always kind of wanted to be a social worker."

The sapphire eyes twinkled. "Always kind of wanted?"

Jamie frowned. "Always **really** wanted."

Sapphire eyes narrowed to a squint. "So, why aren't you one?"

"My mother said social workers don't make any money. She wanted me to be a lawyer."

"And you always do what your mother wants you to?"

"God knows I tried." Jamie shook her head. "Didn't matter—it was never enough." She shrugged. "Anyway, it's moot. She died two months ago."

"Guess you can stop trying now," Brad said, with a wry chuckle.

"Some habits are harder to break than others."

"You're not ready yet?"

Jamie smiled sadly. "Why does everyone always ask me that?"

"Sorry."

"Don't be. It's not your fault I don't know what I'm doing."

"Oh, I think you'll figure it all out soon enough."

"Sure—easy for the computer genius to say."

"Quit your job," Brad said.

"What? I can't do that. My sister would have a fit."

"I could use a good social worker." He leaned in to kiss her softly on the mouth.

Jamie laughed. "God, you're a good kisser," she said, reluctantly coming up for air.

"Speaking of sisters," Brad said, his smile growing cryptic. "Who do you think taught me to kiss like that?"

"Your sister taught you how to kiss?"

"Sisters," he qualified. "I had three of them. I was the baby of the family, and they used me shamelessly." He laughed. "So when they first started dating, they'd try things out on me.

'How was that, Bradley? And how was that?' And then they started bringing over their friends, and that's when things got really interesting."

"I bet."

"Yeah, because then I could be more, what's the term a social worker would use? Proactive? Yeah, that's it. I definitely became more proactive. And that's when they started telling me what **they** liked. They said there was nothing worse than some guy jamming his tongue halfway down your throat, that it was much better to take it slow and gentle. Like this," he said, once again drawing Jamie into his arms and touching her lips with his own.

She felt his tongue playing with the sides of her mouth, felt it brush gently against her own tongue before slowly moving deeper. His arms snaked around her body, pulling her down on the bed as he climbed on top of her. But instead of thrusting into her, she felt him moving down the bed, his tongue tracing a sensuous path from her neck to her breasts, and then moving lower still, until his head was buried between her legs, his tongue working its magic there. She cried out as her body was wracked by a series of spasms unlike anything she'd ever experienced before. "Please don't tell me your sisters taught you that," she said later, when she could find her voice.

He laughed. "No, I figured that one out all by myself. Don't tell me nobody's ever done that to you before."

"Not like that, they haven't." Jamie thought of her former husband. She'd practically had to beg him to perform oral sex, and the few times he had—grudgingly, reluctantly—he'd jumped out of bed immediately afterward to brush his teeth and gargle. It hadn't taken very long for her to stop asking. "So, have you ever been married?" she asked.

"Yep," Brad said easily, although he offered nothing further.

"And?"

"And it didn't work out."

"You don't want to talk about it," Jamie stated.

"No, I don't mind talking about it," Brad

said. "There just isn't a whole lot to say. The marriage was good, and then it wasn't. It wasn't anybody's fault, and luckily, we've managed to stay friends. We talk on the phone pretty much every week."

"You do?"

"Well, we have a son together."

"You have a son?"

"Corey. He's five years old. I have a picture somewhere." Brad beamed with obvious pride as he reached for his jeans at the far end of the bed. He retrieved his wallet, pulled a crumpled photograph out from behind a neat stack of twenty-dollar bills.

A beautiful, towheaded little boy smiled shyly up at Jamie.

"This was taken almost a year ago, on his fourth birthday. He's grown a lot since then."

"He looks like you."

"You think so?"

"Well, his hair is lighter, but he's got your smile."

"Yeah?" Brad returned the picture to his wallet, the wallet to the pocket of his jeans.

"Unfortunately, his mother remarried recently, and they moved up north."

"She took Corey with her?"

"'Fraid so."

"How long has it been since you've seen your son?"

"Almost three months."

"That's got to be so hard."

"Well, Beth asked me to give him a little time to adjust to his new life, which I thought was only fair."

Jamie shook her head. "I think you're amazing."

"Not really," he demurred.

"I don't know many ex-husbands who would be so understanding."

"Yours wasn't?"

"How do you know I've been married?"

"The way you said 'ex-husband.'"

Jamie smiled.

"How long were you married?" he asked.

"Not long. Less than two years."

"No kids." It was a statement, not a question.

Jamie wasn't sure whether to shake her head or nod. "No kids," she agreed.

"Your mother didn't approve?"

"That's putting it mildly."

"Why didn't she like him?"

"She thought he was the reason I left law school."

"He wasn't?"

Jamie shook her head. "He was just the excuse I'd been looking for."

"You didn't love him?"

"I didn't **know** him."

Brad laughed again, a wonderful explosion of sound that assured her everything was going to be all right as long as he was beside her.

"Do you know that when we got divorced, my mother-in-law made me give back all the jewelry her son had given me, including my wedding ring? She said they were family heirlooms, and that she'd sue me if I didn't give them back."

"Charming."

"I thought so."

"And did you give them back?"

"Absolutely. I didn't want the damn things anyway. Except for a pair of gold-and-pearl earrings I used to wear all the time. I really hated giving those back." Jamie made a face of displeasure. Why was she talking about her former husband and his mother? The bed might be king-size, but it wasn't big enough for all of them. "Anyway, it doesn't matter anymore. They're out of my life. I'll never have to see either of them again."

"You're free to do whatever you want," Brad said.

"You make it sound so easy."

"It **is** easy."

Jamie closed her eyes, lay her head against his chest, and allowed herself to be lulled by the steadiness of his breathing.

"You ever think about just getting in your car and seeing where the road takes you?" he asked.

"All the time," Jamie said.

CHAPTER THREE

She dreamed of her mother's funeral.

Except that in her dream the pallbearers consisted not of her mother's assorted friends and colleagues, but rather of her father's subsequent wives, each wearing a bridesmaid's dress of the palest mauve chiffon and clutching a bouquet of odoriferous white lilies. Her sister stood next to the coffin, tall and regal in a deep purple, matron-of-honor gown, occasionally glancing at her watch. She's waiting for me, Jamie understood, trying to locate herself among the mourners.

"I'm coming," she tried shouting from the periphery of her consciousness. "Wait for me." Jamie saw herself racing toward the crowd just as the coffin began its measured descent into the ground. Omigod, I'm naked, she realized, trying to shield her naked flesh from her sister's horrified eyes and tripping on a nearby stone that sent her hurtling through the air. The casket's lid opened wide to accept her.

Inside the white, satin-lined coffin, her mother opened gold-flecked, brown eyes and stared accusingly at Jamie. "Are you ready?" she asked.

Jamie let out a cry and jolted up in bed, a trickle of perspiration trailing its way between her naked breasts, her breathing labored and unsteady. "Damn," she muttered, pushing her hair away from her forehead and trying to reconnect with both her surroundings and reality. Her surroundings were easy: she was in her apartment, in her tiny bedroom, in her king-size bed. Her reality was harder to accept: she was a twenty-nine-year-old woman in a dead-end job, with an ex-husband in Atlanta, a married lover in the hospital, and a virtual stranger in her bed.

Except that Brad Fisher was no longer beside her, she realized, coming fully awake, not sure whether to laugh or cry. Had she dreamed the handsome stranger as well?

The throbbing between her legs quickly convinced her he'd been real, as did the dent in the pillow where Brad's head had been. "Damn," she said again, straining to hear sounds of him coming from another room, then burying her face in her hands, knowing he was gone. On the one hand, she was relieved he wasn't there. At least now she wouldn't have to contend with the moments of awkward silence, the fake promises to get together again soon, the painful kiss on the forehead as he hurried out the door. He'd spared them that. She should be grateful. On the other hand, she couldn't help but feel abandoned, used, and even a bit abused. Again. "Don't be silly," she told herself. You were using Brad Fisher every bit as much as he was using you. What's the old saying? The best way to get over one man is by getting under a new one? Surely she hadn't expected a one-night stand to turn into a lifetime of devotion.

Except that, deep down, that was exactly what she'd been expecting.

Jamie wondered at what precise moment Brad had crept out of her bed and out of her life. Had he left as soon as she was safely asleep, or had he allowed himself the luxury of a few hours slumber before making his escape? He got what he came for, after all. The dearly departed indeed, she thought with an audible sigh, her dream relegated to an unpleasant blur that hovered just out of her mind's reach. Still, it would have been nice if he'd at least hung around long enough to wish her a nice day, she decided, glancing at the clock beside the bed. 8:15. "Oh, no!" she exclaimed as the bright red numbers on the digital clock registered on her brain. "It's eight-fifteen," she shouted to the empty room, knowing that no matter how quickly she showered and dressed, no matter how fast she drove, no matter how many excuses she prepared, she would be late for work, and Mrs. Starkey would be furious.

"You are such an idiot," she said, her sister's wagging finger following her into the bathroom. "You couldn't even remember to set the alarm clock."

I was a little busy, Jamie thought, suppressing a smile as she stepped into the shower and turned on the tap, positioning herself directly underneath the nozzle and opening her mouth to the sudden torrent of hot water. "You are such an idiot," she repeated, the words riding the water out of her mouth as Brad's invisible hands slid the soap across her body, his fingers lingering on her breasts and belly before disappearing into the folds between her legs. God, did he have to be so damn good? she wondered, emerging from the shower seconds later and rubbing herself almost raw with a large yellow towel, trying to erase the memory of his touch. Too good to be true, she reminded herself as she brushed her teeth and hair, then threw on the first things she saw in her closet, which she realized too late were the same navy skirt and powder blue blouse she'd worn to work the day before.

When something seems too good to be true, it usually is, her sister recited as Jamie stuffed a piece of cold, leftover pizza into her mouth and rushed for the door.

No makeup? her mother asked.

Jamie ran down the concrete steps to the parking lot behind the three-story building, surreptitiously checking the lot for Brad's car, although she knew it wasn't there. **How could you be such a moron?** she castigated herself again as she fumbled inside her purse for her car keys. **What were you thinking?** "That's just it. You **weren't** thinking," Jamie said before either her mother or sister had a chance.

You never think until it's too late, they added anyway.

Jamie checked her watch. 8:40. "I'm late all right. Mrs. Starkey is going to kill me."

But Mrs. Starkey wasn't in her corner office when Jamie finally plopped down at her desk at almost ten minutes after nine. The four other claims adjusters who shared the sun-filled space barely acknowledged her entrance, although she thought she detected a slight shake of the head from Mary McTeer.

"Everything okay?" Karen Romanick asked without looking up from her computer.

Karen was Jamie's closest friend at Allstate, although they rarely exchanged confidences and never socialized outside the office. She was reed thin and her hair was a veritable explosion of frizzy blond curls that lent a faintly frantic air to everything she did. Being around her for any length of time made Jamie nervous.

Jamie nodded. "Mrs. Starkey not here yet?"

"Oh, she's here all right." Karen's tone rendered further comment unnecessary. Mrs. Starkey was here, the tone said, and she wasn't happy.

"Great." Jamie turned on her computer, calling up one of the files she'd been working on the day before.

"Did you get to the hospital?" Karen asked out of the side of her mouth.

"I sure did."

"So how's Tim?"

"Married," Jamie said simply, then caught the strange look on Karen's long, triangular face. "You knew?" she asked incredulously.

"You didn't?"

I am **such** an idiot, Jamie thought again. Was she the only person in the world who hadn't known?

You only see what you want to see, she heard her mother say.

The phone on Jamie's desk rang. Maybe it's Brad, Jamie found herself thinking. He's sorry he had to run out so early; he wants to make it up to me. Jamie took a deep breath and answered the phone in the middle of its second ring. "Jamie Kellogg," she announced hopefully. "How can I help you?"

But instead of Brad's soothing voice whispering words of apology in her ear, she heard the nasal New York accent of Selma Hersh berating her for not getting back to her yesterday, as she had promised she would.

"I'm so sorry," Jamie told the woman, trying to remember exactly who she was as she pressed the keys to locate her file. "I was having some problems with the computer yesterday, and I couldn't access the information I needed."

There was a snort of derision from Selma

Hersh. "When can I expect my check?" she barked.

Jamie quickly scanned the woman's file. "It appears we still don't have all the necessary documentation, Mrs. Hersh."

"What are you talking about?"

"We need a doctor's letter stating the cause of your husband's death."

"You have a copy of the death certificate. Why do you need anything else?"

"It's standard policy, Mrs. Hersh. We need a note from the doctor who pronounced your husband dead, stating the exact cause of death."

"He died of pneumonia."

"Yes, but I still need a note, on the doctor's letterhead—"

"My husband died at JFK Memorial. How am I supposed to know what doctor pronounced him dead?"

"I'm sure the hospital can assist you in obtaining that information."

"This is ridiculous."

"I'm sorry, Mrs. Hersh. If you'll just get us

that note, we can release the check to you immediately."

"This is absurd. I want to speak to your supervisor."

"I'll have her call you as soon as she gets in." The line went dead in Jamie's hands. "Have a nice day," she said just before the phone rang again. Jamie took a deep breath, pushed her lips into a smile. "Jamie Kellogg."

"Jamie. Hello."

She recognized Tim's voice immediately, although it lacked its usual resonance. She wondered if he was still in intensive care and if his wife was still standing guard. Hang up, she thought.

"Don't hang up," Tim said, as if reading her thoughts. "Please, Jamie. Just hear me out."

"I see you're still alive," she said coldly.

"I'm so sorry, Jamie," he began, a tremble in his voice that threatened tears.

Jamie shook her head, feeling her body sway, knowing she was perilously close to getting sucked back in. They'd been together for over four months after all. He'd been her lover, her confidant, occasionally even her friend. And now he was in the hospital, having barely escaped death. . . .

What's the matter with me? she berated herself, slamming her fist onto the computer's keyboard, causing the screen to go instantly blank. He was a married man, for God's sake, and he'd lied to her. Had she no pride, no sense of self-preservation? Had her marriage taught her nothing at all? "What are you sorry about, Tim?" Jamie snapped, thinking of Selma Hersh, deciding she could use some of that old woman's gumption right about now. "That you lied to me, or that you got caught?"

"Both," he acknowledged after a pause.

"What did your wife tell you?"

"That I had some visitors from the office. It didn't take a genius to figure out—"

"Are you getting a divorce?" Jamie interrupted.

Another pause, slightly longer than the first, then, "No."

Jerk, Jamie thought. You picked a hell of a time to start telling the truth.

"That must have been some scene last night," he said, chuckling softly.

"You bastard," Jamie said slowly. "You're enjoying this."

The laugh quickly degenerated into a cough. "What? No, of course not."

"You're flattered, you miserable son of a bitch."

"Jamie, you're overreacting."

"Go to hell." Jamie slammed down the receiver.

In the stillness that followed, Jamie gradually became aware of other sounds: the hum of her computer; the slightly grating sound of Mary McTeer's voice as she conferred with a colleague; the clicking of Karen Romanick's fingers across her keyboard; the rhythmic breathing of someone standing directly behind her. Jamie swiveled around in her seat, knowing who was there even before she saw the long, manicured fingers that were Mrs. Starkey's trademark. They tapped impatiently against the sleeves of her beige silk blouse.

"What an interesting way to deal with

clients," Mrs. Starkey remarked, cool hazel eyes glaring at Jamie from behind a pair of square, tortoiseshell glasses. "No wonder you're so popular."

"I'm sorry," Jamie began, not quite sure what she was apologizing for. For being such an idiot, for having an affair with a married man, for sleeping with a stranger, for taking personal calls on company time? Any or all of the above? What the hell—take your pick. She was sorry for her whole misspent, stupid life.

"My office," Mrs. Starkey snapped, turning on her brown flats and marching off without looking back.

"Damn." Jamie glanced at her blank computer screen. "Damn," she said again, unable to move.

"Just go in there and listen and don't answer back," Karen advised out of the corner of her mouth.

"I don't think I can deal with her right now."

"I don't think you have a choice."

"Damn."

"You'll apologize, you'll grovel, you'll keep your job," Karen said.

"I don't want this job," Jamie said loudly.

"What are you saying?"

Jamie pushed herself away from her desk, rose quickly to her feet. "I'm saying I don't want this job."

"What are you **doing**?"

Jamie began emptying her desk of any personal items—a telephone-address book, a tube of pink lipstick, a nail clipper, a spare pair of pantyhose. "I'm quitting."

"Without talking to Mrs. Starkey?"

"She's a smart lady—she'll figure it out." Jamie bent down to give her startled colleague a hug. "I'll call you when the dust settles." She walked from the office in purposeful strides.

"You're sure you want to do this?" Karen called after her. "I mean, you don't think you're being a little rash?"

Jamie saw Mrs. Starkey watching her from her corner office and relished the quizzical look on her angular face. "Have a nice day," she called back to no one in particular, letting the door slam shut behind her.

She was home before ten o'clock. She'd thought of stopping at the Breakers, then thought better of it. If Brad wanted to get in touch with her, he knew exactly where to find her. Besides, his premature departure had pretty much said it all where she was concerned. And who could blame him? It was bad enough to sleep with a man on your first date, but she hadn't even waited that long. Their first **encounter,** for God's sake. "What's the matter with you?" Jamie was muttering as she walked up the outside steps to her apartment. She waved at a stooped old man at the far end of the hall. The man stared back at her, as if he had no idea who she was. And maybe he didn't, Jamie realized, hearing her stomach rumble, and knowing she had nothing in her place to eat but leftover pizza. She should have picked up some cereal and milk. Maybe even some eggs. A cheese omelet sounded awfully good right now. With a toasted sesame seed bagel and a cup of strong, black coffee, she thought, as the aroma of freshly brewed coffee wafted teasingly down the corridor toward her. What a shame she'd never gotten to know her neighbors. She could have stopped in for a friendly cup.

Except she didn't have any friends. And she didn't have a job. "And I don't have any coffee," she wailed, unlocking her front door and stepping inside her living room.

The smell of coffee rushed to embrace her, and for a minute Jamie thought she'd wandered into the wrong apartment. Except that the red, secondhand sofa her sister had passed on to her after she'd redecorated was still sitting against the far wall, at right angles to the black leather chair she'd bought on sale at Sears, and her mother's expensive glass table was still littered with the latest batch of fashion magazines.

So, this **was** her apartment. And the handsome man emerging from her tiny galley kitchen and walking toward her, a mug of steaming black coffee in his outstretched hand, was the man she'd spent the night making mad passionate love to, and here he was, still anticipating her every want and need, and so obviously, this had to be a dream. In fact, the entire morning had been a dream, a dream that was just now starting to get good, and so naturally, this was the moment she'd probably wake up, which was the last thing in the world she wanted to do. Please don't let me wake up, she was thinking as he placed the coffee in her hand and bent to kiss her softly on the lips.

"You came back," he said, kissing her again.

He feels so real, Jamie thought. He sounds so real. "So did you," she heard herself say, her voice pushing her out of her fantasy and into the real world.

Brad Fisher was still there.

"I woke up early and thought I'd surprise you with one of my special breakfasts," he told her, nodding in the general direction of the kitchen. "But the cupboards were pretty bare, so I hightailed it over to Publix to pick up some bagels. . . ."

"You got bagels?"

"Thought I'd make it back before you left

for work, but my car broke down, and I had to get it towed, and by the time I got back, you'd already left."

"You got bagels?"

He smiled. "Somebody sounds hungry."

Jamie stumbled toward the sofa, sank down on the pillow, took a long sip of her coffee. It was the best coffee she'd ever tasted. "How'd you get in?" she asked.

Brad shrugged. "Door was unlocked."

"I forgot to lock the door?"

"Apparently."

"First I forget to set the alarm clock, then I forget to lock the door. My mother used to say I'd forget my head if it weren't attached."

"She ever say anything nice?"

"She said I had a smart mouth."

He laughed. "Not exactly what I had in mind."

"I quit my job," Jamie wailed.

"You did? That's great."

"Great? No, it's not. It was stupid and impulsive. . . ."

"You hated that job."

"I know, but it paid my bills."

"So, you'll get a different job."

Jamie took another sip of her coffee as a sly smile overtook Brad's face. "What?" she asked.

"I have a great idea."

Jamie felt a stirring between her legs. "You do?"

"I think we should do what we talked about last night."

Jamie cocked her head to one side. Very little of what she remembered from last night involved dialogue.

"I think we should just get in the car and go," he elaborated. "Of course we'd have to use your car, since mine's in the shop."

"And where would we go?"

"Wherever."

"You're not serious."

"I'm very serious."

"I can't do that," Jamie said.

"Why not? We're both unemployed and unattached. There's nothing keeping us here. It's the perfect time."

"You **are** serious."

"Deadly."

The phone rang. Jamie grabbed it, pressed it to her ear. "Hello?" Immediately, Brad's hands were around her breasts, his lips tracing a series of tiny kisses along the tops of her shoulders.

"What the hell is going on?" her sister demanded.

"Hi there, Cynthia. How are you?"

"Don't 'Hi there, how are you?' me. What the hell do you think you're doing?"

Jamie wondered if Cynthia had a surveillance camera in her apartment, that even now she was watching Brad's fingers gently outlining the contours of her nipples beneath her blue blouse.

"Todd just phoned to tell me he had an angry call from Lorraine Starkey, that she told him all about that little stunt you pulled. . . ."

"It wasn't a stunt."

"You quit your job without so much as a word? You didn't give notice? You didn't offer any explanations. . . ."

Brad's fingers disappeared underneath her blouse. Jamie moaned audibly.

"What was that? Did you just moan?"

Jamie grabbed Brad's hands to still them, and in so doing, dropped the phone.

"Jamie?" Cynthia called from her lap. "What's going on there?"

"Sorry. I dropped the phone."

There was a slight pause. "Is somebody there?"

"What? No, of course not."

Brad leaned forward, resting his chin on Jamie's shoulder and monitoring the conversation.

"Are you all right?" Cynthia asked. "You're not having some sort of breakdown, are you?"

"I really hated that job, Cynthia."

"You can't keep doing this, you know."

"I can get another job."

"I'm not talking about that. You know what I'm talking about."

"I'm not sure I do."

"You can't keep fucking up."

"I won't."

"Just call Mrs. Starkey and tell her you're sorry."

"I can't do that."

"Why can't you?"

"Because I'm **not** sorry."

"Okay, look," Cynthia said. "Obviously this isn't the best time to be discussing this. We'll talk about it when you get here."

"What do you mean, when I get there?"

"What do **you** mean, what do I mean?"

"What?"

"This is great," Brad said, a small chuckle escaping his mouth.

"What was that?" Cynthia demanded.

"What was what?"

"Are you laughing?"

"Of course I'm not laughing."

"Because this isn't funny."

"I'm not laughing."

"Then what time are you coming over? And don't you dare tell me you forgot and made other plans."

Brad began nodding his head up and down. "You've made other plans," he whispered in her ear.

"What did you say?" Cynthia asked.

"I'm sorry, Cyn. I **have** made other plans," Jamie said.

"You can't do that to me," her sister protested. "You said you were gonna come over and we'd go through Mom's things. You promised."

"We'll do it another time. Tomorrow . . ."

Brad shook his head. "You're busy tomorrow," he said.

"What?" Cynthia asked.

"Not tomorrow. Sorry. Tomorrow's no good."

"And not Sunday either," Brad said.

"This weekend's just not good for me," Jamie said.

"Well, when **is** good for you? We can't keep putting it off forever."

Why can't we? Jamie wondered. Why the rush to dispose of Mom's things? It's not like she was going anywhere. Jamie leaned her cheek against Brad's, felt his morning stubble rough against her skin. "Look, I think I'm going to go away for a few days," she said suddenly, feeling Brad's smile stretch across his face. "Maybe for a week."

"What? What are you talking about? What do you mean you're going away? Where are you going? What are you talking about?" Cynthia questioned angrily.

"I just need a break."

"A break?"

"Not for long. A week. Maybe two," she added as Brad held up the middle and index fingers of his right hand.

"This is unbelievable. When did you decide this?"

"I'll call you in a couple of days."

"Call me when you grow up," Cynthia said before slamming down the phone.

Brad was instantly on his feet. "Way to go, Jamie."

"She's really pissed."

"To hell with her." Brad grabbed her hands, twirled her around the living room. "Come on, Jamie-girl. Time's a wasting. Let's get this show on the road."

"But where are we going? Do we have any plan at all?"

"Of course we have a plan. We'll head

north. Maybe stop for a few nights in Ohio."

"Ohio? What's in Ohio?"

"My son. Wait till you see him, Jamie. You're gonna love him. Come on. You're not having second thoughts, are you?"

Second thoughts were exactly what she was having. Everything was moving so fast. Too fast. She'd already committed one impulsive act today. Was she actually considering driving off into the sunset with some guy she'd just met? In **her** car, no less! She needed to take a deep breath, calm down, think things through.

"I'll take that as a no," Brad said, kissing her gently on the lips.

What was she worried about? she wondered, tossing aside any pesky concerns. "Where in Ohio?" she asked him.

"Dayton," he told her, flashing that wondrous grin. "A street called Mad River Road."

CHAPTER FOUR

The two-story wood house at 131 Mad River Road was like all the other houses on the street: old and slightly shabby. Its gray paint was peeling, and the once-white shutters framing the four front windows were stained and tilted at a variety of precarious angles. The shutters outside the bedroom windows were in particularly bad shape, caked with years of accumulated debris, and barely hanging on. *Just like me,* Emma thought, breathing in the crisp morning air and reluctantly pushing her long legs up the six crumbling front steps. She stopped on the tiny porch before the torn screen door. Beyond the screen door was another door, this one solid and painted black, although the color was faded and the surface scratched. Across the threshold was more peeling, more crumbling, more fading. The old house had definitely seen better days. Emma shrugged. Who hadn't? Besides, what did she expect for the kind of rent she was paying?

Several years ago the street had been bought up by developers with the idea of tearing down the existing houses and erecting a row of pricey townhomes. Gentrification, they called it. Except that someone on the city council had objected, and the project had stalled, mired in a seemingly endless ball of sticky red tape. In the meantime, the developers, reluctant to give up on their investment and hoping to reach a satisfactory accord with the powers-that-be in the near future, had decided to rent out the houses on a monthly basis. The result was that Mad River Road had become something of a haven for women in a state of flux, women whose pasts were murky, whose futures were uncertain, and whose presents were on hold. Not surprisingly, these included a large number of single mothers and their offspring. When Emma and her young son had arrived in town looking for an inexpensive apartment in a safe neighborhood, preferably one within walking distance of an elementary school, the real estate agent had thought for only half a second before directing her to Mad River Road. True, the houses were in less than stellar condition, and you could be booted out with only two months' notice, but the inhabitants of the street had worked hard at sprucing up their surroundings, planting flowers in the front gardens and painting the exteriors of the houses a variety of interesting pastels. Besides, where else could you find a two-bedroom home in the city for this kind of money? "It's a charming little house," the realtor had pronounced. "Lots of potential."

The potential for a fresh start, Emma remembered thinking. Except that potential cost money, Emma thought, and she was going through what little cash she'd managed to hide from her ex-husband at a speed she hadn't imagined. Soon there'd be nothing left.

She tucked shoulder-length dark hair behind her right ear, listening to the sound of birds in the nearby trees, and wondering absently, What kind of birds, what kind of trees? She should know these things. She should know what kinds of birds—robins, blue jays, cardinals?—serenaded her in the mornings as she walked her son to school. She should know the types of trees—maple, oak, elm?—that lined both sides of the long street and threw deep shadows across her small patch of front lawn. She should know stuff like that. Just as she should know the names of the flowers—peonies, posies, pansies?—that old Mrs. Discala had recently planted along the sidewalk in front of her house. Emma fished her house key out of the side pocket of her jeans, pulled open the screen door, and unlocked the next. Both squealed loudly in protest. Probably need oil, she thought, wondering fleetingly, What kind of oil? Animal, mineral, vegetable?

Inside, the house was stuffy, but Emma dismissed the idea of opening a window. In truth, the temperature suited her mood, which was lethargic and verging on depressed. Today was supposed to be the day she went out looking for a job, but her son hadn't slept well last night—another nightmare—which meant, of course, that she hadn't slept well either, and she doubted the bags under her normally vibrant blue eyes would make a good impression on a prospective employer. Her eyes had always been her best and most striking feature. They were large and oval and dominated an otherwise blandly pretty face. Besides, she hadn't really decided what kind of job she was looking for. "I'll look later," she told the morning paper, still lying on the light hardwood floor inside the front door.

She crossed the small foyer that divided the house into two uninteresting halves, the living room to the left only marginally bigger than the dining room on the right, the kitchen behind the dining room barely big enough to accommodate the round white table and two folding chairs she'd picked up at a secondhand shop, along with most of the other furniture. An oddly shaped brown sofa that had probably been some designer's idea of modern took up most of the living room. It sat against the front window next to a surprisingly comfortable beige-and-green armchair, a small set of white stacking tables in between. The dining room consisted of four gray plastic chairs grouped around a square, medium-size table, the table completely covered by a floral tablecloth Emma had bought to hide its deeply scarred surface. The walls throughout the house were dull white, the floors bare and crying for carpets. Still, there was something about the idea of putting down carpets that smacked too much of permanence. How could she think of planting roots, of settling down, of moving ahead when she was always looking over her shoulder? No, it was still too early. Maybe one day . . . "Okay," Emma said. "Enough of that." She mounted the steep set of stairs to the second floor, each step a reminder that one day was pretty much the same as the next on Mad River Road.

Emma entered her bedroom and threw herself across her unmade double bed, wondering why anyone would name a street Mad River Road when the river in question was miles away. Rumor had it there used to be a tributary somewhere nearby, but that it had dried up long ago. Why the name Mad River anyway? What had made the river so **Mad**? Had it seemed angry, wild, uncontrollable? And could the same adjective be used to describe the street's inhabitants? Another one of life's unsolved mysteries, Emma decided, closing her eyes. She had more pressing things to worry about.

Her son, to name one. She had to do something about his nightmares. They were occurring with increasing frequency of late, and it was taking her longer and longer to calm him down. As it was, he insisted on sleeping with the overhead light on and playing his radio all night. Not only that, but a series of nonsensical bedtime rituals was occupying more and more of his time: he brushed his teeth for thirty seconds, using exactly fifteen strokes for the top row, followed by another fifteen for the bottom; he then rinsed out his mouth, starting on the left side and moving to the right, before spitting into the sink three times; he touched the wooden baseboard of his narrow bed twice before he climbed under the covers, then reached behind him to tap the wall above his head. No action could be left out or modified in any way without, he feared, the most dire of consequences. Her son was afraid of everything, Emma realized, groaning out loud and wondering if he'd always been so fearful and just hadn't shown it.

True, the last year hadn't been easy for him. Hell, it hadn't been easy on either of them. They'd moved three times, and Dylan still didn't understand why they'd had to leave home in the first place, abandoning everything that was familiar and comfortable: his nana, his room, his friends, his toys. He was always asking where his father was, and if anyone was looking after him. He didn't like their new names, even after she explained she'd named him after a character from her once-favorite TV show, **Beverly Hills 90210.** And Emma was the name Rachel had given her baby on **Friends,** she'd told him, and didn't he agree it suited her much better than her old name? He had to be very careful, she reminded him regularly, not to slip up and use his old name around strangers. It was important, she'd cautioned him repeatedly, although she didn't say why. She couldn't very well tell him the truth about his father. He was way too young to understand. Maybe if they had to move again, she'd let him choose his own name.

Emma flipped from her back onto her side and opened her eyes to stare out the front window. Delicate wisps of cloud floated across a blue, untroubled sky. A tree branch, newly furnished with leaves, blew toward the glass. It was cool for May. The outside air smelled damp. It carried the threat of rain, which she hated. Emma took the weather very personally, which she knew was stupid. Still, did it have to be so damn unpleasant so much of the time? She'd grown up in a place of warmth and sunshine. Maybe one day she'd be able to go back.

In the meantime, she was stuck here on Mad River Road. Another month, and school would be over. What would she do with Dylan then? Even if she had the money to send him to camp, she doubted he'd go. And she couldn't very well take him with her to work for two months. So how could she even think of getting a job? Maybe she could convince old Mrs. Discala to babysit. Dylan liked her. He said she reminded him of his nana.

This was all her fault, Emma thought, sleep tugging at her eyes. She was the reason her son was so fearful. If she didn't do something soon, they'd both go crazy. Mad River Road indeed.

She drifted into a state that was half torpor, half sleep, fantasy mingling with reality as strange images, together with actual events, began to flit in and around her consciousness. One minute she was frantically packing her bags and fleeing her home, the next minute she was diving into a turbulent stream. Familiar faces lined an unfamiliar shore, calling out to her in a variety of names, vying for her attention. They were throwing sticks and stomping their feet. Some were banging their fists against the heavy air, as if trying to beat down a door.

Someone's at the door, Emma realized as the banging grew louder. Who? she wondered, almost afraid to move. She wasn't expecting anyone, and it wasn't like any of her neighbors to just drop in uninvited. She hadn't exactly solicited anyone's friendship in the months since she'd taken up residence on Mad River Road, shunning the initial overtures of other single mothers on the street. It was better that way. No point in forming attachments, in getting involved in other people's lives, when her own life was so tenuous and fraught, when a surprise phone call or an unexpected encounter could once again cause her to flee into the night. Was it really so surprising this attitude had filtered down to her son? His teacher, Ms. Kensit, regularly bemoaned Dylan's lack of friends. Was it Ms. Kensit who was knocking on her door? Was she here to tell Emma something terrible had happened to her son? That someone had come to spirit him away?

Emma bolted up in bed, trying to shake off the terror that was rapidly enveloping her, but it clung to her like a stubborn cold.

Had he found them?

She checked her watch as she pushed herself off the bed and into the upstairs hall. She'd been asleep almost half an hour. Was it possible that in that half hour, in those thirty minutes when her defenses were down, her world had been once again, and forever, altered? All without her knowledge, and most certainly without her consent? "I do not agree to this," she said as she inched her way down the stairs, her fingers pressing into the wall for support, leaving the sweaty imprint of her fear on the flat, white paint. "I do not accept this." Taking a deep breath and holding it tightly in her lungs, Emma pulled open the front door and stared through the screen. I'll kill you if I have to, she was thinking, staring at the uniformed stranger. I'll kill you before I let you take my son away from me.

"Parcel," a young man with a wide space between his two front teeth announced nonchalantly. "It wouldn't fit through the slot." Emma pushed open the screen door as the man, whom Emma now realized was the postman, handed her a large stuffed envelope along with her regular mail, then turned on his heel and skipped down the front steps to the sidewalk. She quickly closed the door and tore open the padded envelope, pulling out what appeared to be a very long letter, neatly typed and double-spaced. From whom? she wondered, the cloak of fear returning to drape itself across her shoulders as she flipped to the final page. But instead of a signature, there were two words—THE END. "What's going on here?" she asked, returning to the first page. The letter began:

> Dear Ms. Rogers,
>
> Thank you so much for the opportunity to read your short story, "Last Woman Standing." While we found the story to be entertaining and well written, we don't think it is quite right for the readers of **Women's Own.** We wish you the best of luck in placing this piece with another magazine, and hope you will think of us in the future.
>
> Sincerely . . .

What the hell is this? Emma wondered, understanding in that moment that the postman had delivered the envelope to the wrong address. In fact, all the mail belonged to somebody else. To one Ms. Lily Rogers of 113 Mad River Road. **113,** not 131. Emma knew who Lily Rogers was. She lived at the far end of the street, nine houses down, and waved to Emma whenever she saw her. Several times she'd tried to start a conversation, but Emma had always brushed her off and rushed away. "Wait a minute," Emma called out now, pushing open both sets of doors and searching the street for the misguided mail carrier. But he'd already turned the corner and disappeared down the next street, and she wasn't about to go chasing after him. She'd return Lily Rogers's mail to her this afternoon when she went to pick up her son at school. There was no rush. No one was in a big hurry to be rejected.

Emma lifted up the letter of rejection to glance at the story beneath. "Last Woman Standing," she read. By Lily Rogers.

Pauline Brody is thinking of licorice sticks. The long, twisted, red ones that her older sister used to tell her weren't really licorice at all, but some kind of plastic, full

of horrible red dye that would give her cancer when she grew up.

Yuck, Emma thought, returning the story to the envelope and dropping Lily's mail to the floor as she retrieved the morning paper, then carried it into the kitchen at the rear of the house. The sun poured in through the large window above the sink, spotlighting the smooth Formica counter that ran between the small white refrigerator and the oven. There was no dishwasher, no microwave, no fancy grill, for which Emma was almost grateful. She didn't need any of those things. She'd had them during her marriage to Dylan's father. She didn't miss them. Hell, as long as she had her Mr. Coffee machine, she was happy. She rinsed out her mug and poured herself a fresh cup of coffee from the pot she'd made earlier that morning. Well, maybe not so fresh, she thought, taking a long sip and sitting down at the kitchen table, spreading the want ads out before her. Enough procrastinating. She needed a job.

Emma groaned, leaning back in her chair and stretching toward the drawer beside the sink. She couldn't do this alone. She needed fortification. And there it was, at the back of the drawer, hidden among the dishtowels and cleaning rags: a pack of Salems, complete with a half-full book of matches. Talk about things that would give you cancer when you grew up, Emma thought, withdrawing a cigarette from the middle of the pack. She lit it and inhaled deeply, closing her eyes. There were only so many things she could worry about, and the truth was that Emma loved smoking. She loved everything about it—the taste of the tobacco on her tongue, the slow burning sensation that traveled up her throat, the exquisite pressure in her lungs as they filled with smoke, the deeply satisfying release of that smoke back into the air. Emma didn't care what the experts said. Nothing that made you feel this good could possibly be that bad.

Of course, she'd once felt the same way about men.

And then there was her promise to Dylan. Yes, I swear I'll stop smoking. No, I'm not going to die. Yes, that was my last cigarette ever. No, I'll never have another one. I promise. See? Mommy's throwing out all her nasty cigarettes. There. All gone. Stop crying. Please, baby, stop crying.

She'd have to open some windows before he got home and air the room out, brush her teeth. Fifteen strokes, top and bottom, she thought with a sad smile, picturing Dylan going through his nightly ablutions. God, what was she going to do with that child?

"What am I going to do with **me**?" she asked, scanning the list of jobs under **General Help Wanted.**

A BLING BLING DEAL, the first heading began.

Looking for a cool job? Great atmosphere and pay are waiting for you.

"Sounds good to me," Emma said, reading the rest.

14 F/T marketing reps needed for expanding marketing co. No telemarketing.

"What in the world is an F/T marketing rep?" Emma asked, taking another deep drag of her cigarette and perusing the rest of the page.

A travel operator position (22 new jobs), $10/hr + $40–$100 cash daily . . .

Baker required for Portuguese bakery. Call Tony or Anita . . .

Eighteen travel consultants needed for reservations dept . . .

Program Supervisor for Halfway house. $50K a year . . .

"Now that sounds more like it."

. . . Min. 5 years exp. E-mail résumé to . . .

"Shoot. So much for that."

Another knock at the door. Another sharp intake of breath.

"Don't be silly. It's only the mailman, come to correct his mistake." Emma took another long, last drag off her cigarette before throwing it down the sink and walking to the door, coffee mug in hand. She scooped up Lily Rogers's mail from the floor, then opened the door.

The woman who stood on the other side of the screen door was young and blond and pretty. In a bovine sort of way, Emma thought, taking note of the woman's round face, small upturned nose, and more than ample bosom. It was a shame. She'd be beautiful if she lost five pounds, drop-dead gorgeous if she could get rid of ten.

"Hi," Lily Rogers said, brown eyes smiling. She held up a small stack of letters. "These came to my house by mistake. I think we must have a new postman or something," she continued as Emma opened the door just wide enough for them to exchange mail. "The regular guy doesn't make these mistakes. Oh," she said, realizing the large envelope had been opened.

"I'm really sorry," Emma said immediately. "I opened it before I realized. . . ."

"That's all right. Good news, I hope."

Emma said nothing.

"Damn," Lily Rogers said, without bothering to read the letter of rejection.

"They did say the story was entertaining and well written," Emma offered, adding quickly, "Sorry. I didn't mean to snoop."

"That's okay."

She doesn't look okay, Emma thought. She

looks on the verge of tears. Just give her a little nod of condolence and send her on her way. "Would you like some coffee?" she heard herself ask, then bit down on her lower lip. What was the matter with her? She didn't want Lily Rogers in her house. Hadn't she made a pointed effort not to befriend any of her neighbors? What was she doing? She didn't want a friend. She couldn't afford one.

"That'd be great," Lily said, following Emma to the kitchen.

Emma dropped her mail, which she noticed consisted of two bills and a flyer for a vacation resort in Cape Cod, on the counter, then cleared the morning paper off the table and poured Lily a mug of coffee, motioning for the young woman to pull up a chair.

"Thank you." Lily sank into the nearest folding chair and crossed one leg over the other. She was wearing an unflattering gray sweat suit bearing the logo of a local health club. "I work at Scully's four days a week, from ten to three," she said, noticing the direction of Emma's gaze. "While Michael's in school. I think our sons are in the same class. Ms. Kensit?"

Emma nodded, reached into the top drawer next to the sink, withdrew another cigarette. "You want one?"

"No, thanks. I don't smoke."

Emma nodded, lighting her second cigarette of the day and blowing smoke rings into the air. "So, what's with the story?" she asked, nodding toward the stuffed envelope on the table in front of Lily.

Lily shrugged. "You know what they say about hope springing eternal. . . ."

"You want to be a writer?"

"Ever since I was a little girl. I was always the kid being asked to read her compositions out loud in class. Everyone thought they were so great. My English teacher in the tenth grade actually announced to everyone, 'This girl is going to be a writer.'" Lily shrugged again. "Oh, well. I keep trying."

"This isn't your first rejection slip?"

"More like my one hundred and first. I could paper your walls with them."

"Would you?" Emma laughed, realizing she was enjoying herself. How long had it been since she'd relaxed over coffee with another adult, since she'd had a conversation with someone who wasn't five years old? "I had a story published once," she confided.

Lily's brown eyes grew wide. She lowered her mug to the table. "You did? Where?"

"Cosmo." Emma smiled sheepishly. "It was a long time ago. And it wasn't a story like the kind you write. It was about my experiences modeling."

"You're a model?"

Emma wished Lily hadn't sounded quite so surprised. "Not really. Not anymore, anyway. I did some a few years back. Before I got married."

"Why'd you stop?"

Emma shrugged. "No reason in particular."

Lily nodded, as if she understood.

How could she? Emma wondered. "You ever use Maybelline mascara?"

"Sure."

"You remember the packages they used to have?" Emma asked. "The ones with the enormous blue eyes looking up . . . ?"

"Yeah. I think I remember."

"Those were mine."

"Those were your eyes? Are you kidding me?"

Again Emma wished Lily hadn't sounded quite so surprised. "That's exactly what I said when this sleazy-looking guy comes over to me in McDonald's one afternoon and says he's a photographer and that I have these fantastic eyes. So he hands me his card, which I think is a joke, right? But then I showed it to my mother, and she calls the guy, and he turns out to be the real deal, and next thing I know, my eyes are all over the ads for Maybelline mascara."

"That's fantastic."

"Yeah. I did some other stuff as well, but then I got married, and well . . . you know how it is."

Lily nodded, as if she really **did** know.

Emma took another deep drag of her cigarette. "You married?"

"I'm a widow," Lily said, her voice barely audible.

"A widow? Wow. What happened?"

"Motorcycle accident." Lily shook her head, as if trying to shake away an unpleasant image. "So you sold your modeling story to **Cosmopolitan,**" she said, in an obvious attempt to change the subject. "That's terrific. I'd love to see it."

"So would I," Emma agreed. "Unfortunately, I had to leave my copies behind when I moved."

Lily's round face grew pensive as she downed the remainder of her coffee and checked her watch. "I better go or I'll be late for work." She gathered up her mail from the table, rose to her feet. "Listen," she said, stopping at the front door. "I started this book club a few months back. It's just a few women from the street and a couple more from work. We're meeting tonight at my house, if you'd like to drop by."

"No, thanks," Emma said quickly. "Book clubs aren't really my thing."

"Well, if you change your mind. . . ." Lily ran down the steps. When she reached the sidewalk, she turned back, held up her mail. "Seven-thirty," she called out. "Number 113."

CHAPTER FIVE

Jamie stared out the passenger window of her car as it sped north on the Florida Turnpike, wondering if she was in the middle of a total nervous collapse. Not only had she quit her job, alienated her sister, and handed over the keys to her beloved Thunderbird to a man she barely knew, but she hadn't stopped smiling since they'd begun their journey almost three hours earlier. This despite the fact there was absolutely nothing of interest to be seen on this long, boring stretch of highway, and she'd long ago stopped being amused by the seemingly inexhaustible supply of billboards for Yeehaw, a city whose main industry appeared to consist of selling discount coupons to Disney World and Universal Studios. SEE

MICKEY AT A MINNIE PRICE, one such billboard proclaimed proudly, followed in rapid succession by another—DAHLING! Then another—SUCH DEALS! And another—TO DIE FOR! And yet another—AT YEEHAW! Jamie got the distinct impression that if she were to lay all these signs end to end, the territory covered would probably be bigger than the tiny town of Yeehaw itself.

Weaving through all these signs were multiple billboards for Florida orange juice—TO YOUR HEALTH!—Busch Gardens, SeaWorld, assorted wildlife preserves, and that modern convenience known as a Sun Pass, a device that allowed drivers to zip through the many toll plazas en route without having to wait in line. HE'S NOT FAMOUS / HE DRIVES AN OLD CAR / YET HE GOES THROUGH TOLLS / LIKE A MOVIE STAR, a coterie of signs announced, one after the other. There were also billboards trumpeting the politics of special interest groups. One urged drivers to CHOOSE LIFE, before asking, AREN'T YOU GLAD YOUR MOTHER DID? while another warned that THE UNITED NATIONS WANTS TO TAKE YOUR GUN.

Only in Florida, Jamie thought, watching the passenger in the convertible ahead of them lift long, tanned legs into the air to rest her bare feet on the dashboard, revealing toenails painted a variety of bright colors. Like a bunch of M&M's, Jamie thought, switching her attention to the many vanity plates whizzing by—LA GUTS, IPINE4U, LITIG8R—and the ubiquitous bumper stickers boasting of proud parents and their honor-student offspring. There was also SHE'S A CHILD—NOT A CHOICE stenciled in black across the oversize trunk of an old white Lincoln Continental, a poster taped to the inside of the rear passenger window of a Dodge Caravan that announced THERE IS NO GRAVITY—THE EARTH SUCKS, and Jamie's personal favorite, a hand-painted sign that stretched across the entire back window of a bright yellow Corvette and advised fellow travelers to SAVE A HORSE, RIDE A COWBOY. Jamie closed her eyes, realizing she was getting a headache from squinting through the bright sun, and almost drifted off to sleep, lulled by the hypnotic refrains of the country tunes on the radio, songs that invariably had something to do with heartache, drinking, and more of the same. A sudden tweaking in the vicinity of her bladder was an unnecessary reminder that she hadn't been to the bathroom since leaving her apartment.

It was only hour three of her long journey and already she was tired, headachy, and uncomfortable.

Still, she couldn't remember the last time she'd felt so exhilarated.

"What are you smiling about?" Brad asked, smiling himself.

Jamie laughed and opened her eyes. "I just can't believe how good I feel."

Brad's right hand left the wheel and stretched across the front seat to caress her bare thigh. "You sure do."

Jamie flushed as she glanced at the black Jaguar in the lane beside her. The two cars had been taking turns passing each other for the last several miles. HOT DOC, the Jag's license plate read. Jamie wondered if the man behind the wheel was a busy doctor or an in-demand producer of documentaries. Maybe he was a good-looking veterinarian, or possibly a dentist with delusions of grandeur. She wondered if he could see Brad's hand as it burrowed its way beneath the left leg of her white shorts. But the HOT DOC was staring straight ahead, seemingly transfixed by the heavy flow of midday traffic, and was oblivious to the sexual shenanigans taking place right next to him.

"Undo your shorts," Brad directed.

"What?"

"You heard me."

"I can't do that."

"Why not?"

"Because I can't. People can see in."

"Nobody's looking. Besides, I can't get at you like this."

A series of mild electrical shocks traveled up and down Jamie's entire body as she slowly, and reluctantly, removed Brad's hand from inside her shorts and purposefully crossed her legs. "You're supposed to be concentrating on the road."

"How can I concentrate on the road with you sitting there, looking so damned delicious?"

Delicious, Jamie repeated silently, savoring the sound. When had anybody ever told her she looked delicious? The man was getting better by the second. She took a deep breath, stifling a groan of pure pleasure that was building inside her. How had she gotten so lucky? she asked herself as she had asked herself the night before. How had an impromptu one-night stand turned into the best thing that had ever happened to her? LET GO AND LET GOD, she thought, recalling another, perhaps prophetic, bumper sticker she'd seen just after they left Stuart.

After the decision to leave town had been made, everything had proceeded with exaggerated speed, as if someone had pressed an invisible fast-forward button. Jamie had quickly discarded her work clothes in favor of an old pair of white shorts and an orange T-shirt, then thrown a few items into an overnight bag that Brad had subsequently tossed into the trunk of the car. He'd advised her to pack light, told her he'd buy her whatever she needed along the way. Whatever she needed. Whatever she wanted. Whenever she wanted it, he'd said. Nobody had ever said anything like that to her before. Just as no one had ever told her she looked delicious before. And not just delicious either, but **damned** delicious. Her smile widened. "I look delicious?" she asked, hoping to hear the words again.

"Good enough to eat," Brad said teasingly. "In fact, I may just have to pull off the road at this service station coming up, and do just that." Without another word, he transferred the car into the far left lane, signaling his intention to get off at the next exit.

"What? No. You can't. Brad. No. You can't be serious."

"Oh, I'm serious all right. I have a powerful hunger all of a sudden."

"No, Brad. We can't," Jamie protested as Brad left the main highway.

"Why can't we?"

"I just wouldn't feel comfortable."

Brad ignored her continuing protestations as he followed a large transport truck along the gently winding road away from the turnpike toward the service center in the middle of the divided highway. The lot, already crowded with cars and trucks, contained a self-service gas station with three lanes of pumps and a small convenience store at its far end. Jamie wondered if Brad was really serious and, if so, where he intended to park so that they wouldn't be noticed. Did he really intend to go down on her in the middle of a service center in the middle of the Florida Turnpike in the middle of the day in the middle of middle America, an act that would undoubtedly land them in the middle of a holding cell? Was she really going to let him?

Despite her vociferous protests, Jamie found herself strangely thrilled by the notion of making love in such a public place. A service center no less. Surrounded by cars and trucks and weary travelers stretching their legs. She laughed to herself. Talk about being serviced! She'd never done anything remotely like this, and she doubted that all those billboards and bumper stickers advising her to CHOOSE LIFE had had quite this scenario in mind.

And yet, that's exactly what I'm doing, she decided, riding a fresh wave of euphoria as Brad pulled the car into the lane closest to the small convenience store. I'm choosing life. I'm letting go and letting God. Or Brad, as the case may be, she corrected, holding her breath and bracing herself as he turned off the car's ignition and swiveled around in his seat. Was he really going to do it right here, right now?

"I was just teasing you," he said with a slow smile. "You know I'd never do anything to make you uncomfortable."

"I know that," Jamie said, hoping neither her face nor her voice betrayed her disappointment. What was the matter with her? Had she no shame at all?

Brad kissed her on the cheek, then got out of the car, using his credit card to activate the gas pump, then selecting the most expensive gasoline. “You have to use the washroom?” he asked, leaning back into the front seat. “Now’s probably a good time.”

“Good idea.”

“I think it’s around back,” he directed as she climbed out of the car. “You probably need a key.” He pointed toward the convenience store.

The heat slammed into Jamie like a rude pedestrian, the sheer force of it almost knocking her to the pavement. She tripped over her own feet and turned back self-consciously toward Brad, who was standing beside her car, waving with one hand as he manipulated the gas pump with the other, and he was smiling that fabulous grin that outshone even the blistering Florida sun. “You okay?” he called out.

She nodded. “You want anything? A Coke? Some chips?”

“A Coke would be great. You need some money?”

Jamie laughed, held up her tan canvas purse. “My treat.” She entered the small store, a welcome torrent of frigid air rushing to embrace her. In the distance she heard a car door slamming, an engine revving, tires squealing. Someone's in a hurry, she thought, staring at the rows of junk food and magazines. An old and broken video game sat in a far corner behind a stack of unopened boxes. Along the walls were four large, glass-doored refrigerators filled with dairy products and soft drinks. She withdrew several cans of soda pop from the fridge and carried them past a middle-aged couple hunched over a map, arguing about a missed exit. "How much?" Jamie asked the gum-chewing young woman behind the counter.

"Two dollars, fifty cents."

Jamie handed over a five-dollar bill and waited for her change, realizing she had about a hundred dollars in cash. "Can I have the key to the washroom?" she asked the cashier.

"Don't need one." The girl noisily cracked her gum as she dropped the two cans of Coke into a plastic bag and handed the bag to Jamie. "The lock's broken."

Great, Jamie thought, taking the bag and

lowering her head as she stepped back into the bright sun. Out of the corner of her eye, she noticed a rag-covered derelict in a pair of mismatched sneakers standing beside a clump of newspaper boxes, his body swaying before them, as if praying. Creepy, Jamie thought, as tiny rivulets of perspiration gathered at the base of her hairline.

"Hey," someone shouted, and Jamie looked toward the sound, hoping to see Brad waving at her from beside her car. But what she saw was one teenage boy calling to another, and what she didn't see was Brad Fisher or her blue Thunderbird anywhere in sight. Her body did a quick 360-degree turn. Both her trusted steed and her Prince Charming were gone.

Where was he? she wondered, spinning around.

When something seems too good to be true, it usually is, she heard her mother and sister chant in unison.

It didn't make any sense. Brad had had his chance to leave this morning. Hell, he'd already left. Why would he come back—with bagels, no less—if he was planning to abandon her only hours later?

Jamie knew the answer to that one even before the question was fully formed. Because he needed a car, she reminded herself. Because his own car had broken down and he needed wheels to get to Ohio.

Because he'd lied about having money and staying at the Breakers, and God only knows what else.

Because it was a long, boring drive and she was a pleasant diversion.

Because she was an idiot, Jamie thought, as tears sprung to her eyes and fell down her cheeks. She tried to ignore them as she walked around the store to the washrooms at the back. "A **damned** idiot." She pulled open the door marked **adies,** its **L,** like Brad Fisher, long gone.

The room was surprisingly clean, the smell of disinfectant radiating from the off-white walls. A large, green, plastic garbage bin stood in front of a green Formica counter containing two graying, enamel sinks, and someone had obviously tried to brighten up the small, windowless room by placing a Coke bottle filled with plastic flowers in front of the large mirror behind the sinks. Probably the same person had made a hurried stab at cleaning the mirror, and the result was a series of artful streaks that dissected the glass at irregular intervals.

Jamie opened the door to the closest of the two toilet stalls, lowering her purse and the bag of Cokes to the floor, and pulling down her shorts, even as her sister warned her not to let her flesh make contact with the seat. **Squat,** Cynthia instructed.

At the very least, line the seat with toilet paper, her mother urged.

In response, Jamie sat directly down on the seat, lowering her head into her hands and fighting back tears. "What am I doing? What's wrong with me?"

She remained in this position long after she was through, looking up only when she heard the outside door open and someone step inside. And then nothing. No movement, no water running, no opening the door to the second stall. Just the sound of breathing.

The sound of someone waiting.

"Brad?" Jamie asked hopefully. "Is that you?"

Still nothing.

Jamie pulled up her shorts and tried to see through the crack in the door, but all she could see was a sliver of the mirror on the opposite wall, and the hint of something black reflected in its surface. She held her breath as outside her stall, the breathing grew louder, more ragged. A pair of torn and mismatched sneakers shuffled into view beneath her stall door. The derelict from outside the convenience store! she realized. The one swaying aimlessly in front of the row of newspaper boxes. He'd followed her in here. He was standing just outside her stall, waiting for her to come out. Why? What was he planning to do?

Jamie looked frantically from side to side, trying to weigh her options. The safest thing to do was probably nothing—just stay put and wait the stranger out. Surely somebody would have to use the washroom eventually. Or she could start screaming, hope someone would hear her over the din of the surrounding traffic. At the very least, her screams might scare the man away. Or spur him into action, she realized. Maybe she should take her chances and make a run for it. Even though Jamie had only observed the man briefly, her impression was that he had a slight build and was probably feebleminded. Much like herself, she found herself thinking, and might have laughed had she not been so scared. She lowered herself back to the toilet seat, opting to wait the intruder out. A second later, she was back on her feet. What if the derelict tried to break down the door? It wasn't that strong. One good push and he'd probably succeed. Or he might try to climb over the stall.

Jamie's gaze shot toward the top of the door. She braced herself for the sight of mad eyes and an eerily toothless smile. But mercifully, the mismatched, tattered sneakers remained firmly planted on the floor outside her stall. Dear God, what was she supposed to do?

Instinctively Jamie's hand stretched toward the plastic bag at her feet. Her purse might not be heavy enough to inflict any damage, but two cans of Coke just might do the trick. Providing—she had enough room to swing, she had enough time to aim the bag at the man's head, and he didn't overpower her first.

Someone, please help me, she prayed, hearing whimpering and knowing it was hers. Please, God. Just let him go away. If you make him go away, I promise I'll never do anything stupid again. I'll listen to my sister, and I won't sleep with married men or pick up strangers in bars. I'll find another job, and I'll stick with it no matter how uninspiring it might be. I'll even apologize to Lorraine Starkey, if you'll just get me out of this mess.

And then suddenly the feet withdrew. The outer door opened, then closed. The man was gone, Jamie realized, doubling over with relief. "Let go and let God," she whispered gratefully. Then slowly, her purse in one hand, the plastic bag in the other, she pushed open the door to her stall.

No one was there.

She stood in the middle of the airless room, allowing her breathing to return to normal. Was it possible she'd imagined the whole thing?

Jamie went to the sink and splashed a palmful of cold water on her face, pulling a brown paper towel from its dispenser and rubbing the tears from her eyes and cheeks. Then she pushed back her hair and took a deep breath. Her ordeal was far from over. Now she had to figure out a way to get back home. She'd survived one potentially awful encounter only to be faced with another, this time with someone even more frightening than a deranged stranger—her sister. Jamie pulled open the outer door, thinking, Are you ready for that?

He was standing just outside the door, his black rags blocking the sun, his face in shadows. His nose was long, his mouth hidden by a shapeless and unkempt beard, and his eyes were dark and unfocused. The eyes of a madman, Jamie thought, hearing a scream pierce the air. **Her** scream, she realized.

"Get away from me!" she yelled, tears blinding her eyes. "Get away from me."

The man quickly recoiled.

"Jamie? It's okay," a voice assured her. "You're all right. It's okay."

Jamie stopped crying, swiped at her eyes with the back of her left hand, and opened them wide in disbelief. "Brad?"

"Who did you think it was?"

Jamie spun around, her eyes shooting in several different directions at once. "There was a man. You didn't see him?"

"I saw some beggar taking off into the bushes. Why? What happened? Did he hurt you?"

"No," Jamie admitted, taking a moment to catch her breath. "He just scared me." She described what had just taken place.

"Sounds like you scared him more." Brad shook his head in seeming amazement. "You should never have come back here alone. Why didn't you call me as soon as you saw him?"

"I looked for you. Where were you?"

"I noticed one of the tires was looking a little low, so I took it around the side to give it some air. Then I figured I might as well use the facilities myself. Which is when I heard this god-awful racket. . . ." His lips broke into a sly smile. "Feisty little thing, aren't you?"

"Am I?" No one had ever called her feisty before. Foolhardy, yes. Stubborn, often. But never feisty.

"Feisty," Brad repeated, backing her into the washroom and kicking the door closed behind them. "And very sexy." He pushed the large, green garbage bin in front of the door, blocking both entry and escape. "Very, very sexy."

"What are you doing?"

"What do you think I'm doing?" He reached for her, one hand pinning her against the wall while the other one tugged at the side zipper of her shorts. In the next second, he was hoisting her into the air and pushing his way roughly inside her.

Jamie gasped, unable to believe the speed with which everything had turned around.

One minute she was terrified, the next relieved, the next so excited she could barely breathe. She grabbed hold of Brad's shoulders, hanging on for dear life as he spun her around the small room, pummeling into her repeatedly. She caught a glimpse of her face in the mirror, barely recognizing the woman she saw reflected in the glass, her mouth open, her head thrown back in wild abandon. Who are you? Jamie wondered. What are you doing?

"This is all your fault, you know," Brad said later, taking a plastic flower from its container and tucking it behind her ear. "You're just so damned delicious."

Jamie followed him out of the bathroom, her head lowered, her legs wobbling and threatening to give way. Feisty and delicious, she repeated proudly to herself as she walked beside him to the car, happy to accept the blame.

CHAPTER SIX

Her rejected story peeking out from the top of her tote bag, Lily pushed through the thick double-glass door of Scully's gym, located in a small and unassuming strip mall that was only a short bus ride from Mad River Road, at exactly one minute to ten that morning, greeting the deeply tanned woman behind the reception counter with a big smile and a large, skim-milk latte.

"You're a godsend," Jan Scully said, taking the coffee from Lily's outstretched hand and tearing the lid off the top in one sweeping gesture, slurping eagerly at the hot foam. "How'd you know this is exactly what I've been pining for all morning?"

"Because it's what you're always pining for,"

Lily told the forty-two-year-old owner of Scully's.

Everything about the woman was magnificently over-the-top, from her height—Jan was several inches over six feet tall—to the full orange lips she regularly had injected with collagen, to the turquoise blue shadow that coated her upper eyelids, to the raucous laugh that rumbled through her body, like thunder. Photographs of Jan in her heyday—most showing her in a series of skimpy bikinis, proudly hoisting an assortment of bodybuilding trophies into the air above a haystack of flamboyant red curls—covered the wall behind the reception counter, while the trophies themselves—brass dishes, silver cups, stone carvings—filled a locked glass case that sat against the far wall. Today, as was her usual custom, Jan wore a sleeveless gray T-shirt, the better to show off her still-shapely arms and rock-hard biceps, and matching sweatpants that were slung low across her hips to highlight her preternaturally flat stomach. The **Scully's** logo was emblazoned prominently on the chest and butt of each, in bright pink letters, intended to convey the message that a membership at Scully's would result in a flab-free body like Jan's.

Lily tucked her tote bag behind the counter and pulled up one of two high wooden stools, casually scanning the exercise room behind the wall of glass at the back of the small reception area. She counted a total of six people—five women and one man—making use of the various machines, and smiled. She knew something they didn't: that while regular workouts did indeed help keep Jan's body in great condition for a woman over forty, her recent tummy tuck and boob job had accomplished even more. Not to mention the extensive liposuction on her hips and thighs. "After a certain age, there's only so much exercise can do," Jan had confided in a deep, throaty voice that hinted at a wild, misspent youth, swearing Lily to secrecy. Of course it also helped that Jan had never had children, Lily thought, patting the slight bulge around her own middle. No, the gym was Jan's child, won in a hard-fought custody battle with her soon-to-be-ex-husband, a muscle-bound, steroid-addled rogue who'd left her for the twenty-three-year-old nurse of the plastic surgeon who'd recently removed the bags from underneath Jan's disbelieving eyes.

Some might have relished the irony, but Lily refused to entertain such unkind thoughts. Jan had given her a job when she first arrived in Dayton, this despite her total lack of experience. For that alone, the woman deserved nothing less than Lily's kindest thoughts and best wishes, just as she deserved the latte Lily bought her every day. "How's it going?" Lily asked as Jan finished her coffee and started gathering up her belongings.

"It was busy as hell when I first opened the doors. Stan Petrofsky was actually here before I arrived, chomping at the bit to get in. Must have a new girlfriend." She laughed the laugh filled with thunder and glanced toward the exercise room. "It's tapered off a bit since then."

The phone rang and Lily answered it. "Scully's," she said with a smile. "Yes, we certainly are open. That's right, from seven a.m. to ten p.m. Monday through Saturday, and from eight to six on Sunday. Uh-huh. Yes, absolutely, I can do that," Lily continued, responding to the caller's request for more information. "Well, membership is normally an initial payment of five hundred dollars, plus thirty dollars a month, but we're currently offering a special of only two hundred and fifty dollars to join. Plus the thirty dollars a month, yes."

"Don't forget to mention the free mug and T-shirt," Jan said.

"And we're throwing in a free mug and T-shirt," Lily added dutifully.

"Get her name," Jan reminded Lily just as she was about to ask for it.

"Can I have your name?" Lily grabbed a pencil, scribbled **Arlene Troper** on a nearby piece of paper. "Yes, we have several treadmills, as well as a couple of elliptical machines and an extensive collection of free weights." She peered through the glass wall at the rather paltry display of old equipment. "We also have a bench press, a rowing machine, and a stationary bicycle. No, we don't have a Gravitron. We've found that the simpler things work best," Lily improvised quickly. What do you expect for these prices? she was tempted to ask but didn't. "As well, we can provide you with a personalized exercise routine to suit your needs. Yes, that's included in the initial payment. Good. Well, thank you, Mrs. Troper. I look forward to seeing you then. Okay. Thank you." She hung up the phone. "Arlene Troper says she'll drop by sometime this afternoon."

"It's the free mug," Jan said with a laugh. "Gets them every time."

Jan was smiling, but Lily could tell she was worried. Membership had fallen off substantially ever since Art Scully had opened his own gym in a competing mall only several blocks away. Art's Gym was bigger and boasted better and newer equipment. Art was also offering a deal on membership that included a free T-shirt—although not a free mug, as Jan was quick to point out.

Jan slung her large, floral-print purse over

her shoulder, took a long, critical look at her reflection in the glass of the trophy case, and headed for the door. "I'll see you later," she said. "What book are we supposed to have read for tonight?"

Lily sighed. The five women who made up her monthly book club were supposed to come prepared. At the very least, they were supposed to have read the book being discussed. "**Wuthering Heights,**" Lily told her.

"Oh, great. I read it in high school. Cathy and that guy, Clifford . . . ?"

"Heathcliff."

"Right. Good stuff. Anyway, I'm off. Wish me luck."

"Why do you need luck?" Lily asked.

But the front door was already closing, and the only response Lily received was the flutter of Jan's long, orange nails waving good-bye.

"Good luck," Lily called out belatedly, hoping that Jan wasn't about to do anything foolish. Such as consult another doctor about that brow lift she'd been considering ever since she saw a picture of Catherine Zeta-Jones in one of the tabloids and remarked that nobody could possibly look that good without a little surgical help.

"It's unnatural," she'd proclaimed. "Not found in nature," she'd added for good measure.

Lily walked around the reception desk to the small black leather settee, straightening the magazines that were strewn carelessly across the top of the square, oak coffee table in front of it. Julia Roberts smiled up at her from the cover of one magazine, Gwyneth Paltrow from another. They both looked impossibly beautiful, although Lily had seen pictures of Gwyneth in sweats and carrying a yoga mat, looking less than fabulous, and even Julia looked occasionally tired, wan, and downright horsey when she wasn't all dolled up.

"The mark of a truly beautiful woman," Lily's mother had once told her, "is that she doesn't always look beautiful."

It was one of the things her mother used to say that sounded profound on the surface but didn't make much sense upon closer examination. Still, Lily had taken comfort in those words, as she'd taken comfort in so much of her mother's down-home blend of wisdom and common sense. If I can be half the comfort to my son that my mother was to me, I'll count myself lucky, she thought, wishing her mother was beside her right now, reluctantly absorbing the ineluctability of her loss. So many losses, she was thinking, fighting back the sudden threat of tears. Her mother had been the one who'd held everyone together after Kenny had lost control of his motorcycle that awful, rain-soaked night, crashing it into a tree at the side of the road only blocks from home. Her mother had been the one who'd rocked her in her arms in the moments of her deepest and darkest despair, the one who'd tried desperately to assure her that Kenny's death hadn't been her fault, that she wasn't to blame.

And Lily had almost believed her.

Almost.

The phone rang and Lily returned to the reception desk. "Scully's," she announced, her voice resonating with fake cheer. It was important to present a positive front, to remain optimistic. “Yes, we’re open until ten. That’s right. No, I’m afraid you have to take out a membership in order to use the facilities. But we’re having a special introductory offer. . . . Hello? Hello?” Lily shrugged and hung up the phone, no longer offended when people cut her off in midspiel. People were busy after all. They didn’t always have time to indulge others, especially once they realized they had no interest in whatever was being offered. She’d stopped taking such rudeness personally, just as she’d stopped interpreting her scores of rejection slips to mean she was a lousy writer. Reading was subjective after all. Her book club had certainly taught her that. What one person found scintillating and profound, another found disappointing and shallow. You couldn’t please everyone. You shouldn’t try.

Lily watched Sandra Chan, an attractive woman in her mid-to-late thirties, climb off the elliptical machine and wrap a thin, white towel around her equally thin, white neck, then wait for her friend, Pam Farelli, to finish up on the treadmill. Minutes later, the two women, talking animatedly, pushed through the heavy glass door that separated the exercise room from the reception area and proceeded into the small locker room behind the black leather settee without so much as a glance in her direction. I'm invisible to them, Lily thought. "Which is a good thing," she reminded herself in her best Martha Stewart voice.

The front door opened and a rugged-looking man with short, dark hair, a sturdy build, and massive hands protruding from under the sleeves of his tan windbreaker stepped inside. "Good morning," he greeted Lily as she reached underneath the counter to hand him a fresh towel.

"How are you today, Detective Dawson?" she asked, as she asked every Monday, Wednesday, and Friday when the plainclothes police officer dropped by for his regular forty-minute workout.

"Not bad at all," came his standard response. "Even better if you'll agree to have dinner with me tonight."

Lily took an involuntary step back, not sure how to respond. This was a deviation from their familiar banter, and she was unsure how to proceed. It wasn't that she didn't find Detective Dawson attractive. She did, and had, ever since he'd come storming through the doors just after she started working at Scully's, barking, "Is that your white Impala parked illegally in the handicapped zone? Because if it is, it's about to get towed."

"It's not mine," she'd stammered. "I don't have a car."

"No, but you have an awfully pretty smile," he'd replied quickly, with a smile of his own.

"Tonight's my book club," she told him now.

Jeff Dawson narrowed his dark blue eyes and wrinkled his twice-broken nose, as if he'd just stumbled onto something sinister. "Book club? You mean, like Oprah?"

"Except for the cameras and the seven-figure salary." Lily smiled, thinking that he wore his weight well, then shook her head, angry at herself for noticing. It was precisely because she found him so attractive that she could never go out with him. Hadn't she decided that part of her life was over? She had a young son to think about, a life to rebuild. A little innocent flirting was one thing, but she didn't have the energy for the trivialities of dating, the time for the vagaries of the single scene, the patience for the inevitability of disappointment, the stamina to withstand, once again, the horrible sounds of her world crashing down around her.

"How about tomorrow?" he asked.

"Tomorrow?"

"Seven-thirty? Dinner at Joso's?"

Lily had never eaten at the popular, and very pricey, downtown restaurant, although she'd heard wonderful things about it. McDonald's was more her speed these days. And besides, where would she find a babysitter at this late date?

"I have a son," she told Jeff Dawson simply, searching his face for even the slightest hint that this was more than he bargained for.

"A son?"

"Michael. He's five."

"My daughters are nine and ten. They live with their mother. We're divorced. Obviously." He laughed self-consciously. "Almost three years now. You?"

"Widow. Last year. Motorcycle accident," she clarified before he could ask.

"I'm sorry."

"I can't have dinner with you tomorrow night," Lily said.

Jeff Dawson nodded, as if he understood. "Maybe another time," he said easily, moving away from the desk and toward the exercise room at back, almost colliding with Sandra Chan and Pam Farelli, who were now dressed and ready to leave.

"He's cute," Pam said, loud enough to be heard as Sandra's eyes trailed after him. "Great triceps," she continued, watching the detective shed his tan windbreaker to reveal the muscular torso straining against his white T-shirt.

"We always leave too early," Pam pouted.

"Who is he anyway?" she asked Lily, as if suddenly aware of her presence. "Is he a regular?"

Lily felt an unexpected stab of jealousy and fought the urge to run around the desk to trundle these two would-be poachers out of the gym. "I'm sorry. What?" she said instead.

"The guy bench-pressing two-hundred-pound weights without breaking a sweat," Pam said, pointing with her chin. "What do you know about him?"

"Is he married?" asked Sandra Chan.

"I know he has two daughters," Lily said, pretending to be busy with something under the counter. "Nine and ten years old, I believe."

The women shrugged in unison. "Damn," one muttered.

"The good ones are always married," said the other.

Well, it wasn't quite a lie, Lily decided as the two women pushed open the outside door and disappeared in a burst of sunlight. "He does have two daughters. They are nine and ten years old." But why hadn't she simply told the women the truth? She pulled her hair into a tight ponytail, secured it with a black scrunchie from her tote bag, and straightened the stacks of thin, white towels that were already perfectly straight, directing her eyes resolutely away from the exercise area. She didn't want to see an attractive man only a few years her senior, wearing a tight-fitting, white T-shirt, and bench-pressing two hundred pounds without breaking a sweat. That was the last thing she wanted to see, the last thing she **needed** to see. Men like Jeff Dawson might fuel her fantasies in unguarded moments, but what she needed right now was a healthy dose of reality. Lily pulled the large stuffed envelope out of her tote bag and laid it on the counter. Reality it is, she thought, pulling out both her story and its accompanying letter of rejection.

Dear Ms. Rogers,

That would be me.

Thank you so much for the opportunity

to read your short story, "Last Woman Standing."

Dumb title for a story. I should have called it something else.

While we found the story to be entertaining and well written,

And what's wrong with entertaining and well written?

we don't think it is quite right for the readers of Women's Own.

Why the hell not? What's not quite right about it?

We wish you the best of luck in placing this piece with another magazine,

What other magazine? I've tried all the other magazines.

and hope you'll think of us in the future.

Fat chance of that.

Sincerely . . .

"**In**sincerely," Lily stated out loud, returning both the letter and the story to the envelope. That's quite enough reality for one day, she decided, her gaze drifting toward the exercise room despite her best intentions. Ada Pearlman, whose fine, gray hair was pinned into an elegant French twist at the nape of her neck, was trudging along on her treadmill at roughly two miles an hour, which was still faster than Gina Sorbara, a verging-on-obese, middle-aged woman who seemed to be sleepwalking on hers. Jonathan Cartseris was struggling with the rowing machine, and Bonnie Jacobs, an elderly woman who'd recently been diagnosed with osteoporosis, was standing in front of the rows of free weights as if she didn't have a clue what she was doing there. Only Police Detective Jeff Dawson looked as though he belonged, lying on his back with his legs spread on either side of the narrow bench, sturdy thighs tensed inside his black sweatpants, as he repeatedly heaved a two-hundred-pound barbell into the air above his head. He **does** look good, Lily found herself thinking, noticing that Bonnie Jacobs was waving at her. Lily smiled and waved back, but the woman persisted, beckoning her inside. Lily quickly got off her stool and went into the exercise room, careful to avoid a closer peek at the now-grunting police detective. "Is something wrong, Mrs. Jacobs?"

"The doctor says I'm supposed to exercise with free weights, but I have no idea what to do." She grabbed a ten-pound weight in each hand and almost fell to her knees.

"Oh, no, Mrs. Jacobs. That's way too heavy for you. You'll injure yourself. Why don't you start with these?" She lifted two, two-pound barbells from the shelf, transferring them gingerly to Mrs. Jacobs.

"Is that enough?"

"It's all you need. Trust me," Lily said, wondering why Mrs. Jacobs should trust her, why **anyone** should trust her. She then demonstrated several easy exercises for the biceps and triceps, as well as one for the pectoral muscles and several for the back and shoulders. "I'll write them out for you, if you'd like," she offered, returning as quickly as she could to the reception area.

The next half hour passed uneventfully—she said hello to the people who came in, good-bye to those who left, answered the phone, did one load of wash and started another. She wondered how Michael was doing in school, he'd taken his new Kermit the Frog puppet in for show-and-tell; what Jan was doing that she'd needed luck for; and whether she should attempt to write another story. She had lots of ideas, although most of them were pretty far-fetched. What was it they always said? Write about what you know? Could she do that? she wondered. Could she be that brave? That stupid?

She shook her head, inadvertently glancing toward the exercise room just as Jeff Dawson raised himself up and sat straddling the bench. Immediately the bench became a motorcycle.

Lily gasped, brought her hand to her mouth. Of course he rode a motorcycle. He was a cop. Riding a motorcycle probably came with the territory. She turned away, refusing to dwell on such possibilities. What difference did it make, since she had no intention of going out with him?

"Everything okay?" he asked, appearing suddenly at her side.

For such a big man, he moved very gracefully, she thought. "Everything's fine. Why do you ask?"

"You look a little pale. You feeling okay?"

"Do you drive a motorcycle?" she heard herself ask.

If he was surprised by the question, he didn't let on. "No. Not since I had kids."

Lily nodded and looked toward the phone, as if begging it to ring.

"Does this mean you might reconsider going out with me tomorrow night?" he asked after a pause.

"Sorry, I can't," Lily said as the outside door opened and her neighbor Emma Frost walked through. "Emma! Hi," Lily greeted her, smiling at the woman as if she were her best friend on earth. "What are you doing here?"

"Thought I'd check out where you work, maybe see about signing up." Emma's huge eyes wandered aimlessly around the premises.

"That's great. We're having a special introductory offer right now. Just two hundred and fifty dollars to join, and thirty dollars a month."

"Two hundred and fifty dollars?" Emma repeated, eyes coming to a stop on Jeff Dawson.

"It's a good deal when you compare it to other clubs in the city," Jeff chimed in.

"And you are?"

"Jeff Dawson, member in good standing."

"I'm sure it is," Emma said playfully, extending her hand. "Emma Frost."

"Have we met before?" Jeff asked, shaking Emma's hand and staring at her intently.

"I don't think so. Why?"

"You just look so familiar to me."

"Emma's eyes used to be on all the packages for Maybelline mascara," Lily volunteered.

"I don't use a lot of mascara," Jeff said with a laugh. "At least not lately. My boss kind of frowns on it."

Emma dropped her gaze to the floor. "And what is it you do, exactly?"

"Jeff's a police detective," Lily said. Was it her imagination or did she see Emma flinch?

"I better get going," Jeff said, pushing himself away from the reception desk. "You have my number in your files," he told Lily. "Call me if you change your mind." He needed only three steps to reach the front door.

"Nice tush," Emma said as the door closed behind him. Then, "Change your mind about what?"

Lily shook off the question with a toss of her head.

"You two have something going on?"

"No. Of course not."

"Then why are you turning all shades of purple?"

"I am not," Lily said, sounding just like her son.

"Okay." Emma shrugged. "Maybe I will

come to that book club thing you mentioned earlier, if the invitation's still open."

"Sure. Great. Any chance you've read **Wuthering Heights**?"

"Are you kidding? It's one of my favorites."

"Terrific. Then I'll see you later."

Emma walked to the door, stopped, and turned back. "You don't want to get involved with a cop," she said.

"You have something against the police?" Lily asked, trying to sound casual.

Emma shrugged. "Just never found them to be very useful."

CHAPTER SEVEN

The main difference that Jamie could determine between Florida and Georgia, at least along this section of I-75, was in the ubiquitous billboards punctuating the flat landscape along the side of the busy highway. Georgia tree-ripe peaches had replaced Florida juicy oranges as the highly trumpeted fruit of choice; Vidalia onions now filled the void left by the Sun Pass when it disappeared, along with the turnpike, at Wildwood; instead of signs counting off the miles till Yeehaw, there were countless billboards hailing the arrival of peanuts and pecans—WE'RE NUTS! WE SHELL! YOU CAN PECAN! There were also an alarming number of ads for what appeared to be pornographic truck stops—CAFÉ

RISQUÉ—WE BARE ALL, and its sister club, CAFÉ EROTICA—WE DARE TO BARE. COUPLES WELCOME, several signs encouraged, while others bragged of GREAT FOOD along with the nude women. These women—COEDS, one sign promised, although JAILBAIT was probably a more apt description, Jamie thought, judging by the pictures of the puffy-haired, pouty-lipped young girls staring down at her from their cardboard perches—were available all day and night for the jaded traveler's entertainment, along with a wide selection of ADULT TOYS AND VIDEOS. These roadside oases were OPEN 24 HOURS, serving up heaping portions of FOOD-N-FUN.

"Food-n-fun," Jamie repeated, shaking her head at the number of cars parked outside each such establishment they whizzed past. It was almost six o'clock, although the sky was still as blue and as bright as it had been at noon. Jamie stretched her legs, arched her back, and rotated her neck in a wide semicircle, hearing her various muscles groan and her bones crack. She was weary of sitting in the same position, even though it was Brad who'd been doing all the driving.

"Tired?" he asked, as if reading her thoughts.

"A little."

"We can stop at the next 'risky café.' " Blue eyes twinkled mischievously.

"Are you serious?"

"You know I'd do anything to make you happy."

Jamie smiled. "I love it when you say things like that," she said, and he laughed. Jamie loved when he laughed. In fact, she'd pretty much decided there was nothing about Brad Fisher she didn't love. Was it possible to fall head over heels in such a short time? Less than twenty-four hours, to be precise. Her sister would undoubtedly insist she was in the throes of infatuation, that she was rebounding from her last, ill-fated affair, which was also not real love, her mother would have added. Real love was built on a foundation of trust and truth. It took time to develop and was based on common goals and interests, respect as well as chemistry. Besides, any idiot could fall in love, both would have agreed. It was the **staying** in love that was the hard part. "So, what are your hobbies?" Jamie asked now, in an effort to silence their nagging, all-knowing voices.

"My hobbies?"

"Do you have any?"

"Do you?"

"Not really," she admitted after a pause. "I guess I should."

"Why?"

"I don't know. My mother loved to play Scrabble. She used to talk me into playing with her. But then she never liked the words I put down—she said they were too simple and that I needed to make better use of my letters—so she'd end up making the words for both of us, and I'd just kind of sit there until it was over. She always won. And my sister plays bridge. She's always trying to get me to take it up, but I don't know. She and her husband are always screaming at each other when they play. I used to collect Barbie dolls when I was little," Jamie continued, smiling at the distant memory. "Does that count as a hobby?"

"Do you still collect?"

Jamie shook her head.

"Then I don't think it counts."

Jamie frowned, wondering what had become of her collection of Barbies. She hadn't seen the dolls—hadn't even thought of them—since she'd moved out of her mother's house. Probably they were still there, she realized, nestled securely among her mother's belongings. Those same belongings she and Cynthia were supposed to be going through this very evening. "Your turn," Jamie said to Brad, mentally tossing her old collection of Barbies through the car window. They were part of her past. The man beside her was her present. Maybe even her future, she allowed herself to think. "I've talked enough. It's your turn."

"What is it you want to know?"

"I don't know. Stuff."

"Stuff?"

"Yeah. Stuff. Details."

"Details?"

"Life's in the details. Isn't that what they say?" Is that what they said? Or was it God? God was in the details. Or was it the devil?

"Life's in the details," Brad repeated. "I like that."

Jamie felt a flush of pride. She'd said something he liked. No point in changing it now. "What are some of the things you like to do? Aside from . . . you know."

"Aside from making love to you?" His head swiveled toward her, his tongue resting provocatively between his teeth.

"Aside from that," Jamie said quickly, feeling the familiar stirring between her legs. "Watch the road."

"Why? Is it doing something interesting?"

Jamie smiled. "I mean, I already know you like computers."

"Computers?"

"Well, you design software. Isn't that what you said?" Had she misunderstood?

"Sorry, I thought you asked about my hobbies."

"I thought you said you didn't have any."

He smiled. "Well, I like movies."

"Yeah? What kind?"

"The usual guy-kind. Action, war movies, thrillers."

"I like thrillers," Jamie agreed. "Maybe we can go to one later. Maybe there's a drive-in."

"A drive-in? They still have those?"

"I don't know. Maybe there's one along the highway somewhere." She stared at the strip of long grass that divided the north and south traffic, saw nothing but the lines of cars moving steadily in both directions.

"How'd your mother die?" Brad asked suddenly.

Jamie released a deep breath of air. "Cancer. It started in her left breast about five years ago. The doctors operated, thought they got it all. But it was only hiding. Cancer's real sneaky that way."

"It came back," Brad stated.

"This time right between her lungs, so there was nothing they could do."

"Must have been hard for her."

"I guess. She didn't believe in complaining. Said facts were facts, and you had to accept them. She was a judge," she added.

"What kind of judge?"

"Criminal court."

"Sounds like one tough lady."

"She wasn't easy." Jamie shrugged. "I think it's hard when you're in a position of power, you know, when you have that kind of control over other people's lives, and you spend all day telling people what to do, and then you come home and you've got to deal with this wiseass kid who thinks she knows everything. I mean, here the woman is in court, where nobody so much as goes to the bathroom without her permission—I mean that literally—and everyone's deferring to her left, right, and center, hoping to get a favorable ruling, and here she's got this daughter who's always arguing with her, and who never listens, let alone takes her advice, so it's got to be hard."

"On both of you, I would imagine."

"She used to throw her hands up in the air,

like this." Jamie illustrated, extending her arms and stretching her fingers, as if she were tossing confetti. "And then she'd stomp out of the room, muttering to herself. 'Fine. Have it your way. Do what you want.' You could just picture her judge's long, black robes trailing after her." Jamie shook her head. "She said I was incorrigible."

"Meaning?"

"Willful, uncontrollable." She sighed. "Impossible to rehabilitate."

"Impossible to rehabilitate," Brad repeated, smiling. "I like that."

"I don't know. I like to think I'm a good person."

"Which is exactly your problem."

"What is?"

"You think too much."

"What about **your** mother?" Jamie asked, finding it vaguely curious that every time she asked about him, they ended up talking about her. Was she really so self-centered?

The skin around Brad's mouth tensed, pulling back into a stiff smile. His fingers tightened their grip on the wheel. "What about my mother?"

"Well, you told me about your sisters, but you didn't say anything about your mom and dad."

"That's because there isn't much to say. They're just typical, upstanding, hardworking, God-fearing citizens of this great country of ours."

"Are you being sarcastic?"

"Why would I be sarcastic?"

"I don't know."

"You're thinking too much again."

"Where do they live?" Jamie persisted, trying a different tack.

"Texas."

"I've never been to Texas."

"You're kidding."

"I've never been a lot of places."

"Then I'll have to take you there someday."

Jamie smiled. "I'd like that."

"You've lived in Florida all your life?"

"Most of it. My mother wanted me to go to Harvard, of course, but I opted to stay in

Florida. I lived in Atlanta for a while," she added, almost reluctantly.

"What's in Atlanta?"

"My ex-husband."

"And his mother," Brad said, lowering his voice.

It all comes back to mothers, Jamie thought. "Let's not go there," she said.

"On the contrary," Brad said. "We'll be passing through Atlanta in another few hours. Maybe we should drop in and say hello. How'd you like that?"

"I wouldn't," Jamie said. "Is that a cop car?" She pointed toward a black-and-white sedan at the side of the highway.

"Shit." Brad pumped the brake in a futile effort to reduce his speed before being tagged by radar.

Too late. The cruiser was already behind them, lights flashing.

"Shit," Brad said again, banging the palm of his hand against the steering wheel.

Jamie held her breath as Brad brought the car to a halt, frightened though she wasn't sure why. She swiveled around in her seat as the officer approached, a visor and helmet covering his eyes. Brad lowered the window as the officer leaned inside.

"License and registration, please."

Brad reached in his pocket as Jamie popped open the glove compartment and retrieved the car's registration.

"Remove the license from your wallet, please," the policeman instructed Brad, who promptly did just that.

"Any idea how fast you were going?" The officer's gloved hand closed over the license and registration.

"I'm not sure," Brad said. "I didn't think it was too—"

"I clocked you at eighty-four miles per hour," the officer interrupted. "This is a seventy-mile-an-hour zone."

"I was just trying to keep up with the flow of traffic," Brad explained.

"Wait here," the officer directed, returning to his car.

"Bastard," Brad muttered.

"What's he doing now?" Jamie asked.

"Checking to make sure there are no outstanding warrants."

"Are there?" Jamie had heard stories of southern roadside justice, apocryphal tales of travelers being forced to pay exorbitant speeding fines on the spot, and being hauled off to jail if they couldn't produce the necessary cash. She wondered whether her car was about to be impounded, and what it would be like to spend the night in some small-town holding cell. She pictured her mother watching the events from somewhere in the cloudless blue sky, saw her shaking her head. "Brad? Are you all right?" she asked, suddenly aware of his rigid posture, the scowl that had overtaken his jaw.

He didn't answer.

"Brad?" she asked again as the officer reappeared at the side of the car.

The policeman handed back their license and registration. "This area's pretty heavily patrolled. I suggest you slow down if you don't want to get stopped again." He wrote out a ticket, handed it through the window. "Oh, Mr. Fisher," he added, about to back away. "Your rear tire's looking a little low. You might want to stop at Tifton and have somebody take a look at it."

"Will do," Brad said.

"Thank you, officer," Jamie said as the policeman retreated. "It was nice of him to tell us about the tire—"

"Asshole," Brad sneered, stuffing both the license and the registration into the pocket of his jeans.

"How much is the ticket for?"

In response, Brad ripped the ticket into half a dozen pieces, dropped them to the floor at his feet. "What difference does it make?"

"What are you doing?" Jamie protested. "It's not going to just go away."

"It just did." He started the car, waited for a break in the traffic, then pulled into the right lane, quickly increasing his speed until he was driving well above the limit.

Jamie said nothing. Obviously he was upset, and the last thing she wanted to do was say anything that might upset him further. "What do you think is wrong with the tire?" she ventured after several seconds.

"How should I know? It's your fucking car."

Tears sprung to Jamie's eyes, as if he'd slapped her, hard, across the face.

"Sorry," he said immediately. "Jamie, I'm sorry."

"It's all right," she stammered.

"No, it's not all right. I had no business snapping at you like that."

"You were upset."

"That's no excuse. I'm really sorry."

"I don't understand," Jamie said. "I mean, it was just a ticket. We **were** speeding." She glanced toward the dashboard.

Brad quickly brought the car's speed back within the acceptable limits. "Sorry," he apologized again.

"I take it you don't like cops," Jamie stated.

Brad laughed.

Immediately Jamie felt the tension dissipate. She laughed gratefully. Everything was okay. They'd hit a slight blip in the road, courtesy of the Georgia State Police, but now everything was back to normal.

"I hate the bastards," Brad said, instantly shattering the tranquility.

Once again, Jamie's body tensed, her breathing stilled. "Why?"

Brad rubbed the tip of his nose with the back of his hand, narrowed his eyes as he checked the rearview mirror. Clearly he was deciding how much to tell her. "When I was seventeen," he began, "my father got a new car. A Pontiac Firebird," he continued, gradually warming to his subject. "Fire-engine red. Black leather seats. Power-everything. It was a real beauty, and he was so proud of it, always washing and polishing it. God forbid you leaned against it or got your dirty fingerprints on it. He'd go crazy. Well, of course, what do you do when you're a seventeen-year-old boy who wants to impress the girls, and whose father has a new, red Firebird?"

"You didn't."

He glanced at her out of the corner of his eye. "One night, I waited till my parents were asleep, then I took that freshly cleaned, spanking-new car out for a spin, with my favorite girl, Carrie-Leigh Jones, sitting on the black leather seat beside me. And I'm thinking, if this doesn't get me laid, nothing will."

Jamie smiled, although she sensed disaster looming.

"We drove around a while—I was real careful, didn't speed or show off or anything—and then we headed out to Passion Park, or at least, that's what we called it, 'cause in those days that's where everybody went to make out. It was real quiet that night. I think because it was pretty late, and most of the kids had already gone home. Anyway, we start fooling around, and I'm just rounding second base, as we used to say, when I hear this car pull up—I assume it's just some other lucky guy—but before I can even look up, this flashlight is shining in my face, and these two cops are dragging me out of the car, and they're beating the shit out of me, right in front of Carrie-Leigh." Brad's face darkened with the memory of what happened next. "I'm barely conscious when this one officer throws me over his knee, like a little kid, and holds me down while his buddy starts whipping me with his belt. And I'm crying, man. I'm begging them to stop. And I hear one of the policemen say to Carrie-Leigh, 'Why don't you find yourself a real man?' and promising they won't tell her parents where they found her if she keeps her mouth shut about what happened."

Jamie could barely speak. "What happened then?"

Brad shrugged. "'Bout what you'd expect. They drove Carrie-Leigh home. Left me in the dirt to fend for myself." There was a long pause. "Eventually I made it home, terrified of getting blood on those damn black leather seats. Stupid me was still hoping my father was asleep. But there he was, waiting at the front door. Turns out he was the one who'd called the cops, told them to teach me a lesson."

"He told them to beat you up?"

"Saved him the trouble, I guess." Brad smiled. "He laughed when he saw me. Told me if I ever touched his car again, he'd kill me with his bare hands." Brad laughed, a joyless sound that bounced off the car's windows.

"That's so horrible."

"No, that's just life. What'd your mother say—facts are facts, and you gotta accept them? Hey, look." Brad pointed to a large sign on the side of the road.

WELCOME TO TIFTON, the sign proclaimed. THE READING CAPITAL OF THE WORLD.

"I wonder how they know that," Brad mused.

"Maybe we should stop and get something to eat," Jamie said. "Have that tire looked at."

Brad nodded. "I'm really sorry, Jamie," he said again.

Jamie reached over to take his hand. "For what?" she asked.

CHAPTER EIGHT

"All righty, Dylan. Come on up now," Emma called down from the top of the stairs. She was wrapped in a large mustard-colored towel, a smaller one curled around her wet hair. "It's time to get ready for bed."

No answer.

Emma's bare feet padded across the hall at the top of the stairs. She peered into her son's bedroom. The size of a postage stamp, she thought, depression hovering as her eyes passed over the cot-size bed in the middle of the room, the brown shag bath mat that served as a rug lying on the floor beside it, the plain wood dresser propped unsteadily against the opposite wall. One of Dylan's school drawings, an unframed pastiche of colorful images—a big green hill, a stick figure in a red coat and oversize white skates jumping into the air, arms and legs joyously akimbo, a smiling, yellow sun in the far right corner of the page, a bunch of disembodied, pink and blue Smiley Faces scattered throughout—supposedly representing "What Winter Means to Me"—was Scotch-taped to the wall and served as the room's only art. "Dylan, come on, sweetie. Where are you?" Emma checked her watch. It was just past seven o'clock. That gave her almost half an hour to get dressed and dry her hair, then see her son through all his various bedtime rituals before she had to be at Lily's. Hopefully he'd be asleep before Mrs. Discala arrived. Providing, of course, she could find him.

A sudden terror seized her, and she froze. What if their hiding place had been discovered? What if Dylan's father had gained access to the house while she was busy singing in the shower? What if he'd absconded with her son and disappeared into the night? She'd have only herself to blame, she was thinking.

There'd been no reason to wash her hair. It had looked absolutely fine the way it was. Why was she trying to impress a bunch of women she didn't know and cared even less about, women whose company she'd actively shunned until a mix-up in the day's mail had brought a charming and unassuming young woman to her door, a woman offering the renewed possibility of a life filled with something other than running and sleeping and stifling bedtime rituals? A life of friends and conversation, she thought. A life. It had been just too tempting to turn down. "Dylan!" Emma called again, her voice teetering on the edge of hysteria.

"I'm hiding," came a small, muffled voice from inside his tiny closet.

Emma exhaled a relieved breath of air from her lungs. "Well, come on out. It's bedtime."

"You have to find me."

Emma whipped the towel from her head, slung it across her bare shoulders, took a series of exaggerated steps toward the small landing. "I have to find you? But you're such a good hider. It's too hard." She clumped toward her bedroom, made a loud show of opening and closing the bedroom door. "No, you're not there. Where are you? Can you give me a hint?"

Muffled giggles from the next room.

Emma returned to Dylan's room. "And you're not here," she continued, approaching the bed and lifting up the thin, brown-and-white-striped blanket hanging over its sides. "Let's see. Are you under the bed?" She paused. "No, not under the bed."

"Try the closet," her son whispered loudly.

"I think I'll try the closet," Emma announced, crossing the room in several long strides and pulling open the closet door, immediately spotting Dylan curled into a tight little ball on the floor at the back of the closet, his head buried beneath a pile of week-old laundry she kept forgetting to take to the Laundromat. "No, you're not here," Emma said as the laundry shook with laughter. "Where can you be?"

"Look on the floor, silly."

"The floor? There's nothing on the floor but this pile of dirty clothes." Emma bent down. "I better take this stuff to the Laundromat and throw it in a washing machine before it stinks up the whole house."

Dylan screamed in delight, pushing his head through the laundry and scattering the clothes around the small space. "It's me, Mommy," he shouted, jumping into her arms.

Emma stumbled back in shock. "No! Don't tell me you were hiding under the laundry."

Dylan nodded his head emphatically up and down. "Fooled you."

"You certainly did."

"Now it's your turn." Dylan climbed down her body, looked up at her expectantly.

"Oh, sweetie, I can't now. I have to get dressed and dry my hair."

"No. You have to hide." Big blue eyes threatened tears.

Emma knew better than to argue with those eyes. "Okay. But then you have to get ready for bed. Deal?"

"Deal," Dylan agreed.

"Close your eyes and count to ten."

He was already on five before Emma was out the door. Where should I hide this time? she wondered, hurrying into the bathroom and stepping into the still-wet tub, drawing the shower curtains closed around her. What she wouldn't give for a separate shower stall, she was thinking, as he reached ten.

"Ready or not, here I come."

And a Jacuzzi, Emma found herself fantasizing, waiting for her son's footsteps on the tile floor. Instead she heard him clumping down the stairs. Where was he going? He had to know she was hiding in the shower. It was where she always hid. What was he doing? She pulled back the white plastic curtain and inched cautiously out of the tub, tiptoed toward the stairs. She heard him rummaging through the kitchen cupboards. **As if I could squeeze myself into one of those tight little spaces,** she thought with a smile, returning to the bathroom to run a comb through her hair, then applying some blush to her cheeks and mascara to her eyelashes. "Maybelline, of course," she informed her reflection, hearing Dylan run from the kitchen into the dining room.

"I can't find you, Mommy."

"Keep looking," Emma encouraged, lining her lips with a nude pencil, then applying two coats of deep pink lipstick, before reaching under the sink for her hair dryer. A surge of hot air blew against her scalp as she made a mental list of the clothes in her closet. What does one wear to a book club meeting? she wondered. A skirt seemed too formal, while jeans might convey a lack of respect. Probably a simple pair of black pants was the way to go, she decided, although the only pair she had were wool and getting a little heavy for this time of year. What she needed were a few new things, nothing outlandish or impractical, just a few pairs of cotton slacks and some nice tops. Of course Dylan could also use some new things, she thought, feeling a pair of accusing blue eyes gazing up at her.

"You're not hiding," Dylan said, lower lip trembling.

"I was," Emma started to explain, "but—"

"We have to do it again."

"Dylan—"

"Not Dylan!" he protested angrily. "My name isn't Dylan."

Emma was immediately on her knees in front of her son, her fingers digging into the delicate flesh of his skinny arms. "Yes, you are. You're Dylan Frost. Say it."

"No."

"Remember what we talked about? Remember how important it is that you be Dylan Frost? At least for a little while longer?"

"I don't want to be Dylan Frost."

"Do you want them to come and take you away from me? Is that what you want?"

Her son shook his head vehemently, his eyes growing wide with fear.

Emma knew she should stop, but she couldn't. She had to make her son understand how important it was for him to continue with their charade, that their happiness and well-being depended on it. "You don't want to go live with a bunch of strangers, do you?"

"No!" the little boy cried, burrowing deep into her arms, his round little cheeks wet with his tears.

"Okay then, what's your name?"

No response beyond the sound of muffled tears.

Emma pushed her son away, held him at arm's length. "What's your name, little boy?" she asked, as if she were someone he'd met on the street.

"Dylan," the little boy sputtered between sobs.

"Dylan what?"

"Dylan Frost."

"All righty then." Emma closed her eyes and pulled her son close, rocking him gently back and forth. "That's really good, Dylan. You're such a good boy. Mommy is so proud of you."

"I'm Dylan Frost," he repeated for good measure.

"Yes, you are. And you know what?"

"What?"

"It's almost your bedtime, Dylan Frost. So if

you want me to hide, we better do it quickly. You ready?"

He nodded, light brown hair falling into troubled blue eyes.

It was probably time to color his hair again, Emma thought, deciding to leave that battle for another day. "Okay, start counting."

Once again Dylan counted, once again Emma hid behind the shower curtain, and once again Dylan raced down the stairs to check out the kitchen cabinets. Emma looked at her watch, knowing Mrs. Discala would be here in a few minutes and that she was nowhere near ready. She wondered what the protocol for book club meetings was, whether it was acceptable to be ten, even fifteen minutes late. Should she bring cookies, a bottle of wine? I have neither, she realized, hearing Dylan's footsteps clambering up the stairs. **Finally,** Emma thought as he returned to the bathroom and pulled open the shower curtains, looking genuinely surprised to find her there.

"You found me!" Emma wailed in mock consternation.

"Let's play again," Dylan shouted.

"Uh-uh. No. Now it's time to get ready for bed," she told him firmly. "You go get your pajamas on while I get dressed."

Dylan pouted momentarily before giving in and doing as he was told. Emma climbed out of the tub and wiped her feet on the threadbare pink mat before returning to her room and rifling through her closet, ultimately selecting the too-heavy black slacks and a not-too-old peach-colored jersey. Her hair was only partially dry, and several dark strands were already twisting into unruly waves at both sides of her head. "Damn," she said, knowing she didn't have the time to tame them into something more manageable. The story of my life, she thought as her son came bounding into her room dressed in his blue flannel pajamas.

"Where are you going?" he asked warily when he saw her.

"I'm not going anywhere," Emma lied, wishing she didn't have to. But Dylan got so anxious whenever she went anywhere without him, and she just didn't have the time to explain everything right now. It was just easier this way, less traumatic for both of them.

"Then why are you all dressed up?"

"I'm not dressed up."

"Yes, you are."

"Well, I'm not going out," she lied again. "Mrs. Discala is coming over for a visit."

"Why?"

"Because I asked her to."

"Why?"

"Because," Emma said firmly, in no mood to play "why" games. She had only a few minutes to get Dylan in bed and asleep before she had to leave. Normally, Dylan was as quick to fall asleep as he was deliberate in his nighttime rituals, sometimes even nodding off before his head hit the pillow, and not waking up until morning. Unless, of course, a bad dream shook him awake in the middle of the night. No problem, Emma thought, guiding her son back into the bathroom and watching as he slowly twisted the cap from the toothpaste tube, then meticulously spread the white-and-green-striped gel across the soft bristles of his orange toothbrush. She'd only be gone a few hours, back in plenty of time to reassure him if he were visited by nightmares.

Emma studied her reflection in the small, rectangular mirror over the sink as her son began the long process of brushing his teeth. I look so tired, she thought. Not quite thirty, yet sallow and old before my time. What I need is a holiday, she decided. A few days alone. How wonderful that would be, she thought, silently counting out the last of the fifteen strokes her son required to brush his top row of teeth before starting on the bottom. She fought the urge to grab the toothbrush from his hand, finish the job for him, then hurry him into bed. But she'd tried that before, she remembered, and the resultant scene had set them both back for days. At the time, she'd actually considered consulting the school nurse but quickly decided against it. A school nurse understood runny noses and scraped knees, not obsessive-compulsive behavior. And a therapist was out of the question. Therapists cost money, money she didn't have.

Besides, a therapist would ask a lot of questions, and Emma had no answers for those questions. At least, none that she could share.

Dylan half-filled the little pink plastic cup at the side of the sink, stopping the water at a dark grain that ran through the pink plastic, then rinsed his mouth, starting on his left side then transferring the water to his right cheek before spitting three times into the sink. He then returned the plastic cup to its exact position at the side of the sink and wiped the side of his mouth with a flimsy white washcloth. "Finished," he said proudly, as he said every night.

Emma ushered him out of the room with an affectionate pat on his tiny behind, followed him into his room, and watched him touch the wooden baseboard of his narrow bed twice before climbing under the covers and reaching up behind his head to tap the wall. Was he checking to make sure it was still there? she wondered. Was he looking for signs of permanence, however slim? And was she responsible for such irrational behavior? she asked herself again, her own nightly ritual.

Well, I **did** change his name and tell him strangers might come to take him away, she reminded herself, shaking her head in regret as Dylan turned on the radio at the side of his bed. Still, she wasn't to blame for their current situation. Yes, their standard of living had fallen precipitously, and yes, she was often tense and depressed, but she loved her son more than life itself, and she hoped one day he'd understand why she'd had to spirit him away from everything he loved and felt comfortable around. Had she made the right decision? I have nightmares too, she wanted to say. "Good night, sweetie-pie," she said instead, stroking his hair. "Sleep well."

"Tell me a story."

This was a new wrinkle, Emma thought. Something totally unexpected. He senses something is different, she realized, glancing down at her watch, noting it was almost seven-thirty and wondering what was keeping Mrs. Discala. "I don't know any stories," she told him honestly.

"Daddy knew lots of stories."

Emma's entire body tensed. "I know, sweetheart, but—" She broke off, feeling suddenly stupid and inadequate, the way she'd felt throughout most of her marriage to Dylan's father.

"But what?"

Daddy was a liar, she wanted to shout. Instead she said, "How about I tell you a story tomorrow? Maybe we can even go to the bookstore, and you can pick out a book. . . ."

"Tell me a story **now,**" Dylan insisted.

Emma searched her imagination for several seconds, found nothing. What was the matter with her? What kind of mother was she that she didn't know any stories? "Okay, if I tell you a story, you promise you'll go right to sleep?"

Dylan nodded enthusiastically.

"Okay. Just one," she said, stalling for time. Surely she could remember at least one story from her childhood. Except that no one had ever read her a bedtime story either, she realized.

"Mommy?" Dylan was looking at her questioningly.

"Okay. There was once a little boy," Emma began.

"What's his name?"

"His name is Richard."

"I don't like that name."

"No? What name do you like?"

"Buddy."

"Buddy?"

"Yeah, there's this boy in my class named Buddy, and he's cool."

"Cool?"

"Yeah. So can the boy in the story be named Buddy?"

Emma shrugged, once again checking her watch and seeing that it was now seven-thirty on the button. "Buddy, it is." Where **was** Mrs. Discala? She was normally so prompt.

"Mommy?" Dylan prompted again.

"What?"

"There was a little boy named Buddy."

"Right. Once upon a time, there was a little boy named Buddy, who was five years old."

"What did he look like?"

"Buddy was about three and a half feet tall and had soft brown hair that matched his beautiful blue eyes."

"Like me?"

"That's right. He looked just like you." Now what? she wondered. She'd never been very good at this sort of thing, never the girl who, like Lily, had been asked to read her compositions out loud in class. Her imagination just didn't work that way. While she could easily go on about her own experiences—God knows there were plenty of stories she could tell there—she'd never been any good with things like nursery rhymes and fairy tales. "Anyway, Buddy loved licorice sticks," she recited, happily borrowing from Lily's rejected story, "the long, twisted, red ones that his sister used to tell him weren't really licorice at all, but some kind of plastic."

"Plastic?"

Full of horrible red dye that would give him cancer when he grew up, Emma continued silently but didn't repeat out loud. Dylan had enough to worry about. Why couldn't Lily have written something more child-friendly?

"Anyway, Buddy and his mother lived in a small house at the edge of town."

"Where was Buddy's father?"

"Buddy didn't have a father," Emma said curtly. The phone rang. "Close your eyes," Emma directed her son. "I'll be back in a minute." She raced into her bedroom, answered the phone in the middle of its third ring. "Hello?"

It was Mrs. Discala, and she was terribly sorry, she wouldn't be able to babysit after all. She'd hurt her back that afternoon while planting a new rosebush in her backyard, and she'd been lying down ever since, thinking it would feel better soon, but it didn't, and she'd just gotten off the phone with her son, who was a paramedic, and he'd told her to take a few Advil, pour herself a hot bath, and get into bed. She was really sorry, she hated to do this to Emma, especially at the last minute, but she didn't see how she could look after a small child, even one as good as Dylan, even if he was already asleep. She just couldn't do it, she was sorry, she apologized again.

"It's okay," Emma said, hanging up the phone and bursting into tears. "Damn it." She was surprised by just how disappointed she was. Having shut herself off from adult companionship for so long, she hadn't realized how desperately she'd been craving it. Only now did she understand how much she'd been looking forward to tonight. Even if it meant sitting around with a bunch of women she didn't know, discussing a book she'd never read.

Whatever had possessed her to tell Lily that **Wuthering Heights** was one of her favorite novels? Favorite **titles,** maybe, since that was about as far as she'd ever gotten with the damn book. Reading had just never been high on her list of priorities. Probably the result of that tony private school she'd attended—**phony** tony, she amended now—where students were expected to read a book a week, part of a general program to promote excellence. Except when had they ever promoted anything but self-interest and the preservation of the status quo? No, at Bishop Lane School for Girls, to which she'd been granted grudging acceptance because her mother was part of the custodial staff, it was much more a question of where you came from than where you were going. And since she'd come from little, it was generally assumed she wouldn't amount to much.

So it was probably much better that this evening had worked out the way it had, she thought. She'd only have embarrassed herself, said something stupid, revealed herself as a charlatan and an impostor. The women would have shunned her, as her classmates at Bishop Lane had when they found out she was little more than a charity case. The janitor's daughter, they called her. And it didn't matter that her maternal grandfather had once been as rich as any of them, because **their** parents hadn't frittered away their inheritance on a series of bad deals and worse investments, **their** fathers hadn't abandoned them when the money ran out, **their** mothers hadn't been forced to work two jobs to pay off the crippling debt, and then a third job to cover current expenses. Was it any wonder her mother had never had time to read to her when she was a child? Was it any wonder her life had been an ever-twisting, downward spiral of bad choices and worse consequences?

She'd spent almost thirty years railing against the notion that biology was destiny, jumping over the many hurdles constantly materializing in her path, determined to escape the inevitability of her fate. Yet whatever road she took, it seemed she always ended up back where she'd started. The cities might be hundreds of miles apart, the street names might be different, but basically they were all the same. No matter how far she traveled, no matter where she settled, she always found herself back on Mad River Road.

Emma wiped the tears from her eyes and expelled a deep breath of air. She needed a cigarette. My kingdom for a cigarette, she thought, looking around the room, seeing the small television tucked in the corner and wondering if there was anything decent on tonight to watch. Probably she should move the TV down to the living room so that Dylan could have easier access to it, but the truth was that the TV was as much a soporific for her as the radio was for her son.

Emma walked into Dylan's room, prepared to offer him half an hour in front of the TV in exchange for not having to finish her story, but mercifully, he was already asleep. "Thank you, God," she whispered, kissing his cool forehead and making sure his blanket was secure. "Sleep well," she whispered from the doorway.

In the kitchen, she lit a cigarette and carried it outside, watching an old Cadillac pull into a space at the end of the street, and seeing a woman with big red hair and leopard-print pants push herself out of the front seat and hurry across the road. Clearly a **Wuthering Heights** devotee, Emma thought with a laugh. She should probably phone Lily and explain why she wouldn't be joining them tonight. But they hadn't exchanged numbers, and Lily would undoubtedly figure out quickly enough that she wasn't coming. She'd apologize and explain the next time she saw her.

Or she could explain now, she realized. Dylan was sound asleep, and she'd only be gone a few minutes. What could it hurt? Taking a final drag of her cigarette, Emma ground the butt beneath her foot and hastened down the street.

CHAPTER NINE

It says here that Tifton is the birthplace of Interstate-75," Jamie said over a burst of raucous laughter from a nearby table. She was reading from the brochure she'd picked up just inside the front door of the crowded, decidedly down-home Bar-B-Que pit where she and Brad had stopped for dinner. The laughter came courtesy of a group of rowdy young men ensconced in the booth behind Brad.

"You mean, in addition to being THE READING CAPITAL OF THE WORLD?" Brad asked, his voice capitalizing each word while simultaneously managing to reflect his total lack of interest in all things Tifton.

Behind Brad, one of the booth's occupants stood up on his seat in order to get the attention of the obviously harried, middle-aged waitress. "Hey, Patti," the boy called out. "Can we get some more beers over here?"

"Sit down, Troy," the waitress told him without so much as a glance in his direction.

The young man, barely out of his teens, was very tall and equally skinny, with broad, bony shoulders and long, blue-black hair that fell into small, close-set, dark eyes. White boxer shorts ballooned from the top of his low-slung jeans, jeans worn so low on his narrow hips that Jamie feared he was in danger of losing them altogether. As he slithered lazily back into his seat, he caught Jamie looking at him and winked.

Immediately Jamie's eyes returned to her brochure. She wasn't sure but she thought she heard the word **bitch** drop, like a loose penny, into the surrounding air, then roll toward her feet. "Apparently fifteen thousand people live in Tifton," she said, louder than she'd intended.

Brad showed his indifference to the population of Tifton by soaking a potato chip in ketchup, then balancing it on the tip of his tongue.

Jamie glanced around the small diner, careful to avoid the boys in the booth behind Brad, taking note instead of the mismatched, multistained wooden strips of the floor, the dark green vinyl of the seats, and the shiny, beige Formica of the tabletops. Innocent faces with huge, limpid eyes stared down from strategically hung black velvet canvases. A large chalkboard on the far wall listed the specials of the day, which today were black bean soup and a pound and a half of baby back ribs. Sweet-smelling smoke from behind the closed kitchen door wafted through the small space. There was no air-conditioning, and the still-stifling evening heat was kept at bay by two large, overhead fans, spinning at full force.

Out of the corner of her eye, Jamie sensed movement, and she turned back to see the skinny, dark-haired young man in the next booth wiggling his long fingers flirtatiously in her direction. He pushed his mouth into a mock kiss, made a smacking sound with his lips. Jamie looked away, wondering if she should say anything to Brad, deciding against it. Brad was feeling irritable enough. The last thing she wanted to do was upset him more than he already was.

Jamie knew that Brad was frustrated because all the local auto body shops in town were closed until morning, which meant they had to spend the night in Tifton. At first, he hadn't appeared unduly agitated, but a quick tour of the downtown area, which comprised twelve short city blocks, had convinced him that Tifton was THE READING CAPITAL OF THE WORLD because, he'd pronounced impatiently, THERE WAS ABSOLUTELY NOTHING ELSE TO DO. Jamie was more forgiving. She loved the grand old homes, constructed between the late 1800s and the 1930s, that were nestled among the giant shade trees lining the streets. She hoped they'd get the chance to visit at least one of the beautiful, historic churches or meticulously restored buildings before they left town in the morning. Wasn't that the plan? Weren't they supposed to be following the road wherever it might take them? Well, a shaky tire had delivered them to Tifton. Why not make the best of it? "It says here," Jamie said, ignoring the continuing flow of gestures from the next booth and reading from the brochure in a relentlessly perky voice that even she found grating, "that Tifton is the birthplace, not only of Interstate-75, but also of the entire interstate system, since it was the first interstate construction project in the country to receive federal approval and funding. And it all came about because . . ." Jamie watched the young man's two companions swivel around in their booth, the better to get a look at the object of their friend's attention. One had stringy blond hair, pulled into a ponytail. The other boy's head was shaved clean, and when he smiled at her out of the corner of his mouth, his lips pulled up and away from his teeth, exposing his gums, like a snarling dog.

Brad pushed his plate into the middle of the table and leaned forward on his elbows, oblivious to the activity taking place behind his head. "Because?"

"Because it seems the good people of Tifton wanted to cut down on the heavy flow of 'snowbird' traffic from the north, especially in winter," Jamie continued reading, determined to ignore her three dubious admirers. Eventually they'd lose interest in her, she decided, plowing on. "So they decided to build a bypass around the town, and apparently they spent years studying and planning before they finally agreed to go ahead and award contracts and stuff, and bingo!—wouldn't you know it?—a month later, President Eisenhower signed a bill that officially launched the **whole** interstate system."

Brad shook his head in mock amazement, rolling his eyes toward the ceiling as the waitress emerged from the kitchen with a tray full of beer.

"So, because Tifton had already done all this work, they decided to start here," Jamie read. "But get this—at the time, the federal interstate planning regulations allowed for only one exit every eight miles, and construction was already under way in Tifton for **eight** exits, which is why Tifton has more exits than most other I-75 communities." She smiled at Brad, hoping to elicit one of his dazzling smiles in return, a smile that assured her that while he might not give a damn about anything she was saying, he thought she was cute as hell for saying it, but he was staring out the long side window, having mentally opted for one of Tifton's many exits somewhere in the last sixty seconds. The boys from the next booth had lost interest in her as well and were now happily giving the waitress a hard time. "Tifton is also the home of Prestolite Wire," Jamie continued perversely, hoping by sheer force of will to bring Brad back on track, "manufacturers of automobile ignition wiring systems for Ford, Chrysler, Nissan, and Honda, among others. Brad?"

"Hmm?"

"Tifton is—"

"What are you doing, Jamie?" he snapped.

"What do you mean?"

"Am I seriously supposed to give a shit about some armpit of a town we're stranded in overnight?"

Jamie leaned back, felt her T-shirt stick to the dark green vinyl of her seat, not sure how, or even if, she was expected to respond. She was aware that Brad's tone had carried to the booth behind him. She saw bodies shift, heads tilt, shoulders angle subtly toward them. The boy with the shaved head slung one heavily tattooed forearm across the top of the booth, scratched at the side of his ear. In profile, his brow was low and his nose hooked. "It's not so bad," Jamie said defensively, wondering if she was feeling defensive on Tifton's behalf or her own.

"**It's not so bad,**" Brad mimicked. "What are you, a cheerleader for the local chamber of commerce?"

Tears sprang to Jamie's eyes. She lowered her head so no one would see.

"Sorry," Brad apologized immediately. "Jamie?"

Jamie continued staring down at her plate, her concentration centered on keeping her lower lip from trembling.

"Jamie?" Brad's hand reached across the

table, his fingers—still sticky from his pound and a half of ribs—curling around her own. "Did you hear me? I said I was sorry."

Slowly Jamie raised her eyes to his. "I just don't understand why you're so upset," she whispered, trying to keep their conversation private. "It's not like we're on a tight schedule or anything."

"I know."

"I thought part of the fun would be discovering little out-of-the-way places like this."

"Tifton's hardly out of anybody's way," Brad said, a sly grin spreading from his lips to his eyes. "What with its **eight** exits and all."

Jamie smiled in spite of herself.

Brad leaned across the shiny, Formica tabletop and wiped a wayward tear from Jamie's cheek. She smelled tangy barbeque sauce on his fingers and fought the urge to take a lick. "I'm really sorry, Jamie. I guess I'm just in a hurry to see my son, that's all."

"I know you are."

Brad signaled the waitress for the bill. "So, what do you want to do now, my beautiful girl? You think there's a movie theater in Tifton?"

"Well, surely they can't spend **all** their time reading," Jamie answered, and Brad laughed. Jamie was thrilled at being called his beautiful girl, even more thrilled to elicit such a joyous response after the tension of the last hour. "There must be a mall nearby. You think it's okay to drive on that tire?"

Brad shrugged. "We'll give it some more air. It should be okay until morning. You game?"

"You're not too tired? I mean, you're the one who's been doing all the driving."

Brad shook his head as the waitress dropped the bill on the table on her way to the kitchen. He reached into his pocket, tucked a twenty underneath his plate, and stood up. "Just let me use the facilities, and we'll be on our merry way."

He kissed her forehead, then headed for the washrooms at the back of the restaurant. Jamie watched him until he disappeared behind a swinging set of wooden doors, then, aware of three sets of eyes still focused in her direction, she pretended to be searching for something inside her purse.

"Whatcha looking for?" asked a voice from the next booth.

Jamie's body tensed, her fingers freezing on a tube of lipstick. "Found it," she said, forcing a smile onto her face as she lifted her gaze, determined not to be intimidated.

"Need some help putting it on?" The young man with the exposed boxer shorts billowing around his midriff was suddenly out of his seat and sliding into the seat beside her, his narrow hips pushing her into the corner. His buddies quickly filled the seats across from her.

Jamie looked toward the bathroom, but Brad was nowhere to be seen, and the only waitress in sight was busy depositing a full tray of ribs on another table. She thought of screaming, quickly decided against it. She was in a well-lit restaurant, after all, surrounded by dozens of people. Brad would be back any second. What was the point in causing a scene if she didn't have to? "I can manage, thank you."

"She can manage," said the skinhead as Jamie returned the lipstick to her purse.

"I'll bet she can. I'm Curtis, by the way." The ponytailed young man extended his hand across the table.

"Wayne," said the skinhead.

"Troy," said the boy beside her.

"Jamie," Jamie told them, deciding to play along, although she kept her hands in her lap.

"Is that your blue Thunderbird in the parking lot?" Curtis asked.

Jamie nodded.

"Thought so. Didn't look familiar."

"What's wrong with the tire?" Wayne asked.

"We're not sure. Hopefully we'll find out in the morning."

"Whatcha doing tonight?" Troy asked.

"We were thinking of a movie." Jamie looked toward the back of the restaurant. What was taking Brad so long?

"We saw a great movie the other night, didn't we, guys?" Troy said.

"Great movie," the others agreed.

"Really? Which one was that?"

"The new Tom Cruise. Over at the multiplex on North Central."

"Is that far from here?"

"Five minutes." Curtis smiled, baring his gums.

"How'd you like the ribs?" Wayne began playing with the edge of the twenty-dollar bill protruding from underneath Brad's plate.

"They were delicious."

"Best in Georgia," Curtis said proudly. "Troy's dad owns the place."

So she could relax, Jamie thought. Clearly they wouldn't start any trouble in Troy's father's restaurant. Assuming, of course, this really was his father's restaurant, she realized, her body tensing up again. "Well, please tell him how much we enjoyed everything. Now, if you'll excuse me . . ."

"How about some dessert?" Troy asked, refusing to budge. "They serve a mean peach cobbler."

"Sounds really good," Jamie said, "but I couldn't eat another thing. Now, if you don't mind . . ."

Troy grudgingly slid from her side. She thought she felt a hand on the back of her thigh as she scrambled to her feet. In the same instant, she saw Brad emerge from the washrooms at the back.

"Is there a problem here?" Brad asked, his eyes quickly sizing up the three young men.

"We were just trying to help your girlfriend out," Curtis said with a lazy shrug of his shoulders.

"Apparently there's a multiplex nearby," Jamie interjected, sensing the renewed possibility of danger and wanting to get out of its way as fast as possible.

"Is that right?" Brad said.

"Over on North Central," Wayne added. "They're playing the new Tom Cruise."

"Sounds good."

"Is good. Real good," Curtis agreed.

"Well, maybe we'll do that," Brad said. "Thanks for your help."

"Y'all come back and see us again real soon," Troy drawled with exaggerated southern flourish as Brad took Jamie by the elbow and led her from the restaurant, into the parking lot.

"Everything okay?" Brad asked as they approached her car. A slight drizzle had started to fall.

Jamie nodded, although her legs felt wobbly and she was glad for Brad's supportive arm.

"First the derelict in the bathroom, then three hoodlums in a diner. I can't leave you alone for a minute."

Jamie laughed, recalling how many times her mother had said the same thing. "Probably not a good idea."

"I'll keep that in mind." Brad glanced at the wayward tire.

"What do you think? Can we risk a trip to the multiplex?"

Brad smiled his killer grin. "What's life without risks?"

They were waiting by her car when Jamie and Brad exited the movie.

"So, what'd you think of my boy Tom Cruise?" Troy asked. Curtis stood to Troy's left, a cigarette stuck to his bottom lip. Wayne was leaning against the passenger door. They were parked at the far end of the large lot, and there was nobody else in sight. The drizzle had stopped, although a damp wind was blowing, threatening more.

Jamie felt Brad's hand grow tense on top of her own. "He was terrific," Brad said, drawing her protectively behind him.

"Tom Terrific," Curtis agreed with a laugh.

"What are you guys doing here?" Brad asked, keeping his voice light, even friendly.

"We were worried about your tire," Troy said. "Thought we'd come by, make sure you were all right. In case you needed a lift or something."

"Well, that's very kind of you, but we'll be fine."

"Will you?" Wayne asked, pushing himself away from the car and ambling menacingly toward them. "Are you sure? Your girlfriend seems like a bit of a handful." The other two boys fell into step beside him. "Thought you could use a little help."

Oh, God, Jamie thought, taking an automatic step back, her eyes cutting across the empty parking lot, wondering where the hell everybody was. Why had they parked so far away from the theaters? "Brad . . ."

"It's okay, Jamie."

"Yeah, Jamie," Troy said, drawing nearer. "It's okay. We're gonna show you a real good time."

"I think you've gone far enough," Brad warned.

Something about the tone in Brad's voice brought the young men to a temporary halt. "Oh, you do, do you? You gonna stop us?" Wayne asked after a moment's pause.

"If I have to."

"Brad, let's just run," Jamie whispered.

"Don't worry, Jamie," Brad said, loud enough for everyone to hear. "This is gonna be fun. Ain't it, guys?" He reached into his pocket as once again, the boys advanced, Curtis the first to reach them.

Jamie heard an unfamiliar click, saw the blade of a knife as it flashed in the darkness and slashed through the air. She saw a flurry of motion as she was pushed to one side, and she fell, looking up just as Brad grabbed Curtis by his ponytail and spun him around, locking him in a stranglehold, and pressing the blade of the knife against his exposed throat.

"Now **this** is my idea of a good time," Brad said, pressing the blade into the boy's skin, drawing blood.

"Hey, mister," Troy began, drawing back and tugging anxiously on his low-slung jeans. "Take it easy. We were just kidding around."

"Didn't sound like you were kidding to me."

"Please," Curtis whimpered.

"Way I figure it," Brad was saying, clearly enjoying himself. "You got about three seconds to apologize to my girl here before I slit your friend's throat."

"Brad . . . ," Jamie said. "No . . ."

"It's okay, Jamie. Well, boys? What's it gonna be?"

"We're sorry," Wayne said quickly.

"We're really sorry," echoed Troy.

"How about you, big shot?" Brad took a tiny nick out of Curtis's flesh. "You gonna apologize to the lady?"

"I'm sorry," Curtis managed to croak out.

"Good boys. Now I'm gonna suggest you get the hell away from here as fast as possible." He released his grip on Curtis's neck, simultaneously twisting the boy's ponytail around his fingers, then slicing it off with one quick flick of his wrist, as easily as if it were sliding through butter. Instantly the boys took off. Brad watched them until they disappeared, then helped Jamie to her feet. He tossed the severed clump of hair into the air, watched it fall to the ground and scatter in the breeze, like flecks of ash from a fire. "I think his mama's gonna like that look a whole lot better, don't you?"

"I still can't believe what happened," Jamie was saying later. She was curled up in Brad's arms, their naked bodies glistening with the sweat of their recent lovemaking, in the middle of the motel room's king-size bed while the **Late**

Show with David Letterman played silently on the small TV attached to the dark, imitation-wood dresser on the opposite wall.

"It was fun, wasn't it?"

She sat up. "No, it wasn't fun. Are you crazy?"

"Crazy about you," he said, dragging her back down.

Jamie couldn't help but smile, although she was still trembling and hadn't stopped trembling since they'd checked in. "What if they go to the police?"

"They won't."

"How do you know?"

"'Cause I do."

Jamie pulled the dark floral bedspread up around her breasts. In the corner of the generically decorated room, an air-conditioning unit rumbled loudly at irregular intervals, switching on and off without notice. Beside her, a remote control unit lay glued to the end table, probably to prevent theft. In retaliation, some enterprising soul had absconded with its batteries, rendering it useless. Which meant they'd have to get out of bed to turn off the television. Which meant it would probably be on all night. "Can I ask you something?"

"You want to know where I got the knife," he stated, as if he'd been expecting this question all night.

"I thought switchblades were against the law."

Brad gently brushed some hairs away from her forehead. "Did I tell you that before I got into the computer business, I spent some time working with underprivileged kids?"

"What? No."

"There was this one kid everybody said was . . . what's that word your mother used in describing you?"

"Incorrigible?"

"That's the one. I preferred 'free spirit.' Like you," he said, kissing the tip of her nose.

Jamie felt herself melting. She wasn't incorrigible. She was a free spirit.

"Anyway, kid claimed I turned his life around, that if it hadn't been for me . . ." Brad stared absently at the television screen. "And as a parting gift, he gave me the knife. Said he wouldn't be needing it anymore. That I should always carry it—for good luck."

Jamie shook her head. The man was one surprise after another. "Well, it was certainly lucky we had it tonight."

"Sometimes you have to protect yourself," he said. "And the people you love."

Jamie held her breath. Was he saying he loved her? "No man's ever looked out for me the way you do," she whispered, huddling in against his side, silently thanking God for bringing this man into her life. A kindred spirit who saw into her soul, who understood who she really was. A man who looked after her, protected her, took care of her. She could have been raped tonight, she realized. Or worse. She closed her eyes, choosing not to think about the awful things that could have happened had Brad not been there to rescue her. I'm so lucky, she thought, sighing deeply and giving in to sleep.

CHAPTER TEN

"Hi. Come on in," Lily said, grabbing Emma's hand and ushering her inside.

"I can't stay very long," Emma said, thinking, I shouldn't have come, I must be out of my mind to leave Dylan alone, even for a few minutes.

"I was afraid you'd changed your mind."

I only came to tell you I can't stay. "I had to make sure Dylan was asleep," she said instead, allowing Lily to lead her toward the living room. Her house is so cheery, Emma was thinking, marveling at the pale pink wallpaper with its endlessly repeating pattern of delicate little flowers, and wondering idly how much it had cost. I should do something like that with my hall, she was thinking.

The living room was painted a deeper shade of pink than the hall, and the furniture, while clearly not new, was warm and comfortable-looking. At least the four women occupying the two pink-floral love seats facing each other in the middle of the small room looked comfortable enough. As did the wild-haired, leopard-clad amazon she'd seen exiting the old Cadillac parked across the street, and who was now twisted into a pretzel-like position on the beige carpet in front of the fireplace. Emma wondered how anyone achieved that kind of flexibility. She wondered if the fireplace actually worked. She wondered what she was doing with these women when she should be home with her son.

"Ladies, this is Emma Frost," Lily began, leading Emma into the center of the room. "If she looks familiar, it's because hers were the eyes on the Maybelline mascara packages a few years back."

"You're a model?" one of the women asked.

"Not so much anymore."

"I use Maybelline mascara," someone chirped. "It's the best."

"Well, well, you must have made a bundle from that. What are you doing on Mad River Road?" This from the leopard-clad diva on the floor.

"It's a long story," Emma told her.

"We're a book club," the woman said. "We love stories."

The other women laughed.

"You **do** have lovely eyes," someone offered.

"Let me introduce you to your neighbors," Lily continued proudly. "Emma, this is Cecily Wahlberg. She lives in the lilac-colored house."

"Number 123," Cecily elaborated, as if there was more than one. She crossed one skinny leg over the other and weaved bony fingers through her fine, blond pageboy.

". . . Anne Steffoff . . ."

"Number 115," Anne stated, her voice a deep baritone that went well with her short, geometrically cut hair. "I wanted to paint it purple."

"I wouldn't let her," said the woman beside her. "Carole McGowan," she said, offering Emma a strong handshake and a toothy grin. "Anne's significant other."

Emma recognized the three women, all of whom were casually dressed in jeans and pastel-colored T-shirts, and felt a pang of guilt for having so actively avoided them in the past. Of the three, Cecily was closest to her own age, and if memory served, she had a daughter slightly older than Dylan, while Anne and Carole were approximately a decade her senior. She pictured the women as they regularly walked their two overweight schnauzers up and down Mad River Road.

"And this is Pat Langer, who used to work at Scully's, but left to have a baby."

"Traitor," the amazon sneered from her position on the floor.

"Hi." Pat waved shyly before sinking back in her seat.

"How old's your baby?" Emma asked her.

"Two months." Pat smiled proudly. "His name's Joseph."

She's not much more than a baby herself, Emma thought, wondering who was at home looking after Joseph right now.

"What am I—chopped liver?" Jan demanded, uncrossing her leopard leotards and extending her hand. "Jan Scully," she announced. "Owner of Scully's. Lily tells me you're thinking about taking out a membership."

"Well, I . . ."

"Now would be a good time to do it."

"We're offering a free T-shirt and a mug," the other women chimed in unison. Once again, easy laughter filled the room.

Such a seductive sound, Emma thought, longing to curl up inside it, then vanish with it into the air. Or maybe she could bottle it and take it home with her, open it whenever she was feeling sad and lost, which was most of the time these days. How long had it been since she'd been with people who laughed out loud? She should tell them that her sitter canceled, that she can't stay. They'd understand. They'd also insist she leave, and she so desperately wanted to stay. If only for a few minutes more.

"Okay, so forgive me for trying to drum up a little business," Jan was saying, a pout playing with her enormous lips. "I was at the bank today. Bastards turned down my loan application."

"No!" Carole said.

"They didn't," Anne agreed.

"Did they say why?" Lily asked.

Jan shrugged. "Didn't have to. I'm a woman, and this is a man's world."

"It sure is," Cecily agreed.

"You want to know what really pisses me off?" Jan asked.

"What really pisses you off?" Anne and Carole asked together.

"If I don't sign up some new members soon, I'll have to close up shop, which is exactly what my ex-husband is counting on. I can just hear him saying, 'I told you Scully's was my baby. I told you you couldn't make it without me. Should've let me buy you out when you had the chance.' May he rot in hell. You married?" she asked Emma in the same breath.

"Divorced."

"So you agree—men are jerks." It was a statement, not a question.

"Absolutely," Emma said.

"You said it," chimed in Cecily.

"We're probably not the best ones to ask about men," Anne said with a sly nod at her partner. Carole smiled her toothy grin and patted Anne's substantial thigh.

"I'm sorry, ladies, but I just can't agree," Lily demurred.

"That's because you were married to the perfect man," Cecily told her.

"I know a lot of wonderful men," Lily protested. "My father was one, my brother . . ."

"Then you cornered the market," Jan pronounced. "Why'd you get a divorce?" she asked Emma.

"Take it easy, Jan," Cecily cautioned. "Emma just got here. You'll scare her away."

"Oh, she's not scared away that easily, are you, sweetheart?" Jan asked.

This is my cue, Emma thought. My chance to hightail it out of here. Instead she heard herself say, "My ex-husband, or the pervert, as

I like to refer to him, was a compulsive liar who slept with anything that had a pulse. Although frankly, I'm not even sure that was a requirement, since there was many a night when I just lay there like a dishrag, and he didn't seem to notice or mind. I left him when I discovered a huge stash of child pornography hidden among a bunch of golf magazines at the back of his closet." She stopped. She could elaborate, she thought, but judging from the slightly stunned looks on all their faces, that was probably enough for one night.

"What about Heathcliff?" Lily ventured.

"Who?" Pat asked.

"The hero of the book we're supposed to be discussing?" Lily pointed out.

"Oh. Him."

"Yes, him."

"Isn't she cute?" Jan said, unraveling her body with remarkable ease and getting up from the floor to give Lily a hug. "She still thinks we meet every month to discuss books."

"Isn't that what book clubs are supposed to do?"

"Isn't she cute?" Jan said again.

"I think Lily's right," Pat said meekly, her voice soft and tremulous. "I don't think men are so bad."

"How can you say that?" Jan demanded. "After all the times you've cried on my shoulder because of that imbecile you married!" She continued before Pat had a chance to answer. "How many times did he tell you he wasn't ready for a commitment, even after you told him you were pregnant? What about the time he took off in the middle of the night, didn't call for a week?"

"He came back," Pat said proudly. "We got married."

"Call me when you live happily ever after," Jan advised bitterly.

"Can we get back to **Wuthering Heights**?" Lily tried again.

"I just don't see how we can be so disparaging of men," Pat continued. "Some of us are raising sons of our own."

I should be home with Dylan, Emma thought, a fresh wave of guilt washing over her.

"Daughters are worse," Cecily chimed in. "At least according to my mother, who had two of each. She said all you had to do was get a boy interested in sports, and you'd be okay. Unless of course, you had one who was artistic. Then you were doomed."

"And speaking of doomed," Lily ventured, waving her copy of **Wuthering Heights** in the air. "Is Cathy's relationship with Heathcliff doomed because their love is so intense? Or is it so intense precisely because it's doomed?"

The women looked at her as if they had no idea who she was.

"I think it's a bit of both," Emma said, sensing Lily's growing frustration with the direction of the conversation and amazed at how authoritative she could sound when she had absolutely no idea what she was talking about. "I think one thing plays off the other, so that it's almost impossible to say where one leaves off and the other begins."

"It **is** a great love story," Anne said.

"Only because it ends badly," Carole said.

"You're saying there's no such thing as romantic love?" Pat asked.

"There's no such thing as romantic love that **lasts,**" Jan corrected.

"You really can't imagine Heathcliff and Cathy sharing toothless kisses in some old-age home, now can you?" Anne said.

"You wouldn't want to," Carole said.

"No. You want them haunting the moors as these forever-gorgeous, young ghosts," Cecily agreed.

"What do all the great love stories have in common?" Emma asked, emboldened. "Romeo and Juliet? Tristan and Isolde? Hamlet and Ophelia?"

Jan smiled triumphantly. "Everybody dies," she said.

"Well, that was an interesting evening," Lily said as she and Emma sat sipping coffee on the outside steps of Lily's home.

It was almost ten o'clock. The other women had departed en masse five minutes earlier. Emma had fully intended to leave with them, but instead she'd found herself lingering, allowing herself to be coaxed into one more cup of coffee, even though she had enough caffeine in her body to keep her awake for a week. She was feeling better, having run home to check on Dylan during an earlier cigarette break, and finding him sleeping soundly. Besides, her house was easily visible from where she and Lily were sitting. She had nothing to worry about. "It was fun," Emma agreed.

"Took a while to get to the book." Lily laughed. "I guess that happens a lot whenever a bunch of women get together."

"I wouldn't know."

"You don't have a lot of girlfriends?"

"Don't have a lot of friends, period."

"You're more of a loner," Lily observed.

"Well, we've moved around a lot this past year, and it's hard, you know."

"I think friends are so important. I love my women friends."

"No men friends?"

Lily shrugged delicate shoulders. "Not lately."

"What about Detective Dawson?" Emma asked.

Again Lily shrugged. "Seems like a nice man."

"So, have you changed your mind?"

"About what?"

"About whatever the two of you were discussing when I walked into the gym this morning. I'm assuming he asked you out."

"For tomorrow night. Dinner at Joso's."

"And you turned him down? Are you crazy?"

"I thought you didn't like cops."

"I don't. But I can appreciate a good dinner as much as the next girl. Why'd you say no? I mean, I know it's none of my business, but you seemed to have a certain chemistry. . . ."

"I don't know why I said no," Lily said. "I've been asking myself that question all day."

"Have you dated at all since your husband died?"

"A few times. Nothing serious."

"But you sense this could be different, that with this guy, it could get serious?"

"What? No. Who said anything about serious?"

"You did," Emma reminded her.

"I hardly know the man."

"But you think maybe you'd like to."

Lily exhaled, looked toward the star-filled sky. "I don't know what I think."

"Well, I think you should call him. You owe it to the rest of us."

Lily laughed. "How do you figure that?"

"Give us something to talk about at our next meeting. Along with the Steinbeck."

Lily laughed again, a clear, bell-like sound. "So, you'll join our little group?"

"Can I think about it?"

"Absolutely. Your comments tonight were really insightful. What you said about Romeo and Juliet, and Tristan and Isolde, really got the discussion going."

Emma smiled, recalling her mother's enormous collection of opera recordings. While she herself had no patience for opera and had no idea who Tristan and Isolde were, or what exactly their story was, she'd just assumed it ended badly. Operas usually did. Funny how seemingly insignificant memories could sometimes come in really handy, she thought, taking another sip of her coffee and wishing she could stay here, right here on this front step, sipping coffee all night and feeling wonderfully, gloriously free. From care. From responsibility. From the past.

"So you think I should call Jeff Dawson, tell him I've changed my mind?"

"Have you?"

"I don't know. I don't have a sitter," Lily said in the next breath. "And it's a Saturday night."

"So bring Michael over to my place," Emma heard herself offer.

Lily glanced toward Michael's bedroom. "I couldn't do that."

"Why not? I'm home anyway. The boys can have a sleepover. I'm sure Dylan would be thrilled." Would he? Emma wondered. Would her son be thrilled about such a disruption to his nighttime routine? "They can sleep in my bed. They'll have a blast." Would they? Would they have a blast? Or would it be an unmitigated disaster?

"Can I think about it?" Lily asked, borrowing Emma's earlier question. "I mean, Michael was an angel tonight, but he can be a bit of a handful."

"Not to mention Detective Dawson."

The sound of dogs barking cut through the ensuing silence. Both Emma and Lily looked toward the sound, saw Anne and Carole leaving their house, their two overweight schnauzers straining on their leashes, pulling them down the street.

"Who's taking who for a walk?" Lily called after them as the dogs pulled them past her house, only to stop abruptly at the next lamppost. First one dog lifted his leg to mark his territory, then the other, then the first again.

"Men," Anne said with a laugh as the two women linked arms and continued on down the street.

"You ever been hit on by a woman?" Emma asked.

"What?" Lily's eyes widened.

"I was," Emma continued. "Long time ago. One of the teachers at this private school I went to."

"My God. What happened?"

"I was thirteen, maybe fourteen. Just starting to fill out. More than a little self-conscious about it. And there was this gym teacher, Mrs. Gallagher, who everybody loved. She had long, shiny, blond hair that she used to let all the girls brush. I mean, can you imagine? We actually thought it was some kind of honor to brush this woman's greasy hair. And one day, that honor fell to me. And so I'm standing behind her, brushing away. My arm feels like it's about to fall off, but I keep brushing, and she tells me I do it better than any of the other girls, that I have a real feel for it, which of course makes me brush even harder, and she asks me to come back at the end of the day. So I did. Only instead of me brushing **her** hair, she starts to brush mine. And I have to admit, it feels great. And she's telling me I have this fabulous hair, so soft and pretty. And then suddenly I feel something brush against my neck, only I know it's not the brush."

"She kissed you?"

Emma nodded, raised one eyebrow, folded one lip inside the other.

"What'd you do?"

"Nothing. I was terrified. I just sat there. And she's saying stuff like, 'Does that feel good? Do you like that?' And then suddenly, I just bolted off that chair and ran. Didn't stop running until I got home."

"Did you tell anyone?"

"I told my mother. She was the school principal."

"And? Did she fire her?"

"She didn't believe me, said I was making the whole thing up to get attention."

Lily looked horrified. "How awful for you."

Emma shrugged.

"You've had a very interesting life," Lily remarked after a pause of several seconds.

"A little too interesting at times." Emma finished the last of her coffee, pushed herself to her feet. She handed the Scully's mug to Lily. "I guess I should be getting home."

"I'm really glad you came tonight."

"Me too. Let me know what you decide

about tomorrow." Emma walked down the steps, waved good-bye from the sidewalk. "I had a wonderful time," she called back, forcing one reluctant foot in front of the other. When she reached her house, she turned back, but Lily was no longer standing on her front steps. She probably shouldn't have told Lily her mother was a school principal, she thought, unlocking the front door and tiptoeing inside. Was she afraid that Lily wouldn't like her if she knew the truth? That was silly. Lily wasn't like the girls she'd grown up with. She wouldn't think any less of her if she found out her mother had been part of the custodial staff.

And did one more lie really matter all that much, when she'd told so many lies already?

Emma checked Dylan's room and saw he was sleeping soundly. If only I could sleep like that, she thought enviously as she undressed and climbed into bed.

She closed her eyes and waited for the demons.

CHAPTER ELEVEN

In the few minutes of twilight between sleeping and waking, Jamie relived the almost two years of hell that had been her life with Mark Dennison. It began, fittingly enough, on their wedding night, when a series of frantic phone calls from the groom's mother repeatedly interrupted their attempts to consummate their marriage.

"How could you do this?" Jamie heard her new mother-in-law wail through the phone wires. "How could you marry a girl you just met, a girl you know absolutely nothing about?"

Jamie waited to hear her new husband say "I know everything I need to know. I know I love her." But instead what she heard were a string of abject apologies—for the rashness of his decision, the unnecessary speed of his elopement, the stunning disregard for his mother's feelings—and his assurances that he and his new wife had no intention of settling in Palm Beach, that they'd abandon their plans for a honeymoon in the Bahamas and fly to Atlanta first thing in the morning in order to reassure her. Jamie even heard herself trying to console her new mother-in-law by offering to let her tag along when they went apartment hunting, telling the clearly distraught woman that she welcomed her input and was looking forward to being part of such a close-knit, loving family. What she heard in return was the stony silence of a phone going dead in her ear.

Needless to say, their lovemaking that night had been a disaster, her husband unable to sustain an erection, no matter what she tried. "Where'd you learn that little trick?" he'd demanded, angrily pushing her away. "Your college boyfriends teach you that?"

That was the first time she thought of leaving. Pack your bag and walk out the door, she remembered thinking as she huddled on the other side of the bed. Swallow your pride and go back home to Mama. It's been less than twenty-four hours. You can get an annulment, go back to law school, reenroll for the spring term. Just get out of this mess you've gotten yourself into, and get out now.

Except how could she leave him when he was so vulnerable, when he was literally crying for her to stay, apologizing to her over and over again for the awful things he'd said? He was upset, confused. He hadn't meant any of it. Surely she knew that. Please understand, he'd begged. If she would only be patient, give him another chance. His mother had had a hard life, he explained. She'd been widowed when she was only thirty-six, and he'd become her sole source of comfort, the one she turned to and relied on, the only thing that kept her going, allowed her to get out of bed in the morning. At the tender age of eight, he'd become her little man. For the last two decades, it had been just the two of them. Naturally it was going to be hard for her to accept a virtual stranger into their lives. If Jamie could just be patient . . .

Jamie agreed to try. He was right after all. His mother was just upset because of the suddenness of their union. It had nothing to do with her. She shouldn't take it personally. Hadn't her own mother been almost apoplectic when Jamie announced her intention to marry a man she'd known barely two weeks?

"Mom, this is Jamie. Jamie, this is my mother, Laura Dennison," her new husband said, proudly introducing the two women in his life to each other.

Jamie was surprised at how small her mother-in-law actually was. Despite her towering voice on the telephone, in person she measured a scant five feet two inches tall and couldn't have weighed more than 100 pounds. At almost five feet seven and 120 pounds, Jamie loomed over her like a large building. *What was I so afraid of?* she wondered, extending her arms magnanimously toward the woman with the short auburn hair and cold blue eyes.

"You don't look anything like I pictured," her mother-in-law said, stiffening inside Jamie's embrace.

"It's great to finally meet you," Jamie ventured, pulling back. "Can I call you Laura?"

"I'd prefer Mrs. Dennison," came the chilling reply.

"You just went a little too fast," her husband advised as they were settling into his old bedroom. "My mother has never been overly demonstrative."

"She hates me."

"She doesn't hate you."

" 'I'd prefer Mrs. Dennison,' " Jamie repeated in her mother-in-law's steely voice.

"Give her time," her husband urged. "She's still a little shell-shocked. Just take it nice and slow. Have a little patience."

"I'm going as slow as I can," Jamie said with a mischievous smile, her arms reaching out to encircle her husband's waist, her hands dropping to his buttocks, pulling him closer.

"This probably isn't a good idea." He pointed with his chin toward the closed bedroom door.

"It's okay. I locked it."

"You locked it? Why?"

"Thought we could use some privacy." She brought her hands around to the front of his pants.

He smiled, began nibbling the side of her neck. "Oh, you did, did you?"

And then he kissed her, and she remembered what it was about him she'd found so appealing. She'd always been a sucker for a good kisser.

They were halfway out of their clothes when a knock on the door interrupted them. It was followed immediately by a second knock, then the frantic turning of the doorknob. "Mark." Mrs. Dennison's voice cut through the solid wood. "Mark, are you in there?"

"Just a minute, Mom," he said as he began struggling back into his clothes.

Jamie wrapped her arms around his slender hips, tried pulling him back toward the bed. "Tell her you're busy," she whispered.

"Get dressed," was his response.

"Is something wrong?" his mother asked, still twisting the doorknob back and forth.

Mark broke free and walked to the door, stealing a last look back at Jamie. "Your buttons," he scolded, pointing to her half-open blouse.

"Why was the door locked?" Mrs. Dennison stared accusingly at Jamie.

"Force of habit," Jamie said, forcing a smile onto her lips.

"We don't lock the doors around here," Mrs. Dennison said.

"Is something wrong?" Jamie wondered what was so urgent.

Mrs. Dennison looked both confused and conflicted, as if she were debating with herself over what she was about to do. "I thought you should have these," she said after a long pause. She held out her hand. Inside it were the most exquisite gold-and-pearl earrings Jamie had ever seen. "They belonged to my great-grandmother, and I always promised my son they'd go to the woman he married." She pulled back her shoulders, cleared her throat, spit out the last few words. "So now, I suppose, they're yours."

"Mother, that's so thoughtful."

"They're beautiful," Jamie agreed, feeling

suddenly light-headed and grateful. Her husband was right. His mother was a wonderful woman who just needed a little time to adjust to her son's surprise wedding. She just had to be patient. "I'm so touched."

"You understand, of course, that if this doesn't work out," Mrs. Dennison said matter-of-factly, "it's your duty to return them."

That was the second time in two days of marriage that Jamie considered leaving. Instead she again allowed herself to be cajoled into giving her new mother-in-law the necessary time to adjust; she told herself that it was her fault for expecting too much too soon, that she was the one who'd rushed into this marriage, and now it was up to her to slow things down. She'd had unrealistic expectations. You don't marry a man you barely know and move with him to another city and expect everything to just fall into place.

Except that's exactly what she'd been expecting.

That the tall young man with the shy dimples and long, aquiline nose whom she'd met at an automobile show—he was there for a convention of car salesmen; she was there to view the display of antique cars—wasn't the sexy, knight-in-shining-armor he'd first appeared to be, but was rather a timid and insecure mama's boy still living at home, was a thought too painful to dwell on.

Everything will be all right as soon as we get our own apartment, she assured herself. Things will be different. He'll change back into the man I married—the man I **thought** I was marrying—as soon as I get him away from his mother.

But Mark Dennison had proved remarkably resistant to severing the apron strings. "I don't understand why you're in such a hurry to leave," he told her. "She cooks for us, she does the housework, the laundry. She knocks herself out, for God's sake. Why can't you just appreciate it? What's wrong with you?"

"I just think it would be nice to have a place of our own. You know, where we could have a little more privacy. A little more sex," Jamie whispered, stroking his thigh. A lot more sex, she was thinking, aware that their love life had dwindled to almost nothing in recent weeks.

"Is that all you ever think about?" he asked accusingly. "Why don't you get a job?" he suggested in the next breath, as if one were a viable substitute for the other.

She did. It was as an administrative assistant for a property management company, and it bored her to tears. She quit after less than a month, took another job as a receptionist to a busy developer, lasted barely six weeks. She talked about going back to college, getting her MSW.

"Why would you want to be a social worker?" her mother-in-law asked.

Her husband became even more withholding until she dropped the idea of college altogether, found another job as an administrative assistant, this time for a small insurance company.

Her husband finally agreed to at least look at some apartments in the neighborhood, but then his mother got sick, some vague problem the doctors couldn't quite pin down, probably stress-related, they said, so how could they leave her until she was well again?

She'll live to be a hundred, Jamie thought, realizing she would never have any chance of a normal life until she took matters into her own hands. So she found an apartment, signed a lease, and told her husband she was moving out at the end of the month, with or without him. Reluctantly, he agreed to the move. They'd been married one year.

Year two was more of the same.

She was working at a job she hated, married to a man she barely knew and rarely saw—he'd taken to stopping by his mother's every evening after he finished work, sometimes having dinner there without even bothering to call her—and cut off from her family and old friends. She tried making new ones, found a circle of girlfriends in whom she could confide and commiserate. They told her to cut her losses and run. "All you've done is exchange one overbearing mother for another," they told her.

They were right. After fortifying herself with several glasses of wine, she'd called him at his mother's to tell him she was moving back to Palm Beach. An hour later, he showed up on their doorstep with flowers, apologies, and tears. "Please don't leave," he begged. "This is all my fault. I've been a complete idiot. I promise you that things will be different. I'll change. Please, give me another chance. Things will get better. I promise."

He was right. Things did get better. For a few weeks anyway.

Then they got worse.

That's enough of that, Jamie thought now, turning over onto her side in bed and coming fully awake. Once was more than enough, she was thinking, refusing to relive those last agonizing months. It was over. She never had to see Mark Dennison again. She had a new life now, and after several false starts, a new man. She reached over to stroke Brad's back.

He wasn't there.

"Brad?" Jamie climbed out of bed, her eyes searching the obviously empty room, her ears straining above the air-conditioning unit for sounds of a shower running, a shaver humming, a toilet flushing. There was nothing.

She ran to the window and pulled back the drapes. The sun exploded in her face, like a camera's sudden flash, temporarily blinding her. But even through the ensuing blur of white light and purple dots, she could see the parking space outside her motel room window was empty and her car was gone. Had last night's unsavory trio somehow discovered their whereabouts and returned, lying in wait to ambush Brad?

And then she saw it, a large piece of white paper hanging over the blank TV screen and held in place by the Holy Bible. The note read:

Took the car to the auto body shop. Back soon. Grab some breakfast in the lobby. It's included.

Jamie smiled, held the note against her chest, like a shield of armor, using it to still the wild beating of her heart. You see, she assured herself. I told you you have nothing to worry about. He's safe and sound and thinking of your welfare. As always.

Jamie quickly showered and washed her hair, then got dressed, choosing a white shirt and a pair of pink capris. Then she packed her overnight bag so that she would be ready when Brad returned, and, after taking a cautionary look around, proceeded to the hotel lobby. "Are you still serving breakfast?" she asked the prematurely balding young man behind the reception desk. The clock on the wall above his shiny head said it was already 9:36.

"Around the corner." He pointed with the index finger of his right hand. Jamie noted he was missing the tip of that finger and wondered what had happened to it. She walked around the corner to the designated breakfast area. The green-carpeted space consisted of several small tables and chairs as well as an old beige canvas sofa and a large-screen TV. A narrow food table ran along one wall, filled with an unappetizing display of cold bagels and slices of dry, white bread for toast. There were a couple of danishes, one whose center was filled with cheese, the other with strawberry jam. Jamie selected the one with cheese, then filled a Styrofoam cup with lukewarm coffee and carried both to the nearest table, realizing she was the only one there. Well, it's late, she thought, taking a sip of her coffee and turning her attention to the TV screen, where a man in a big-brimmed cowboy hat and blue-and-white-checkered shirt was lovingly embracing an assault rifle and passionately defending his right under the Constitution to bear arms. Did that include a knife? she wondered.

"What do you think?" a male voice asked from somewhere beside her.

Jamie looked up as the balding young man from the reception desk helped himself to a cup of coffee, then sat down at the next table, stretching his long legs out in front of him and taking a long drag of an unlit cigarette. A sign on the wall next to the television announced that smoking was prohibited. "What do I think about what?" Jamie asked. The ban on smoking? Gun control? Switchblades?

"The coffee," he answered. "We're trying a new brand."

"It's okay."

"Just okay?"

Jamie took another sip. "Just okay."

"Yeah, that's what I was thinking," the young man agreed, scratching the side of his short, pug nose and lowering his Styrofoam cup to the small, round table before taking another drag of his unlit cigarette. "Nothing special. Name's Dusty, by the way."

"Jamie," Jamie told him. "Danish is really good though." She took a bite, as if to emphasize her point.

"Yeah? I like the cinnamon rolls best. They got lots of raisins."

"I didn't see any of those."

"Nah, you wouldn't at this hour. They're always the first to go."

Jamie took another bite of her danish, another sip of her coffee. Dusty took another hit off his unlit cigarette. The man in the cowboy hat on TV was explaining that guns didn't kill people. People killed people, he was saying. Would Brad really have slit that boy's throat? she wondered.

"So, where you headed?" Dusty asked.

"Ohio."

"You from there?"

"No. I've never been there before."

"Me neither. Never been out of Georgia." Dusty's small brown eyes narrowed, as if he wasn't quite sure why that was. "So what's in Ohio?"

"My boyfriend's son," Jamie said, loving the feel of the word **boyfriend** on her tongue, the sound of it in her ear. No way he would have used that knife.

Dusty tapped his fingers on the table. Charlton Heston had replaced the man in the cowboy hat. He was speaking at some sort of rally. "From my cold, dead hands," he was shouting to thunderous applause.

What does that mean? Jamie wondered. "What happened to your finger?" she asked.

Dusty held up his right hand, examining his index finger as if he couldn't quite remember. "Accident with a lawn mower," he said after a lengthy pause.

Jamie flinched. "Yikes."

Dusty laughed. "Yikes?"

"Must have hurt like hell."

"Nah, not so much. At least not till later. I didn't even realize what had happened until I looked down and saw all the blood." He shook his head. "There sure was a lot of blood."

"They couldn't reattach it?" Jamie asked.

"Couldn't find it. Damn thing just took off."

Jamie pictured Dusty's fingertip flying through the air in the same arc as Curtis's severed ponytail. She heard the sound of laughter, realized with horror it was her own. "Oh, my God, I'm so sorry. I didn't mean to laugh. That's terrible. I'm so sorry."

"Don't be. It was pretty funny." Dusty laughed with her.

"You never found it?"

"Not till the next day. By then it was too late. I still have it though."

"You have it?"

"Not with me."

"Thank God," Jamie said.

"Yikes," Dusty said, and they laughed again.

A shadow fell across the TV screen. Jamie looked over, saw Brad leaning against the far wall. "What's so funny?" he asked, his eyes darting between the two.

Jamie was instantly on her feet. "Long story," she said, still chuckling.

"We've got lots of time," Brad said. "Seems the mechanic can't work on the car till this afternoon."

"You can probably keep your room till around four," Dusty offered. "That's when we start to get busy."

"Appreciate it," Brad said as Dusty returned to his desk.

"Well, we can just relax then," Jamie began. "Maybe go for a walk. There are those churches—"

"You really think it's a good idea to get so familiar with these people?" Brad interrupted. "Didn't last night teach you anything?"

It took Jamie several seconds to understand what Brad was talking about. "You mean Dusty?" She laughed. "Trust me. He's harmless."

"Trust **me.** There is no such thing."

Jamie inched forward until she was standing

directly in front of Brad. She stood on her tiptoes, her lips touching briefly on his. It was sweet of him to be so protective, so concerned for her welfare. "I **do** trust you."

He smiled, produced a white plastic bag from behind his back. "Bought you something."

"You did? What is it?"

"Open it."

Jamie took the bag from Brad's hands and reached inside it, extricating the box and bursting into tears at the sight of the platinum-haired doll with the impossible figure and red plastic, high-heeled shoes. "I don't believe it. You bought me a Barbie!"

"Thought you might want to start a new collection."

Jamie threw herself into Brad's arms. "I can't believe you," she said, delighted.

Brad squeezed Jamie tightly to his chest as the sound of televised gunfire ricocheted throughout the room. "Come on," he said. "Let's take Barbie to church."

CHAPTER TWELVE

"All right, Dylan. Time's up," Emma called from outside the locked bathroom door. It was almost six-thirty. Lily would be bringing Michael over any minute.

"Go away," a small voice responded.

"What are you doing in there, sweetie? Is your tummy okay?"

No response.

"Dylan, you know Mommy doesn't like it when you lock the door."

"Go away," Dylan said again.

Emma took a deep breath and made herself smile. She remembered reading that if you forced yourself to smile, regardless of how you were actually feeling, it would make you feel better. Act positive and you'll feel positive.

Some such rot. "Sweetheart, your friend Michael will be here any second."

"He's not my friend," came the immediate retort.

"He's in your class. I thought you liked him."

"I **don't** like him."

Emma smiled harder. "Well, he likes **you.** And he's been looking forward to this sleep-over all day."

"He can't sleep in my bed."

"I already told you, you'll be sleeping in my bed. Both of you."

"I don't want to sleep in your bed."

"Okay. We'll work something out later. In the meantime—"

"He can't play with my toys."

"Then you'd better get out here so that you can keep an eye on him, because he'll be here any second."

"No. Tell him to go home."

"I can't do that. I promised his mother—" She stopped. What am I doing arguing with a five-year-old? she wondered. "Dylan, get out of there this minute or you'll be very sorry." **I'll huff and I'll puff and I'll blow down your door!** "Dylan, do you hear me?"

Silence. Followed by the reluctant sound of a lock turning, the slow creak of the bathroom door as it fell open. Dylan stood glaring at his mother from the middle of the tiny room, his lower lip trembling.

"Good. That's quite enough silliness for one day. Now come downstairs. I'm making macaroni and cheese for dinner."

"I hate macaroni and cheese," Dylan said, refusing to budge.

"What are you talking about? You love macaroni and cheese."

"No, I don't. I hate it."

"Come downstairs." Emma reached for her son's hand, then stopped abruptly, recoiling in dismay as her eyes absorbed the wet tile in front of the toilet. "What happened in here?"

"It was an accident." Dylan looked away, his cheeks blushing bright pink.

Emma glanced from the floor to the toilet seat to the wall behind the toilet. A decorative splash of urine, like spray-painted graffiti, covered the various surfaces. "This was no accident, young man. You did this on purpose."

"No," Dylan insisted. "I just missed."

"Well, then, you just better clean it up." Emma soaked a washcloth, then forced it into her son's hand. "Right now."

"No."

"Dylan, I've had just about enough nonsense out of you for one day."

In response, the fingers of Dylan's hand opened, and the washcloth slid to the floor.

"Okay, mister, pick it up."

"No."

"You want a spanking? Is that what you want? Because I'd be more than happy to give you one."

"You're mean," Dylan shouted suddenly, pushing past Emma and running from the room. "You're a mean mommy."

"And you're a little stinker," Emma countered, catching up with her son at the top of the stairs. Frustration had already wiped the smile from her face, and now tears were obliterating whatever shadow of it remained. She grabbed Dylan's arm and spun him around, slapping him repeatedly on his backside as he screamed his indignation.

The doorbell rang.

Emma's hand froze in midair. What am I doing? she wondered. Didn't I promise myself that no matter how bad things got, I'd never take it out on my son? She took several deep breaths, followed immediately by several more, trying to calm herself down. "Okay, now, we are going downstairs," she began, speaking very softly and deliberately, "and you are going to say hello to Michael, and then you're going to go into the kitchen and eat every bit of the macaroni and cheese I put on your plate, and what's more, you're going to like it. And then you're going to say thank you, Mommy, thank you for making me that delicious macaroni and cheese. And you're going to take Michael up to your room and you're going to let him play with whatever toys he wants, or tomorrow morning when you wake up, there won't be any toys left to play with. And that includes Spider-man. Is that clear? Dylan, is that very clear?"

"I hate you," came Dylan's response.

"Fine. But I'm all you've got."

"I want my daddy," Dylan shouted in her ear, freeing himself from her grasp and running back into the bathroom, slamming the door.

"Dylan!"

The sound of the lock snapping into place.

"Dylan, don't do this. Please."

"I want my daddy!"

The doorbell rang again.

Emma stood in the middle of the hallway, fighting back tears and trying to regain some sense of equilibrium. What the hell had just happened? What had she done? "Dylan, I'm sorry, honey. I didn't mean—"

"Go away."

Emma shook her head, wiping the tears from her cheeks with both hands as the doorbell rang a third time. "Just a second," she called out, her feet following her voice down the stairs. What was the matter with her that she had so little self-control these days? Yes, Dylan had awakened in the middle of the night again with his usual quotient of bad dreams. As a result, he'd been tired and cranky all day, and yes, she was equally exhausted. It wasn't easy being a single parent, but that was precisely the point: **she** was the parent and **he** was the child. She was the grown-up in this equation, and she couldn't go flying off the handle every time Dylan misbehaved. After all it had been **her** decision, and not his, to invite Michael to spend the night. She hadn't consulted Dylan, hadn't taken his wishes into account, even though she'd known, deep down, that her son would be resistant to the idea. Just as she knew she was the one who'd made him that way, that she was responsible for Dylan's wariness, his lack of friends. How could she have expected him to react any other way to the news that, on a whim, a sudden, ill-advised impulse, she'd invited a relative stranger into their midst? And it didn't matter that it was a harmless five-year-old boy, or that they were in the same class in school, or that he lived just down the street. He was **other**, and therefore, he was someone to be feared, and ultimately rejected.

Like one of Lily's stories, Emma thought as she pulled open the front door, seeing Lily and her son smiling on her doorstep. Lily was wearing navy sweats and no makeup, and her hair was pulled into a careless ponytail, stray blond hairs sticking out from everywhere. Still, she had a glow of anticipation on her round face that almost took your breath away. Emma felt a stab of jealousy and thought how nice it would be to be in Lily's shoes, if only for one night. To be actually looking forward to something—how long had it been since she'd looked forward to **anything**?—to have dinner with a man who'd look at her with longing, and not loathing. If only it were **my** husband who'd died in a motorcycle accident, Emma was thinking as she ushered Lily and her son inside. "Hi, guys. Come on in."

"Sorry about the buzzer," Lily apologized. "I thought maybe you didn't hear me. And then

I thought maybe the buzzer wasn't working, so of course, I kept pressing. Makes a lot of sense."

"I was in the bathroom."

"Oh, sorry."

"No, don't be silly." Emma glanced at the little boy standing just behind his mother, tightly clutching his overnight bag in one hand and Kermit the Frog in the other. She fought the urge to bend down and take a large, suction kiss out of his round, apple-red cheeks. Were all five-year-old boys so magnificent? What the hell happens to them when they grow up? "This must be Michael."

"This is Michael," Lily agreed, her voice filled with motherly pride.

"This is Kermit." Michael pushed the large green doll toward Emma.

"Well, I'm delighted to meet you, Michael. And Kermit." Emma looked toward the stairs. "Dylan, Michael's here!"

No response.

"He'll be down in a minute. Are you hungry?" Emma asked Michael.

Michael nodded, lowering his small overnight bag to the floor.

Emma wondered if he was as angelic as he looked. Perversely, she hoped not. "I hope you like macaroni and cheese."

"His favorite," Lily said.

"Mine too," Emma agreed.

"Mine too," Dylan said, appearing at the top of the stairs.

Emma felt her heart grow large in her chest, as if it were about to burst with love and gratitude. "Dylan, sweetie, look who's here."

Dylan clumped gracelessly down the stairs, his fingers leaving a sticky trail on the side of the wall. "Hi," he said.

"And this is Michael's mother, Mrs. Rogers."

"You can call me Lily."

"Is that okay, Mommy?" Dylan asked.

Emma felt a surge of love so great, she had to grip the floor tightly with her toes to keep from falling over. Her son was the best thing that had ever happened to her. How could she have been so careless with him, so **mean,** as he had rightfully accused? He was just a little boy, for heaven's sake, and she expected way too much from him. I'm so sorry, baby, she told him silently. Forgive me. I promise I'll never raise a hand to you again. "Of course it's okay, sweetheart."

"I'm hungry," Dylan announced, taking Michael by the hand and leading him toward the kitchen, the women following after them. "My mom makes the best macaroni and cheese," he was saying. "Don't you, Mommy?"

"Old family recipe." Emma smiled at Lily. "The Kraft family, but still . . ."

Lily laughed as Emma spooned heaping portions of Kraft dinner onto the boys' plates.

"You have time for a drink?" Emma asked, lifting the glass of white wine she'd been nursing all afternoon from the counter where she'd left it earlier. When had she started drinking in the afternoons? she wondered suddenly, feeling the cheap wine warm in her throat.

"No. I wish I did, but I really should get going," Lily demurred.

"My mom has a date," Michael informed Dylan.

"What's a date?" Dylan asked.

Michael leaned toward him conspiratorially. "Dates are when you eat in a restaurant."

Dylan's eyes grew wide. "Can we go on a date too, Mommy?"

"Sounds good to me," Emma said, taking another sip of her wine.

Lily gave her son a good-bye hug. "Okay, so have a good time, do what Mrs. Frost tells you . . ."

"Emma," Emma corrected quickly, although, truthfully, she would have preferred Mrs. Frost. Her mother had always drummed into her the importance of addressing one's elders with the proper respect.

". . . and I'll see you in the morning." Lily kissed her son on the cheek as he continued spooning the Kraft dinner into his mouth. "Here's my cell phone number, if you need to reach me." She handed Emma a piece of paper with her number carefully printed across it. "If you decide, for any reason, that you want me to pick up Michael on my way home, don't hesitate."

"I'm sure that won't be necessary."

They stopped at the front door.

"You really think I should be doing this?" Lily asked, large brown eyes pleading for reassurance.

"Stop worrying. Michael will be fine."

"I don't mean Michael. I mean Jeff Dawson."

"You'll do great." Emma reached out to pat her new friend's arm.

"I don't know. Do you have any idea how long it's been since I was on an actual date with anyone?"

"I think I might."

"I won't know how to act. I won't know what to say."

"So you'll listen. What is it they used to tell us in health class? Get him talking, find out what his interests are, laugh at his jokes."

"What if he doesn't tell any?"

"Then you tell one."

"Oh, God. I don't know any. Do you?"

"What's black and white and red all over?" Emma offered.

"A newspaper?"

"A nun rolling down a hill."

"Oh, God. That's the dumbest joke I've ever heard," Lily wailed.

"Really? It's a big hit with the kindergarten crowd."

"I think I'm going to be sick."

"You're going to be fabulous." Emma opened her front door, gently pushed Lily onto the landing. "Just remember, if all else fails . . ."

"What?"

Emma smiled, took another sip of her wine. "Lie."

After the boys were asleep, Emma relaxed in the living room with another glass of wine. Despite Dylan's fears—and hers—the evening had progressed without a hitch. The boys had finished their dinner, then raced upstairs to play with Dylan's toys. And although there weren't a lot of toys to choose from—his beloved Spider-man doll, a small army of G.I. Joes, some Legos, a bunch of plastic cars and trucks—they seemed happy enough. There was the obligatory game of hide-and-seek before bedtime, followed by Dylan's nightly rituals, all of which he performed with a minimum of fuss and a maximum of subtlety. If Michael noticed anything was strange, he hadn't voiced his concerns. Instead, he and Dylan had climbed into her bed as she was watching a rerun of **Friends,** the episode in which Ross says, "I take thee, Rachel," when he's marrying somebody else. The only worrisome moment of the evening had come when Dylan had turned to Michael as the program concluded and proudly announced, "My mother was named after Rachel's baby." Luckily, the dubious logistics of that one had gone sailing clear over Michael's head.

"Cool," was all he'd said.

"Cool," Dylan had repeated with a laugh.

Now Emma sat, sipping on her wine and wondering what she was going to do for the balance of the evening. She could read a book.

If she had one, she thought. She topped off her glass, wondering how Lily was doing on her date. "To the happy couple," she said, wishing now she'd moved the TV downstairs so she'd have something to occupy her time. She couldn't just sit here, talking to herself and drinking all night. Could she? "Why not?" she asked out loud, kicking off her shoes and curling her legs around the various angles of her brown sofa, trying to get comfortable. I don't belong here, she was thinking as she closed her eyes. I don't belong on Mad River Road.

Had she ever belonged anywhere?

She certainly hadn't belonged at the Bishop Lane School for Girls, that god-awful bastion for the spoiled daughters of the elite, where the title of posture queen was as coveted as the position of valedictorian, which shouldn't have come as any surprise, considering the numbers of poles stuck up the students' perky asses. Now that's the speech she would have given had she been selected valedictorian. Hah! Fat chance of that.

Although her first term had held such

promise. Those first few months before anyone knew who she really was, before it was discovered that she was a charity case, that her mother was part of the custodial staff. **The janitor's daughter!** they whispered in the halls as she walked past, as if she were a communicable disease.

All she'd wanted was to fit in, to be like the other girls, but how could she be like the others when they had everything and she had nothing, when even the cheapest pair of designer jeans was well beyond her means? Was it really so surprising she'd started shoplifting? Just little things at first. A lipstick here, some nail polish there. "That's a great color," Sarah Johnson had commented the next day in class. The first sign of affirmation she'd had from her peers in months. That faint hint of acceptance had been enough to carry her through the day and sustain her through many subsequent slights. So why not help herself to this pair of neat leather gloves, especially when the salesgirl was being so snooty? And these sneakers? Weren't they just like the ones Lucy Dixon received such compliments on? And what about this skirt and sweater? She looked good in them, felt even better. In these clothes, she was as good as anybody else. She'd show them—the janitor's daughter was nobody's charity case.

How ironic that in order to belong, she'd had to take things that didn't belong to her, Emma thought now, remembering the rush, the feeling of sheer exhilaration, of power, she'd experienced each time she secreted an item inside her oversize bag.

She also remembered the subsequent anguish, the guilt, the promises she'd made to herself to stop.

Except, she hadn't. **Couldn't,** despite her best intentions. Then one day, exiting Neiman Marcus with three miniskirts under her school uniform, she was detained by a female guard who'd been monitoring her stroll through the store. They found the three skirts, the two bras, the cashmere sweater set, even the stupid tube of moisturizing cream she'd pocketed on her way out, a last-minute impulse, a gift for her mother on Mother's Day. Some gift. The store called her school, her mother, and the police, although they ultimately declined to press charges.

It was her first run-in with the police. But not her last.

The following year, she'd skipped school one afternoon to sneak into the local multiplex. Of course she got caught, and the theater, deciding to make an example of her, had called the school. She'd been suspended for two days and warned that any future transgressions would not be tolerated. She was lucky her mother was a well-regarded employee, the principal said.

Six months later, her mother was let go, and she found another job, forcing Emma into another school. Emma colored her hair, altered the spelling of her name, told everyone her mother was dying of cancer. For a while this gained her a measure of acceptance. But then some good samaritan from the guidance office called her mother and asked if there was anything she could do to help her during this difficult time, and Emma was exposed as a liar and a fraud. Several days after that, she ran into some former classmates from Bishop Lane. "Is it true you have such big boobs because you wear twelve bras?" asked one of the girls.

Emma responded by punching her in the face. "Served her right," Emma snorted now, remembering all the blood and finishing what was left of the bottle of wine. Of course, the school had been notified and her mother informed. This time, the police were summoned, although again no charges were filed. "You're lucky," the arresting officer had told her, lecturing her on the error of her ways before asking her to blow him in the backseat of his cruiser.

And now she was babysitting the son of the only friend she'd made in years so that said friend could go out to dinner with—**ta dum!**—a cop. Another of life's little ironies. As was the fact her mother had died of cancer after all, not long after Emma's ill-fated marriage. Emma struggled to her feet, as if trying to escape the man she'd married. You can run, but you can't hide, she was thinking as the room spun around her. She quickly sank back down. Where was she going anyway? No matter how fast she ran, no matter how far she traveled, her past went with her. She could make all the fresh starts she wanted. She'd still end up in the same place.

CHAPTER THIRTEEN

"Some more wine?" Jeff Dawson reached past the thick, cream-colored candle in the middle of the pink linen tablecloth for the bottle of expensive Merlot.

Lily shook her head, then quickly changed her mind. How often did the opportunity to drink good wine with a nice man in a chic restaurant present itself these days? And who knew when it would happen again? She might as well take advantage of the opportunity. "Okay. Just a bit."

Jeff poured an inch of wine into her glass before adding a similar amount to his own. "How's your salmon?"

"Fabulous. Your lamb?"

"Perfection." Jeff cut a piece, dangled it on

his fork, the knot of his burgundy tie straining against his linebacker's neck as he proffered it across the small table. Even the tailored, navy blazer he wore over his powder blue shirt wasn't enough to camouflage the massive expanse of his chest and arms. "Here. Try some."

Lily opened her mouth to accept the offering. "Oh, that **is** good. You want to try the salmon?"

"No, I've never been much of a fish eater," Jeff confessed, almost guiltily. "I blame my mother."

"Oh, sure. Everybody always blames the mother."

Jeff laughed. "Actually, she was a great mother, just not much of a cook. And I'm afraid the only fish she ever served us were these awful salmon patties that I hated."

"I never liked those either."

"So I never developed the taste."

"There's still time." Lily motioned toward the salmon on her plate.

"Nah. I'm just a meat-and-potatoes kind of guy, I guess." He popped another piece of meat into his mouth, as if to underline his point.

Lily watched him chew, enjoying the enthusiastic movement of his jaws. He has a nice mouth, she thought, her eyes sweeping up from his soft, full lips, past the twice-broken nose to the small, Y-shaped scar in the middle of his right cheek, then stopping to admire the straightforward look in his close-set, dark blue eyes. Not handsome exactly, not even handsome **remotely,** and curiously, all the more appealing because of it. Lily had never been particularly partial to handsome. She'd always preferred a man with flaws. "How'd you get the scar?" she asked. "If you don't mind my asking."

"Don't mind at all," he told her. "Knife fight with a dope-crazed drug dealer."

"Oh, my God. Really?"

"No." Mischievous eyes twinkled in the candle's soft light. "But I've always wanted to say that. Sounds very dramatic, don't you think?"

"I've never been a huge fan of dramatics."

"No? That's good then, because the truth is really very mundane."

"What is it?"

"I had this small tumor growing on a nerve on my cheekbone. Ten, eleven years ago. They had to cut it out."

"Sounds scary."

"Not quite as scary as having to subdue a dope-crazed, knife-wielding drug dealer, but yeah, I guess it was a pretty scary time," he admitted. "Luckily, the damn thing was benign. So . . ."

"So," Lily repeated, stabbing at a piece of lettuce and surreptitiously checking the front of her melon-colored blouse to make sure she hadn't inadvertently sprayed herself with salad dressing. Which is just the sort of thing she would do, she thought, tucking her hair behind her left ear and wondering if Jeff was enjoying himself as much as she was.

The restaurant was lovely, everything the ecstatic newspaper reviews had claimed. Intimate without being claustrophobic, romantic without being cloying, sophisticated without being pretentious. The walls were deep purple, the floor and ceiling light oak. Classical jazz played quietly in the background. There were fresh flowers everywhere. And the food was wonderful, although Lily had almost gagged when she saw the prices.

"So," Jeff said again, and they laughed. "Have I told you how beautiful you look tonight?"

Lily felt her cheeks grow warm. Again she tucked her hair behind her left ear, although it was already secure, then stared down at her plate. "You have, yes."

"Is it okay to tell you again?"

"Be my guest."

"You look beautiful."

Lily smiled, tossed aside the compliment with a wave of her fingers.

"You don't believe me?" Jeff leaned forward in his seat, rested muscular forearms on the table.

"Well, I could stand to lose a few pounds."

"You gotta be kidding me."

"At least five pounds."

"No way."

"Well, that's very sweet of you, but—"

"Hey, I'm a cop. I never lie."

"Really?"

"Well, no. I guess I lie occasionally, same as everybody else."

"On what occasions?" Lily asked.

"What?"

"On what occasions do you lie?"

Jeff put down his fork, looked toward the ceiling, obviously giving the question serious consideration. "Well, professionally, I lie in order to get information or extract a confession."

"Is that ethical?"

"Absolutely. There's nothing in the Constitution that says I have to be honest when I'm dealing with thieves and murderers."

"You deal with a lot of murderers?"

He shrugged. "Not too many. Statistically, murder is still a pretty rare occurrence."

"Thank God for that."

"The murderers I **have** dealt with weren't a whole lot different from you and me. At least on the surface."

"And below the surface?"

"Well, that depends."

"On what?"

"Circumstances. How can I explain this?" He looked around the crowded room, as if searching for someone he knew. "Okay, see that couple in the corner?"

Lily glanced casually to her right. "The man with the beard and the woman in the polka-dot dress?"

Jeff nodded. "Okay, so suppose tomorrow morning, you're reading the newspaper, and you find out Mr. Beard's been arrested for killing Mrs. Polka Dots."

"Okay," Lily said, stealing another look at the middle-aged couple in the corner and wondering if they had any inkling they were the subjects of such unsavory speculation.

"Okay, so, scenario number one: Beard tells Polka Dots he has to go back to work for a few hours after dinner; Polka Dots goes home; Beard works for a while, then decides he's had enough and returns home earlier than expected; Beard walks in and finds Polka

Dots in bed with his best friend; Beard goes berserk and sprays Polka Dots all over the walls."

"A crime of passion," Lily said, imagining polka dots all over the deep purple interior and trying not to laugh. "Not to mention, very colorful."

Jeff smiled. "Lawyer's going to argue that, ordinarily, Beard would never do such a horrible thing, that he's this upright citizen who pays his taxes and loves his dog and takes care of his widowed mother, but that the shock of finding his wife in bed with his best friend rendered him temporarily insane, and therefore, he isn't responsible for his actions. Chances are pretty good the jury agrees with him. Mr. Beard may have killed someone, but he's not really a murderer. It could happen to any one of us. Okay?"

Lily nods.

"Okay, scenario number two: Beard and Polka Dots go home; she accuses him of flirting with the waitress all night; he says she's crazy; she calls him a bastard; he calls her a bitch; the fight escalates. They're screaming and pushing each other. Next thing you know she grabs a knife and stabs him through the heart. He's dead before he hits the floor, and she's sobbing to the arresting officer she didn't mean to do it. The lawyer gets up in court, details Beard's assorted infidelities and Dottie's abject apologies. She's a God-fearing woman who's never had so much as a parking ticket; she'll never do it again, et cetera, et cetera."

"She may have killed someone, but she's not really a murderer," Lily continues. "It could happen to any of us."

"Scenario number three: they go home; he's had too much to drink; he starts using her as a punching bag, something he does on a regular basis, except this time it's worse; he says he's going to kill her, but during the struggle, she breaks free, grabs a gun . . ."

"Dottie shoots Beard in self-defense."

"Exactly. She kills him, but is she really a murderer?"

"Scenario number four?"

"Same as number three, except this time, Beard makes good on his threat and beats Dottie to death with his fists."

"Well, this case is different."

"How so?"

"This time he really is a murderer."

"You don't think it's something that could happen to any of us, given the right—or **wrong**—set of circumstances?"

"I think we can all be **victimized,**" Lily argued, choosing her words carefully. "I think we all make bad choices now and again, but in this case, you're talking about a history of abuse, a conscious and repeated decision to brutalize another human being, and ultimately take another life." Lily shuddered, took a soothing sip of her wine. "I think it's different than the other cases you described. There's no reasonable doubt here."

"I agree," Jeff said. "Beard's a cold-blooded killer who deserves to be put away for life. But looking at him now, sitting there, laughing and enjoying his coffee, how can you tell? He looks just like you and me. Which brings us to scenario number five, and the most dangerous killer of all—the psychopath."

"And what makes him more dangerous than the others?"

"A total lack of conscience. Plus he's a chameleon. He changes personalities as easily as you or I change clothes. He studies you, gives you the guy you want to see. He has no real feelings, but he's great at pretending. You can be married to a guy like Beard for years, and then one morning you wake up to discover he's been lying to you since day one, that he never went to medical school, that he has another family up in Canada, that his last three wives have all disappeared under mysterious circumstances. That's if you're lucky. The unlucky ones are the ones who never wake up, who disappear while walking the dog and turn up months later in a nearby lake or a stinking pile of landfill. Turns out Beard's just been biding his time."

"But why does he kill?"

"Insurance money, another woman, fear of being found out. Sometimes he kills just because he likes it. Hell, to him it's no different than swatting a fly."

"Talk about scary." Lily glanced back at the man with the beard as he popped a piece of apple flan into his mouth and continued talking to his companion in the polka-dot dress. "I guess you never know about people."

"Think about it. What does everyone always say when they hear about some particularly grisly crime?" Jeff asked. "The people who live down the street from the wacko who's just been arrested for burying twenty people alive in his backyard? They always say the same thing: 'He was so nice, so quiet. We never would have suspected him in a million years.'"

"So you're saying everyone has a secret life?"

"Well, I don't," Jeff said with a laugh. "With me, what you see is definitely what you get."

I like what I see, Lily thought, taking another bite of her salmon to keep from saying it out loud. "And personally?" she asked instead.

"Personally?"

"What do you lie about?"

"What do I lie about?" he repeated. "Little things, mostly."

"Such as?"

"Such as my mother knit me this sweater last Christmas, and it's this wild, pink-and-burgundy-striped thing—God only knows what she was thinking—and, of course, she's proud as punch, and she keeps asking me if I like it. What am I going to say? 'It's the ugliest damn thing I've ever seen, I wouldn't be caught dead in it?' No, of course not. I tell her it's beautiful, that I love it."

"So you lie to protect someone's feelings?"

"And I guess sometimes I might exaggerate a little," he admitted after a pause. "You know, to make a story sound better."

"You mean like the fish that got away?"

"Or, in my case, the perp."

"The perp?"

Jeff laughed. "Perpetrator, felon, crook. The guy I'm chasing—'He must have been an Olympic champion. Superman couldn't catch this guy.' That kind of thing."

Lily's turn to laugh. "So you like being a policeman?"

"I do. Yes, very much."

"What is it you like?"

"Truthfully?"

"Unless you're worried about protecting my feelings."

He smiled. "Honestly, I like everything about it. I like solving mysteries, saving somebody's dog, finding somebody's kid. I like arresting bad guys and putting them away. I like going to court. Hell, I even like lawyers, which is not information I share with a lot of people."

"I'll be sure to keep it quiet."

"And you?" Jeff asked. "What do you like?"

"Well, I certainly like this salmon." Lily finished what was left on her plate, knowing she was evading his question. She knew he was watching her, waiting for her to continue. "And I like this restaurant." She paused, lowered her fork, raised her eyes to his. "And I like that I changed my mind about going out with you tonight."

"Why did you?"

"Truthfully?"

"Unless you're worried about protecting my feelings," he said, and they both smiled.

"Well, it wasn't that I didn't want to go. I always wanted to go."

"Which, of course, is why you said no."

"It's just that it's been a long time since I've been out on an actual date with anyone, and I wasn't sure it was such a great idea."

"Why?"

"Why wasn't I sure it was a good idea?"

"Why haven't you been dating?"

Lily arranged her knife and fork across her plate, then massaged the back of her neck with the fingers of her right hand. "Long story."

"You told me your husband was killed in a motorcycle accident last year."

Lily nodded.

"How long were you married?"

Lily hesitated. She didn't really want to talk about her marriage. Still, not talking about it might make it seem more mysterious than it needed to be. And hadn't Jeff already said he liked solving mysteries? "Four years. I was pregnant when we got married," she added, although he hadn't asked.

"Was it a good marriage?"

Lily shrugged. "Let's just say it had its ups and downs."

He nodded his understanding. "Still, the accident must have been a horrible shock."

"Yes. It was," Lily heard herself say, her voice distant and lacking substance, like an echo on its third repetition. "I remember the policeman coming to the house. I remember the look on my mother's face as we were leaving for the hospital. I remember the policeman saying we should prepare ourselves, that Kenny hadn't been wearing his helmet, so his face was all torn up, and there was lots of blood. They said nearly every bone in his body was broken, but that miraculously, he was still alive. We got to the hospital a few minutes before he died."

"I'm sorry."

"It was my fault," Lily said flatly.

"Your fault? How could an accident like that possibly have been your fault?"

"Because we'd been fighting. We'd been fighting all afternoon."

Jeff reached across the table, covered her hand with his own. "People fight, Lily. That doesn't make what happened to Kenny your fault."

"You don't understand. He was so upset. I should never have let him get on that motorcycle."

"Could you have stopped him?"

"No," Lily admitted, sliding her hand away from his to wipe several stray tears from her cheek. "I'm sorry. Can we talk about something else?"

"Absolutely. And I'm the one who should be apologizing to you."

"For what?"

"For not minding my own business."

"You're a cop," she reminded him. "I would think not minding your own business is part of the job description."

"That's very generous," he said. "Now, what would you like to talk about?"

Lily checked her watch. "Actually, it's getting kind of late. I probably should be heading home."

"Jan told me Michael was at a sleepover."

"Good old Jan," Lily remarked, deciding to speak to her in the morning. "What else did she tell you?"

"That you're the best employee she's ever had, but that what you really want is to be a writer."

Lily nodded, wondering, How often do we get what we really want? "Do you think we could save that discussion for another time? I told Emma that I'd try to stop by her house, see how the boys were making out."

"Emma's the one I met yesterday? The one with the Maybelline eyes?"

Was she wrong, or had she detected a note of cynicism in Jeff's voice? "You sound like you don't believe her."

Jeff shrugged. "I'm a cop, remember? It's part of the job description to be suspicious."

"You think she's lying?"

"I don't know."

"Why would she lie?" Lily persisted.

"I don't know," he said again. "Maybe she isn't."

Well, well, you must have made a bundle from that, she heard Jan say. **What are you doing on Mad River Road?**

"The modeling business isn't the most secure profession in the world," Lily said in an effort to silence them both. "You can be hot one minute, ice-cold the next."

"No doubt about it."

"She even wrote a story about it for **Cosmo** magazine."

"Really? Did you read it?"

"No. Why? You think she's lying about that too?"

"I just asked if you'd read her story."

"No, I haven't. But why would she make that up?"

"To impress you?" Jeff offered.

"Impress me?"

"Kind of like the fish that got away."

Lily shrugged, uncomfortable with the idea that her new friend might be lying to her.

"I tell you what," Jeff said as he reached into

his jacket pocket and pulled out his cell phone. "Why don't you call your friend and make sure the boys are okay. If there's a problem, I'll take you home immediately. If not, we'll stay for dessert. I hear the chocolate cake is out of this world."

Lily took the phone from his hand and quickly pressed in Emma's number. It rang once, twice, three times before being picked up in the middle of the fourth ring.

"Hello?" Emma's voice was groggy and coated with sleep.

Lily checked her watch. It was only a few minutes after nine o'clock. "Emma, it's Lily. Did I wake you up?" She pictured Emma at her front door, a glass of wine in her hand.

"No, of course not," Emma said, clearing her throat. "Sorry. Frog in my throat."

"I was just calling to make sure everything's okay."

"Everything's great. The boys are sound asleep. How's your date going?"

"Fine. I just thought I'd check in."

"Okay, consider me checked. Now stop

worrying and start having a good time. The boys are fine."

Lily returned the phone to Jeff's outstretched palm, glancing toward the table where the man with the beard and his companion in the polka-dot dress had been sitting, only to discover they were no longer there.

"Well?" Jeff asked. "Is everything okay?"

Lily smiled, pushing any unpleasant thoughts to the back of her mind. "Everything's just fine," she said.

CHAPTER FOURTEEN

"I gotta tell you, this is the best chocolate cake I have ever tasted." Jamie forked another piece of the three-layer cake with the caramel icing into her mouth, her taste buds luxuriating in the rich, moist goodness of the chocolate, even as her eyes tried not to notice the scowl that had ambushed her companion's normally playful features. The scowl had also infected his posture, lending an almost menacing cast to the slant of his shoulders, the tilt of his head. Cool blue eyes verged on ice-cold, refusing to make contact with her own. Soft, full lips had disappeared into a hard, thin line, obliterating even the hint of his glorious smile. Clearly something was bothering him. "You sure you don't want any?"

Brad turned away, took a disinterested sip of

his coffee, and played with the Hi-Q game the restaurant had thoughtfully provided for each table.

In case conversation starts to wear thin, Jamie thought, watching him move the brightly colored plastic pegs around the small, triangular board. The object of the game was to leave only one peg standing. "I think it's true what they say about chocolate releasing all these endorphins to the brain that make you feel good," she persisted. "Like when you exercise. Apparently endorphins give you a natural high. **Endorphins** is kind of a funny word, don't you think?" Jamie continued when Brad failed to respond. "I always wonder where they get words like that."

Brad continued playing with the game, jumping one tiny blue peg over a tiny yellow one, then tossing the yellow peg onto the shiny wood table beside two previously discarded white ones.

"Brad, what's wrong?"

"Nothing's wrong," he said, although, obviously, something was.

Jamie swallowed another bite of cake as she looked around the crowded restaurant. "Why do you think they call it Cracker Barrel?" she wondered out loud.

Brad shrugged, his eyes following after an attractive waitress whose jet-black hair was a nice complement to her bright orange uniform, as she wiggled her way through the tables toward the kitchen. "It's a restaurant chain, Jamie," he said. "Who cares why they call it anything?"

Jamie studied the large, well-lit room with its lacquered wood floors, varnished wood furniture, and assorted wood trimmings. "Maybe because the wood is the same kind of wood they make barrels from," Jamie postulated, although this sounded lame, even to her own ears. Besides, that didn't explain the Cracker. "Is Cracker a kind of barrel?"

Brad blinked several times in her direction. "What are you talking about, Jamie?"

"I was just wondering. . . . Never mind."

Brad finished his latest attempt at Hi-Q, leaving one peg on each corner of the triangular board.

"Three pegs—that's not bad."

"It's lame," he said, setting up the game again.

"I think you're supposed to be some sort of genius if you manage to leave only one peg."

"Guess I'm no genius."

Jamie popped the last piece of cake into her mouth, then gathered up the remaining crumbs of chocolate on the ends of her fork, thinking, No amount of endorphins is going to be enough to lighten this mood. "Are you mad at me about something?" she broached, when she could no longer stand the tension.

Brad lifted his eyes from the table for the first time since they'd sat down. "Why would I be mad at you?"

"I don't know, but you seem kind of distant."

"Distant?"

"You've been pouting for the past hour," she said, deciding to take the bull by the horns.

"I don't pout." He quickly discarded several blue pegs on the tabletop.

"Yes, you do. You get this major upper-lip thing going." She hoped he'd smile.

He didn't. "You're imagining things, Jamie."

"I don't think so. You've hardly said two words to me since I said I didn't want to stop in Atlanta overnight. Are you mad because I don't want to stop in Atlanta?"

Brad shrugged, his eyes returning to the table. "It's no big deal. I just thought it would be a nice place to stop, that's all. You said your-self, we're in no rush."

"I really don't like Atlanta," Jamie de-murred.

"Fine."

"Fine?"

"I understand."

"Do you?"

"Well, no, I guess I don't," he admitted, wav-ing his hands in obvious frustration, the back of one hand sending the multicolored pegs scattering across the table to the floor. "I mean, what's the problem here? Are you afraid of running into your ex-husband?"

"It's not that."

"What is it?"

Jamie watched one of the yellow pegs roll

across the floor, coming to a stop under the heavy, black shoe of a nearby diner. "I don't know."

"What is it, Jamie? Aren't you over this guy?"

"What? Are you kidding me? Of course I'm over him."

"Then I don't get it."

"It's just that I don't have very pleasant memories of Atlanta."

"So, we'll make new memories."

"Look, if we just drive another forty minutes, we'll get to Adairsville. There's this fabulous place outside Adairsville called Barnsley Gardens that's supposed to be the most romantic place in Georgia. You know, very **Gone With the Wind**-ish. It's got all these ruins that are supposed to be haunted, and water gardens, and acres and acres of flowers. And it has this five-star resort with, like, all these nineteenth-century cottages. We could stay there. Unless, of course, you think it would be too expensive, then we could stay somewhere else—"

"Jamie," Brad interrupted. "I'm tired. I don't think I can drive for another forty minutes."

"I'll drive," she offered happily.

He shook his head. "I just want to relax. It's been an exhausting day."

It has? Jamie quickly replayed the day's events in her mind. They'd spent a lovely morning in Tifton, visiting all the churches and shops in the downtown core, then enjoyed a nice, leisurely lunch in a local café before picking up the car at around three o'clock, its leaky tire replaced by a brand-spanking-new one, the cost of which Brad had insisted on putting on his credit card. Then they'd resumed their journey north on I-75, stopping for an hour in Macon after a sign advertising the Georgia Music Hall of Fame caught her eye, and where Brad had bought them matching blue T-shirts, before continuing on their way. Everything had been perfect until he mentioned spending the night in Atlanta.

"I guess last night finally caught up with

me," Brad said now. "But, hey, I guess I can tough it out for another half hour or so, if that's what you want."

"You don't feel well?"

"I'll be fine."

"Maybe you should eat something."

"I just need to lie down for a little while."

"Well, I'll drive, and you can have a snooze," Jamie suggested.

"**I'll** drive," Brad insisted, signaling to the waitress. "It's getting dark, and the traffic around Atlanta can get pretty hairy. It's too risky. I don't want anything happening to you."

Jamie reached across the table, covered his hand with her own. What was the matter with her? Couldn't she see that the man was bone weary? Why was she behaving so selfishly? Was he right? Was she afraid of running into her ex-husband, or worse, his mother? And what if they did run into them? So what? She had a sexy, new man on her arm to show off. A man who was everything her ex-husband was not. One glance would tell Laura Dennison that.

Hell, it might be fun to run into them after all.

This is gonna be fun, ain't it, guys? she remembered Brad saying.

"Okay, we'll stay overnight in Atlanta."

"What? No," Brad countered. "You hate Atlanta. You won't be comfortable."

"I'll be fine," she assured him.

"We'll go to this Beardsley Gardens—"

"Barnsley," she corrected with a laugh. "And we can go another time. Maybe tomorrow night. Or on the way back. You probably need reservations anyway. Place like that is probably booked months in advance."

He nodded, as if agreeing with her only reluctantly. "You're probably right. I'll call first thing in the morning, see what I can do."

"That'd be great."

The waitress approached with the bill.

"I'm suddenly really hungry," Brad exclaimed. "I think you might be right about my needing something to eat. Would you mind? I'll have the all-day breakfast, with extra-crispy bacon and two sunny-side-up eggs," he told the waitress before Jamie had a chance to respond. "Oh, and some of your delicious biscuits, and another cup of coffee. What about you, Jamie? Another piece of endorphin-filled chocolate cake?"

"No, thanks." Jamie couldn't help but marvel at Brad's abrupt change in moods.

"So, where's a good place to stay in Atlanta?" Brad leaned forward, resting his elbows on the table and taking her hands inside his own.

"There's a ton of motels."

"Nah. Forget motels. Let's stay somewhere special."

"There's a Best Western—"

"Better than Best."

"Well, there's the Ritz Carlton over on Peachtree Drive, but—"

"But?"

"It's in Buckhead."

"Butthead?"

Jamie laughed. "I should tell my former mother-in-law you said that. She was always going on about how Buckhead was the **only** area in Atlanta to live. I'm not sure she'd feel the same way if it were called Butthead."

"Well, Butthead sounds pretty good to me, and you can't beat the Ritz. What do you say?"

Jamie smiled. "You can't beat the Ritz," she agreed.

The sumptuous white-and-gold lobby of the Ritz Carlton Hotel was crowded with Japanese tourists as Jamie followed Brad to the front desk. "We'd like a room for tonight," Brad told the clerk as soon as the young man in the dark suit and crisp white shirt finished with the guest who was registering. "A suite, if you have one." Brad snapped his credit card down on the marble counter.

"Very good, sir. Just let me check what's available."

A suite, Jamie was thinking. A suite at the Ritz Carlton Hotel. "My ex-mother-in-law would probably have a heart attack and die if she saw me now," Jamie whispered, unable to keep the glee out of her voice.

"We have a lovely, nonsmoking suite available on the tenth floor, overlooking the Galleria."

"What do you think, Jamie?" Brad asked. "A suite overlooking the Galleria?"

"Why not?" Jamie replied with a laugh.

"The lady says, Why not?" Brad repeated. He turned back to Jamie, whispered in her ear, "What's a Galleria?"

"If you'll just sign here, Mr. Hastings," the clerk said, glancing at the credit card and pushing a form forward for Brad's signature.

Mr. Hastings? Jamie wondered, about to correct him. But the clerk was already taking a swipe of Brad's credit card. She watched him pause, try it a second time.

"I'm sorry, sir. Would you have another card, by any chance?"

"What's the matter with that one?"

"I don't know. It's not going through."

"That's impossible. Try it again."

The clerk tried it a third time. "I'm sorry, sir. Perhaps another card . . ."

"What's the problem?" Jamie asked.

Brad's face darkened. "It's the stupid card.

The magnetic strip must be on the fritz."

"A fritz at the Ritz?" Jamie asked, hoping for a smile, receiving only a tense pursing of his lips. "That happens to me all the time. Do you have a piece of cellophane?" Jamie asked the clerk. "Sometimes if you wrap the card in cellophane . . . Or if you have a plastic bag . . ."

"Jamie, forget it. We'll just go somewhere else."

Jamie felt her heart sink. She'd had her heart set on the Ritz. "I have a credit card," she offered, reaching into her purse and handing her card to the clerk. What the hell? How much could one night cost?

"I don't want to use your card," Brad said.

"Come on. You've paid for everything else."

"I'm sorry." The clerk looked from side to side self-consciously, as if appealing to his colleagues for help. "I'm afraid this card has also been declined."

"Shoot," Jamie muttered. She hadn't gotten around to paying her last bill, and the cost of the suite had probably put her over her limit. "How about just a regular room?"

"I'm afraid there are none available," the clerk said, his voice so tentative even Jamie knew he was lying. "Perhaps you might try the Embassy Suites. They're only several blocks away."

"Shove your goddamn Embassy Suites," Brad said.

"Brad—"

"Come on, Jamie." Brad threw Jamie's bag over his left shoulder, his own over his right, then grabbed her elbow, dragging her through the crowd of Japanese tourists still milling about the lobby, toward the revolving glass door. He tossed his parking ticket at the valet and began pacing restlessly back and forth in front of the entrance.

"It's okay, Brad. We'll find another hotel."

"I'm not staying at any fucking Embassy Suites."

"There's a million hotels in Atlanta. I'm sure we'll find a nice one."

"Fucking credit card."

"These things happen, Brad. It's okay."

"It's not okay. This is very embarrassing,"

Brad said, shaking his head and running his hand through his tightly cropped hair. "Shit!"

Jamie bit down on her lower lip to keep from offering further words of encouragement. Just let him stew, she thought. Let him get it all out of his system. Of course he was embarrassed. He wasn't used to such things happening. In a few minutes, he'd calm down. Everything would be back to normal. "He called you Mr. Hastings," she said, suddenly remembering.

Brad stopped his angry pacing, spun around toward her. "What?"

"The clerk. When he asked you to sign in. He called you Mr. Hastings."

"He did?"

"I was about to correct him, but then he said the card had been declined, and well . . ."

Brad shook his head. "Hastings is my middle name. Brad Hastings Fisher," he elaborated. "Stupid clerk can't even read. No wonder he screwed up."

Jamie smiled. Brad Hastings Fisher, she repeated silently as the valet pulled her blue

Thunderbird into the long, circular driveway. Such a distinguished-sounding name. "Look, you're tired. Why don't you let me drive—"

"Get in the car, Jamie," Brad directed gently, climbing behind the wheel as the valet opened the passenger side of the car. "I'll drive. You play tour guide."

"Now? But you're exhausted."

"My adrenaline's pumping like crazy. Maybe if we drive around the city for a bit, it'll give me a chance to calm down."

Jamie thought of suggesting they continue on to Adairsville, then thought better of it. She had no interest in rehashing their previous argument. "You really want me to show you the sights?"

"How about we just drive around Butthead for a while? You could show me where you used to live."

Jamie sighed. The last thing she wanted to do was drive around Buckhead. What she wanted was to climb into a nice hot bath and then inside a nice warm bed. Still, if all he needed was a few minutes to calm down . . .

"Turn left," she said as Brad pulled the car away from the curb. "Now right. Okay. Keep going to the next corner, then make another right. Follow it around the bend in the road."

"Wow, these homes are really something," Brad remarked. "Talk about **Gone With the Wind.**"

Jamie glanced at the parade of palatial estates surrounded by long, sweeping lawns and all but hidden behind high, wrought-iron gates. "It's hard to see them in the dark. We really should wait until tomorrow."

"Nah, this is good enough. You actually lived in one of these castles?"

"No. I lived in a small apartment about five blocks away. You can get to it if you turn right at the next light."

"Where's your mother-in-law's house?" Brad asked, ignoring her directions and continuing on straight ahead.

Jamie felt every muscle in her body tighten. "My mother-in-law?"

"Didn't you say she lives in Butthead?"

Jamie nodded. "About a mile from here."

"Show me."

"Brad—"

"I'm just trying to get to know my girl better. Come on. Then we'll find a motel, call it a night."

My girl, Jamie repeated silently, savoring the sound. She nodded, guiding him around the hilly twists and turns that made up the upscale suburb of Buckhead. It occurred to her that she could point to any house, say this is it, this is where I spent possibly the worst year of my life, but she sensed he would know if she was lying, and what was the point? Within minutes, they were on Magnolia Lane, the houses growing smaller, less majestic the farther away they got from Peachtree Drive, although still nice, still more than respectable. The real irony was that after she and Mark had divorced, Mark hadn't moved back with his mother but rather found an apartment of his own. "That's it. Number ninety-two. Right-hand side. Second from the end."

Brad pulled the car to a stop in front of the white wood house, the car's headlights illuminating the large FOR SALE sign on the manicured front lawn. Two stately, concrete pillars stood on either side of the black front door. The drapes in all the rooms were closed. The downstairs rooms were dark. There was a light on in one of the upstairs bedrooms. Mrs. Denison's room, Jamie realized, suppressing a shudder. "So the old witch has finally agreed to sell."

"What do you think?" Brad asked. "Should we knock on the door, make her an offer she can't refuse?"

Suddenly the curtains in the upstairs bedroom parted, and a lone figure appeared at the window, her magnified silhouette staring through the darkness toward the street. "Let's get out of here," Jamie whispered to Brad. "Brad, please," she urged when he failed to move. "Before she recognizes my car."

"Can't have that," Brad agreed, making a quick U-turn and speeding down the quiet road.

CHAPTER FIFTEEN

Jamie. Hey, Jamie, wake up."

"Hmm?" Jamie rolled over onto her back in bed, her eyes refusing to open. "What?"

"Wake up, Jamie."

Jamie suddenly shot up in bed, as if she'd been doused by a glass of cold water, her heart racing wildly, a torrent of words rushing from her dry mouth. "What's happened? What's the matter? Is something wrong?" Had the boys from Tifton found them, broken into their room?

Brad laughed quietly beside her, ran a reassuring hand across her bare back. "Hey, hey. It's okay. Take it easy. I didn't mean to scare you."

Jamie fought to bring the cheap motel room into focus, but it was dark and wouldn't stop spinning. It was still night. She knew that much, because she could see the moon peeking through the crack in the heavy drapes, and the neon red numbers of the digital clock beside the uncomfortable double bed quickly confirmed it was only 3:02 in the morning. The middle of the night, for God's sake. She gathered the flimsy, white sheet around her as her eyes adjusted to the darkness, and waited for Brad to explain what was going on. But he said nothing. He just sat there with this dopey grin on his handsome face and stared at her. "Brad, what's the matter? Has something happened?"

"Nothing's happened."

"Then what's wrong?"

"Nothing's wrong."

"I don't understand. Why did you wake me up?" Unless she'd been dreaming and only imagined his voice prodding her awake, and it was she, not he, who'd thrown the room into sudden chaos. He'd been sleeping soundly. It was her fault they were both awake at this ridiculous hour. "Was I having a bad dream?"

"You looked to be sleeping very peacefully to me," Brad said.

So he **had** woken her up. Why? "I don't understand. Why—"

"I love you," he said simply.

Whatever vestiges of sleep had been clinging to her body suddenly vanished. Jamie was now fully, completely awake. "What?" she asked, although she'd heard him clearly the first time. "What?" she asked, hoping to hear it again.

"Look, I know it's happening awfully fast. You probably think I'm crazy. . . ."

"I don't think you're crazy." Tears welled up in her eyes.

"I was just sitting here," he continued, wiping her tears away with the tips of his fingers, "watching you sleep, and it came over me like a wave—I love this woman. I love her. I love you," he said, leaning forward to kiss her. It was a kiss of almost unbearable gentleness, as if a butterfly had fluttered against her lips, then taken flight.

"You woke me up to tell me you love me?"

"I was afraid I'd lose my nerve if I waited till morning."

"You love me," Jamie repeated, cupping the

invisible words to her chest and holding them against her skin, feeling them creep into her pores, into her blood, then float toward her heart. It had been so long since anyone had said anything like that to her, so long since she'd felt loved. "Why?" she couldn't help but ask. "Why do you love me?" **What's there to love?** she asked silently.

"Why do I love you?" he repeated incredulously. "I don't know. Why does anybody love anyone?"

"What do you love about me?" Jamie asked, hoping that by rephrasing the question, it might encourage his response.

"What do I love about you? Well, let me see." He paused, as if giving the question serious consideration. "I love the way you look," he began, teasing her now. "I love your eyes . . . your hair . . . your breasts." His fingers traveled from her face to her shoulders, tracing a delicate path along her newly electrified flesh. "I love the way you throw your head back when you get excited, and I love the sound of your laugh. Kind of like wind chimes. And I love the way you kiss," he said, kissing her again, this time harder. "And the way you moan when I touch the back of your neck in one particular spot. Right here," he said, touching her there, and she moaned, as if on cue, then laughed softly.

Wind chimes, she thought, listening for the sound.

"But best of all, I love your sense of adventure, the way you're not afraid to take chances, the way you go after what you want. I love your fearlessness, your willingness to try anything."

Jamie smiled. What her mother and sister had viewed as reckless and impulsive was fearless and adventurous in his eyes. "You inspire me," she said.

"It's **you** who inspire me." He kissed her again, longer this time, his tongue playing with her own. "So you're not mad at me?"

"Mad at you?" She laughed. "Why on earth would I be mad at you?"

"For waking you up. You were sleeping so soundly."

"Are you kidding? You can wake me up anytime to tell me things like that."

"You're very beautiful when you sleep. So peaceful. So still."

Jamie snuggled in against him, laying her head against his chest, listening to the steady beating of his heart. "Couldn't you sleep?"

He shrugged. "My mind's been racing around like crazy all night."

"What were you thinking about?"

"Oh, just a little surprise I've been cooking up."

"A surprise? What kind of surprise?"

He pulled out of her arms, reached for his jeans. "Time to get dressed, Jamie-girl."

"What?"

Brad jumped to his feet. "Come on, Jamie. Throw on some clothes and get that gorgeous ass in gear." He pulled his jeans over his slender hips.

"No, wait. Brad. Stop. What's happening? What are you doing?"

"You'll see."

"Can't I see in the morning?" This was crazy. It was the middle of the night.

He laughed. "It's more fun in the dark."

"What is?"

"Come on, Jamie. You really want to spoil the surprise?"

Which was when it hit her—they were going to Barnsley Gardens. Somehow he'd made the arrangements, waiting until after she was asleep to make the necessary calls, and now he was standing in front of her, having just confessed his love, for God's sake, barely able to stand still he was so excited, his weight shifting from one foot to the other, eager to get a move on, to get out of this crummy motel room and on their way. "Okay," she agreed, swinging her feet out of bed.

Brad let out a whoop of glee. "That's my girl!"

Jamie stepped into the bathroom, where she threw some cold water on her face and quickly ran a comb through her hair.

"Leave that," Brad urged, watching from the tiny hall. "You look great."

"I look like somebody woke me up in the middle of the night." She didn't want to scare the check-in people at Barnsley Gardens. How late did these people work anyway? For that matter, how had Brad cleared up the problem with his credit card so quickly? She was about to ask when she thought better of it. She didn't want to ruin the surprise after all.

"Come on, Jamie. You can brush your teeth later," he said as she was reaching for her toothbrush.

"I'm not going anywhere without brushing my teeth." She brushed her teeth, then began packing her toiletries into their small leather case.

"What are you doing now?"

"Getting ready to go."

"You can do that stuff in the morning."

"What do you mean? I thought we were leaving."

"We're trying," he said, tossing the clothes she'd been wearing all day in her direction. Jamie caught them before they hit the floor.

"We're coming back here?"

"Of course we're coming back. Gotta get **some** sleep."

"I don't understand."

"Do you trust me?" Brad asked, a hint of impatience creeping into his words.

"Of course I trust you."

"Then let's get this show on the road."

Jamie pulled some fresh underwear out of her overnight bag, then got dressed. Brad had the motel door open before she'd finished tying her sneakers. The damp night air rushed inside, as if trying to hustle her out. So they weren't going to Barnsley Gardens after all, she was thinking, trying not to be disappointed as she followed him to the car. Hadn't he just told her he loved her? And didn't he love her, at least in part, because of her adventurous spirit, her fearlessness, her willingness to try anything?

Did she really want to risk letting him down?

"Let's get this show on the road," she repeated as they climbed into the car.

Minutes later, they were on the road again, although where they were going Jamie had no idea. They seemed to be driving around in circles. Ten minutes later, they were still driving, and she was having a hard time keeping her eyes open. She thought of asking if she could be of help, but the determined look on Brad's face—even in profile, even in the dark—told her to let things be. Obviously he had a plan. Another surprise in a night full of surprises. Might as well relax, she told herself, closing her eyes and listening to the voices on the all-night talk-radio station.

I don't know what to do about her, man. She's sexy as hell, but she's been lying and cheating on me for months.

The way I see it, Buddy, you have two choices. You can stay and continue to be lied to and mistreated, or you can be a man and leave her.

But I love her, man.

Hey, Buddy. Ever hear the expression pussy-whipped?

Jamie opened her eyes as the car swerved suddenly to the right. Where were they?

"Brad—"

"Ssh." He put his fingers to his lips. "I want to hear this."

Nah, man, it's not like that.

It never is, Buddy.

She thought she recognized the tall white columns of a palatial corner house, tried telling herself she didn't. "Where are we?"

"Ssh. Almost there."

She's really terrific.

The bad ones always are.

"Brad—"

"Ssh."

She's got me all tied up in knots. I can't think clearly.

That's 'cause you're not thinking with your head, Buddy. You're thinking with another part of your anatomy. And that part isn't always the best judge of character, as we all know.

Were they back in Buckhead?

You don't get it, man.

Sure I do. Hey, we've all been there. She's gorgeous. She's great in the sack. Best sex you ever had. But it comes with a price, Buddy, and you've got a decision to make. How much is her crap really worth?

Jamie sat straight up in her seat. They were back in Buckhead. Why?

You don't know her, man. Sometimes when we're together, she's like this angel.

She's the devil, Buddy. Get out while you still can.

Jamie reached over and switched off the radio. The voices fell silent. "Brad, what's going on? What are we doing here?"

"I've been thinking a lot about the things you told me."

"What things?"

"About your former mother-in-law."

Jamie found herself holding her breath. "My ex-mother-in-law? Why on earth would you be thinking about her?"

"I don't know. I guess it was driving over there earlier and seeing her in the window, and remembering how she made you give back your wedding ring. . . ."

"Believe me, I didn't want it anymore."

"And those gold-and-pearl earrings?" he reminded her.

Jamie pictured the magnificent, heart-shaped pearl earrings outlined in gold. "Yeah, well, what can you do?"

"Well, that's what I've been thinking about." He turned his face toward her, flashed his killer grin. "I'm thinking we can get them back."

"What?" Jamie tried to laugh, but the look in his eyes froze the laughter in her throat. "You can't be serious."

Brad shook his head. "On the contrary. I'm dead serious."

Jamie twisted around in her seat as the streets grew ever more familiar. They were only blocks from Magnolia Lane. "Brad, stop. Turn around. This is insane."

"What's insane is that this woman got away with making my girl miserable for almost two years. I mean, you can't tell me you haven't at least thought about getting even."

"Getting even? What are you talking about?"

"I'm talking about taking back what's yours."

"But they're not mine."

"Sure they are. She gave you those earrings, didn't she?"

"Yes, but then she took them back."

"Something she had no right to do."

"Maybe so, but—"

"No maybes about it."

They turned the corner onto Magnolia Lane.

"Brad, please. You have to stop. We can't do this."

"Of course we can. We can do anything we want."

"But I don't want this."

"What's the matter, Jamie? Lose your sense of adventure already?"

Even in the dark, Jamie could make out the disappointment in his eyes. "No. It's not that. It's just . . ."

Brad pulled the blue Thunderbird to a stop several houses short of number ninety-two. "Forget it," he was saying. "You're right. It was a stupid idea."

A deep sigh of relief escaped Jamie's lungs. It trembled out of her mouth and shattered upon contact with the air. She could almost see it scatter, as if it were trying to escape in all directions at once. What had Brad been thinking, for God's sake? He was a computer expert, not a thief who broke into people's homes in the middle of the night. "Let's go," she urged quietly.

"I was just doing it for you, you know," he said.

"I know that. But—"

"But?"

"You're tired. You're not thinking straight. In the morning, this is all going to feel like some crazy dream."

Which, of course, was exactly what it was, Jamie realized. There wasn't the remotest possibility that any of this was actually happening. In another minute, she'd wake up, and everything would be back to normal. So she could relax, stop hyperventilating. It was all a silly dream.

With one arm, Brad drew Jamie into a tender embrace. With the other, he switched off the car's ignition.

Instantly Jamie pulled back. "What are you doing?"

"I'm getting your earrings back." He pocketed the car keys, opened the door, and jumped out.

In the next second, he was gone.

"Brad, wait! Stop! Please!" Jamie caught up with Brad as he neared the front of Laura Dennison's house. He's having some kind of breakdown, she was thinking. Either that or it was all a big practical joke. Either way, she had to stop him before things went too far.

"That's my girl. I knew you'd change your mind."

"Brad . . ."

"I knew I could count on you."

"Brad, please. Come back to the car."

"Only place I'm going is in there." He pointed toward the house.

Why? she wanted to scream. "How?" she asked instead. "How are you going to get in? We don't have a key. She has an alarm."

This new information gave him a second's pause. "You must remember the code."

"She's probably changed it by now."

"Why would she? It's not like she thought you'd ever come back."

"What if she changed it anyway? What if it goes off?"

"Then we hightail it out of there."

"And if we're not fast enough? If we get caught?"

"Not gonna happen," Brad said confidently. "Come on, Jamie. This is gonna be fun." He took her in his arms, kissed her with a passion that was both invigorating and contagious. "We're not gonna hurt anybody. We're just going to take back what's rightfully yours. She won't even know we've been here."

"Brad, listen to yourself. You're talking about breaking into somebody's house. You're talking about theft. You're talking about the possibility of getting caught and going to prison."

"Come on, Jamie. Where's that free spirit I fell in love with?"

The question tugged at Jamie's heart. "Please, Brad, this isn't right."

"You think what **she** did was right?"

"No. But you know what they say about two wrongs."

Brad laughed. "It's what your mother would say."

Jamie bristled, although he was right. It was exactly what her mother would say.

"And your sister," he added for good measure. "I thought you weren't like them."

"I'm not."

"Looks like the apple doesn't fall far from the tree after all."

"Brad, I'm serious."

"You think I'm not?"

"I don't think you've thought this through."

"Thought what through exactly?"

"This whole thing," Jamie said, watching the smile slowly seep from Brad's face, leaving only a cold, hard mask in the spotlight of the moon. "It isn't a game."

"'Course it is. It's an adventure."

"No, it isn't. It's a **crime** to break into somebody's house."

"Only if you get caught." The beginnings of

a smile began creeping back onto his face. "And we aren't going to get caught. I promise. Now, are you ready?"

Jamie hesitated. **Are you ready?** The question she'd been hearing all her life. Was she? For what exactly? Who was this man? What had she gotten herself into?

"You gotta have faith, Jamie. You gotta decide—are you your mother's daughter, or the woman I thought I fell in love with?"

The woman he **thought** he fell in love with. "Brad, wait. Please . . ."

"I'm counting on you, Jamie." He cut across the lawn. "I'm doing this for you, babe," he called back.

He's the devil, Buddy, she heard the radio announcer intone. **Get out while you still can.**

Yet how could she let him walk into that house alone? Even if he succeeded in getting inside, he didn't know the code, he wouldn't be able to turn off the alarm, and he'd be caught, end up spending years in jail. For what? Because he was determined to retrieve a pair of gold-and-pearl earrings he felt were rightfully hers? Because he was grandstanding, trying to impress her? Because his pride wouldn't let him back down?

Besides, where was she going without him? The keys to her car were in his pocket, and she wasn't about to start wandering the streets of Atlanta alone at three o'clock in the morning. Nor could she just stand here, hoping for him to come back. She might not have finished law school, but she understood enough about the law to know she'd still be considered an accomplice.

Are you your mother's daughter or the woman I thought I fell in love with?

I **am** her. I am the woman you fell in love with.

He's the devil. Get out while you still can.

He's the man I love, Jamie thought. He's the man I love, and he's giving me the choice: I'm either my mother's daughter or the woman he fell in love with. This is a test. That's all it is. He's testing you. He has no real intention of breaking into Laura Dennison's house. He's just waiting to see who you really are.

Are you ready?

Jamie cut across the interlacing red bricks after him. "Brad," she cried, his name a whisper that raced through the warm darkness, slicing through elusive shadows, chasing after playful ghosts. Where was he? Was he waiting behind the nearest tree, preparing to jump out at her?

She stopped in the middle of the long driveway, glancing over both shoulders to make sure no one was watching her from nearby windows. But the houses on the wide street were all dark, save for the lights over their front doors. She glanced toward the second floor, checked the curtains in Laura Dennison's bedroom for the slightest sign of movement, but all was still. In the background, crickets chirped, traffic reverberated, the night hummed. Jamie held her breath as she stared at the house, remembering the first time she'd seen it, how impressed she'd been, how full of hope. She'd been so young, she thought, although it was only a few years ago. When did I start feeling so damn old? she wondered, proceeding cautiously. Where had all that optimism gone?

"Brad?" she called again, cringing at the sound, although she'd been careful to keep her voice low. She looked toward the front door, but he wasn't there. Had he already slipped around the back? Or had he simply taken off on foot, left her to her own devices, when she'd failed his test? "Brad?" she called again, approaching the side door.

And suddenly someone was at her back, and a hand was reaching around her neck to cover her mouth and nose. She couldn't breathe. She couldn't move. Somebody help me, her insides screamed, although the only sound to emerge was a stifled cry.

"Jamie, it's okay," Brad was whispering in her ear. "It's me." He released her, and she spun around, buried herself in his arms. "I couldn't have you waking up the neighborhood."

"You scared me half to death."

"How many burglars do you think are working this street?" he asked playfully.

Jamie might have laughed had she not been so terrified. Then suddenly he pulled away, reached into his pocket. Was he reaching for the car keys or the switchblade? Jamie wondered, taking an involuntary step back. Instead, he withdrew his wallet and extricated his credit card. "What are you doing?" she asked.

"Damn thing should be good for something." Immediately he began maneuvering the card around the lock in the door.

"Come on, Brad. The joke's gone on long enough. Besides, that only works on TV," she advised as the lock clicked and the door fell open. "Oh, God," she said as a piercing sound signaled the alarm had been activated and they had exactly thirty seconds to tap in the code before the sirens began their sickening wail. "Oh, God," she said again.

Brad grabbed her and kissed her full on the mouth, his face radiating excitement. "I love you, Jamie-girl," he said.

CHAPTER SIXTEEN

Emma awoke to the sound of screaming.

She jumped out of bed, her eyes shooting toward the clock on the end table before she realized there **was** no clock on the end table. It took a few seconds to orient herself to her surroundings: she wasn't in her room; she was in Dylan's room, in Dylan's bed; her son was sleeping in her room, with Lily's son, Michael, tucked in beside him. Or at least, he'd **been** asleep. At the moment, however, he was screaming his little head off, which meant he was having another one of his nightmares, which meant it was approximately three o'clock in the morning. You could set your watch by those damn nightmares. And if she didn't get at least one night of uninterrupted sleep soon, she thought as her bare feet padded across the hall, **she'd** be the one screaming.

Emma quickly checked to make sure she'd remembered to put on a pair of pajamas before climbing into Dylan's tiny bed last night. Wouldn't do to go bursting in on two five-year-old boys when she was naked. Talk about giving the poor kid nightmares, she thought, her head pounding, which meant she was in for one hell of a hangover come morning. That was assuming she'd be able to get back to sleep tonight. "It's okay, Dylan," she said, snapping on the overhead light and gathering her sobbing son in her arms. Beside him in her bed, Michael slept soundly, his blond hair spiraling against the white pillowcase like a series of delicate quotation marks. "Ssh. It's okay, Dylan. Mommy's here. Ssh. You don't want to wake up Michael, do you?" Emma stared at Lily's son, wondering how anyone could sleep so soundly with someone caterwauling beside him.

"I had a nightmare," Dylan cried, hugging her tightly.

"I know, baby. But it's over. I'm here, and everything's fine now."

"There was this man," Dylan began.

This was a new wrinkle, Emma thought. Before this, Dylan had never actually remembered any of his dreams. "A man? Did you recognize him?"

Dylan shook his head vigorously. "I couldn't see his face. He was wearing a hat."

"A hat?"

"A baseball cap. You know, like Daddy has. Except it wasn't Daddy," he added quickly, as if to reassure her. Emma shuddered, trying not to picture her former husband, although it was already too late. He stood grinning at her from the other side of the room.

"He was standing at the end of the bed, watching me."

"Well, you can see there's nobody there now." Emma extricated herself from her son's clinging arms and walked to the window, peered down at the street below.

The ghost of her former husband stared up at her from beside a nearby streetlamp. **You**

can run, the apparition warned. **But you can't hide.**

Dylan ran to her side, burying himself between her legs and digging his fingers into the soft cotton of her pajamas, his nails scratching at her thighs. "Mommy, no! Don't look. Don't look!"

"Nobody's there, sweetheart." She picked him up in her arms, held him up to the window. "See? Just a bunch of insects flying around the streetlamps."

"Why do they do that?"

"Because they're attracted to the light."

"Why?"

Oh, God, not now, Emma thought, too exhausted to play the "why" game at three o'clock in the morning. She should know things like this, she thought. "I don't know, sweetheart." Because they can see better? Because they like the warmth? Because they have a death wish?

"The man said he was going to carve me up into a thousand little pieces and feed me to the sharks," Dylan said.

Sharks in Ohio, Emma thought. No wonder the kid wakes up screaming. "I would never let him do that," she assured her son. "You know that, don't you?"

Dylan's head bobbed up and down against her neck, his tears wet against her skin.

"You're safe now, baby," she told him, carrying him back to the bed. "Nothing bad can happen to you as long as you're with me. I will always protect you and keep you safe." She laid him back down in her bed beside Michael. "Now try to sleep, sweetie. See how soundly Michael sleeps?"

"He doesn't have nightmares."

"No."

"He's lucky."

"Yes." Emma kissed her son's forehead, pushing the hair away from his eyes with the tips of her fingers. "No more nightmares for you either. Okay?"

"Stay here," he urged.

"I can't, sweetheart. There isn't room for all of us."

"Yes, there is." Dylan scooted closer to

Michael. Michael promptly rolled over on his side, as if to accommodate the new entrant. "See?"

"Okay." Emma climbed into her bed beside Dylan. Immediately, he threw one hand over her stomach and one leg across her thigh, as if locking her in place. Great, Emma thought. Now I'm really trapped. She closed her eyes, prayed for sleep. But every time she came close, Dylan kicked or twitched or groaned, and she was jolted back into consciousness. The pounding in her head kept getting louder, and Emma knew she wouldn't sleep again this night.

She was barely twenty when she met the man who would become Dylan's father. He was older and more worldly, although like her, restless and confused about what he wanted to do with the rest of his life. Emma related to the lost, little boy camouflaged by the outward swagger of the man, eloping with him to Las Vegas. "Are you pregnant?" was the first question her mother had asked upon their return.

Not, Are you happy? Not, Are you sure? Not even, Are you crazy? But, Are you pregnant? As if there was no other reason anyone could have for marrying her.

"Is that your way of congratulating us, Mother?" Then, although her mother hadn't asked, "We love each other. We're in love," Emma repeated, as if trying to convince herself this was the case. Which, of course, was exactly what she was trying to do. Because the truth was that she wasn't sure if she loved her new husband or not. They had little in common, he was occasionally moody and preoccupied, and she never knew what he was thinking. But she did know that she loved the sound of his voice when he said **he** loved **her**; she loved the way he looked at her, loved the image of herself that she saw reflected in his eyes.

And while it might have been true that she didn't know her husband very well, the bigger truth was that **he** didn't know **her** at all.

She hadn't meant to lie. The stories she'd told about her privileged upbringing, her scholastic accomplishments, her acceptance into Princeton—she'd just said those things to impress him. And then, when he was beyond impressed, when he was head over heels and they were husband and wife, well, what choice did she have but to continue the charade? Soon it was easier to lie than to tell the truth. And it was becoming increasingly difficult to distinguish between the two.

"Are you ashamed of me?" he asked shortly after their marriage.

"Of course not."

"I mean, I know I'm not as smart as you are. I didn't get accepted into Princeton. . . ."

"So?" Emma asked. "I didn't go, did I?"

"Only because your mother was so sick."

"Please don't talk about that in front of her. She gets very upset. . . ."

"Don't worry. I won't bring it up. But why'd you have to tell her I went to Yale? I just about fell off my chair."

"I didn't hear you deny it."

"I was too stunned to say anything."

Emma shrugged off his concerns with a toss of her long, dark hair. "I told her you went to

Yale because I knew it would make her happy. She's impressed by stuff like that."

"Well, we have to tell her the truth."

"Why?" Emma asked.

"Because the truth will out," he told her.

"The truth will what?"

"The truth will out," he repeated.

"That doesn't make any sense."

"Sure it does."

"What does it mean? That the truth's been hiding in a closet, like it's gay or something?"

He smiled self-consciously. "You know what it means."

"All I know is that I married the handsomest, sexiest man in the world," Emma said, wrapping her arms around her new husband and grinding her hips against his. He smiled and buried his head in her neck. Somehow he had no trouble swallowing that whopper, she thought. So much for outing the truth.

And the truth was that he was withdrawing more every day. He repeatedly accused her of lying to him. She countered with accusations that he was cheating on her. Their sex life dwindled, then disappeared entirely after she announced she was, indeed, pregnant. After their son was born, her husband started sleeping on the couch. On those rare nights when he bothered coming home at all.

At first, she'd tried rekindling their romance, buying exotic lingerie, and even handcuffs, in an effort to entice him, but all such efforts proved futile. One night, she'd confronted him as he stumbled in drunk from a night with the boys. "Who is she this time?" she'd demanded.

"What are you talking about?"

"You know what I'm talking about."

"Don't be ridiculous."

"I'm not ridiculous," she countered. "And I'm not stupid either."

"Then stop acting that way."

"Are you going to tell me where you've been all night?"

"I went out with David and Sal. You know that. Look, I'm tired. . . ."

"So am I."

"Then go to bed."

"Alone? **Again?**"

"Look, we've been through this. I can't give you what you want."

"What I want is a little attention. Am I so awful that you can't even touch me anymore? Come on," she cried, slapping at his arm with her closed fist. "Touch me." She began pummeling the sides of his arms, swatting at his face with her open palm. "Pretend I'm David or Sal."

"Stop that," he told her, grabbing her arms and pinning them to her sides.

"You're hurting me," she cried, and he released her.

She slapped him hard across the face.

He slapped her back.

It went from bad to worse.

"You told your friends I beat you?" he demanded, incredulously, the following week.

"Why not? It's true."

"You wouldn't know the truth if it fell on your head."

"Serves you right," Emma muttered now, flipping onto her side in bed. Everything that happened after that was your fault. All I asked for was a little attention. All I needed was a little love.

"What?" Dylan asked groggily, his little body tensing against her own. "Are we going away again?"

"No, baby. Everything's okay. Go back to sleep, sweetheart."

"I love you, Mommy."

"I love you too."

Lily was dreaming of ice cream. She was standing outside a 1950s-style diner, eating a small cone of strawberry ice cream, and the ice cream was dripping onto her clean, white shirt, leaving a long, pink stain that stretched lazily from the middle of her breasts to the bottom of her blouse. Beside her, Jeff Dawson stood nursing a monstrous sugar cone wrapped in rich, dark chocolate. Suddenly he leaned forward, as if to help himself to some of her ice cream, but instead he grabbed her hand and began licking her open palm. A motorcycle sped by as her mother came running out of the diner waving an American flag and nattering on about tax returns. Seconds later, a giant coconut fell from the sky, and someone yelled, "There's been an accident." Lily looked down at the front of her white blouse. The pink stain had turned bright crimson. Blood was leaking from her heart, as if she'd been shot.

Lily bolted up in bed, the front of her pink, cotton nightshirt soaked with her sweat. "Dear God," she whispered, her eyes searching through the dim light for the clock. Ten after three in the morning. "Wonderful." She climbed out of bed and went to the bathroom, applying a cool compress to her neck and toweling off the sweat. "Okay, so that wasn't too hard to figure out," she muttered, even as the dream began to fade, its images smudging, as if someone were rubbing at them with an eraser.

Obviously she was feeling guilty about how much she'd enjoyed her date with Jeff tonight, and her subconscious was warning her. . . . What? What exactly was her subconscious trying to tell her? That Jeff was potentially dangerous to her health? Or that she was dangerous to his? That if she allowed him to get too close, a large coconut would come falling out of the sky and kill him as surely as it had killed Kenny?

Except that a wayward coconut hadn't killed Kenny.

She shook her head. It was just a stupid dream. A bunch of unrelated images that didn't add up to anything. How else to explain her mother running around waving an American flag and ranting about her latest tax return? If dreams were supposed to serve as some sort of portent, it would be nice if occasionally they made sense.

"Now, strawberry ice cream makes sense," Lily said, heading for the stairs. It was strange being alone in the house without Michael. The small space felt so empty without the sound of his voice, the raucous peal of his laughter, the steady rhythm of his breathing. She caught sight of the many finger paintings and watercolors covering his bedroom walls as she passed by, and she took a few steps back, entering his room and flipping on the overhead light, amazed, as she always was, by what talent he possessed. And she didn't feel this way just because she was his mother. Everyone else thought so as well. His teacher, Ms. Kensit, had told her that Michael was the most artistically gifted student she'd had in her nine years of teaching. She'd even taken one of his paintings, a watercolor of a group of deer munching wildflowers at the side of a stream, to the school principal, who'd stuck a gold star in the top right-hand corner and told Michael he was going to be a famous artist one day, and the principal would be able to say, I knew him when. That painting now hung proudly on the wall opposite Michael's bed, between a chalk drawing of a boy and his mother running hand in hand through a field of tall grass, and an abstract finger painting of lime green swirls that almost danced off the page.

Lily moved from one wall to the other, studying each picture as carefully as if she were visiting the Louvre. There was a painting of a vase filled with purple and red flowers, one of a boy jumping out of an airplane, the boy twice as big as the plane, his parachute opening wide behind him. Beside it was a charcoal sketch of a young boy and his mother standing proudly in front of a small, triangular-shaped house. Another picture, this one taped over his bed, depicted a mother tucking her young son into bed, the full moon smiling at them from outside the window. There were no stick figures in Michael's artwork, as there were in the drawings of most young children. The people who inhabited Michael's world were fully formed, if dubiously proportioned. Some had huge heads, others had heads no bigger than a pillbox. Some had enormous hands, while others had legs that stretched clear up to their necks. Lily noticed something else. There were no men in any of Michael's paintings.

That was her fault.

Lily grabbed her son's pillow from his bed and raised it to her nose, inhaling his sweet scent. "I'll make it up to you, Michael," she whispered. "I promise." She fluffed out the pillow and returned it to his bed, then flipped off the light and headed down the stairs to the kitchen, where she helped herself to a large bowl of ice cream and sat down with it at the kitchen table. "I can't believe I'm eating again," she said. Hadn't she told Jeff she was so stuffed, she doubted she'd ever look at food again. "Sure. Fat chance of that." So much for losing five pounds, she thought, deciding to hit the gym the next day, although tomorrow was her day off and she'd promised to take Michael to a movie. Maybe she'd ask Emma if she and Dylan would like to join them. Or even better, she'd offer to take Dylan and give Emma the afternoon off. The poor woman looked as if she could use the break, and it was the least she could do. It was hard raising a child all by yourself. Especially a boy. Especially when you didn't have a clue what went on in their little heads.

Not much, Jan would probably say, then rumble with laughter. Jan had never had any children, although she had a nephew in California with whom she spoke regularly.

What would Michael be like when he got older? Lily wondered. Would he still look up to her the way he did now? Would he still love her once he was in possession of all the facts, when he was old enough to understand the unimaginable? Or would he resent her, blame her for his not having had a father during his formative years? Would he run away to Europe at the first opportunity, call her only rarely from parts unknown, think of her less and less while blaming her more and more?

Lily helped herself to another scoop of ice cream, thinking that there wasn't enough ice cream in the world to mitigate her guilt, that all the double chins in the world couldn't provide enough folds for her to hide behind. Although she could certainly try, she decided, continuing to spoon the ice cream into her mouth, relishing the cold on the insides of her cheeks.

She reached for a pen and a piece of paper, began doodling a series of interconnecting hearts down one side. She used to draw when she was a child, she remembered, although she was never very good at it. No, her talent was with words. She loved making up stories, creating a character out of nothing and then watching that person take shape and grow. Yes, she was going to be a writer, just as her teacher had proclaimed. "I'm going to be a writer," she'd told Kenny proudly, and for a while, he'd seemed proud as well. Of course, then she got pregnant, and that pretty much took care of her writing career. The pundits all advised writing about what you know, but what did she know, after all, when she didn't even know enough not to get herself knocked up? as Kenny had so eloquently shouted at her that fateful, rain-filled night. "It's easier to write about what you don't know," she said now, pushing herself away from the kitchen table. What she didn't know could fill volumes.

Although Jeff seemed to find her interesting enough.

"He was just hoping to get lucky," Lily said, slowly mounting the stairs. He did get lucky, she thought with a chuckle. Lucky she **hadn't** invited him to come inside.

Why hadn't she?

It would have been so easy. The opportunity was there. She had the house to herself. Who knew when that would happen again? And she found him attractive. No, more than attractive. Desirable. And it was pretty clear he felt the same way about her. They'd had a wonderful meal, then gone for a drive to the new RiverScape Park, at the sight where Dayton's five rivers meet—Twin Creek, Wolf Creek, Great Miami, Stillwater, and Mad—then walked along one of the well-lit paths.

"Did you know that Dayton is the number one city in the U.S. for inventors?" Jeff had asked, pointing out the many gold stars honoring these inventors that were set into the concrete.

"Really? What kind of inventors?"

"Well, it was in Dayton that the Wright brothers, who owned a printing and bicycle repair shop over on South Williams Street, worked on and refined their famous Flier."

"That's right. I remember reading that. What else?"

"Well, you probably don't know that parachutes, office building mail chutes, stepladders, cellophane tape, ice cube trays, parking meters, cash registers, movie projectors, gas masks, as well as a host of other indispensable everyday items were invented in Dayton," he enumerated, pausing to catch his breath. "Not to mention chocolate-covered potato chips."

"Chocolate-covered potato chips?"

"You can buy them over at Kroger's."

"No, thanks. I'm so stuffed, I don't think I'll ever look at food again." They continued walking for another ten minutes, stopping to admire the whimsical Wright Brothers weather vane of a metallic paper doll clinging to a pole and blowing sideways in the breeze. "That's how I feel most of the time," Lily confessed.

"Then you'd better hold on tight," Jeff said, taking her hand.

His touch was electrifying. It was all Lily could do to stay upright as her hand disappeared inside his and he led her back to the car. How long had it been since she'd held hands with someone who wasn't five years old?

"Have you been to the Art Institute yet?" he

asked as they drove past the warm stone building with the beautiful red tile roof just north of exit 54B, seemingly oblivious to the chaos he'd unleashed inside her body just a few moments ago.

"No, not yet," Lily managed to sputter. "I keep meaning to take Michael."

"Your son likes art?"

Lily nodded proudly. "He's very talented."

"I'd like to meet him. Maybe one day you'll introduce us."

Lily smiled and said nothing. For the rest of the drive home, she concentrated on the lingering feel of his fingers interlaced with hers, wondering what she would do if he tried to kiss her good night.

"I had a wonderful evening," he said as he walked her to her front door.

"Me too." She felt as nervous as a teenager on her first real date.

"I hope we can do it again sometime."

"I'd like that." She fished inside her purse for her keys. *Is he going to kiss me now?* she wondered. *Or is he waiting for me to invite* him inside? That's what I should do. I should invite him inside. "Thanks for the tour of RiverScape Park. If you ever decide you don't want to be a policeman anymore, you'd make a great tour guide," she said instead, unlocking her door and stepping over the threshold, the screen door a convenient barrier between his lips and hers.

"It was my pleasure."

And then he was gone. She waited until his car had disappeared down the street, then locked the door behind her and headed straight up the stairs to bed.

And now it was after 3 a.m. and she was back where she had started. She reached the top step and stopped. Outside, the evening's soft breeze had picked up, become wind. It carried the threat of rain. Lily walked into her room, crawled back into bed, and brought her covers up around her head to protect herself from the ghosts and shadows blowing against the window, trying to get in.

CHAPTER SEVENTEEN

"Quick, what's the code?" Brad hissed over the shrill, flat-line, warning sound of the alarm.

Jamie vaulted toward the keypad on the wall just inside the door and tapped in the four-digit code. **Please be the right numbers,** she was praying, her hands shaking so badly she could barely feel the pads beneath her fingertips. **Please don't have changed the code. Please let this god-awful noise stop.**

And suddenly the house fell silent.

"You did it, Jamie," Brad whispered, taking her in his arms and spinning her around, kissing her cheek before releasing her. She stumbled back, losing her footing, and almost crumbling to the small patch of tile floor. "Whoa, there, careful," Brad said, reaching out to grab her arm before she crashed into a nearby closet.

Jamie's heart was racing so fast and beating so loudly, it was several seconds before she understood their break-in had gone undetected. They were safe. No harm had been done. They could walk away now and no one would be the wiser. "Brad, let's get out of here," she pleaded, pulling on his arm.

"Ssh." He raised his fingers to his lips and cocked his head to one side, listening.

The house was completely still. No wary footsteps padded around overhead. No hushed voices were making frantic 9-1-1 calls. Everything appeared to be calm and peaceful, as it should be at just past three o'clock in the morning. The goddamn middle of the night, she was thinking, when sane people the world over were sound asleep in their beds.

What were they doing here? How had this happened?

And could Laura Dennison really have slept

through that dreadful warning wail? Or was she even now sneaking stealthily toward the front door, her cell phone pressed tightly to her lips, giving the police a detailed description of the blue Thunderbird parked just down the street? **My former daughter-in-law drove a car just like it.** Surely she couldn't still be asleep. Although the woman had always been a remarkably sound sleeper. How many times had Jamie heard her boast of being "dead to the world" the moment her head hit the pillow? No, no sedatives for her, she'd declared smugly when Jamie once complained of not sleeping well and asked if she had any Tylenol PMs. And Mrs. Dennison **did** sleep with her door closed, Jamie remembered, the only time closed doors were permitted in the house on Magnolia Lane. So it was entirely possible she hadn't heard the warning wail of her alarm after all.

Or maybe she wasn't home, Jamie thought, hopefully. Maybe she was on vacation somewhere with Mark, or with one of the women with whom she played bridge every week, maybe even the whole damn bunch of them. They'd always talked about taking a trip together one day, going off to some bridge tournament to earn some much desired master points, whatever that meant, so maybe that's exactly what they'd finally done, and so the house was empty, there was no need for her to be worrying herself almost sick, the wicked witch had hopped on her broomstick and taken off for parts and bridge hands unknown.

Except she hadn't.

Because if she had, who was that woman Jamie had seen standing at her bedroom window earlier in the evening? No, Mrs. Dennison was here all right. Jamie could feel her presence in the etherlike pall of the air. The poison filled her nostrils and invaded her lungs, making every breath not only painful, but also dangerous. Brad tugged gently on her hand, pulling her forward, even as her body continued angling toward the door. "Brad," Jamie began as he suddenly dropped her hand and abruptly left her side. She watched him skip up the three carpeted steps into the main part of the house. Fearless, she was thinking. In the next second she was racing up the three steps after him.

Even in the dark, Jamie could clearly make out every piece of furniture in the large living room. There was the pink-and-white chintz sofa in front of a long front window, framed by matching drapes, a green-and-white-striped wing chair to either side of it, and a light pine coffee table in front of it. A huge brick fireplace occupied much of the opposite wall, two dark green, embroidered Queen Anne chairs in front of it. A black baby grand piano was stuffed into a far corner, facing toward the center of the room. To Jamie's knowledge, nobody had ever played it. Nor had anyone ever used the gorgeous ivory chess set, imported from Italy, that sat in the middle of the pine coffee table, or the beautiful set of brass candlestick holders that stood on top of the mantel next to an empty, pink-striped, glass fruit bowl and several framed photographs of mother and son. The walls were white, as was the thick pile rug. The artwork consisted of two muted landscapes, one on either side of the fireplace. There were silk pink and purple orchids everywhere. Mrs. Dennison had regularly boasted that no one could distinguish them from the real thing.

"Brad, let's get out of here."

"A white rug," Brad remarked, as if she hadn't spoken. "Pretty brave or pretty stupid." Slowly and deliberately, he kicked the dirt from his sneakers onto the side of the rug.

"Brad, don't."

"Why not?"

"Because she'll know someone was here."

"Someone **was** here."

"I know, but—"

"Hand me one of those things." He pointed toward the mantelpiece.

"What?"

"One of the candlestick holders."

"Why?"

"I have an idea."

"What sort of idea?" Jamie's voice echoed against her ears, like a shout, and she winced. Her former mother-in-law might be a sound sleeper, but there were limits to everything. The less they talked, the better. The sooner they were out of here, the better.

"Trust me," he said.

Jamie reluctantly lifted a candlestick holder from the mantel. It was heavier than she anticipated and it almost slipped from her fingers.

"Careful," Brad warned.

Jamie tightened her grip. "What are you going to do?"

"Put it over there." He pointed at the piano.

"Why?"

"Just do it."

"I don't understand."

"Put it on top of the piano. Yeah, right there," he said as Jamie deposited the candlestick holder on the closed top of the ebony piano. "The old bat'll spend days wondering how the hell it got there," he said, answering her silent question.

"She'll probably just fire the cleaning lady," Jamie said, already feeling guilty.

"What's through here?"

"Brad, no. Let's just . . ." But Brad was already pushing open the swinging door into the dining room.

A traditional walnut table surrounded by eight, high-backed wooden chairs, upholstered in blood-red leather, occupied the center of the rectangular room. A tall, matching walnut cabinet stood against one wall, filled with expensive china and glassware. Brad glanced casually in the cabinet's direction before pushing through the next set of swinging doors to the kitchen.

"I'm really thirsty," he said, striding toward the refrigerator.

Jamie followed after him, peeking back over her shoulder. "Brad, I really think we should get out of here."

"I could use a glass of milk."

"Milk?"

He pulled open the refrigerator door, leaned forward, began inspecting the contents of the fridge. "Let's see. There's orange juice, eggs, cranberry juice, a plate of what looks like leftover spaghetti." A flash of white glistened in the dark. It was at that moment Jamie realized Brad was wearing latex gloves.

"You're wearing gloves?" she asked incredulously.

He pulled a carton of 2 percent milk from the top shelf. "Where does she keep her glasses?" he asked, ignoring her question.

"Where did you get the gloves?" Jamie persisted.

Brad shrugged, as if the question was as irrelevant as it was unimportant. "The glasses?" he asked, opening the closest set of cupboard doors.

"Over there." Jamie pointed to the correct cupboard on his right above the stovetop. "Brad, what are you doing?"

"Having a glass of milk." He retrieved a glass, filled it with milk. "You want some?"

"What I want is to get out of here."

"And we will. Just let me finish this milk." He gulped it quickly down, deposited the glass in the sink.

What the hell was going on? What was he doing? Why was he wearing gloves? "Brad, I don't like this. I'm leaving."

Instantly he was at her side, taking her in his

arms and kissing her. She tasted the milk on his tongue as he transferred it to hers. "No," he whispered. "You can't leave yet. Not yet." His hands reached for her buttocks and he pressed her to him. "Fun's just starting."

Jamie's head was spinning. Only several days ago she'd been a relatively ordinary young woman working at a boring, unfulfilling job and involved in an everyday affair with a run-of-the-mill married man. Then, in rapid succession, she'd picked up a handsome stranger in a bar, quit her job, and taken off for the open road. And now she was making love in public restrooms and breaking into people's houses. Somewhere along the interstate, Jamie Kellogg—daughter of Anne, sister of Cynthia, a judge and a lawyer, for God's sake—had gotten lost. She no longer had any sense of who she was or what she was doing, almost as if some alien force had taken over her body and seized control of her brain.

No, she heard her mother scold. **You're not getting off that easily.**

When are you going to start accepting

responsibility for your actions? her sister asked.

Jamie put her hands over her ears. "Brad, I want to go. Please. I'm tired."

"My baby's tired?"

"Exhausted."

"Okay."

"Okay? We'll leave?"

"Soon as we get what we came for." He pulled away, disappeared from her side, returned to the dining room.

Jamie was right behind him. "Brad, please. I'm a little dizzy. . . ."

"It's just stage fright." Already he was past the dining room and halfway out the living room, heading for the stairs to the bedrooms. "Okay. Stay put. Wait for me there." He stopped at the foot of the stairs. "Of course, since I don't know where she keeps the damn earrings, I'll have to go through everything, and who knows how long that might take. She might wake up, and then I'll get caught, probably spend the rest of my life behind bars, all for the woman I love," he continued, teasing her now. "Come on, Jamie. You don't want to see me spend the rest of my life in jail, do you?"

"I just want to get out of here before it's too late."

"It's already too late," he said, taking the stairs two at a time.

Run, Jamie thought. Get out of here. Get out while you still can.

It's already too late.

He stood waiting for her at the top of the landing, his eyes pulling her toward him as steadily as a fisherman reeling in a prize catch. Jamie felt one foot lifting in front of the other as she mounted the first step, her hand tightly gripping the wooden banister, the imprint of her sweaty fingers staining the dark wood. **He's wearing latex gloves,** she reminded herself. **Why? Where did he get them? When did he get them?**

Who is this man? she wondered, inching her way up the stairs.

He's the devil.

"Which way?" the devil asked when she reached the top.

Jamie glanced to her right. She might not be sure exactly what she was doing or how she'd gotten herself into this predicament, but one thing was certain, she was in it up to her eyeballs, and she might as well get it over with as soon as possible. The sooner they located the damn earrings, the sooner they'd be out of here, the sooner she'd be back in the safety of the motel room, and she could get some sleep, clear her head, and decide in the morning what to do next. Clearly, Brad Fisher wasn't the man she'd thought he was. Computer experts, software designers, wealthy businessmen didn't go around breaking into people's houses in the middle of the night. They didn't know how to open a locked door with a credit card. They didn't keep switchblades or a spare set of latex gloves in their pockets. **Who are you?** she wondered, watching Brad tiptoe down the hall and stop in front of Mrs. Dennison's closed bedroom door. **Who the hell are you?**

"Coming?" he asked, his hand on the knob.

Jamie didn't move.

Brad twisted the knob, pushed open the bedroom door, extended his hand toward her.

Jamie took a deep breath, forced one foot in front of the other, and then followed him inside.

Instantly the smell of Laura Dennison's perfume filled her nostrils. That awful, cloying scent of too many gardenias pushed its way down her throat, like a finger, and she gasped to keep from gagging.

"Ssh," Brad cautioned, tiptoeing toward the queen-size, four-poster bed with the lace canopy and staring down at its occupant.

Mrs. Dennison was asleep on her back, her head turned to her left, her face all but hidden behind a large, black mask that covered her eyes and most of her forehead, her auburn hair longer than Jamie remembered it, her white roots visible even in the dark. Jamie stared down at her former nemesis, her body filling with loathing and revulsion. *Would it have been so difficult for you to be nice to me?* she demanded silently of the sleeping woman. *Did you have to go out of your way to be so mean, to make my life miserable?*

"Ugly old thing, isn't she?" Brad said with a sneer.

Jamie's eyes widened with alarm at the sound of his voice. She raised her fingers to her lips in an effort to silence him.

"It's okay," he said easily, his gloved fingers motioning toward Laura Dennison's face. "See? She's wearing earplugs."

"What?"

"Look for yourself."

Brad was right. Stuffed into each ear was a tiny sponge. No wonder the woman never had any trouble sleeping. Between the mask and the earplugs, she really was "dead to the world." How I despise you, Jamie thought, overwhelmed by the unexpected intensity of her feelings.

"Think she sleeps in the nude?" Brad was already nudging the covers down from around the woman's neck.

"Brad, don't."

"Just a little peek."

"Please. She could wake up. . . ."

She didn't, although she stirred slightly, her

right shoulder twitching as Brad drew the heavy, down comforter toward her chest. "Figures," he said, sneering at the long-sleeved, blue nightgown Laura Dennison was wearing. "Guess we should be grateful." He chuckled.

Jamie was dismayed to hear herself chuckling along with him. You hateful old witch, she was thinking, her mind flooded with almost two years' worth of indignities and slights—the time her mother-in-law had refused to eat more than two bites of the dinner Jamie had painstakingly prepared, then claimed the next morning those few nibbles had made her violently ill; the time she'd pointedly "forgotten" to introduce her to some old friends they'd run into when Jamie had taken her out for lunch; the way she looked just past her whenever she deigned to speak to her; the condescension in her voice; the subtle put-downs; the unrelenting undermining of Jamie's position in the family; the constant competition for her son's attention and affection; the escalating animosity; all of it culminating in that awful, final night.

Jamie shook her head in an effort not to remember it, but already the cast of characters was moving into position, and the scene was being replayed before her tired eyes: In another of her ill-advised, last-ditch efforts to save her marriage, Jamie had invited friends of Mark's—Bob and Sharon Lasky, Pam and Ron Hutchinson—over for dinner. Naturally Mark was late, having stopped off at his mother's first. "I come bearing gifts," he'd explained to their guests as he strolled casually into their apartment half an hour after they'd arrived. "My mother's famous lemon meringue pie."

"Only my favorite thing on earth," Bob said.

Jamie had smiled, relegating the chocolate cake she'd made that afternoon to the freezer, determined to give her mother-in-law the benefit of the doubt, to prove to her husband that she was capable of compromise.

After dinner, they'd sat around talking and watching the Miss America pageant on TV. Mark had made some stupid comment about wanting to go out with one of the contestants, a big-haired, big-bosomed campaigner for world peace whose enormous dimples bracketed a mouth filled with Chiclets-size teeth.

"You're kidding me," Pam had said, laughing. "What on earth would you talk about?"

Mark had looked genuinely horrified. "I don't want to **talk** to her," he'd exclaimed to much laughter.

"Did you like dinner?" Jamie had asked later, after everyone had gone and they were getting ready for bed. She'd made a chicken with cumberland sauce, and everyone, including Mark, had had second helpings.

"It was okay."

"Just okay?"

"What is this, a fishing expedition? You looking for compliments?"

"Just that you never said anything."

"I said it was okay. Dessert was fabulous," he added, climbing into bed and pulling the blanket up around his shoulders, a clear signal he wasn't interested in making love. "Don't forget to call and thank my mother."

"She knew I was making a chocolate cake."

"What?"

"I spoke to her today. I told her we were having company tonight and that I was making a chocolate cake for dessert."

"What are you saying? That she did it on purpose?"

"Why would she make a dessert when she already knew I was making one?" Jamie persisted.

"I don't know. Maybe to be nice? Because she knows it's Bob's favorite? Because she figured you'd fuck it up."

"I didn't fuck it up."

"You fuck everything up."

"That's not fair."

"That's not fair?" he repeated. "What are you—five years old? Christ, Jamie, do you ever listen to some of the stupid things you say?" He was suddenly out of bed, pacing the floor in the boxer shorts he'd begun wearing to bed every night. Another signal he wasn't interested in making love. "My mother makes you a fabulous dessert, which most people would accept for the kind gesture it was, and you make it out to be an act of sabotage. Hell, she goes out of her way to be nice to you. . . ."

"She goes out of her way to make me look incompetent."

"You **are** incompetent," Mark shouted. "Besides being an ungrateful bitch."

The words slapped at Jamie's cheeks, brought tears to her eyes.

There followed more words, more accusations, more tears. Finally, mercifully, there was silence. Ultimately Mark had gotten dressed, thrown some clothes into an overnight bag, and stormed from the apartment. No need to ask him where he's going, Jamie thought, falling into bed, eventually drifting into a restless sleep.

The twisting of a key in the front door woke her about an hour later. "Mark?" she asked, sitting up in bed, her eyes swollen almost shut with her tears.

Without a word, Laura Dennison walked into the bedroom and flipped on the overhead light. "I've come for my jewelry," she said, as if this were the most natural of announcements.

Jamie couldn't believe her ears. She must be

dreaming, she thought, pinching herself underneath her blankets. "What?"

"The wedding ring, the bracelet, the earrings," Mrs. Dennison enumerated.

"Surely this can wait till morning."

"I'd rather get this out of the way now, if you don't mind."

"I **do** mind."

"They're family heirlooms, as you know. I'll sue you if you try to keep them."

Numb with anger, fatigue, and disbelief, Jamie climbed out of bed, pulling off her wedding band as she walked toward the dresser. Wordlessly, she dropped the ring into her mother-in-law's outstretched palm, along with the gold bracelet and the pearl-and-gold earrings she'd worn just this evening. I **do** mind, she repeated silently as her mother-in-law dropped the jewelry into her purse and marched from the room.

"I mind very much," Jamie said now, staring at the hateful woman as she slept. "The earrings are in her dresser," she told Brad. "Top drawer, at the back."

CHAPTER EIGHTEEN

Brad traversed the plush, white broadloom to the dresser in one graceful arc, almost like a dancer, Jamie thought. As if his entire life he'd been breaking into people's homes as they slept. As if rifling through their belongings and stealing their most prized possessions was something with which he was intimately familiar. As if it was all in a night's work. He was a little too comfortable with the situation, she thought, as he seized the ornate brass handle of the polished wood dresser and pulled open its top drawer, exposing its contents to the scrutiny of the night. Just as he'd looked a little too comfortable with a knife in his hands last night in Tifton.

Jamie's eyes had grown slowly more used to

the darkness, and she had no trouble making out even the smallest details of the room: the myriad shapes of the glass perfume bottles that lined the top of the dresser; the silver-embossed title of the softcover book on the night table beside the bed; the small crack in the pale blue-and-white wallpaper between the door frame and the ceiling. Although maybe she was just remembering this last detail. She couldn't be sure. She'd worked so hard to blot out everything about her time here.

And now here she was, right back in the middle of it.

And what else? What else had she gotten herself into?

Beside her, Mrs. Dennison stirred, made a slight munching sound with her mouth. For a second, Jamie feared she was about to wake up. Nature giving her a middle-of-the-night wake-up call. But she only flipped onto her left side, her right arm reflexively reaching out to pull the comforter back up around her shoulders. What would she do if Mrs. Dennison were to wake up right now? Or maybe she was already awake. Maybe she was just pretending to be asleep.

"You'd like to kill her, wouldn't you?" Brad said from beside the dresser, fistfuls of the woman's intimate apparel overflowing his cupped hands.

"What? No! Of course not." A line of sweat suddenly materialized across Jamie's forehead, like a fever breaking. She was thinking of the switchblade in his pocket.

"Bullshit," Brad countered. "It's written all over your face." He laughed. "Your hatred for this woman glows in the dark." He laughed again, although this time the laugh was silent.

Jamie was about to protest but stopped when she realized he was right. She did hate Laura Dennison.

"You could do it, you know," Brad continued, his voice a seductive whisper. "All you'd have to do is grab that pillow next to her head and hold it over her face for a couple of minutes. It'd be so easy."

Jamie stared down at her former mother-in-law. Was Brad seriously trying to encourage her to commit murder? **Would he really have slit that boy's throat?** Don't be ridiculous, she told herself, forcing the troublesome thought from her brain. "Let's just get the earrings and get out of here."

Brad dropped the bras and panties in his hands to the top of the dresser, his hand sweeping soundlessly across the inside of the top drawer. "There's nothing here."

"There's no jewelry box?"

"See for yourself."

Jamie tiptoed to his side, knowing even before she reached her hand inside the drawer she'd find nothing. "She must have moved it," she muttered, hating the sleeping woman even more. You couldn't let anything be easy, could you? she was thinking as she returned the underwear to its former position. Silently, she searched through the bureau's second drawer, and then the third, coming up empty. "Okay, it's not here. Let's just leave."

"Nah. It's gotta be somewhere. Where would she keep it?"

"I don't know. My heart is racing; my head

is pounding. I think I'm going to be sick," Jamie rattled off, her body suddenly acutely aware of her predicament. You've overstayed your welcome, her body was telling her. You're pushing your luck, courting disaster.

Get out while you still can.

Brad's arms were immediately around her, his voice soft in her ear, advising her to calm down, take deep breaths, pull herself together.

"I'm going to be sick," Jamie repeated forcefully, feeling the bile rise in her throat. She tore out of his arms and vaulted toward the en suite bathroom, pulling the door closed after her and flipping on the light, temporarily blinded by the eight spotlights framing the tall, rectangular-shaped mirror over the sink. "Oh, God," she said to the terrified young woman trapped inside the glass, gasping for air. "What the hell are you doing?"

And then she saw it. The ivory-inlaid, red enamel jewel box that housed the so-called family heirlooms. It was sitting on the bathroom counter at right angles to the sink, beside a plethora of antiwrinkle creams and expensive moisturizers. A large bottle of hair spray stood on its other side, like a sentinel, and beside it a round, glass bowl stuffed with cotton balls. An impressive collection of makeup brushes, foundations, lipsticks, and blushes occupied the balance of the counter space. This from a woman who'd once criticized her for wearing too much mascara. "Jealous old bat," Jamie whispered now, her fear of being sick suddenly subsiding. She opened the door a crack, wincing when she saw a streak of light cut across Mrs. Dennison's face, like the blade of Brad's knife. "Brad," she whispered. "It's here. I found it."

There was no response.

Jamie stepped back into the bedroom, closing the bathroom door behind her, her eyes quickly readjusting to the dark. "Brad?" Was he hiding? She braced herself for his sudden reappearance, her shoulders hunching around her ears in anticipation of his popping up like a jack-in-the-box and slicing at her hair. But nobody jumped out at her, and the only sound she heard was the steady hum of Mrs. Dennison's breathing.

Where was he?

She heard a noise and she froze, sensing Mrs. Dennison leave her bed to inch up behind her. Dear God, what could she say to the woman? How could she even begin to explain what she was doing here? But when she glanced over at the bed, she saw that her former mother-in-law was still sleeping soundly. She spun around just as Brad appeared in the doorway.

"Where the hell have you been?" she demanded angrily.

"Ssh," Brad cautioned, moving back into the room and nodding toward the sleeping figure.

"Where did you go?"

He shrugged, pulled a tall, brass candlestick holder out from behind his back. "Thought we'd have some fun."

"Fun? What are you talking about?"

He put the candlestick holder on the

dresser. "That ought to freak her out pretty good when she wakes up."

"Then she'll know for sure someone was here. She'll realize her earrings were stolen."

"You found them?" Brad asked, smiling in anticipation.

Jamie looked toward the bathroom.

"In there?" Already he was walking toward the small room, pulling open the door.

Light flooded the bedroom.

"Brad, for God's sake, close the door."

"Stop worrying," he said, leaving it open. "Zorro's sound asleep. Where are the earrings?"

Jamie hurried to the bathroom, deliberately closing the door after her and grabbing the enamel box from the counter, lifting its lid.

"Wow," Brad said with a low whistle. "Ain't this a pretty sight."

Ain't this a pretty sight, Jamie repeated in silent disbelief, wondering when the southern good old boy had replaced the sophisticated computer programmer and software designer she'd run away with. She forced her eyes to the small but impressive collection of jewelry in the box. Several gold bracelets, a delicate necklace made up of tiny diamond flowers, a star sapphire ring, a pair of diamond studs, some silver hoops, the gold-and-pearl earrings, a wide, antique, gold, wedding band. **Her** wedding band, she found herself thinking. **Her** gold-and-pearl earrings.

"Take them," Brad said, as if her thoughts were etched across her forehead in bright fluorescent letters. "They're yours."

With trembling fingers, Jamie lifted the earrings out of the box, before returning the box to the counter. What in God's name was she doing?

"Put them on," Brad directed.

Jamie brushed her hair away from her ears, pushing first one earring, and then the other, through the tiny holes in her lobes, then admiring the result in the mirror.

"Back where they belong," Brad said, and Jamie couldn't help but smile.

He was right. The earrings **were** back where they belonged. She'd paid for them with two years of her life. She'd earned the right to wear them.

"They suit you." He came up behind her and kissed the side of her neck, his arms wrapping tightly around her rib cage. "You look beautiful."

She **did** look beautiful, Jamie thought. The sad little girl who wore her fear like a heavy veil had disappeared. In her place stood a confident young woman wearing gold and pearls. "We should get out of here."

"You're not going to leave those diamonds behind, are you?"

"Those were never mine," Jamie explained.

"They are now." Brad dropped the diamond studs into the palm of her hand.

"No. I can't. I don't want them."

"Sure you do."

The cold stones felt strangely warm against her skin. She felt them burning holes in her flesh, like tiny drops of acid, and quickly returned them to the jewelry box. "No. I don't. Please. Let's just get out of here."

Brad shrugged. "Okay. If you're sure. . . ."

"I'm sure." Jamie started from the room, turning back to see Brad stuff something into the pocket of his jeans. She quickly switched off the light so that she couldn't see any more.

"Good night, Mrs. Dennison," Brad whispered as they passed by her bed. "Sleep tight, you old witch."

He's taken on my anger as if it were his own, Jamie thought, wondering why, and realizing that under different circumstances, she might have felt flattered. She stepped into the hall, relief struggling to replace the terror in her lungs, to allow her enough space to breathe. Another minute and they would be out of here. They could put this Bonnie and Clyde act behind them, go back to the people they really were.

Except, who were they?

Who was **she**?

"Show me your old room," Brad said suddenly, his voice a cold glass of water dripping down her back.

"What?"

"Show me your old room," he repeated, tugging on her arm.

"No. Let's just get out of here."

"Not until you show me your room." He plopped down in the middle of the beige carpeted hall, crossed one leg over the other.

"What are you doing? Get up, for God's sake."

"Not till you promise you'll show me your room."

"It's just a room," Jamie insisted. Then when it became obvious he wasn't going to budge until she complied, "Okay. Fine. I'll show it to you."

Instantly he was on his feet, following her down the hall, grinning from ear to ear.

This is all a big game to him, Jamie realized. He's enjoying himself. "You think this is fun?" she asked incredulously, stopping in front of her old bedroom.

"Don't you?" Brad stepped inside.

"No. I just want to get out of here."

"Come on, Jamie. It's a kick. Admit it." He grabbed her hand, pulled her inside the room, stopping at the foot of the queen-size bed. "Is this where you used to do it?" He bounced down on top of the quilted brown-and-black patterned bedspread.

Jamie would have laughed had she had enough breath. "Yeah, right," she scoffed as her eyes swept across the room. A boy's room really, with its heavy, dark furniture, its dull, beige walls and slightly darker broadloom, the modern stereo equipment propped against one wall, a large flat-screen TV on the wall across from the bed. No frills or soft touches anywhere in sight. She'd tried to soften it once by buying a Klimt reproduction she'd seen in an upscale poster shop. Even though she'd never formally studied art, she found the painting of a young couple both passionate and tender, and hoped it would inspire some of that in her marriage. She'd hung it over the bed. "It's beautiful, isn't it?" she'd asked her husband, and he'd nodded, but the next day the poster was gone.

"Come sit beside me," Brad said softly now.

Jamie shook her head. She just wanted to

get out of here. Seeing this room again made her queasy with unwanted memories: the times she'd spent reaching for her husband in the dark, only to be rejected; the nights she'd spent crying herself to sleep; the mornings she'd awakened to find him already finishing breakfast with his mother. Was she truly so unlovable, so unworthy of even the slightest sign of affection?

Brad patted the space beside him on the bed. "Come on, Jamie. Sit with me."

Tears filled Jamie's eyes as she allowed the tenderness in Brad's voice to seduce her. She sank down beside him on the bed, felt the comfort of his arm as it snaked across her shoulder. He drew her to him, kissed her forehead, cradled her hands inside his own.

"Poor Jamie," he was saying as she buried her face in his chest, crying into the dark cotton of his T-shirt. "Poor little Jamie-girl." And then he was kissing her hair and the side of her face, her forehead and her eyelids, her nose, her cheeks, and finally her mouth, the kisses becoming more urgent, more insistent, his hands leaving hers to caress her breasts. What was he doing? What was **she** doing?

"Brad, no. Don't do that."

"It's okay, Jamie. Relax."

"No. What are you doing?"

"You know what I'm doing." One hand reached between her legs.

"No. Stop."

"Why?"

"Why?" **Why?** "Because it's not right."

"It feels right to me."

Jamie tried to push him away, but his arms were like vines that had grown wild and entrapped her, his mouth a pesky insect that wouldn't go away. "We can't do this here."

"Of course we can."

"No. What if she hears us? What if she wakes up?"

"She won't hear us. Not if you stop making such a fuss." He was pulling at her T-shirt, tugging at her pants.

"Brad, stop it."

"Tell me what you did with him in this bed, Jamie," he was saying, ignoring her protests.

"Brad, I don't like this. I want you to stop."

"No, you don't. You're enjoying this as much as I am." He pushed her back on the bed, climbed on top of her, pinned her arms above her head. "Tell me if you sucked his cock."

Jamie shook her head, torn between screaming and going limp. Dear God, how had she gotten herself into this mess? Just let me out of here in one piece, she prayed. I promise I'll never do anything stupid again.

"Tell me if you sucked his cock," Brad repeated, pulling her T-shirt up over her breasts and kissing her nipples.

"I sucked his cock," Jamie said dully, hoping it would be enough to satisfy him, to get him off her. The touch of Brad's tongue on her bare skin was starting to nauseate her. For the second time that night, she felt she might throw up.

"And did he like it?"

"I don't think so, no."

"But you liked doing it, didn't you?" Brad unzipped the zipper of her jeans, pulled them down over her hips, quickly burying several fingers deep inside her. It hurt and she cried out. "Ssh," he warned, forcing his fingers higher still. "You like this, don't you?"

"No. I don't like it," she said truthfully, crying now.

"Sure you do. I know you do. You like it rough and dirty."

"No, I don't. Please, stop." She heard his zipper opening, felt him tugging at his clothing.

"You like the danger. Admit it. You loved last night in the parking lot, didn't you? Those guys looking at you the way they did." He withdrew his fingers, only to force himself inside her, pounding into her relentlessly, whispering in her ear the whole time. "You like the threat of being discovered. You like doing it in this bed, leaving your scent, your juices all over the bedspread. You love picturing that old bat coming in here tomorrow and sniffing her nose in the air, and saying, 'What's that smell?'" Brad laughed. "Hey, Jamie-girl," he said, continuing to ride her—SAVE A HORSE, RIDE A COWBOY, she thought as a fresh flood of tears sprung from her eyes—"you think she still remembers what sex smells like?"

Jamie turned her head to one side, closed her eyes, and tried to pretend she was on a beach somewhere, buried up to her neck in sand, numb from the neck down, but every time she tried to convince herself this wasn't happening, Brad picked up the tempo of his pounding, the ferocity of his thrusts, and she was forced to acknowledge the truth of her situation, that she was in her former mother-in-law's house, in her ex-husband's bed, being raped by a man she'd willingly run away with only days before, a man with whom she'd made love in every possible position in every possible place, a man with whom she'd actually thought she might be falling in love. It would be funny if it weren't so pathetic. So **damned** pathetic, she thought, as once again his mouth returned to her breasts. He bit her nipple, and she cried out.

"Ready?" he asked, as if mistaking her pain for passion.

Was that possible? Could he really think she was enjoying this?

Jamie held her breath as Brad suddenly pulled out of her and flipped her onto her stomach, spreading the cheeks of her buttocks apart with his fingers and forcing himself inside her, drilling a hole through her body clear up to her heart. She felt as if she were being split in two, as if someone had lit a torch to her insides, and fire was racing through her, burning up everything in its path. The pain was unbelievable, and she chewed on the bedspread in an effort to silence her screams.

And suddenly he was collapsing on top of her, laughing with satisfaction. "It's your fault for having such a great ass," he told her as he slipped out of her, slapping playfully at her rear end. The tips of his fingers stung like a whip, and she whimpered. "Hey, Jamie. You all right? I didn't realize I was invading virgin territory."

Jamie said nothing. She lay on the brown-and-black bedspread, unable to move.

"It's your fault, you know, for being so

damn sexy," Brad continued, zipping up his fly and straightening his clothes. "You make me crazy. You know that?"

It's my fault, Jamie repeated silently.

"Come on, girl. You better get up and get dressed. We've been here long enough."

Jamie struggled to get up, pushing herself off the bed and onto her feet, her legs giving out as soon as they hit the floor. She crumpled to the carpet, as if paralyzed. "Oh, God."

"Careful there, Jamie-girl. You don't want to go getting blood on the carpet."

Blood? Jamie thought. She was bleeding?

"We'll clean up back at the motel," Brad was saying as he pulled her to her feet, maneuvering her jeans back over her hips, then zipping them up when her fingers refused to cooperate. "Come on, let's get out of here."

They were halfway down the stairs when they heard footsteps overhead and looked back to see a light come on in Mrs. Dennison's room.

"Oh, God."

"Mark? Is that you?" Mrs. Dennison called

warily, flipping on the hall light as Brad and Jamie reached the bottom step. Then, "Jamie?"

Jamie froze, as if a giant net had suddenly descended on her head.

"Jamie, is that you?"

"Get out of here," Brad yelled, galvanizing Jamie into action.

She tore open the front door, fleeing into the night without stopping or turning around.

It was only as she was being sick on the side-walk next to her car that Jamie realized Brad wasn't beside her. She looked back up the street just as the light disappeared from Laura Dennison's room.

CHAPTER NINETEEN

At first Emma couldn't decide what to do with her newfound freedom. It had been so long since she'd had an entire Sunday all to herself. When Lily had first suggested taking the boys for the day—breakfast at the International House of Pancakes, followed by a trip to the Art Institute, then lunch at McDonald's, and finally a movie—Emma had been against it. She disliked fast food almost as much as she disliked art galleries, and a vague but persistent headache at the base of her neck made the idea of sitting in a movie theater with a bunch of noisy five-year-olds something less than appealing, but how could she refuse when Dylan was staring at her with those big eyes filled with such obvious longing and Lily was smiling that sweet smile of hers? "It's just that I have so much to do," she demurred as Dylan's features pinched together in disappointment and his eyes welled with tears. Not to mention my profound shortage of cash, Emma refrained from adding. The thought of wasting what little money she did have on something she wouldn't enjoy . . .

"Oh, you don't have to come," Lily had assured her brightly, as if she'd been expecting Emma's response. "Let me take the boys. My treat."

"Oh, no. I couldn't let you do that." Her protest sounded weak even to Emma's ears.

"Of course you can. You looked after Michael last night. Today is my turn."

"Well, if it wouldn't be too much trouble."

"I want you to come too, Mommy," Dylan had piped up.

"I can't, sweetheart. I have way too much to do."

"What do you have to do?"

"All sorts of things." Emma knelt down beside her son. "But it's up to you, sweetheart. You can spend the day with Michael and his mother, going to the movies and all that other fun stuff, or you can spend the day with me, running errands and all that boring stuff. It's your choice." Some choice, she thought, hoping Dylan would feel the same way.

"I want you to come with us," he'd responded, as if she hadn't spoken at all.

"That's not an option."

"What's an option?"

"It means you either go with Lily and Michael or stay home with me."

Dylan didn't like her definition of **option,** and they spent the next five minutes going around in increasingly tight circles, but ultimately he'd made the only sensible choice and left with Lily and her son for breakfast at the International House of Pancakes.

"I'll have him home by five o'clock," Lily promised as Emma watched her son disappear down the street with his new friends.

Emma was surprised by the ease, even the eagerness, with which she'd let him go, considering the tight reins she'd held on him this past year. But Lily was so sweet and so reliable, Emma couldn't imagine anything bad happening to her son while he was in her care. Lily would guard Dylan as if he were her own, Emma knew, feeling giddy and light-headed at the prospect of eight whole hours with no one to answer to but herself.

It was only later, as she stood in the shower, letting the hot water cascade around her head and shoulders, that she realized she hadn't even asked Lily about her date last night. Not that she'd had to. Lily had been positively glowing when she'd shown up outside her screen door at barely eight o'clock this morning, so obviously the date had gone well. She'd just tell Lily she hadn't wanted to question her about her evening in front of the children. Hopefully Lily might have a few salacious details to divulge later, although the fact that she'd shown up so early this morning probably meant the detective hadn't slept over. Emma swallowed two Excedrin as she wiped the steam from the bathroom mirror. "I look awful," she said.

Her reflection nodded its agreement. *How long's it been since you had a decent haircut?* the face in the mirror asked.

Emma pictured the new hairdressing salon that had recently opened in the same plaza as Scully's. What was its name? She'd walked past it just the other day. Nan's Place? Nancy's? Nadine's? "Natalie's," Emma remembered, the large white poster in the small salon's front window coming into sharp focus, proudly announcing it was now open for business, including, for a limited time only, Sundays from ten to five. Emma wondered how much Natalie charged for a trim. "It doesn't matter. I can't afford it, no matter what it costs."

Sure you can, her image argued. *How long's it been since you treated yourself to anything?*

"Too long," Emma said out loud, tugging on her hair and deciding to walk over to the strip mall as soon as her headache disappeared. First she'd have her hair styled and trimmed, and then maybe she'd go shopping. Hell, she had eight hours. Might as well get started.

* * *

The salon was surprisingly busy for a Sunday morning, and Natalie was booked until noon, so Emma settled for a stylist named Christy, even though Christy looked to be suffering from an even worse hangover than Emma. Maybe it was the loud reggae music playing in the background, Emma thought as Christy led her to the sinks at the back of the salon. Christy was a skinny young woman in a yellow-and-black-striped jersey, a black mini-skirt, yellow tights, and heavy, black combat boots. She looks like a giant bumblebee, Emma thought, settling into the chair at Christy's station as Christy threw a black cape across her shoulder and ran a comb through her freshly washed hair. The yellow-and-black motif continued into Christy's geometrically cut, chin-length bob, which was dark yellow with an inch of black roots, as well as in the mustard yellow ring that ominously circled her left eye.

"I tripped," Christy said before Emma had a chance to ask. "Not that anybody believes me," she continued, unprompted. "Everybody assumes my boyfriend clocked me one, but Randy's the sweetest guy you ever met, I swear. He wouldn't hurt a fly. But people give him such looks when we're out together. You wouldn't believe. It's funny, but it's embarrassing too. I feel like wearing a sign that says 'He didn't do it,' with an arrow pointing in his direction. You know, like those T-shirts that say 'I'm with Stupid.' It doesn't help, of course, that he looks like such a bruiser."

"Same thing happened to me once," Emma volunteered. "I tripped over my son's toy and went flying into the corner of the kitchen door. Everyone assumed my ex was responsible."

"So, you're divorced," Christy stated, combing out Emma's shoulder-length dark hair and studying her in the mirror. She reached around to guide Emma's chin to her right and then her left.

"A year ago."

"Yeah? I've never been married. I mean, why bother, you know? It's just a piece of paper. All this fuss they're making about gays getting married? I say, if they want to, let them. I mean, pretty soon they're going to be the **only** people who want to get married. What are you thinking of?"

It took Emma a few seconds to realize that Christy was referring to her hair. "I don't know. Maybe a few inches off the bottom?"

"I think we should thin out the sides a bit too. Give 'em some shape. Right now they look a bit too much like cocker spaniel ears for my taste."

Emma felt her spine stiffen. Her hair resembled the ears of a cocker spaniel? This from a woman who looked like a bumblebee? "Whatever you say."

"Oh, I just love it when people say that." She began combing Emma's hair with greater purpose and determination. "So, what do you do?"

Emma ran through a silent list of possibilities. She could be anything her little heart desired. Doctor, lawyer, police detective. Anything but the failure she was. "I'm a writer." Surely Lily wouldn't mind if she borrowed her identity for half an hour. She might even be flattered.

"Yeah? Cool. What sort of things do you write?"

"Short stories, articles for magazines. I'm working on a novel."

"That's so great. I really admire people who have a talent like that." She began snipping away at Emma's dark hair. "Where do you get your ideas?"

Emma sighed. Why was it that people were never satisfied, that they always felt the need to know more? More to the point, why was she always putting herself in this position? She knew how stupid, how ultimately destructive her behavior was. Still she couldn't help herself. Because the truth—the whole truth and nothing but the truth—was that it hurt too much when the lying stopped. "It's hard to say."

"They just come to you out of the blue?"

Emma almost laughed. "Apparently."

"Wow. That's so interesting." Christy began cutting into the sides of Emma's hair. "So, you got a boyfriend now?"

Emma nodded. Hell, she was already in pretty deep. Might as well go all the way. "He took me to Joso's last night for dinner."

Christy looked unimpressed, as if she'd never heard of Joso's. And maybe she hadn't. "Yeah, so, where'd you meet him?"

"Over at Scully's."

"Yeah? That Jan's quite a character, isn't she? I'd love to get my hands on her hair, drag her into the twenty-first century. And all those trophies!"

"They're pretty impressive."

"I heard her husband left her for her plastic surgeon."

"I think it was his nurse," Emma corrected.

"That'd be interesting, don't you think? Working for a plastic surgeon?"

"Not really. I worked for one a few years ago," Emma said, thinking, here we go again. "It wasn't that interesting. Except for the movie stars coming in."

"Yeah? Like who?"

Emma shook her head. Would she never learn? "I really shouldn't say."

Christy made a face of disappointment that was a duplicate of Dylan's face when he didn't get his way. "So, what were all these movie stars doing coming to Ohio?"

"I was living in California at the time."

Christy made a face that said, Of course. I should have realized that. "I guess you've moved around a lot."

"I guess."

"Probably gives you lots to write about."

"I guess," Emma said again, growing bored with the conversation. That was the other thing about lying. It was exhausting. She closed her eyes, grunting at appropriate intervals to indicate she was still listening, although in truth, she'd pretty much tuned the now one-sided conversation out. Luckily, Christy didn't seem to notice, and if she did, she didn't seem to mind. She continued babbling the entire time Emma was in her chair, her voice a sedative, lulling Emma into a state of blissful semiconsciousness.

Emma pictured herself floating on a pink rubber raft in the middle of a bright, blue sea.

The reggae music emanating from an overhead speaker became a live band playing from the upper deck of an imagined nearby yacht. A party was in full swing. Someone threw a glass of champagne overboard, and Emma caught it and lifted it into the air, toasting the ship's handsome captain as a hot wind blew into her ear, and mermaids played with her hair.

"So, what do you think?" a voice was asking, slicing into her reverie with surgeonlike precision.

Emma opened her eyes as Christy returned the blow dryer to its table. She leaned forward in her chair, mesmerized by her shapely new cut, shorter by several inches and softly layered at the sides. "It's beautiful. I love it."

Christy smiled proudly as she whipped the black cape from Emma's shoulders. "Would you like to book now for your next appointment? Six weeks should be about right."

Six weeks? Emma tried to remember how long it had been since she'd planned anything that far in advance. Who knew, after all, where she'd be in six weeks? And yet, suddenly, for the first time in more than a year, she was feeling, if not secure, then at least a little settled. She was feeling, if not exactly happy, then at least a little hopeful. Her world no longer felt so insular and circumspect. It showed signs of expanding. She had a new friend, and the possibility of more. Even more important, her son had a new friend. Perhaps his nightmares would soon cease, and along with that, the nightmare that had been the last year of their lives. She smiled at her reflection. Nothing like a new haircut to make you feel that all was right with the world. "Six weeks. Sure. Why not?"

Emma floated out of the salon, stopping to linger in front of Marshalls discount department store—how she'd love a new spring wardrobe to go with her new haircut, she thought—before reluctantly continuing on her way. She passed Scully's, waving at Jan, who stood behind the reception desk, wearing a fluorescent orange headband that matched the bright orange of her lips, the neon color clearly visible even through the thick glass of the front window.

Jan smiled and waved her inside. "Hi there. Thinking about taking out a membership? We're having an introductory special. Only two hundred and fifty dollars to join and thirty dollars a month, plus a free mug and T-shirt." She reached under the counter, pulled out a large black mug with **Scully's** scribbled in gold lettering across each side, and sat it on the counter.

Emma laughed. Did the woman never give up? "Actually I was just over at Natalie's. Having my hair done," she added when Jan failed to comment. "You like it?"

"Very nice. Now all we have to do is get that tummy in shape." Jan patted her own flat abdomen for emphasis. "I could personalize a program for you, if you'd like, have you in the best shape of your life in no time."

It suddenly occurred to Emma that Jan had no idea who she was. Even though they'd spent an entire evening together only two nights before, Jan didn't recognize her. It's the new haircut, Emma assured herself, wondering what it was about her that failed to register. "Jan, it's Emma," she said, unable to disguise the impatience in her voice. "We met the other night. At Lily's."

"Of course we did," Jan said without missing a beat, although her eyes betrayed her. "I was just teasing. Are you looking for Lily?" she continued, looking longingly toward the exercise room, as if she were wishing she could slip through the glass. "She doesn't come in on Sundays."

"Neither do a lot of people, from the looks of it," Emma said, observing the lone, middle-aged woman on the treadmill, and trying to keep the smirk out of her voice. Payback, she was thinking, for Jan's failure to recognize her. "Is it always this quiet on Sundays?"

"It's early. It'll start to get busy soon."

Emma walked over to the cabinet containing Jan's many trophies. "You actually won all these?"

Instantly Jan's face brightened. "I certainly did." She sashayed around the counter, walking toward the trophy cabinet. Open-toed, hot pink stilettos peeked out from beneath her hip-hugging, gray sweatpants.

"How many are there?"

"Oh, I've lost count. At least thirty." Jan unlocked the cabinet with the key that dangled from a coiled, lime green, rubber bracelet on her wrist. "I have at least as many at home."

"What are they for?"

"Oh, all sorts of things." Jan reached inside the cabinet, extricated a small bronze statuette of a preening female bodybuilder. "This one is for Mrs. Ohio Bodybuilder. And this one"—she exchanged one trophy for another, this one a large silver bowl—"was from a competition I won in Boulder, Colorado, four years ago." The phone rang. "Can you excuse me a minute?" She returned the bowl to the cabinet, ran around the counter to pick up the phone. "Hello? Noah?" She covered the receiver with her hand, turned back to Emma. "My nephew," she said proudly. "Just graduated from M.I.T."

Emma nodded, as if she were impressed.

"You got two job offers?" Jan repeated, smiling and raising two fingers in Emma's direction. "That's wonderful. And you want my advice?" She straightened her shoulders, winked at Emma. "Okay, so offer number one is for a job that's not all that exciting but it's with a large company and it pays megabucks. And offer number two pays next to nothing, but it sounds really interesting, and you think you'd really enjoy it. And you know which one I'd tell you to choose, but you're still not sure what to do." Jan looked a little taken aback. "Which one do you think I'd tell you to pick?" There was a pause, followed by an impatient shake of fiery red curls. "You think I'd tell you to pick the job that pays nothing but that you'd enjoy? Are you crazy?" Jan demanded, throwing her hands up in the air. "Who says you've earned the right to enjoy yourself? I want you to make a living, for God's sake. I want you to be self-sufficient. I want you to be able to support yourself."

Emma began tiptoeing toward the front door. "I'll leave you alone," she whispered, opening the door and stepping outside.

"Wait," she thought she heard Jan say as the door closed behind her, but Emma had no interest in hearing any more about Jan's nephew or seeing any more of her trophies.

"Who says you've earned the right to enjoy yourself?" she repeated in amazement, about to head back to Mad River Road, when she stopped, turned around, marched purposefully back toward Marshalls. "Damn it, why **shouldn't** we enjoy ourselves?" She pulled open the door to the discount department store and stepped inside, headed for a rack of summer dresses to her right. It's not like she did this sort of thing every day. It's not even like she did it once a month. When was the last time she'd gone shopping for herself? When was the last time she treated herself to a smart summer dress? She checked the price tag of a mauve-and-white flowered halter dress, noting that even at $120, it was at least a hundred dollars more than she could afford. Oh well, it wouldn't hurt to try it on, just for fun. She located her size and threw the dress over her arm, moving on to the next rack, and doing the same with a pale peach sweater set. She took her time going through the aisles, eventually piling all the items she'd selected into a shopping cart, except for a delicate, green chiffon scarf that she wrapped around her neck. She could always claim she'd tried it on and forgotten to take it off, she decided, although the fuchsia-colored silk blouse that she'd stuffed surreptitiously into her purse might be harder to explain.

She pushed her cart toward the dressing rooms, then waited in a small line of women for an empty stall.

"Only five items at a time," the attendant told her.

Emma rifled through the various items in her cart. "I don't know what to pick first."

"I know. They got such nice things in this time."

Emma selected five items, including the mauve-and-white flowered dress, and offered them to the attendant for perusal.

"I just love this dress," the woman said, handing the items back.

"It's gorgeous, isn't it? Could you check the size? A six? I'm blind as a bat without my glasses," Emma lied.

The attendant fumbled for the tag as Emma slid the peach-colored sweater set underneath the other items she'd be taking into the dressing room. "Yeah, here it is. Size six. Wish I could fit into a size six," she said wistfully.

"I think you look great," Emma said, managing to sound as if she really meant it. She should have worn a skirt. One of those long, billowy numbers that was easy to hide things underneath. That way she could have walked out with half the store. This way, she'd only be able to manage a few items. Hopefully, that would include this peach-colored sweater set, she thought, pulling off her white T-shirt and replacing it with the sleeveless pullover, then pushing her arms through its matching cardigan and admiring herself in the mirror, deciding she liked what she saw. "Sold," she said to her reflection, determined to ignore the unsolicited little voice in her head reminding her she'd sworn off this kind of behavior. She tried on the rest of the items, then repeated the whole process again, managing to secrete two items the next time.

"You're not taking the dress?" the attendant asked as Emma exited the fitting room for the last time.

"It doesn't fit right," Emma said. Thank goodness. She would have been heartbroken to leave it behind had it looked good, but there was simply no way she could have managed to get it out of the store undetected. Not on this trip anyway.

"So, nothing worked?"

"Some days are like that."

"Well, better luck next time," the attendant said.

Emma was smiling as she left the changing room area. The day was shaping up to be a great one. Not only did she still have a whole free afternoon ahead of her, but she also had a flattering new haircut and the beginnings of a brand-new wardrobe. As soon as she got a job, as soon as she started making some decent money, she'd send Marshalls an anonymous check to cover the cost of the items she was taking.

And since she'd ultimately be paying for

everything anyway, she might as well select a few items of jewelry to go along with her new clothes, she thought, stopping to admire a pair of dangling pearl earrings. "Can I see those?" she asked the salesgirl behind the counter.

The teenage girl, whose own lobes were ablaze with multicolored crystal studs, withdrew the earrings from their glass case with surprising care. Emma noted similar crystals decorating the girl's frighteningly long, magenta-colored nails, and one large, red crystal perforating the side of her wide nose, like a large freckle.

"How much are these?" Emma held up the earring, staring at her reflection in the small mirror that sat on the counter.

"Fifty-five dollars."

"That's a lot."

"They're pearls," the girl said.

Emma almost laughed. As if the girl could tell pearls from peanuts, she thought. "What about those?" She pointed toward a pair of pink rhinestone hearts. "And those." She indicated a pair of tiny blue flowers. "Could I see those as well?" Emma held the different pairs of earrings up to her ears, turning her head from side to side, pleased with the way each set highlighted the graceful bend of her long neck. Maybe they weren't as expensive as the "pearls." Maybe she'd actually be able to afford them. "How much are these?"

"The hearts are sixty-five, and the flowers are fifty."

"Ouch." So much for affordable. She returned them to the counter, suddenly resolving to return the other items she'd stolen as well. I'm not that girl anymore, she reminded herself. I don't take things that don't belong to me.

"Excuse me," a customer called from the other side of the counter. "Is there anyone here who can help me?"

The girl turned her head, and without a second thought, Emma swept the pink rhinestone earrings off the counter and into the pocket of her jacket. "You go," she told the salesgirl magnanimously. "I'll come back another time." So much for turning over a new leaf.

She was almost at the front door when she felt the hand on her shoulder. "Excuse me," a male voice said ominously. "I think you'd better come with me."

CHAPTER TWENTY

Jamie opened her eyes to find Brad standing beside the bed, staring down at her.

"Well, well. Look who finally decided to open her eyes."

Jamie said nothing.

Brad plopped down on the bed next to her. The motion tore through Jamie's torso like a bayonet, and she had to bite down on her lower lip to keep from howling out in pain. "Aw, come on, Jamie. You're not still mad at me about last night, are you?" His hand reached out to gently brush away several stray hairs from her forehead.

Every muscle in Jamie's body tensed and recoiled, sending agonizing spasms from the bottom of her toes to the tips of her fingers, although she barely moved. "What time is it?" she asked, her voice heavy and without inflection.

"Almost twelve o'clock," Brad said, and laughed. "Do I get points for letting you sleep in?"

"Twelve o'clock," she repeated, although the words meant nothing and refused to resonate. What did it mean that it was twelve o'clock? What did anything mean?

"Time to get this show on the road."

Time to get this show on the road, Jamie repeated silently, wondering, what show, what road?

"Come on, Jamie. Checkout time's one o'clock."

Brad stood up, walked to the dresser, threw the same clothes Jamie had been wearing yesterday toward the bed. "Get dressed. It's time to go."

Jamie could tell from the flatness of his voice that he was running out of patience, and she tried to move, to push one foot over the side of the bed, to prop her body up on her elbows, but it was as if each limb had been encased in plaster casts while she slept. Her arms were like anchors, weighing her down, each faint exertion causing her to sink lower and lower into an endless abyss. If only that were true, she was thinking as Brad's hand whipped the thin blanket from her naked body. Cold air from the air-conditioning unit blew noisily against her newly exposed flesh. Goose bumps rose along her skin.

"Get up, Jamie. Now."

"I have to take a shower," she muttered without moving.

"What—are you kidding me? Another shower? You spent half the night in the damn shower."

"I need a shower," Jamie reiterated, surprised to find herself suddenly on her feet. She shuffled along the side of the bed, hugging the wall for support and trying to ignore the gauntlet of invisible razors slashing at her thighs, the knives poking at her backside.

"You got five minutes," Brad said.

Jamie caught a brief glimpse of herself as she

passed the mirror, although she barely recognized the swollen face and haunted eyes staring back at her. Were it not for the gold-and-pearl earrings peeking out from underneath her tousled hair, she might have been able to dismiss the apparition as nothing but a figment of her overly fatigued imagination.

"Hey, Jamie," Brad said as she walked past. "I love you. You know that, don't you?"

Immediately Jamie's body jackknifed, doubling over on itself, and she was overcome by a succession of dry heaves that pushed her to her knees and left her gasping for air.

Brad was instantly beside her, wrapping her in a smothering embrace and pulling her to her feet. "Whoa there, Jamie-girl. That's no way to react when a man professes his love."

Jamie wiggled free of his arms.

"Aw, come on, Jamie. Don't be that way."

Jamie spun around, her eyes shouting what her voice could not. **Don't be that way? Don't be that way?!**

"Come on, Jamie. It wasn't that bad. It was

really kind of fun, when you think about it."

Jamie could scarcely believe the words she was hearing. Was he serious? Had he really used the word **fun** to describe what he'd done to her last night? **"Fun?"** she heard herself cry. "You raped me, for God's sake."

"Aw, don't call it that. Come on, Jamie. You enjoyed it. At least a little bit. Admit it."

"How can you say that? How can you even think it?"

"'Cause I know women," he said ominously. Then even more ominously, "'Cause I know you."

Was that true? Jamie wondered. Was it possible a virtual stranger could know her better than she knew herself? That he'd recognized something inside her—or more likely, that he'd recognized a **lack** of something—the moment he saw her and simply acted on his instincts? **This is all your fault,** she heard him say as she stepped onto the cold tile of the bathroom floor and closed the door.

"Don't lock it," Brad called after her.

Jamie stood with her hand on the lock. One

twist was all it would take to keep him out, at least temporarily. And maybe he'd get tired of waiting, of coaxing, of banging on the door. Maybe the maid would come to clean the room. Maybe if she started screaming, screaming at the top of her lungs, he'd panic and take off. More likely, he'd just kick in the door, grab her by the hair, throw her down on the bed. And then what? A repeat of last night's **fun**?

"Oh, God," she moaned, her hand dropping to her side as tears traced familiar lines down the length of her cheeks.

"Hey, Jamie," Brad said from just outside the door. "You want me to come in there and wash your back?"

Jamie said nothing as she pulled back the clear, plastic shower curtain and stepped into the tub, turning on the spigot and feeling the water shift abruptly from cold to hot. She thought of opening her mouth and letting her throat fill up with water. Could one actually drown that way? she wondered, turning around, feeling the water racing down her back to hide between her buttocks. "Oh, God," she cried again, as a fresh flood of tears escaped her eyes. She lifted her hands to push the wet hair away from her face, her fingers brushing up against the gold-and-pearl earrings at her ears. "What have I done?" she cried.

She'd been asking herself the same question all night.

What happened? What had she done?

She'd been asleep in her bed at the motel. Not the Ritz exactly, but clean, and the bed was comfortable. And suddenly Brad was whispering in her ear, telling her he loved her, the words coaxing her out from under her covers and into the cool night air. Driving through the city, turning onto Magnolia Lane, Brad telling her his plans, ignoring her protests as he got out of the car, she following after him, trying to assure herself that he would stop, turn around, tell her it was all a joke.

Except he hadn't stopped, and soon they were in the house, the warning wail sounding, then ceasing when she pressed in the code. The code Mrs. Dennison could easily have changed, the code she **should** have changed. Why hadn't she changed the damn code? This whole mess could have been avoided if Laura Dennison had simply changed her code. The wail would have mushroomed into a full-fledged siren. She and Brad would have taken off down the street, escaped into the night, laughed all the way back to the motel. **How stupid was that?** she could hear them giggling as they tumbled into bed. **How stupid was that?**

Except Mrs. Dennison hadn't changed the code. And she hadn't woken up. Not when Jamie and Brad were roaming through the downstairs rooms, not when they were standing beside her bed, not when they were rifling through her dresser drawers.

From underneath the shower's steady spray, Jamie saw herself reaching for the gold-and-pearl earrings in the red enamel box and fitting them into her ears. She saw Brad pocketing the diamond studs as they fled the room, watched him sit down in the middle of the hallway, stubbornly refusing to move until she showed him her old room. And then the room itself, with its beige walls and horrid black-and-brown patterned bedspread.

Come sit beside me.

Brad, no. Don't do that.

It's okay, Jamie. Relax.

No. Stop.

Tell me what you did with him in this bed, Jamie.

Brad, I don't like this. I want you to stop.

No, you don't. You're enjoying this as much as I am. You like it rough and dirty.

No, I don't. Please, stop.

Ready?

The stale smell of the quilted fabric pressing against her nose as he mounted her from behind. The searing pain, the fire rampaging unchecked through her body, razing her insides, leaving her torn and bleeding. Leaving her for dead.

It's your fault, you know.

It's my fault.

A loud banging on the door. "Hey, Jamie, how long you gonna be in there?"

Jamie's head snapped toward the sound. She grabbed the soap, began massaging it across her breasts, trying to wash away the sting of his teeth on her nipples.

She heard Mrs. Dennison's voice at the top of the stairs—"Jamie?" she'd called. "Is that you?"—then watched herself bolt from the house and run down the street to her car. She saw herself double over, then throw up by the side of the road. She watched herself collapse onto the pavement, unable to move.

Where could she go?

The police? And say what? That she'd been raped? Sodomized by her lover in her former mother-in-law's house, a house they'd broken into, the woman's pilfered gold-and-pearl earrings grinding painfully against her ears? That she'd fled the scene, leaving her lover to deal with the woman? That everything that happened that night was her fault?

"Two more minutes, Jamie. Then I'm coming in," Brad warned.

And then he was beside her, gently helping her into the car, and her face was pressing against the passenger window, her eyes catching the reflection of his smile in the glass. She felt the car's engine turning over, humming around her as he pulled away from the curb. She heard his laughter, the excited snap of his fingers as they tapped triumphantly against the steering wheel. "Wow. That was really something," he'd said, and laughed again.

Somehow she'd found her voice. "What happened?"

"What do you think happened?"

"Oh, God." A low moan escaped her throat, reverberated through the car.

Brad reached across the seat, squeezed her thigh. "Relax, Jamie. Nothing happened." He laughed again.

"What do you mean?"

"I mean, nothing happened."

"But she saw us. She saw me."

"She **thought** she saw you. I convinced her she was mistaken."

"How? How did you do that?"

"I can be very persuasive."

"You didn't hurt her?"

"Didn't have to." He shrugged, turned right at the next corner.

"I don't understand. What did you say to her?"

"I explained that it was all a mistake, and that if she promised not to call the police, I promised not to come back and wring her neck. She seemed most agreeable."

"That's it?"

"More or less."

"How much more?" Jamie asked, holding her breath.

"Nothing for you to worry about, Jamie-girl."

"But you promise you didn't hurt her?" Jamie asked again, her voice a plea.

"Told you I didn't, didn't I?"

Was it possible? Jamie wondered now, as she had somehow managed to convince herself last night.

They'd driven back to the motel. She'd been unable to muster the strength needed to open the car door, so he'd had to do it for her, holding the door open and helping her to her feet, supporting her elbow as she stumbled toward the motel. Once inside their room, she'd staggered into the bathroom and stripped off her clothes, gasping at the sight of the blood staining her panties, the dark red bruises on her breasts and arms and thighs, the splotches of dried blood around her buttocks. She'd been sick again, although there was little left in her stomach. Then she'd curled up in the middle of the tiny white squares of bathroom tile, hugging her legs to her chest, and cried, using her knees to muffle the sound. It was only when Brad threatened to come inside that she'd scrambled to her feet and into the shower, staying there until the water turned cold, and even after, until she heard the door open and saw Brad step inside the room, his features distorted by the translucent plastic of the shower curtain. The real Brad Fisher, she'd thought as he'd pulled back the curtain and turned off the tap, suddenly very much in focus. The devil, she thought.

And she, the devil's disciple.

He was surprisingly gentle with her, using all the available towels to pat her dry, then tucking her into bed and pulling the blanket up around her ears before climbing in beside her, wrapping her in his arms and holding her until her shivering stopped, and she succumbed to sleep.

"Jamie," Brad called again, a whoosh of cold air accompanying his entrance into the room.

Jamie turned off the shower, gathering the shower curtain around her body like a giant shawl.

"It's time to go," he said.

She nodded, waiting until he retreated back into the main room before climbing out of the tub, using a blood-streaked towel to dry herself off. Where were they going? she wondered. Was he really serious about continuing their trip? As if last night never happened? As if they hadn't broken into Laura Dennison's house and made off with her jewelry? As if he hadn't raped and sodomized her in her ex-husband's bed?

Come on, Jamie. It wasn't that bad. It was really kind of fun, when you think about it.

The door opened a crack as Brad threw her

jeans and T-shirt inside, along with some clean underwear. Jamie got dressed, then brushed her teeth until her gums bled, combed her hair until her scalp hurt. She pulled the gold-and-pearl earrings from her ears, tearing her lobes, leaving dots of blood in their place. Then she abandoned them at the side of the sink.

"Where are we going?" she asked, returning to the bedroom.

Brad looked quizzical. "What do you mean? You know where we're going."

"We're still going to Ohio?"

"Of course. I thought you wanted to meet my son."

"But after last night . . ."

"How long are you going to obsess about last night?" Brad asked impatiently, holding the front door open for her, then guiding her toward her car, dragging her overnight bag behind him. It bumped along the pavement, occasionally spinning off its wheels and ultimately turning on one side, as if it too were reluctant to proceed. "Get in," he instructed Jamie, who thought only fleetingly of trying to make a run for it. What was the point after all? Where was she going?

The sky was a brilliant shade of blue, with only a few large, fluffy clouds on the horizon. The temperature was warm, the air dry. A perfect day, Jamie thought as they pulled out of the parking lot, her eyes scanning the intersection for police cars, her ears straining for the sound of sirens. But there were none. Was it possible Brad had been telling the truth about Mrs. Dennison? That he'd managed to convince her it would be in her best interest to pretend last night hadn't happened?

On the radio a woman was singing about lost love, and Brad started singing along. He has a nice voice, Jamie realized. A gentle voice, she thought with a shudder, turning away.

"Should probably stop for gas," Brad said, pulling into a station just before the entrance to the highway. He jumped out of the car, withdrawing his wallet from the back pocket of his jeans. "Let's see if we can get this stupid card to work today." He pushed the credit card into the appropriate slot. "Come on, Gracie-girl. One more time." Seconds later, the card was once again declined. Brad made a derisive snort, then tossed the card back onto the front seat. "You got any cash?" he asked Jamie. "I'm running a bit low."

Who is Gracie-girl? Jamie wondered, reaching into her purse and withdrawing a twenty-dollar bill, handing it through the open window to Brad.

"Thatta girl," Brad said.

Gracie-girl, Jamie repeated silently, glancing at the credit card on the seat beside her, then lifting it to her eyes.

G. HASTINGS.

Who was G. Hastings?

If you'll just sign here, Mr. Hastings.

I'm sorry, sir. Would you have another card, by any chance?

Gracie-girl.

He just called you Mr. Hastings.

Hastings is my middle name. Brad Hastings Fisher.

Brad Hastings Fisher. Such a distinguished name.

"Who's Gracie Hastings?" Jamie asked as Brad climbed back behind the wheel.

His answer was to take the credit card from her hand and bend it in half, folding it back and forth until it split in two. He tossed the two halves from the window as they pulled onto I-75, heading north.

Jamie turned away, said nothing, concentrating on the scenery as it sped by. I could open the door, she was thinking, throw myself out of the car. In her mind's eye, she watched her body tumble from the front seat, wafting through the air like a discarded Kleenex toward the dark pavement; she felt her head hit the hard surface and split apart, her face disappearing into the back of her skull as her broken body bounced along the highway, setting off a wave of sparks before being hit by a second car and catapulted to the side of the road, like an errant football. Would such an ignominious end be enough to quell the fire still tearing through her? She closed her eyes, feigned sleep.

"Hey, Jamie," Brad said about half an hour later. "Look where we are."

Reluctantly Jamie opened her eyes.

"Barnsley Gardens, next cutoff," he announced. "Still feel like going?"

Jamie shook her head. Was he serious?

"You're sure? 'Cause I'm more than happy to go, if it'll make my girl love me again."

"I don't want to go."

"I've been thinking about that five-star restaurant. Thought you might be hungry. You haven't had anything to eat all day."

"I don't want anything."

They drove past the exit to Barnsley Gardens in silence. "So . . . what? You're not going to talk to me all day? You're just gonna keep giving me the silent treatment?"

"I'm tired, Brad. I don't feel like talking."

He said nothing for several minutes. Then, "You know, I read somewhere that all women fantasize about being raped."

Jamie said nothing, although she thought there was probably some truth to the assertion. She herself had occasionally entertained such fantasies. There'd been something strangely enticing, even liberating, about the idea of being taken against one's will, about not being given a choice, of being forced to submit, to do what was forbidden. But what might have been erotic, even pleasurable, in fantasy had proved both terrifying and repulsive in real life.

In Jamie's fantasies, no matter how violent, how perverse the attack, she never actually got hurt. She felt no discomfort, no humiliation, no fear. There was no real pain. Her insides didn't burn; her heart didn't break. The fantasy rapist had no real power over her. He did only what her imagination would permit. Ultimately, he was as concerned with her pleasure as his own. Ultimately, she was the one in control.

Reality was a different matter entirely.

There was no pleasure in this reality.

"Oh, by the way," Brad was saying, reaching into the side pocket of his jeans. "You forgot these at the motel." Two gold-and-pearl earrings winked up at her from the palm of his hand. He gave her the coldest of grins, then dropped the earrings into her lap.

CHAPTER TWENTY-ONE

Emma froze, the massive hand weighing heavily on her shoulder, threatening to sink through the denim of her jacket, the wool of her sweaters, the cotton of her T-shirt, to rub through her skin and cut through her bones, like an eraser through chalk, to bring her to her knees. Her breathing grew labored and her head light as the air turned cloying and miasmal. The store blurred around her, one aisle merging with another, the menswear colliding with the jewelry, women's casual garments tumbling into the shoe department, the checkout counters collapsing one on top of the other like a row of dominos. Was she going to faint? "Look, I can explain." She swiveled around, the heavy hand tightening its grip on her jacket, preventing her total collapse.

The eyes Emma found herself staring into were navy blue and closely set around a nose that had been broken at least several times and never properly reset. A small, Y-shaped scar cut through the middle of the man's right cheek, and his dark hair was closely cropped. A policeman's hair, Emma realized, as the room around her stopped spinning, and she was able to put a name to the face. "Jeff," she said, the word floating from her lips on a sigh of relief.

Detective Jeff Dawson stared at her as if he had no idea who she was.

"It's Emma. Emma Frost. We met the other day at Scully's. You're the member in good standing," she joked, hoping to elicit a smile. "I'm Lily's friend," she continued when he failed to respond. Why did she always have to keep reminding people who she was? Her hands flew skittishly to her head. "I changed my hair. It's probably why you didn't recognize me."

"Oh, I recognized you, all right," he said

coldly. "I just couldn't believe my eyes. What the hell are you doing?"

"It's not what it looks like," she stammered. "I was going to pay for the earrings. Of course I was going to pay for them."

"And that's why you put them in your pocket?"

"I was afraid of dropping them."

"And the scarf you're wearing?"

Emma's hand shot to the green chiffon scarf tied casually around her neck, her fingers fumbling with the knot at her throat. The damn thing was starting to feel like a noose, she thought, whipping it off. "I was just trying it on, trying to make up my mind." She held it out for him to see. "The price tag is still on it, for God's sake. Don't you think I would have removed it if I were planning to steal it?" Was he going to arrest her?

The salesgirl with the multiple crystal studs in her ears approached warily. "Is there a problem?"

Emma glanced from the police detective to the salesgirl, then back again. "These must have fallen on the floor," she improvised, reaching into her pocket and withdrawing the pink rhinestone earrings, then depositing them on the counter.

"Oh, my God. Thank you." The salesgirl quickly returned them to their proper place behind the glass.

Detective Dawson leaned forward, whispered in Emma's ear. "And the purple blouse in your purse?"

Emma closed her eyes in defeat, shook her head in frustration. "How long have you been watching me anyway?"

"At least half an hour."

Damn, Emma thought, wondering if he was going to take her to the station to be strip-searched. She couldn't let that happen. Not now. Not when everything was just starting to come together for her. "Please," she begged as Jeff Dawson began leading her away from the jewelry counter. "You can't arrest me. It would kill Dylan. He's my son, and he's got all these problems. If you arrest me, I don't know what will happen to him." If she could only make herself cry, she was thinking. Like those actresses on the daytime soaps who are able to cry on cue.

"You should have thought of your son earlier," Jeff said, as she'd known he would.

Cops were so predictable, she thought. "I know. It was stupid. I was stupid. Please, I'm begging you—"

"You don't have to beg." Jeff Dawson let go of Emma's arm, scratched at the side of his head. "I'm not going to arrest you."

"What?"

"I said I'm not going to arrest you."

"Oh, thank God. Thank **you.**"

"Providing you put everything back."

"Of course."

"Believe it or not, I actually came in here to find you."

"What? Why? Has something happened? Dylan . . . ?"

"Nothing's happened."

"I don't understand," Emma said.

"Look, why don't we grab a coffee over at Starbucks."

"You want to have coffee?"

"I want to talk."

"About?"

"We'll talk over coffee."

"Coffee it is," Emma agreed, thinking, He's not taking me to the police station; he's taking me to Starbucks. She started toward the front doors.

"Aren't you forgetting something?" Jeff Dawson glanced at Emma's purse.

Emma carefully reached inside her bag, managing to withdraw the fuchsia-colored silk shirt without disturbing the yellow cotton blouse she'd also managed to sneak out of the changing room, reluctantly dropping the shirt into a nearby shopping cart.

He seemed like a decent enough guy, she thought, as they walked briskly to the Starbucks at the far end of the mall. No wonder Lily liked him. She wondered if she'd ever have a man like Jeff Dawson in her life, then quickly dismissed the idea. Men like Jeff didn't fall for the Emmas of this world. They preferred the Lilys, who were simpler, and purer of heart. At the very least, they preferred women who didn't shoplift and tell lies.

Jeff's arm brushed against hers. Can he feel all the layers of clothing beneath my jacket? Emma wondered, happy the outside air was as cool as it was. Any warmer and she'd be in deep trouble.

"What'll it be?" Jeff asked as they entered the always busy café and approached the counter.

"I'd love a cappuccino."

"One cappuccino, one regular coffee." He pushed a twenty-dollar bill across the counter. "You want anything to eat? A muffin or something?"

"No, thanks." The last thing she wanted was to get crumbs all over her new sweater. She glanced down, began casually doing up the buttons of her jacket as they waited for their order to be readied. No point drawing any more unnecessary attention to herself.

"Cold?"

"Just not used to air-conditioning, I guess," Emma lied.

"Then I suggest we sit near the window. At least that way, you'll get a little sun."

Emma smiled, retrieved her cappuccino from the young man behind the counter, and sprinkled it with cinnamon. Was he playing with her? she wondered, following Jeff to a small, round table at the front of the café, the sun settling on her shoulders like a well-worn shawl as she sank into her chair. All around her, people were chatting and reading the morning paper. She took a slow sip of her coffee, watched Jeff do the same. Was he going to tell her what they were doing here? "What is it you wanted to talk about?" Emma ventured reluctantly.

"I was in Scully's just after you left," he began.

Emma felt her heart stop. Oh, God, she thought.

"Jan wanted you to have this." He reached into the pocket of his tan windbreaker, pulled out a black mug with the **Scully's** logo scribbled in gold across its sides, placed it on the table between them. "She said you left before she had a chance to give it to you."

Emma stared at the mug in amazement.

"She said to tell you it was her way of apologizing for not recognizing you right away. Apparently, she ran after you, but you were already on your way into Marshalls and she couldn't leave the gym, so I volunteered to find you."

"Well, you found me all right."

"I was looking around the store when I saw this woman wrap a scarf around her neck, and my instincts told me to keep an eye on her. I didn't realize it was you until I saw you slip that purple blouse inside your purse."

"Fuchsia," Emma corrected.

"What?"

"The color. It's fuchsia. Not purple. Sorry, I guess that's hardly relevant."

"Why'd you do it?"

Emma squirmed, traced the embossed gold letters of the **Scully's** logo with her fingertips. "Temporary insanity?" Her eyes sought his. "I don't know. The blouse was pretty. The silk felt good. I knew there was no way I could afford it."

He nodded, although his eyes told her he was far from convinced. “I don’t have to remind you that shoplifting is a serious offense.”

“I know that.”

“If you’re convicted, it means a criminal record, possible jail time.”

“Oh, God.”

“I came this close to arresting you.” He indicated with his fingers how close he’d come.

“So why didn’t you?”

“Because you caught me off guard. Because I felt sorry for your kid. Because you’re Lily’s friend, and I figured I owe you one.”

“You owe me?”

“For last night.”

Emma nodded. “Thank you. Thank you so much.”

“Don’t thank me.” Jeff glanced around the crowded café, as if afraid someone might be monitoring their conversation. “Just don’t do it again.”

“I won’t.”

“If I ever catch you at it again, I won’t care whose friend you are.”

"It'll never happen again. I promise." Emma took another sip of her cappuccino, wiping the foam from her upper lip with her tongue, and leaning back in her chair, perspiration beginning to seep through the layers of clothing beneath her denim jacket. She wondered if there was anything else Jeff wanted to talk to her about. He'd given her the mug and the lecture. Was there more? "So, did you and Lily have a nice evening?"

"Yes, very nice." He offered nothing further.

"I've never been to Joso's. I hear it's fabulous."

"It's very nice," he said again. Obviously it was the adjective of choice.

"I think Lily had a nice time." When in Rome, she thought.

Jeff lifted his eyes from his coffee, his interest clearly piqued. "You've talked to her?"

"Just briefly. When she came to get Michael. She offered to take Dylan for the day, which was really . . . nice." She wondered if Lily had ever been caught shoplifting.

Jeff nodded his agreement, took a long sip of

his coffee. "So, tell me about Emma Frost."

Emma took a deep breath. Had she misread his intentions? Was it possible he was coming on to her? Was threatening to arrest her his idea of foreplay? And how did she feel about moving in on her friend's, her **best** friend's, her **only** friend's, territory? "What is it you want to know?"

"Whatever." He shrugged, leaned forward in his chair, his elbows resting on the table, and balanced his chin on the backs of his huge hands.

"Well, I'm twenty-nine. Divorced. Have a five-year-old son. . . ."

"Dylan," Jeff said.

"Yes. Dylan," Emma repeated. Didn't he believe her? Was this some sort of fishing expedition? "And aside from that, there isn't a whole lot to tell."

"Now, why do I have trouble believing that?"

"You'd have to tell me."

"Where are you from?"

"I was born in Buffalo."

"Buffalo?"

"Yeah, but we moved when I was two."

"Where to?"

"Cleveland, Detroit, Los Angeles, Miami. Name a city, I've probably lived there. We moved around a lot when I was a kid. Army brat," Emma said with a shrug.

"I didn't realize Detroit and Miami had army bases."

Emma felt several beads of perspiration forming at her hairline, threatening to disrupt the smooth lines of her new cut. "We moved there after my dad died."

"He must have died very young."

"Yes, he did."

"How'd he die?"

"He was killed in Vietnam."

Jeff nodded. "Must have been hard, all that moving around."

"Yeah, it was. It seemed like every time we got settled into a new neighborhood, we'd have to move, and I'd have to start all over again, making friends, getting used to new schools, new teachers. It wasn't easy."

"Why'd you have to move?"

"What?"

"You said that every time you got settled into a new neighborhood, you had to move."

"I didn't mean we **had** to move. We just moved, that's all."

"Any particular reason?"

Why was he asking her all these questions? Emma was growing impatient and was tempted to gulp down the balance of her cappuccino, make her excuses, and hightail it out of there. Except she'd already used up all her excuses, and a hasty retreat was probably not the best way to handle Jeff Dawson. "My mom got transferred a lot."

"She was in the army too?"

Emma laughed. "In a manner of speaking, I guess. She was a school principal."

"She got transferred between cities? Isn't that unusual?"

"Unusual kind of sums her up," Emma said.

"How so?"

"Let's just say she was one of a kind and leave it at that, shall we?"

"If that's what you'd like."

What I'd like is to get out of here, Emma

thought. Was he never going to finish his coffee?

"So, how long have you lived on Mad River Road?" he was asking.

"About a year."

"You like it?"

"It's okay."

"Thinking of moving again?"

"Who knows?"

"There can't be much in the way of modeling jobs here in Dayton," he remarked.

"I haven't really looked into it."

"No. Why is that?"

"Been there, done that, I guess."

"You didn't enjoy it?"

"Not really. I mean, I liked it for a while. It was great having people fuss over me and tell me how beautiful I was and stuff, but there's a lot of pressure involved that people don't realize."

"What kind of pressure?"

Emma took a deep breath. "Well, the pressure to be thin, of course. And not **just** thin, but really, **really** thin. Unhealthy thin."

"Thin eyelashes?"

"What?"

"I thought the whole point of mascara was to make your eyelashes look thick."

You think too much, Emma wanted to shout. "I did other stuff besides Maybelline."

"Yeah? What other stuff did you do?"

"Some hair products. L'Oréal. **I'm worth it,**" she said, and laughed again.

"You're kidding. I've seen those ads."

"The one I did was years ago. Before they started using celebrities. I'm not even sure they aired it in this part of the country."

"I'm surprised the Maybelline people let you do ads for a rival company."

"Well, they're not exactly rivals. I mean, they were totally different products."

"That's true."

"I don't think the rules were as strict as they are now."

"You were lucky."

"I guess."

"You're never tempted to get back into it?"

"Not really. Besides, I'm getting a little long in the tooth, as they say."

"Twenty-nine is old?"

"For a model, yes. Unless you're Cindy Crawford or someone like that."

"So, what do you do?"

"What?"

"To support yourself. Do you have a job?"

Emma stared longingly out the front window, the sun shining its harsh spotlight directly into her eyes as she watched a carefree young woman striding toward her car in the parking lot, arms waving freely at her sides. *Take me with you*, she called silently after her. "I'm not working at the moment, no."

"You're between jobs?'"

"I guess."

"Trust fund?"

"What?"

"I'm just curious how you support yourself."

"I have some money saved up. From when I used to model. Not much left," she added, hoping to ward off future questions. Enough was enough. "I plan to start looking for a job in the fall, when Dylan goes back to school."

"What sort of job are you interested in? I might be able to help."

"Oh, that's so sweet of you. I'll keep that in mind. Now, I hope you won't think I'm being terribly rude, but I really have to get going. I have all this stuff to do before Dylan gets home. The laundry and groceries . . ."

"All of which you'll be paying for, I trust."

Emma forced her lips into a smile, fighting the unkind urge to toss the mug from Scully's at his head. "Absolutely. You don't have to worry about me." She rose to her feet. "Thanks for the coffee."

"Don't forget the mug."

Emma dropped the mug inside her purse. "Thanks again."

"Have a nice day," he said.

"Damn it, damn it, damn it!" Emma exclaimed as she threw open her front door and tore off her jacket, pulling off the layers of clothing beneath it as if her flesh were on fire. "I'm so hot, I'm going to explode," she shouted at the empty house. Seconds later, she stood naked in front of her kitchen sink, guzzling water from the tap, as if it were a water fountain. "Damn it," she said again, catching her reflection in the polished steel of the toaster and noting that her hair had started to flip up at the sides, so that it looked as if she were about to take flight. "That's just great." She marched back to the front hall, began retrieving her discarded clothes from the floor. "Fifty-five dollars for a haircut and it's ruined, and it's all your fault, Detective Do-Good," she said, snatching the peach-colored sweaters from the floor and throwing them over her arm, along with the yellow cotton blouse, a white T-shirt, a pair of white shorts, and a pair of black capris, all of which she'd managed to hide underneath her regular clothes. "You think you're so damn smart, Detective Dimwit. What do you think this is? Kiddies' day at the Exhibition? You think you're dealing with amateurs? Shit!" She grabbed her purse from where she'd dropped it just inside the front door, then marched everything up the stairs to her bedroom, throwing her purse on the bed and hiding the stolen items at the back of her closet, to be retrieved at a later date.

She sank down on her bed and opened her purse, withdrawing the mug from Scully's and dropping it on the bed. She didn't accept Jan's pathetic attempt at an apology, a conciliatory gesture for not remembering who she was. Stupid thing almost got me arrested, Emma thought, shaking her head at the irony. If it weren't for that mug, she'd have a beautiful pair of rhinestone earrings and a gorgeous silk shirt. A **fuchsia** silk shirt. "Fuchsia you, Detective Dawson." She dug deep into her purse, her fingers quickly locating the object she was looking for. "You think you're so damn smart." Emma smiled, her first genuine smile since leaving Natalie's, as she extricated a small, but surprisingly heavy, brass bowl from her purse and examined it in the afternoon sunlight streaming in from the window.

WOMEN'S BODYBUILDING COMPETITION, CINCINNATI, OHIO, 2002. SECOND PRIZE

Emma would have preferred a trophy for first prize, but she hadn't had the time to be choosy. She'd selected something small, from the back row, fairly nondescript, so that it wouldn't be immediately missed. Hadn't Jan herself admitted she didn't know exactly how many trophies she had? It might be weeks, even months, before she discovered the trophy was missing. Possibly not even then.

Emma's smile flipped into a frown. Why had she stolen the worthless trinket? It was ugly, and she couldn't very well leave it lying around for anyone to see. Besides, Jan was Lily's boss, and Lily was Emma's only friend. She had to take the trophy back. What was the matter with her? Why did she do such things? She carried it into the bathroom, hid it inside the small cabinet beneath the sink. She'd take it back as soon as she got the chance, figure out a way to return it to its rightful place without Jan noticing.

And then she'd never steal anything ever again.

CHAPTER TWENTY-TWO

"Well, what do you know?" Brad asked, breaking over an hour of silence. "We're about to drive by the Carpet Capital of North America."

Jamie looked aimlessly toward the side of the highway, her still-swollen eyes eventually focusing on the sign announcing the exit for Dalton, population 21,800. THE CARPET CAPITAL OF NORTH AMERICA, the sign read. Well, why not? she thought absently. America seemed to have a capital for everything else. Why not carpets?

"An amazing sixty-five percent of the world's carpets are made in Dalton," Brad said, his voice full of fake enthusiasm, as if he were auditioning for a job as a TV pitchman.

Jamie wondered if he was stating a fact or making up one to impress her. Yesterday she would have found either alternative endearing.

"I read it in a pamphlet back at the motel," he said, as if monitoring her thoughts. "Apparently, some farm girl supported her family during the Depression by making bedspreads and rugs at home, and other women soon joined her, and before you could say 'magic carpet ride,' Dalton had this booming cottage industry that eventually grew into a multi-billion-dollar business. Pretty impressive, huh?"

Jamie said nothing. Did he really expect her to talk about carpets? Was he trying to charm her by taking over her role as tour guide? Did he really think she could be placated so easily?

"I thought you'd be interested in that stuff, seeing as you're the one who's usually spouting off about these things," he said, once again reaching inside her head.

Jamie froze, afraid to allow her thoughts the freedom to form words, for fear he would usurp them, claim them as his own. Without language there is no thought, she remembered reading somewhere, trying to fill her mind with white noise but unable to ignore the tone of Brad's last statement. The tone warned he was getting impatient with her silence, starting to feel hard done by, as if he were the injured party. Worse—he was getting angry, which meant he could explode at any moment. Jamie decided her best approach was to try not to antagonize him further. If she could just hang on until their next stop, make pleasantly innocuous conversation, convince him that he was on the road to forgiveness, get him to let down his guard, she might be able to make a run for it. "What else did you read about?" she asked, forcing her eyes in his direction. He doesn't look any different, she thought in amazement. He's still handsome. Still radiating that boyish charm. Still smiling that devastating grin. Only her response to him was different. Longing had turned to loathing. Disgust had replaced desire. Fear had banished any thought of love.

"Well, did you know, for example, that this

whole stretch of Georgia is full of Civil War battlefields? We're doing it backward, but I-75 actually follows the route of Sherman's march toward Atlanta. Coming up in another couple of miles is Rocky Face Ridge." He stared at her, as if this should mean something. "That doesn't register with you?"

"Should it?"

"Hell, weren't you paying attention in history class?"

"History was never my strong suit."

He shook his head, as if she'd disappointed him. "I can't believe you don't know this."

Jamie shrugged, afraid to say anything for fear of offending him further.

"Rocky Face Ridge was the scene of a huge battle between General Sherman's army and the Rebel forces. Something like a hundred thousand men fought here. Think it was in 1864, maybe '65."

"Were there a lot of casualties?" Jamie asked, trying to inject some enthusiasm for the topic into her voice.

"Couple thousand, I think."

Jamie nodded, not sure how much longer she could keep up her end of the conversation without bursting into tears.

"And coming up soon, right before we get to the Georgia-Tennessee border, is Ringgold, scene of the great locomotive chase. Surely you remember that."

"Was that where Union soldiers stole a train, and it was chased through the countryside by its crew, half of them on foot?" Jamie couldn't imagine what recess of her brain she'd managed to pull that one out of.

"Hey, pretty good."

"I think I saw a movie about it."

"I saw that movie too," Brad agreed enthusiastically. "They played it on the History Channel one night. It starred Fess Parker. You know who Fess Parker was, right?"

Oh, God, Jamie thought. Who the hell was Fess Parker?

"Fess Parker was the guy who played Davey Crockett and Daniel Boone on TV," Brad answered. "Now if you tell me you don't know who they were—"

"I know who they were."

"Tell me."

Was this some sort of test? Was he going to pull off the side of the road and rape her again if she didn't get the right answer? "Davy Crockett was a frontiersman. . . ."

" 'Davy, Davy Crockett,' " Brad sang. " 'King of the wild frontier.' Go on."

"He was born in 17—" She couldn't do this. What if she made a mistake? What if she got her dates confused? Her voice broke off, threatened tears.

"Born in 1786 in Limestone, Tennessee," Brad recited easily. "Served under Andrew Jackson against the Creek Indians in the war of 1813 to 1814, was elected to the state legislature in 1821, served three terms in Congress, eventually becoming a political opponent of Jackson and a voice of conservatism, ultimately defeated in 1835. He then moved to Texas, where he died defending the Alamo in 1836."

"Wow," Jamie said, impressed in spite of herself.

"Daniel Boone," he continued, obviously

enjoying himself. "Born in 1734, in a little town near Reading, Pennsylvania."

"Another king of the wild frontier," Jamie interjected, noticing Brad's shoulders stiffen with the interruption. She held her breath.

"His family were Quakers, and they left Pennsylvania and settled in the Yadkin valley of North Carolina, where Boone became something of an explorer. He founded Boonesboro on the Kentucky River, and was elected a captain of militia in 1776. Captured by Shawnee Indians during the American Revolution and adopted as a member of the tribe, he escaped after four months and founded a new settlement, Boone's Station, near what is now Athens, Kentucky. He served several terms as representative in the Virginia legislature."

"He was quite a guy," Jamie said, when it became evident she was expected to speak.

"Well, it turns out that a lot of the heroic stories you hear about him aren't true, but so what? Man's a legend, right?"

Jamie smiled with what she hoped passed for admiration. "Right."

"And Fess Parker became this big-shot wine-maker in California."

"Fess Parker," Jamie repeated, shuddering with the realization that just yesterday morning, she would have been hopelessly enthralled by Brad's easy command of historical trivia. "How do you know all this?"

"About Fess Parker? I read it in **People** magazine."

"About Davy Crockett and Daniel Boone," she corrected.

He shrugged. "I had a lot of time on my hands last year. Did some brushing up on my reading."

"A man of many talents," Jamie said.

"What's that supposed to mean?"

"Nothing," Jamie said quickly. "Just that I'm surprised that between running your computer business and designing software programs, you actually found any time to read."

"Sometimes it finds you," Brad said cryptically.

Jamie nodded, too tired and too afraid to ask what he meant. "You're also a man of many surprises," she said finally, all she could muster.

"Not all of them bad, I hope."

Jamie forced herself to smile. "No, not all of them."

"Does this mean we're friends again?" Brad asked after a pause of several seconds.

"Friends?" Jamie strained to keep the incredulity out of her voice.

"You gotta know how sorry I am about what happened."

About what happened, Jamie repeated silently. As if it had been something beyond his control. As if he'd had nothing to do with it. "It didn't just happen," Jamie reminded him.

"I know that. I know I got a little carried away."

"You hurt me, Brad."

"I know that."

"You really hurt me."

"And I'm sorry. I'm so sorry, Jamie. Please. You gotta forgive me. I've been kicking myself all day about it. It's making me crazy. You know I love you, don't you?"

Jamie's eyes filled with tears. Was she going crazy? Could they really be having this discussion? "I'm not sure what I know anymore."

"Aw, come on, Jamie-girl. You gotta know I love you. You might not know anything about Daniel Boone or Davy Crockett, but you gotta know that."

Jamie smiled tentatively.

"That's better," Brad said. "That's more like my Jamie-girl." He reached over and grabbed her thigh.

Instantly Jamie recoiled.

"Hey, take it easy. I'm not trying to start something here." He managed to look both surprised and hurt. "I thought we were past that."

"I guess I just need a little time," Jamie said, her voice a plea.

"Sure. We got time." He grinned. "At least until tonight."

Jamie's stomach lurched at the implications of that sentence.

"You okay?" Brad asked.

"Do you think we can stop soon? I could use some water."

"There's some Coke in the backseat. I bought some when we stopped for gas."

"I'd really prefer water."

"Maybe later."

Jamie closed her eyes, tried counting to ten, and when that failed to calm her, to twenty. "Think we could listen to some music?" she asked when she felt more calm. Somewhere along the way, he'd turned off the radio. At the time, she'd welcomed the silence. Now it felt oppressive. As if she was expected to fill it.

Brad pushed a button and the radio sprang to life, the upbeat twang of Shania Twain filling the car. Jamie hummed along, pretending to be engrossed in the insipid lyrics. "Up, up, up," Shania was singing.

"That's not her real name, you know," Brad said.

"It isn't?"

"No. Her real name's Eileen, if you can believe it. She comes from some little town in northern Ontario. Her parents were killed in a car crash, and she raised all her brothers and sisters by herself."

Jamie nodded. The story sounded vaguely familiar. "**People** magazine?"

"**Entertainment Tonight.**"

"You watch a lot of TV?"

"Some. You?"

"More than I should."

"Says who? Your mother and sister?"

"I don't remember my mother ever watching television. My sister claims she never watches anything but PBS."

"She's a liar."

"I don't think so. She's a lawyer and—"

"What? Lawyers never lie?"

"I just meant that between her practice and her family, I don't think she has a lot of time for TV, so she's very picky about what she **does** watch."

"Bullshit."

Jamie shrugged. She never thought she'd find herself in the position of having to defend her sister. Or wanting to.

"What do you call a hundred lawyers at the bottom of the ocean?" Brad asked, already smiling at the punch line to follow.

Jamie shook her head. She didn't know. She didn't care.

"A start." Brad laughed.

She wondered if her sister had heard that one. Cynthia hated lawyer jokes. She claimed they were no better than racist slurs. "My sister says everybody hates lawyers until they need one."

"And then they hate them even more." Brad took a deep breath. "Lying, scum-sucking bastards. Somebody should round them all up and shoot them."

Jamie gasped at the vehemence of his assertion.

"Okay, we won't shoot your sister," he said, softening.

She tried to smile. "You sound like you've had some bad experiences with lawyers."

"Everybody has bad experiences with lawyers."

"I think my sister is a very good one."

"Yeah? How would you know? You ever watched her in court?"

"She doesn't go to court. She's not a litigator." LITIG8R, Jamie thought, remembering the first day of their trip, how long ago that seemed now, her misplaced hope, her lost innocence.

"What kind of law does she practice?"

"Corporate-commercial mostly, tax law, stuff like that."

"Sounds like a lot of laughs."

"She seems to like it."

"She likes the money."

"Everybody likes money."

"Ain't that the truth."

The truth, Jamie thought. What did that mean? Had anything he'd said to her over the course of the last few days been the truth?

Did you really sell your computer business for an outlandish profit? she wanted to ask. Did you even **own** a computer business? Are you really a designer of software? Were you really staying at the Breakers because the lease on your apartment was up?

Do you really have an ex-wife and a young

son in Ohio? What really happened after she fled Laura Dennison's house?

"Who's Grace Hastings?" she asked, the question jumping the queue to fall from the tip of her tongue.

"What?"

"Grace Hastings," Jamie repeated. "Who is she, Brad?" She spoke his name in a conscious effort to show that she was starting to relate to him again on a more personal level, that they were beginning to reconnect.

It seemed to work. He smiled, patted her hand as Jamie tried not to flinch or pull away. "Nobody you have to worry about."

"You had her credit card."

"Yeah, a lot of good it did me."

"Still . . ."

"Grace was a friend of Beth's."

"Beth?"

"My ex."

"Oh, right." Jamie paused. Less than twenty-four hours ago, she'd considered Beth Fisher both the luckiest and stupidest woman on earth. Lucky for having been married to

Brad, stupid for having left him. As for the title Stupidest Woman on Earth—it was all hers now. "What does she look like?"

Brad yawned, as if the topic were of little or no concern. "She's pretty enough, I guess. What difference does it make?"

"I'm just curious."

"Yeah, well, you know what they say about curiosity."

"Just that I have these opposing pictures in my mind."

"What kind of pictures?"

"One is tall, blond, kind of ethereal."

"Ethereal? What's that?"

"Extremely delicate, kind of angelic."

Brad shook his head. "Delicate, huh? Angelic?" He laughed derisively. "And the other picture?"

"She's shorter, darker, stronger."

"Guess she's a bit of both," Brad said, and laughed again.

"And your son?" Did he even have a son? she wondered.

"What about him?"

"I forget what you told me his name is," Jamie lied.

"His name's Corey," Brad said as his face went dark.

So he **did** have a son, Jamie thought. He wasn't lying about that.

The song ended, Shania disappeared, and the DJ announced it was time for the news. There followed a story about the latest skirmish in Iraq and the most recent suicide bombing in Israel. A woman in Oklahoma had been awarded a substantial settlement against a local furniture store after she'd tripped over an unruly child and broken her leg while shopping for a new sofa, this despite the fact the unruly child was her own.

"I should have had **her** lawyer," Brad remarked.

"Why did you need a lawyer?"

"**Still no answers in the brutal slaying of an Atlanta woman early this morning,**" the announcer continued.

Brad switched the channels.

"Wait. What was that?" Please let there be a mistake, Jamie was thinking, her mind racing in several different directions at once. Please let me have misheard. Let the newscaster be talking about somebody else. Don't let it be what I think it is.

"**Fresh crisis in the Middle East,**" another announcer was saying.

Again Brad changed the channel.

"I'm Margaret Sokoloff and this is the four o'clock news."

Once more, the channel abruptly disappeared, to be replaced by another. "**Police are still puzzling over the brutal murder of an Atlanta woman in the early hours of the morning,**" a man intoned.

"Leave it," Jamie urged as Brad's hand ran out of buttons to push.

"Jamie—"

"Leave it."

Brad shrugged. "Whatever you say."

"The body of Laura Dennison, age fifty-seven, was discovered by her son, Mark

Dennison, at eight o'clock this morning when he stopped by for breakfast on his way to work."

Jamie felt her body go instantly numb. Please God, this wasn't happening.

"The Buckhead resident had been beaten to death. Police say they are currently without suspects in the vicious slaying and are refusing to speculate—"

The sound of Jamie's ragged breathing filled the car as Brad snapped off the radio. "Now don't start getting all upset."

"You killed her," Jamie whispered as the scenery began spinning around her.

"Hey, she had it coming, after all the mean things she did to you."

"You killed her."

"It was an accident, Jamie."

"An accident?"

"I was just trying to protect you."

"Protect **me**?"

"She recognized you, Jamie. I tried to reason with her. I tried to tell her I'd never heard of anybody named Jamie, but she just laughed in my face. I tried to explain that we only wanted what was rightfully yours, and that's when she started screaming, said she was going to call the police, said she was going to see you rot in jail for the rest of your life. And I couldn't let that happen. So I hit her. But the old bitch kept on screaming. So I had to keep hitting her until she stopped."

"You told me you were able to persuade her. . . ."

"You were freaking out. What else was I supposed to tell you? You didn't really believe any of that crap. I know you didn't."

He was right, Jamie realized, the revelation rendering her mute. She'd known the truth all along. What other truth could there be?

"I did it for you, Jamie-girl."

Jamie pressed her forehead against the car's side window. She closed her eyes and prayed for oblivion.

CHAPTER TWENTY-THREE

Lily sat at her kitchen table, pen poised over a blank sheet of paper, trying to corral the series of random thoughts that were circling her brain like a bunch of noisy insects, to give them structure and direction, infuse them with something approaching drama. Except how much drama could she create out of a Sunday afternoon spent chaperoning two five-year-old boys at the movies? Unless she was a deranged, sexually repressed babysitter and one of the boys an alien spawn or a precocious serial killer. And hadn't those ideas been done already?

Not that it mattered. Give a hundred writers the same idea and you'll get a hundred different stories, she recalled one of her creative writing teachers saying. So while a good idea was always an asset, what was even more important was what one did with it. And right now, unfortunately, she wasn't doing much of anything.

Stick to what you know, she thought. "Well, I know sexual repression, that's for sure." Or at the very least, sexual frustration, she silently amended, wondering how long it had been since she'd had sex. Who was she kidding? she thought impatiently. She knew exactly how long it had been. Her mind raced back to that March night almost fourteen months ago, and she jumped to her feet, refusing to think of it further. She went to the sink and poured herself a glass of cold water, although she wasn't thirsty, and stared out the back window at the darkening sky. It was almost eight o'clock. The days were definitely getting longer. Time was moving so quickly. Summer would be here before she knew it. And then fall. And then another winter. Another March. How much more time could she afford to waste? "At some point I have to get on with my life," she announced to the surrounding silence. "Get moving," she said. "Get laid." She wondered what Jeff Dawson was doing, wondered what he'd look like naked. "Oh, please," she groused, gulping down her water, as if to douse whatever fires might be smoldering inside her, then returned to her seat at the kitchen table. She regripped her pen, tighter than required, so that the nail from her index finger was digging uncomfortably into the side of her middle finger. She thought for several seconds, then scribbled down a few words, underlining them with exaggerated care.

Moving On
By Lily Rogers

"So far, so good." She looked to the ceiling. "Now what?"

I should probably check on Michael, she decided, half out of her chair before she reminded herself she'd looked in on him less than ten minutes before. He was sound asleep, exhausted from his busy day. She glanced at her watch, noting barely a minute had passed since her last peek. She could watch TV, she thought. Or read. Or phone Jeff Dawson, tell him again how much she'd enjoyed their evening together, maybe suggest he might like to drop over for a cup of coffee. Naked. "Oh, for God's sake. Get a grip."

Moving On
By Lily Rogers

It suddenly occurred to Nancy Firestone as she was walking her young son home from school that three of the men she'd slept with in the last five years were dead.

"Oh, my," Lily said, staring at the piece of paper. Where had that come from?

She was supposed to be writing about what she knew, and the truth was she'd only been with one man in the last five years.

One had died of a heart attack, one had succumbed to a brain tumor, and the third had driven his motorcycle into a massive, and massively unforgiving, trunk of a tree.

"Oh, that's great. Just great." Lily ripped the paper from its pad and tore it into half a dozen pieces, crumpling the pieces in her fists before throwing them to the floor. What had she just decided about moving on? She started again.

Moving On
By Lily Rogers

It suddenly occurred to Nancy Firestone as she was walking her daughter home from school that three of the men she'd slept with in the last five years were dead. One had been hit by a car as he was crossing a busy intersection, one had been felled by a sudden heart attack, and the third had been shot in the head by person or persons unknown.

"That's better." If she wasn't going to stick with what she knew, she might as well go all out. Except, where exactly was she supposed to go now? "I should describe her."

At five feet ten and a half inches, Nancy Firestone was taller than she should have been, considering neither of her parents

stood taller than five and a half feet. Her nose was long, her lips full, her hair a shade too black for her pale complexion. But by far her most outstanding feature was her eyes, which were big and blue and always seemed to know more than they were letting on. Her eyes were full of secrets, a man had once whispered in her ear, and Nancy had thrown her head back and laughed out loud.

Lily lowered her pen to the table, wondering at what point Nancy Firestone had morphed into Emma Frost. And what had Dylan meant this afternoon when he said his mother had been named after Rachel's baby on **Friends**?

"You mean they have the same name," she'd corrected absently as the lights in the movie theater grew dim. She'd watched Dylan dig his little fist into his large bag of buttered popcorn, scattering almost half the popcorn into her lap in the process.

"No," he'd insisted, scrambling to scoop up the errant kernels, shoveling one handful of popcorn after another into his mouth, as if he were afraid she might snatch the whole bag away from him without warning. "She had another name before, except I'm not supposed to tell anybody that."

He'd then gone on to state that Dylan wasn't his real name either, that it was the name of some kid who lived in Beverly Hills, and he didn't like it, so his mother had promised he could choose his own name next time. Except he wasn't supposed to tell anybody that either. Lily had smiled and assured him his secret was safe with her.

Lily shook her head in grudging admiration. She could use some of Dylan's overactive imagination right about now.

He was such a strange little boy, she decided. Silent and wary one minute, voluble and open the next. Fearless in so many ways, and yet afraid of his own shadow. He blew hot and cold, as her mother used to say. Rather like Emma in that regard, Lily thought. You never quite knew what either of them was thinking or where you stood. Like tonight, when she'd brought Dylan home. Emma had been polite but distant, looking through her instead of at her, barely acknowledging Lily's compliment about her hair, the unmistakable odor of freshly smoked cigarettes clinging to her pretty, peach cardigan like adhesive tape. "That's a pretty sweater," Lily said, trying again. "Is it new?"

"No, of course not," came Emma's sharp response, when a simple no would have sufficed.

"You stink!" Dylan had suddenly shouted, bursting into tears and accusing his mother of reneging on her promise to quit smoking.

Emma had insisted she reeked of tobacco only because she'd had coffee with an old friend who "smoked like a chimney."

"What old friend?" Dylan asked, although his question went unanswered, even after he asked it a second time.

Two angry, red circles had materialized on Emma's cheeks, and she'd hurriedly thanked Lily for showing her son such a good time. Then she'd effectively showed Lily the door. "Thanks again," she'd said as the screen door closed in Lily's face.

What was that all about? Lily wondered now, trying not to make too much of it. After all, Emma had always been more than a little aloof. It wasn't until the mix-up with the mail that she'd deigned to acknowledge Lily with more than the occasional wave. Still, Lily had hoped they were on the road to becoming friends. Had something happened today to make Emma change her mind?

"Okay," Lily said, turning her attention back to her writing and picking up her pen, flipping to a new, blank page. "How about we try something a little different?"

Moving On
By Lily Rogers

It had been almost two years since Nancy Firestone had sex.

Uh-oh.

The last time had been, as the saying went, nasty, brutish, and short. A fitting end to a marriage that had been an ill fit from the start.

Lily stared at the sentences she'd just written, her breath freezing in her lungs. What was she doing? She tore the page from the pad in one determined swipe, squishing the offending words into a tight ball before hurling the paper across the room, where it bounced toward the previous reject. What the hell was she doing?

She regripped her pen, began scribbling furiously on the next page.

Moving On
By Lily Rogers

It had been almost two years since Nancy Firestone had sex. Two years of loneliness and longing and lies.

Again Lily's hand reached out to shred her own words. "What's the matter with you, for God's sake? Now don't write anything stupid."

Moving On
By Lily Rogers

It had been almost two years since Nancy Firestone had sex. She decided the time had come to do something about it.

"Thatta girl, Nancy. That's more like it." Lily jumped to her feet with such vehemence, the chair she'd been sitting on fell backward to the floor. She left it lying on its side as she grabbed her purse from the kitchen counter and ferreted around inside, her fingers brushing against the card she was looking for. She pulled it out and stared at the numbers printed neatly across it, committing them to memory without meaning to, then punching in the numbers on her phone before she had a chance to think too long about what she was doing. "Two years without sex is two years too long," she said out loud, listening as the phone rang once, twice, three times.

It was answered in the middle of its fourth ring. "Hi, there," Jeff Dawson said, as if he knew it was her, as if he'd been expecting her to call.

Well, of course. Caller ID, Lily thought. Was that what had taken him so long to pick up the phone? Had he been deciding whether or not he wanted to speak to her? "Hi, it's Lily. Lily Rogers," she added, in case he knew more than one Lily, in case he'd already wiped her from his memory. Maybe she should have said Nancy Firestone, she thought. Nancy Firestone would know what to say next.

Except that Jeff Dawson wasn't listening. He was still speaking. **"This is Jeff Dawson, and this is a recording."**

"Oh, great." She hadn't had sex in so long, she was no longer able to differentiate between a recording and the real thing.

"I can't come to the phone at the moment, but if you'll leave your name and number, and a short message after the beep, I'll get back to you as soon as possible."

"I don't think so." Lily hung up the phone. Well, of course he's out. Why wouldn't he be? You didn't really expect him to be sitting home, waiting for you to call, did you? "Would have been nice." She stood for a few minutes in the middle of the kitchen, then marched from the room.

A minute later, she was perched on the end of her bed, flipping through the channels of her small TV. "Surely I can find **something.**" Except after zapping twice through all the channels, she was dismayed to discover there wasn't a single program on television she was interested in watching. What was the matter with her? Why was she so restless? She'd had a nice day—the art gallery had been as wonderful as Jeff had intimated, and the movie, an animated film about fast-talking sharks and other assorted, deep-sea wheeler-dealers, had been a pleasant diversion. She'd feasted on McDonald's fries and movie popcorn, and Michael had given her no trouble at bedtime, so why was she feeling so out of sorts?

Was Emma's mood contagious? Was she upset because Jeff hadn't called? Or was she just horny? Lily shrugged, unable to shake the unwelcome feeling that something was about to happen. Something unpleasant.

She laughed. How many times had she had that feeling over the last year? And had anything ever happened? No. In fact, the only time things seemed to happen was when she least expected them, when she was least prepared to deal with them. Had she had any inkling of her husband's terrible secret? Had she had even a flicker of precognition that Kenny was about to crash his motorcycle into a tree?

Lily stared at the television set, her thumb releasing its pressure on the remote control as a lovely old house at the end of a tree-lined lane came into sharp focus.

"Does Atlanta have another serial killer on its hands?" a sonorous, male voice asked as a photograph of an attractive, older woman replaced the view of the quiet street. "No further developments in the brutal slaying of a wealthy Atlanta widow in the early hours of the morning," the announcer from CNN continued solemnly as a scroll of the day's headlines raced across the bottom of the screen. "Laura Dennison, age fifty-seven, was found by her son, Mark Dennison, at approximately eight o'clock this morning. The Georgia woman had been struck repeatedly in the head by a blunt instrument. At this time, police are refusing to speculate whether this latest killing is related to two other killings of elderly women in the Atlanta area in the last eight months."

"At this time, we have no reason to suspect these cases are in any way related," a police officer insisted with obvious impatience, trying to escape the microphone bobbing frantically up and down in front of his face.

"But residents of this upscale suburb of Atlanta are far from convinced," the announcer continued, the camera zeroing in on a number of concerned Atlanta residents.

"Of course I'm scared," one senior citizen railed at the camera. "What are the police doing to protect us?"

"Three women have been murdered in the last eight months," another said angrily. "Of course it's the work of a serial killer. How long can the police keep denying the obvious?"

"One doesn't expect this sort of thing to happen in a place like Buckhead."

Lily turned off the TV. She didn't want to hear about serial killers prowling the streets, especially when the police seemed as powerless as everyone else.

Might as well start the Steinbeck, she decided, pushing herself off her bed and heading back down the stairs, wondering how many of her fellow book club members would actually read the book this time. At least I'm getting some exercise, she thought, jumping off the bottom step and turning into the living room, spotting a man's shadow through the sheer curtains.

She gasped, and the figure froze, tilting his head toward her. "Oh, God," she whispered as the figure dashed out of sight. Almost immediately, there was a knock on her front door, tentative at first, and then stronger, more insistent.

Lily moved warily into the hall.

"Lily?" a man's voice asked through the double set of doors. "Lily? It's Jeff Dawson. Are you there?"

Lily pulled open the front door, stared through the screen at the detective.

"I'm sorry. Did I scare you?"

Lily laughed, feeling simultaneously foolish and relieved. "I was watching this story on TV about a serial killer in Atlanta. . . ."

"And you thought he'd taken a detour onto Mad River Road?"

"I guess it spooked me. Come on in."

"I'm not disturbing you?"

"Not at all."

"I was in the neighborhood," he began, then stopped. "Actually, I was on the other side of town." He stepped inside, and Lily closed the door after him. "How's that for playing hard to get?"

Lily smiled. "I was never very big on games."

"Good. I was never very good at them."

"Actually I called **you** a few minutes ago," she admitted.

"You did? Why?"

"I was hoping you might like to come over for a cup of coffee."

"I'd love a cup of coffee."

"Well, good thing I called then." They laughed as Lily led the way to the kitchen, feeling giddy and light-headed.

"My God, what happened in here?"

Lily's eyes took in the overturned chair and

discarded clumps of paper scattered across the floor. Quickly, she righted the chair and tossed the paper balls into the garbage pail underneath the sink. "I got a little frustrated with a story I was working on."

"Anything I can help you with?"

You can take your clothes off and make mad, passionate love to me right here on the kitchen table, Lily thought, measuring out enough coffee for six cups and pouring cold water into the coffeemaker, concentrating on keeping her hands steady. Not playing hard to get was one thing; making a fool of herself was quite another. "Is decaf all right?" she asked, turning around as he stepped toward her.

The kiss that followed was both soft and urgent, everything she'd been fantasizing about all day. She fought to keep her hands at her sides, afraid if she touched him, she wouldn't be able to stop until she'd succeeded in ripping off all his clothes. Maybe they could do it standing up, she found herself thinking. Then, what was the matter with her? What if her son were to wake up and come downstairs, find them passionately going at it against the kitchen cupboards? "So, I took the boys to the art gallery today, like you suggested, and it was great, they loved it," she whispered in a conscious effort to slow things down.

"Boys?" he asked, finding her lips, kissing her again.

"Michael and Dylan. Emma's son." She suddenly felt Jeff stiffen, his lips retreat. "Jeff? What's wrong?" Had talk of her son succeeded in not only slowing things down but in killing them altogether?

Jeff took a step back, leaned against the kitchen table, staring at her through a policeman's eyes. "How well do you know this Emma Frost?"

What was happening? "I don't understand."

"Your friend, Emma. How long have you known her?"

Why was he asking that? "Well, we've been neighbors for a while, but it's only in the last few days that we've become friendly. Why? What's going on?"

"What can you tell me about her?"

"Why should I tell you anything?" Lily heard the defensiveness in her voice and wondered what exactly she was defending.

"I saw her earlier today."

"Oh?" Was he the old friend Emma had spoken of having coffee with, the one who supposedly "smoked like a chimney"? "You had coffee with her?"

"Yes, but only after. . . ."

"After?" Dear God, Lily thought. After what?

"After I caught her shoplifting."

"What!"

"In Marshalls. I almost arrested her."

"What!" Lily said again, the only word her tongue seemed capable of formulating.

"The only reason I didn't was because she's your friend."

"This is ridiculous. I can't imagine Emma ever stealing anything."

"She stole a blouse and a scarf, and a pair of earrings, and God only knows what else she had on underneath her clothing," Jeff enumerated.

Lily suddenly pictured Emma in her pretty,

peach-colored sweater. Was that why Emma had refused to look her in the eye when she'd brought Dylan home?

"Tell me what you know about her."

"I don't know much," Lily conceded. "Just that she used to be a model."

"What else?"

"That she sold a story to **Cosmopolitan** magazine."

"You saw it?"

"Well, no. She left it behind when she left her marriage."

"And she left her marriage because . . . ?"

"Because her ex was some kind of pervert. He was into child pornography. That kind of stuff."

"She ever say where he lives?"

Lily shook her head. He was starting to scare her. "You think she's lying?"

"She told me her family moved around a lot because her father was in the army."

"Well, that's not unusual, from what I understand about army brats."

"Except there are no army bases in Miami

and Detroit, two of the places she says they lived, and when I called her on it, she made up some crazy story about her mother being transferred between school boards."

"Her mother was a school principal," Lily confirmed. "Maybe she just went wherever opportunity took her."

"Emma said her father was killed in Vietnam when she was a child," Jeff countered.

"So?"

"Kind of difficult, since the war ended before she was born."

"Oh, God." She'd left her son with this woman, Lily was thinking. "Her son said something kind of peculiar this afternoon," she said, remembering. "I thought it was just his imagination. . . ."

"What did he say?"

"That his real name wasn't Dylan, that his mother's name wasn't really Emma, but that he wasn't supposed to tell anybody. Do you think that could be true?"

"I think I trust Dylan more than I trust his mother," Jeff said.

"But if she isn't Emma Frost," Lily began, "then who is she?"

Jeff said nothing. It was his silence that did the talking. I don't know, his silence told her. But I'm going to do my damndest to find out.

CHAPTER TWENTY-FOUR

Jamie sat huddled against the ugly, dark wood headboard of the lumpy double bed, trying not to cry. Brad had told her to stop crying, and it was important that she do as she was told because she didn't want to make him angry. If she made him angry—and she had made him angry many times over the course of the long afternoon—then he might hit her again. And she couldn't risk that. Especially now. Now when he was finally relaxed and happy, his fists resting comfortably at his sides as he lay stretched out along the foot of the bed, his feet dangling over one end of the hideous, mustard-and-green quilted bedspread, his eye glued to the TV screen.

He let out a sudden whoop of laughter and

turned his head toward Jamie. "Hah!" he shouted. "Did you hear that, Jamie-girl?"

Hear what? she wondered, her spine stiffening against the hard wood of the headboard. Was it real wood or imitation? she wondered absently, afraid to allow her mind to consider other, more urgent, matters. Like how to get out of this terrible little room in this horrible, cheap motel. Like how to get away from this awful man who continued to profess his love while slapping her so hard across the face, she'd heard her teeth rattle against her ears. To think she'd ever found him handsome, she marveled now, seeing his poisonous smile slither into the blue of his eyes, then quickly banishing such unwanted thoughts from her mind. He'd see them there, she was thinking. He'd see them there and hit her again.

"You didn't hear that?" he asked.

"I'm sorry," Jamie said quickly. She should have heard. She should have been paying attention.

"What are you sorry about?"

"Nothing. I'm sorry," Jamie apologized again.

Brad propped himself up on his elbows and laughed. "It's good news, Jamie-girl," he said. "You're home free. The Atlanta police think they got a serial killer on their hands. Can you beat that?"

"What?" What was he saying?

"They think your mother-in-law was murdered by some dumb-ass serial killer."

Why would they think that? Jamie wondered.

"Apparently two other old ladies got their heads beat in this past year," Brad answered, as if she'd asked the question out loud.

He sees inside my brain, Jamie understood. He knows my every thought. That's why it was so important to keep her mind blank, her head clear.

"Dumb cops." He laughed again. "Hey," he said, glancing at the round, wooden table that stood between the bed and the window. "You still haven't eaten your dinner."

"I couldn't." The thought of food made her sick.

Brad swung his feet off the bed and walked

to the table, picking up the paper bag containing a by-now cold cheeseburger and fries, and tossing it toward the bed. It landed in Jamie's lap, the unmistakable odor of McDonald's bouncing nauseatingly toward her nose. "You gotta keep up your strength, Jamie," he said, as if her welfare was his chief concern. "Come on. Eat up."

Jamie dragged the bag up her chest, unfolding the cellophane wrapping and fighting back the almost overpowering urge to gag as she nibbled tentatively at the bun.

"That's my girl," Brad said, and Jamie remembered how thrilled she'd been the first time he'd called her his girl. "Come on. Have some fries." He walked to her side, stood over her, waiting.

"I don't think I can," Jamie ventured.

"You didn't eat any lunch, Jamie," Brad scolded. "Now, come on. Don't give me a hard time."

Immediately Jamie scooped a bunch of fries into her hand and forced them between her lips. Whatever you do, don't be sick, she told herself. He'll get mad if you get sick, say you're doing it on purpose, that enough is enough, and if you're going to keep acting like a child, he's going to have to treat you like a child. Words to that effect. The same words he'd used when they checked into this miserable place. The same words he'd used just before he hit her again. She stuffed another handful of fries into her mouth, took a bigger bite of her burger.

"That's better." He returned to his previous position at the foot of the bed. "Hey, maybe there's a Chuck Norris movie on we can watch." He began zapping through the channels, although there wasn't much choice, and he quickly found himself back at CNN. "Cheap bastards. What kind of motel doesn't even carry TNT?" He laughed. "Things'll be better tomorrow. We'll get us a fresh infusion of cash tomorrow, then we can head for the nearest Ritz. No more of this shit."

"How?" Jamie wondered, dropping her cheeseburger to her lap when she realized she'd spoken the word out loud.

Brad winked back in her direction. "You let me worry about that. How you making out with that burger?"

Once again Jamie lifted the Big Mac to her mouth, forcing herself to chew even as her taste buds grew numb. With any luck, the numbness would spread to her entire body. With any luck, the numbness would overtake her soul.

She closed her eyes, leaned back, felt her body sway, as if she were still in the passenger seat of her car. They'd driven more than six hours today, stopping only once, outside of Williamsburg, for gas, and so that she could use the bathroom. Brad had actually gone inside the bathroom with her, standing just outside her stall, like that deranged derelict in Florida on the first day of their trip. How long ago had that been? Jamie wondered. A lifetime ago, she thought.

Laura Dennison's lifetime ago.

"Oh, God."

"What's the matter?" Brad asked impatiently. "You aren't gonna be sick again, are you?"

Jamie shook her head, took another bite of her Big Mac, as if offering proof of her stomach's newfound stability.

"Well, thank Christ for that. Don't think I could take any more of that nonsense."

She'd thrown up three times since they'd left Dalton, once just outside of Knoxville, where Brad had barely managed to get the car over to the side of the road in time, and again as the car was mounting the steep uphill grade of the highway that had been cut right into the side of Pine Mountain, not far from the Tennessee-Kentucky border. That time Brad hadn't even bothered to pull the car over, reasoning, correctly, as it turned out, that there was nothing left in her stomach to worry about. He told her then that he thought she was doing it on purpose, and that the sound of her retching was starting to get on his nerves. Jamie laughed in disbelief, a derisive snort that escaped her lips before she had time to censor her reaction. That was the first time he hit her, the back of his hand catching the side of her head, causing a series of vibrations, like shivers, to shoot between her ears. She cried out, and he hit her again, this time splitting her lip. He told her that if she made any more noise, he'd snap her neck like a twig, then ditch her body at the side of the road.

She was quiet after that.

At Berea, population 9,200, they passed the first of half a dozen police cars they were to see that day, and Jamie held her breath, as she did each subsequent time a state trooper came into view, praying one would pull them over. But Brad stuck resolutely to the speed limit, and her tires stayed stubbornly full of air, and so the police took no notice of them. They drove past the exits for Lexington, population 241,800, Georgetown, population 11,400, and Florence, whose population was too small to consider noteworthy, despite its enormous water tower with the words **FLORENCE Y'ALL** printed in huge letters across it—until they reached Cincinnati, population 1,820,000. "Almost there," Brad said, announcing, with something approaching glee, that Dayton was a mere half hour drive away.

Which was when Jamie threw up the third time. This time Brad waited until he'd checked them into a rundown motel just south of Middleton, population 46,000, to hit her again.

Jamie lowered the food to her lap, brought her fingers to her mouth, gingerly patted the spot where he'd hit her. No one had ever struck her before. Not her mother. Not Tim Rannells. Not even Mark Dennison.

"Stop playing with your lip," Brad told her, although she hadn't seen him turn around. "You'll make it bleed again."

Jamie dropped her hand as Brad crawled up the bed to her side.

"Here," he said, leaning his head toward her. "Let me kiss it and make it better."

Jamie held her breath as his lips touched hers, burning into her bruised and tender flesh, like acid.

"You finished your dinner?" he asked, checking inside the paper bag.

"I can't eat any more, Brad," she cried softly.

Please don't make me eat any more, she begged silently.

"That's okay, Jamie-girl," he said soothingly. "Looks like you did a pretty good job for somebody who said she wasn't hungry."

Jamie nodded gratefully. She'd done a pretty good job. He was happy with her.

"You know what I think you should do now?" he asked suddenly.

Jamie shook her head, afraid to ask what.

"I think you should call your sister."

"My sister?"

"You told her you were gonna call her in a few days, and I think you should do that."

"You want me to call my sister?" Jamie repeated in disbelief.

"Well, she's probably heard the news about that old bitch in Atlanta getting her head bashed in, and we don't want her getting any funny ideas, now do we? So I think you should call her, set her mind at rest." He reached for the phone, handed it to Jamie. "Tell her . . . tell her you're in Savannah—that's somewhere I've always wanted to go—and that you're having the time of your life. Go on," he directed, grabbing the phone from the end table and dropping it in her lap. "I think you gotta press eight or nine first for an outside line."

Jamie slowly lifted the receiver and dialed her sister's number, pressing the phone tight against her ear. What could she say to her? she wondered. How could she begin to tell her the kind of trouble she was in?

"Remember I'm hanging on your every word," Brad warned, extricating the knife from his side pocket and waving it lazily back and forth as he snuggled up against her.

The phone was picked up as it was beginning its second ring. "Hello?" a tiny voice chirped.

A press of a button. The blade of a knife.

"Melissa?" Jamie asked, her eyes welling at the sound of her three-year-old niece's voice.

"Yes. Who's this?"

"It's your auntie Jamie, honey."

"**Who** is it?"

"It's Jamie," Jamie repeated, louder this time.

"Who is it, Melissa?" she heard her sister ask in the background.

Maybe if she started screaming, Jamie thought. Except that once she started screaming, she knew she'd never stop.

Until he stopped her.

The way he'd stopped Laura Dennison.

"Melissa, let me speak to your mother," she said sharply.

"Hello?" Cynthia said in the next second.

Jamie pictured her sister in the middle of her spotless kitchen, a law book in one hand, a recipe book in the other, little Tyler perfectly balanced on one hip, Melissa playing happily at her mother's feet.

"Hello?" Cynthia said again. Her tone said she didn't have time for games. "Hello?"

"Say hello to your sister, Jamie," Brad whispered.

"Cynthia, it's me."

"Jamie? Jamie, where are you? Todd, it's Jamie."

"Where is she?" she heard Todd bellow.

"Where the hell are you?" Cynthia repeated. "We've been worried sick."

"Tell her you're in Savannah," Brad directed, his hand covering the receiver. "Tell her you're fine."

"Everything's fine, Cynthia. I'm in Savannah."

"Savannah? She's in Savannah," she heard Cynthia tell her husband. "Thank God. We've been so worried. I didn't know what to think, especially after . . . Have you been watching CNN?"

Brad nodded.

"Yes," Jamie said, following his lead. "I couldn't believe it."

"We didn't know what to think. I mean, obviously I never believed you had anything to do with what happened to Mrs. Dennison, but you'd been acting so strangely lately, quitting your job and taking off the way you did, and I know how much you hated that woman, and then not hearing from you, well, let's just say I'm really glad you called. When are you coming home?"

Brad shrugged.

"I'm not sure."

"What do you mean, you're not sure?"

"Another week or two," Brad whispered.

"Another week or two," Jamie mimicked.

"A week or two? Jamie, what's going on?"

"There's nothing going on."

"Please promise me you didn't get married again."

"What?"

"We both know how impulsive you can be. I'm just hoping you learned your lesson after the last time."

"I didn't get married again." The conversation was becoming surreal.

Brad put a hand over his mouth, in an effort to keep from laughing out loud.

"You swear?"

"Goddamn it, Cynthia . . ."

"Okay, good enough. She didn't get married," Cynthia told her husband. "So, what are you doing exactly? Are you alone?"

"You're with friends," Brad mouthed.

"I'm with some friends."

"What friends? You don't have any friends."

Oh, God, thought Jamie. This would be funny if it weren't so pathetic.

"Tell her you have to go," Brad said, making circle motions with his knife, signaling her to speed things up.

"I have to go now, Cynthia," Jamie told her sister.

"Wait! Something's wrong. I can feel it."

"There's nothing wrong."

"You promise?"

"I'm fine, Cynthia. You don't have to worry about me."

"Oh, sure. Like that's ever gonna happen."

"Give my love to the kids, and give Todd a really big, sloppy kiss for me."

"What?!"

"I love you."

There was a pause. Jamie could almost see the confusion on her sister's face.

"I love you too," Cynthia said.

"I'll call you in a couple of days." Jamie quickly hung up the phone, her heart racing.

"Good girl," Brad said.

Jamie nodded, wondering if Cynthia had understood her pitiful cry for help. Surely she would know that the last thing Jamie would ever advise her to do was give her husband a big, sloppy kiss, even if she liked the man. It wasn't much, but along with the equally uncharacteristic expression of sibling love, it might be just enough for Cynthia to twig to the fact that something was indeed terribly wrong. Was it enough to have her call the police, alert them to the possibility her sister was in some kind of trouble, that they should be on the lookout for an old blue Thunderbird? Jamie tried imagining the conversation between Cynthia and her husband.

That was peculiar, she heard Cynthia say.

And that surprises you? Todd asked in return. **This is your sister we're talking about, remember?**

She just told me to give you a big, sloppy kiss.

She's probably been drinking, her brother-in-law said, dismissing his wife's concerns.

She told me she loves me.

For sure, she's been drinking.

Yeah. I guess you're right, she heard Cynthia agree. **God, do you think she's ever gonna get her act together?**

Jamie closed her eyes. Her sister wouldn't be calling the police. Instead she'd finish feeding her husband and children their dinner, then she'd tidy up some legal work from the office, maybe return a couple of phone calls, then read for a while before going to bed. Maybe she and Todd would make love, maybe not. Maybe she'd wonder about her older sister for a few minutes before drifting off to sleep. Probably not. Thinking about her big sister was too frustrating, too exhausting. It was the stuff of nightmares.

She's not your problem, she heard Todd say as Brad returned the phone to the end table beside the bed.

"So, what's the problem, Jamie-girl?" Brad was asking now. "Feeling a little homesick?"

Jamie stared up at the man standing beside the bed. She watched him as he raised his arms high in the air above his head in a protracted stretch, the knife a natural extension of his hand, as if it were part of his flesh, an extra finger. "Who are you?" Jamie asked, the question escaping her mouth on a sigh. She shuddered, bracing herself for the back of his hand.

Instead Brad laughed. "What kind of question is that?"

"You never designed any software, did you?"

He laughed louder. "I don't know a goddamn thing about software."

"And there's no computer company. . . ."

"That I sold for a vast fortune? No, 'fraid not."

Jamie nodded acceptance of what she already knew. "Is your name even Brad Fisher?"

"Well, the Fisher part's real. I borrowed the Brad from Mr. Pitt. Didn't think he'd mind. Pitt," he repeated. "Terrible last name. Can't understand why he didn't change it. Sounds like something you spit out." He snapped the knife closed, returned it to the pocket of his jeans.

"What **is** your name?"

"What difference does it make?"

"None, I guess," Jamie said. What difference did anything make anymore?

"Ralph's the name on my birth certificate,"

he told her, staring at his reflection in the mirror on top of the dresser across from the bed. "Same name as my father." He ran a hand through his short-cropped, brown hair. "Always hated that name. I'm **Brad** Fisher now. New name. New haircut. New girl."

"Those things you told me about your father," Jamie began, ignoring his last statement and emboldened by his unexpected willingness to talk.

"What about them?"

"Were any of them true?"

"You mean about the time I took Miss Carrie-Leigh Jones out for a spin in my dad's new car?"

Jamie nodded, watching Brad's hands form fists at his side.

"Yeah. That one's true."

"He beat you?"

Brad said nothing, although the face in the mirror grew dark.

"What about your mother?" Jamie asked.

"What about her?"

"Did she ever try to stop him?"

"Oh, yeah." Brad laughed. "And she's got the scars to prove it."

"He beat her too?"

"It was kind of what you'd call a family tradition."

"What about your sisters?"

"I never had any sisters," Brad admitted with an amused shake of his head. "That story I told you about them teaching me how to kiss? Well, I got that out of some magazine interview with our boy, Tom Cruise. Can't tell you how many times that story got me laid." He laughed. "Anyway, Tom's the one with the sisters. Me, I had a little brother."

"Had?"

"He got himself killed about eight years back. Drug deal gone bad," he explained before Jamie could ask.

"I'm sorry," Jamie said, and she was. For all of them.

"What are you sorry about? It was his own damn fault. Anyway, who cares? It was a long time ago."

"Where are your parents now?"

"My mother's still in Texas. My father's dead." Brad smiled. "He was lucky. His heart attacked him before I could."

Jamie shuddered as she absorbed this latest piece of information. "That story about how you got your knife . . ."

"Was a damn good one, don't you think? I'm getting pretty good at thinking on my feet." He laughed, swiveled back toward her. "Why are you asking me these things?"

"Just trying to get to know you," Jamie said, realizing this was true.

Brad returned to the bed and sat down, taking her hands in his. "You want to know the real me, is that what you're saying?"

Jamie felt her body stiffen and recoil at his touch, and she fought to keep from snatching her hands from his. "I want to know the real Brad Fisher," she repeated. I want to know the man I've been sleeping with, she added silently. The man I put my faith in, the man I gave my heart to. The man who raped me, who hit me, who brutally murdered a total stranger in cold blood.

Maybe if she could get this man to talk about himself long enough, she'd find a key to getting herself out of this nightmare.

"Well, okay then," he said, kissing her softly on the lips before leaning back on his elbows and crossing one foot over the other. "Ask away."

CHAPTER TWENTY-FIVE

"Are you going to kill me?" Jamie asked, all her questions melting into one.

"Kill you?" Brad seemed genuinely shocked. "Why on earth would I want to kill you? I love you, Jamie. Don't you know that?"

Tears filled Jamie's eyes. She opened her mouth to speak, but no words came.

"Is that what's been bothering you all day? Is that why you've been acting so strange?"

Jamie looked toward the window, trying to make sense of what she was hearing. Was he serious? Had he really been puzzling over her behavior, wondering **what was bothering her**? Was that possible?

"Aren't you a funny little thing," he said, scooting up beside her in the bed and surrounding her with his arms, chuckling as he kissed her forehead. "You really thought I was going to kill you?"

"I don't know what to think. I've been so scared."

"Of me?"

"I don't understand what's happening." The tears she'd been keeping at bay began dropping freely from her eyes, spilling down her cheeks.

"What don't you understand, Jamie?"

"Anything." She began rocking back and forth. "I don't understand what happened in Atlanta."

"I got a little carried away, that's all. I already apologized for that." A familiar note of impatience edged into the corner of his voice.

"Not just that."

"What then?"

"Everything," Jamie said. "I don't understand anything that's happened, Brad. How could it have happened?"

"There isn't always a reason for things, Jamie."

"A woman is dead, for God's sake!"

"A woman you hated. A woman who treated you like dirt."

"That doesn't mean she deserved to die."

"It does in my book."

"You're saying you killed her because of me?" Oh, God, Jamie thought. Oh, God. Oh, God.

"What difference does it make why I killed her? She's dead, no matter what."

"Please, Brad. Just help me understand."

Brad leaned back against the headboard, folded his hands behind his head, as if he were relaxing in the sun. "I don't know if I can do that, Jamie-girl."

Jamie struggled to put her fears into thoughts, her thoughts into words, her words into coherent questions. "Tell me what happened," she said finally, when no other words made sense.

"I'm not sure where you want me to start."

"Why did we go to Atlanta?"

"What do you mean?"

"Why did we go to Atlanta?" she repeated.

"We were driving through, Jamie," he reminded her. "On our way to Ohio."

"No," she corrected. "I wanted to keep going till we got to Barnsley Gardens. You were the one who insisted we stop in Atlanta."

"I was tired. I wanted to relax."

"You wanted to go to her house," Jamie said, unable to speak Laura Dennison's name out loud. "You were planning to go there all along."

"Well, yeah," he admitted after a pause. "After you told me that story about your earrings, I decided it might be fun to pay the old bat a visit."

"You'd already decided to break into her house," Jamie stated.

"**We** broke into her house," he reminded her.

"You've broken into homes before." Another statement.

Brad smiled. "Once or twice."

"You've been in trouble before."

"Once or twice," he said again.

"But why did you have to kill her?" Jamie asked.

"She saw us, Jamie. What else could I do?"

"You could have run. You could have come with me."

"I had to take care of business first."

"How . . . how did you kill her?" Jamie asked.

"You know how. You heard the news reports."

"You beat her to death."

"It wasn't as bad as those reporters made it out to be. I just hit her a few times. It didn't take much."

"With the candlestick," Jamie said, her voice a monotone.

"Hey—Mr. Fisher with the candlestick in the bedroom!" Brad laughed. "You remember that game, Jamie? The one where you had to figure out who killed who, where, and with what? What was it called? Clue?"

"Clue?" Were they really talking about some stupid board game?

"Yeah, that's the one. I used to love that game."

"You planned on killing her all along, didn't you?"

Brad wrinkled his brow and tilted his head to one side, as if seriously considering the question. "I was kind of playing that by ear."

"That's why you brought the candlestick up to her room."

"You mean the candlestick with your fingerprints all over it?" he asked mischievously.

The question hit Jamie like a blow to the head. She gripped the bedspread tightly with her fingers to keep from falling over.

Brad smiled. "Yeah. I guess I did."

He'd set her up. "Why?" she whispered.

"Why what, Jamie-girl?"

What did he want from her? "Have you ever killed anybody before?" she heard herself ask.

There was a pause of several seconds. "Once or twice," he said, as he had said before.

"Oh, God."

"Hey, now, don't start freaking out on me again."

Jamie fought to keep the scream building in her throat from escaping. She pictured a gold credit card, read the name printed across it. "Grace Hastings?"

"Whoa! Jamie-girl! Give that girl a gold star. You're a real little private detective, aren't you?"

"Who's Grace Hastings? What did you do to her?"

"Hold on. One question at a time."

"Who is she?" Jamie asked again, trying not to think of the poor woman in the past tense.

Brad shrugged. "A friend of Beth's. Although I always suspected she had a hankering to be more. Hey, Jamie, you ever had a three-way?"

"What?"

"You heard me."

"What happened to Grace Hastings, Brad?"

"Uh-uh. You've been asking all the questions. It's my turn."

"Please . . ."

"Have you ever had a three-way?" he repeated.

"No," she answered. What was the point of protest?

"Ever been with another woman?"

"No."

"Never been tempted?"

"No," she answered.

"Not even a little bit?"

"No."

"Just not your thing, huh?"

Jamie nodded. What was he thinking now?

"What about if I told you it excited me, the idea of you with another woman? What if I asked you to? Would you do it for me?"

Oh, God. "I don't know."

"Something to think about," Brad said, hunkering down on the bed, extricating a pillow from beneath the bedspread and fluffing it up behind his head. "Beth was the same way. You should have seen how upset she got the first time I suggested it."

"So there really is an ex-wife in Ohio," Jamie said, trying to regain control of the conversation.

"Sure is."

"And a son?"

"Yes, ma'am. Corey Fisher. He's five years old."

"But you're not on good terms with Beth, are you?"

Brad scratched the back of his neck. "Not really. No."

"She ran away from you, didn't she?" Jamie stated, knowing the answer before she posed the question.

The mark of a good attorney, her sister would say.

Jamie wondered what Cynthia was doing, if she'd been bothered enough by Jamie's strange behavior on the phone to investigate further. Except, what could she do? How would she even know where to begin?

"She took my kid," Brad was saying. "She should never have done that."

"Tell me about her," Jamie said. "Tell me about your marriage."

Brad yawned, as if the story held little interest for him. "Standard boy-meets-girl stuff. We met, fell in love, got married, had a baby. Things were fine in the beginning, although her family never approved of me. I wasn't good enough for their precious little girl, I guess. She kept telling them I was a 'diamond in the rough,' but they weren't buying it. And her friends, it was the same thing with them. They were nice enough in the beginning, tried killing me with kindness, if you know what I mean, probably hoping I'd go away if they just left well enough alone. Bad enough alone, they'd probably say." He chuckled at his own play on words. "Except I fooled them. I didn't go anywhere. And that really ticked them off. Yes, ma'am, that ticked them off something fierce." His voice trailed off, as if he were following some distant memory into a far recess of his brain.

"But why did they hate you so much?"

"You tell me. I mean, I can be a pretty charming guy. Isn't that right?"

"You charmed me," Jamie conceded.

"Yeah, well." He shrugged. "What can you do, right?"

"What **did** you do?" she asked.

"Nothing."

"Did you hit her, Brad?"

"What?"

"Is that why they hated you?"

Brad's expression soured. "People fight," he said.

"Is that why she divorced you?"

"Who says we're divorced?"

"You're not?"

He sat up, the muscles in his back rippling with tension beneath his black shirt. "According to her, we are."

"And according to you?"

"Just because she sends me a goddamn lawyer's letter telling me she's filing for divorce doesn't mean I agree to it." He slid off the bed and walked to the door.

Where was he going? Was it possible he was going to open the door and walk out? Leave her there?

But if that had been his intention, he stopped when he reached the door. He turned around, pressed his back against the far wall. "Relax, Jamie-girl," he said, misreading the look on her face. "I'm a free man."

Jamie nodded, trying her best to look relieved. "She sent you a lawyer's letter?"

"First she has me locked away, then she files for divorce."

"You were in prison?" Jamie held her breath.

"Better part of a year."

"Because you beat her?"

Brad shook his head wearily, as if he were tired of being so misunderstood. "I never beat her." He inched away from the door, still shaking his head. "Why would you say something like that."

"I didn't mean—"

"Women, shit. You always stick together, don't you?" He shook his head. "It takes two people to make a fight, Jamie. She wasn't some innocent bystander, you know. She wasn't some punching bag, just hanging around waiting to get hit. That woman had a mouth on her, I'll tell you. Once she'd start in about something, there was nothing you could say or do that was gonna shut her up. Sometimes all I wanted was for her to be quiet. You know how that is? When all you want is a little peace and quiet, and your damn kid won't stop screaming, and your wife's giving you a hard time about something you said to one of her stupid friends. . . ."

"She left you no choice," Jamie said.

"It's not like she just stood there. She threw some pretty good punches herself. Hell, I was as abused as she was," Brad said with conviction.

"That must have been awful for you." Good for her, Jamie was thinking, praying for the opportunity, the strength, the nerve.

"Yeah, well, what goes around comes around."

"What does that mean?"

"Means I'm very good at biding my time."

Jamie lowered her chin to her chest, stared at a long, torn thread on the quilted bedspread, wondering what would happen if she were to pull it. Would the whole thing unravel and come apart? "Why were you in prison?"

"Long story," Brad said, pacing back and forth between the bed and the door.

"I'd like to hear it."

Brad suddenly pulled a chair away from the table and twisted it around, sitting on it backward, his arms leaning on the top of its back, his legs straddling its sides. He gazed at the heavy, mustard-colored drapes as if he could see right through them. Beyond those drapes was Dayton, less than a thirty-minute drive away.

He's looking at tomorrow, Jamie thought. She closed her eyes, tried not to see.

"You're not gonna like it," he said quietly.

"Was it because of what you did to Grace Hastings?"

"Gracie? No." He laughed, the thought clearly amusing him. "Trust me—nobody's ever gonna find old Gracie-girl."

"Why were you in prison?" Jamie asked again, too afraid to question him further about Grace Hastings.

Gracie-girl, she thought.

Jamie-girl.

Were they going to meet the same fate?

"Well, you gotta promise me you're not gonna get all upset. It was a long time ago, right after I moved to Florida."

"What happened?"

"I was new to Miami, didn't know anyone," Brad began. "One night, I'm in a bar, and I meet this fat, middle-aged guy, and we get to talking.

He tells me he's in town for some sort of appliance convention, wife and two kids back home in Philly, the usual crap. So it takes me a while to realize this asshole's coming on to me. I'm not too thrilled about this, believe me, but I decide to play along. I mean he's the one buying the drinks, and he has a wad of bills on him this big." Brad demonstrated how big with his hands. "He had this solid gold money clip. I'd never seen anything like it, before or since." He shook his head at the memory. "Anyway, a few drinks later, he invites me back to his hotel room, supposedly to show me some catalogs, like I give a shit about a bunch of stovetops and refrigerators, and I'm thinking, not only is this moron cheating on his wife, he's a goddamn faggot, and somebody's got to teach him a lesson, right? So I go back to his room, we have another couple of drinks, then as soon as he puts a hand on me, I let him have it." He shrugged. "Guess I hit him a little too hard."

"He died?"

"Papers said it was a massive brain hemorrhage."

"And you were arrested?"

"Hell, no."

"I don't understand."

"There was nothing linking me to what happened. No one knew me. Nobody saw me go into his room. We were very discreet," he said with a wink.

"Then how . . . ?"

". . . did I get caught?"

Jamie nodded.

Brad's face darkened. "Never trust a woman," he said ominously.

"You told your wife," Jamie said, suddenly piecing it all together.

"We'd been fighting all day. Don't ask me about what. She told me she wanted a divorce. I told her I'd see her rot in hell first. I guess she didn't believe me." Brad shook his head in genuine amazement. "She moved out. Next thing I know she's talking about taking my son and going to California. That's when I believe I mentioned what happened to that queer in the bar. Kind of as a cautionary tale. Few days later, the police are at my door. They find this guy's money clip at the back of some drawer. I'd forgotten I even had the damn thing. Anyway, the long and the short of it is I'm arrested and denied bail, they haul my ass off to jail, and I spend over a year in some stinking cell before a judge decides the evidence they have is inadmissible. Turns out it was an illegal search, and the money clip is considered fruit from a poisonous tree. Something like that." He laughed. "Kind of ironic, isn't it? I'm arrested because of one fruit, and I get off because of another." He laughed again, banging his hand on the tabletop for emphasis. "Anyway, they had to let me go."

"When was that?"

"They released me a few weeks ago."

He'd gone from a jail cell to her bed in only a few weeks?

"I came home to find a couple more faggots in my apartment, if you can believe it, and my wife and son vanished into thin air."

"How did you find out where she'd gone?"

"Well, now, that's where our little friend, Gracie, proved very helpful."

"She told you Beth was in Ohio?"

"I didn't give her much choice."

"I'm sure she called Beth to warn her. . . ." Jamie heard what she was saying, stopped when she realized how ridiculous those words were. Grace Hastings hadn't warned anyone. She'd never had the chance.

He was smiling, as if reading her thoughts. "My turn," he said.

"What?"

"My turn to ask a question. Like in **Silence of the Lambs.** You remember **Silence of the Lambs,** don't you, Jamie?"

Jamie nodded. Were they really talking about movies? First board games, and now movies?

"Great movie. **Great** movie," he said again, agreeing with his own assessment. "You don't think so?"

"I guess."

"What do you mean, you guess? **Silence of the Lambs** was a great movie, no question about it."

"It's been a while since I've seen it."

"Well, we'll have to rent it one night, after all this is settled."

"After what is settled?"

"After we pay a little visit to Mad River Road."

Jamie nodded understanding. "You're going to kill her, aren't you?"

"That's the plan," Brad said easily.

"And where do I fit into your plan?"

Brad pushed himself out of his seat, returned to the bed, stroked Jamie's cheek as he sat down beside her. "You? Why, you're my girl, Jamie. You fit right beside me."

What does that mean? Jamie wondered. What was he saying? "You expect me to help you kill your wife?"

"I expect you to help me," he said. "Same way I helped you in Atlanta."

CHAPTER TWENTY-SIX

Emma lay on top of her bed, staring at the far wall, watching her childhood play out across its bare white surface, like an old-fashioned home movie. She saw herself as a chubby-cheeked child of three or four, being catapulted high into the air above her father's head, confident hands extended skyward to catch her, then tossing her across his broad shoulders like a sack of grain, and racing with her back and forth across their expansive backyard, her joyous squeals trailing after them. In the background, she heard her mother's voice cautioning her father to slow down, be careful, watch where he was going. "No," she heard the child protest as her father's booming laugh filled the sky. "Faster. Faster."

Next she saw herself tucked inside her twin-size brass bed, listening to her parents argue in the room next to hers. The child brought the pale pink blankets up over her head in an effort to silence their anger, and when she emerged, she was several years older, the once-chubby cheeks now thinner, a newfound wariness filling her big, blue eyes. She heard her mother's angry voice, followed by a loud noise, and then another, and she jumped from her bed, afraid that the house was collapsing around her. Which, of course, it was, although not in the way she imagined. Emma watched her younger self climb out of bed and hurry to her parents' room, pushing open the door and catching just a glimpse of a shattered mirror on the floor beside an overturned chair, as her father, sweat-streaked, dark hair falling into furious, dark eyes, rushed toward her and carried her back to bed. "What's wrong?" she asked him repeatedly. "What's wrong? What's wrong?"

"Everything's fine," he assured her. "Go back to sleep, baby. Everything's going to be all right."

Except the next day he was gone, and nothing was ever all right again.

Emma blinked, watching the sad little girl morph into a shy child of nine or ten, as she bounced a rubber ball off the concrete wall behind the six-story apartment building in a mostly gray part of town, where she and her mother lived. Emma's imaginary friend, Sabrina, watched from the sidelines, patiently waiting her turn. Sabrina was named after the Kate Jackson character on **Charlie's Angels,** which was Emma's then-favorite TV show. It was on several times a day in reruns, and Emma watched it as often as she could. She'd seen some episodes so many times, she knew the lines by heart and could recite whole scripts word for word. The early episodes were her favorites, the ones with the original angels, although she liked Cheryl Ladd almost as much as she'd liked Farrah Fawcett. And Jaclyn Smith was certainly pretty, although she couldn't act her way out of a paper bag, as her mother had pronounced caustically after only several seconds of viewing. While her mother didn't like her watching so much television, the fact was she was rarely home. In the days following Emma's father's desertion and the subsequent foreclosure on their home, her mother had been forced to work two, and sometimes even three, jobs to make ends meet, going from one job to the next without a break, leaving first thing in the morning and sometimes not coming home until Emma was already in bed. Emma was rarely asleep when her mother came home, but she often pretended to be. She didn't want to talk to the woman she held responsible for all the losses in her life.

The one friend she managed to make at her new school was a heavyset girl named Judy Rico, who was also new, although that friendship came to an abrupt halt when Judy, in an effort to make herself more attractive to the popular girls at school, announced one afternoon at recess that Emma's mother was **her** mother's cleaning lady. Emma winced at the image of herself pushing Judy Rico to the ground and jumping on top of her, pounding

Judy's face with her fists until blood dripped from her nose and down her white blouse, and a teacher had to come to Judy's rescue, dragging the still-flailing Emma off her and carrying her to the principal's office. After that, everyone left her alone. But that was all right. Who needed friends when she had Charlie's Angels?

Things improved, at least for a little while, after they moved to Detroit, and her mother got the job at Bishop Lane School for Girls. Emma pictured herself in her neatly pressed school uniform, remembering the initial flush of pride she'd felt when she first slipped her arms into the sleeves of her dark green jacket. This is where I belong, she remembered thinking as she took up her position in the back row for her class photograph with the other teenagers, smiling proudly for the camera.

And then everything went blurry.

Emma closed her eyes, rolled over in bed, refusing to see more. What was there to see after all? The episode with the libidinous gym teacher? It had happened all right, but to Claire Eaton, not to her, and the teacher had been summarily dismissed after Claire's mother complained to the school principal, who was definitely **not** Emma's mother. And the photographer she'd met in McDonald's, well, he was all of seventeen years old and his camera was his dad's Polaroid, and she doubted he'd noticed her eyes at all, so busy was he staring at her newly developed chest.

"Why did I tell everybody I modeled for Maybelline?" she moaned at the ceiling.

Because she'd been telling that lie for so long, she almost believed it herself, she realized. It had started innocently enough. A boy, eager to impress her, and no doubt, hoping to get lucky, had told her she had beautiful eyes and asked playfully if those were her eyes on the packages of Maybelline mascara. It was an easy leap from there. The next time someone told her she had nice eyes, she filled in the rest herself. It wasn't that far-fetched, after all. Her eyes were the same color, the same shape as the girl's in the ads. Who would know the difference? How would anyone ever find out the truth?

God, what other lies had she told lately? That she'd written a story about her modeling days and sold it to **Cosmo**? That she was an army brat, that her father had been killed in Vietnam?

That was the trouble with lies. They bred like rabbits. And that was okay, if you told those lies to someone like Lily, who was naive and trusting and pretty much believed whatever you said. But when you told those same lies to someone as jaded as Jan Scully or as experienced as Jeff Dawson, then you were just asking for trouble. All those questions he'd asked. And he'd looked far from convinced at her answers. "Damn it," she said, swinging her legs off the bed and marching to her closet, extricating a beat-up, brown canvas suitcase from the back and throwing it across the bed. I've got to get out of here, she was thinking as she flung back the top of the case and started hurling clothes in its direction. It wouldn't take her long to pack. She didn't have a lot of things, even counting her latest "purchases," and Dylan had even less. She quickly emptied her dresser drawers, then started removing the clothes from their hangers. In less than twenty minutes, every piece of clothing she owned, except the blue cotton pajamas she had on, were in the suitcase. "Well, that was smart," she muttered, realizing she'd left herself nothing to wear.

Besides, where was she going?

"Anywhere," she said, reaching into the suitcase and extricating a pair of jeans and a navy sweater. Her underwear was harder to find, and she ended up unpacking virtually the whole valise and having to fold everything again. "Anywhere but here." She might not have much, but she still had her instincts, and her instincts were telling her it was time to cut her losses and run, that it was no longer safe for her here on Mad River Road.

Still, her rent was paid up until the end of the month, she thought, sinking down on the bed, suddenly overwhelmed with fatigue, and if she left now, in the middle of the night, she'd have to leave behind all her furniture and other belongings, and she didn't have enough money to buy more things, even secondhand. Besides, how could she take Dylan out of school when the school year was almost over? Hadn't she just been lying awake, remembering how painful it had been being constantly uprooted? Hadn't she hated her mother because of it? Did she want Dylan to hate her too?

"Damn it," she said again, pushing the suitcase off the bed and watching her clothes spill out across the floor. She couldn't leave. Nor did she really want to. No—what she wanted was to make a fresh start. Tomorrow morning, she'd tell Lily the truth, about everything, and hope that Lily would understand and find it in her heart to forgive her. And then she'd go to Scully's, return the stupid trophy she'd stolen, apologize to Jan. In another few months, when she thought it was safe, she might even let Dylan start using his real name, and so would she, and they'd make a new beginning by reclaiming their former selves. She'd rediscover the person behind all the lies.

Emma flopped down on her back and stared at the ceiling. There was only one problem with that, Emma thought: she had no idea who that person was.

Lily turned over in bed and opened her eyes. Jeff Dawson was smiling at her from the pillow beside her. She wondered how long he'd been watching her as, wordlessly, he reached for her, and she felt herself melting into his arms.

"What the hell do you think you're doing?" Kenny demanded from the foot of the bed. "He's a loser, for God's sake. Get out while you still can."

Lily gasped and bolted up in bed, her eyes scanning the darkness for men she knew weren't there. Jeff wasn't lying beside her; Kenny wasn't yelling at her from the foot of the bed. "Good God," Lily said, listening to the sound of a motorcycle in the distance and wondering if that ghostly sound had propelled Kenny into her dream.

What would Kenny have thought of Jeff Dawson? she wondered. Would he really have considered him a loser, or would he have liked him?

"I like him," she whispered softly, as if afraid to give the words too much resonance.

"You two have something going on?" she remembered Emma asking the first time she'd seen the two of them together.

"Of course not," Lily had replied, but Emma had sensed the truth even then.

Although what did Emma know of truth? Lily wondered now. Who exactly was Emma Frost, and how many lies had she told?

Once again she replayed her earlier conversation with Jeff, that unbelievable story he'd told about catching Emma shoplifting. That couldn't be right. Then again, why couldn't it? Lily really didn't know Emma very well. She knew virtually nothing about her life and hadn't been around her enough to have any clear understanding of the way her mind worked. In fact, the more she learned of Emma, the more of an enigma she was becoming.

Lily climbed out of bed, walked to the window, and stared out at the dark street, asking herself the same question she'd been asking ever since Jeff had made his startling pronouncement: If Emma Frost wasn't who she said she was, then who was she? Why all the lies and subterfuge?

Lily almost laughed. Who was she to judge others? Who was she to complain about people not telling the truth? And if Jeff had been that quick to detect Emma's fabrications, how long before her own answers proved less than satisfactory?

She walked to her closet, opened it, stared at the few items hanging inside. Maybe it was time to leave. She'd never intended that her stay in Dayton be anything but a temporary stopgap, until she was able to earn some money, figure out what she wanted to do with the rest of her life. She'd always hoped that one day she might be able to go back home. Although not yet. It was still far too early to be thinking of that.

Besides, she liked it here. She had her circle of friends, a job, and even her book club. And Michael was flourishing. So why leave? Because she'd met a man she liked and sensed the possibility of something more? Because it was too early to be thinking about such things? Or because it was too late, she thought sadly, closing her closet door and plopping down at the foot of her bed.

You can't build a relationship on lies, she was thinking. Just as you couldn't run from the past forever. Sooner or later, she had to start telling the truth. About her marriage. About Kenny's death. About her part in everything that happened.

The truth will set you free. Isn't that what they said?

Didn't they also say that **freedom's just another word for nothing left to lose?**

Lily closed her eyes. She had a great deal to lose, she thought, climbing back under the covers and staring up at the ceiling, wondering what Jan would think of her when she learned her trusted employee was a liar, what her friends would think when they learned the extent of her lies. What would Jeff Dawson say, she was wondering as sleep began gnawing on the perimeter of her consciousness, if he were to find out that Emma Frost wasn't the only imposter on Mad River Road?

Jamie waited until she was confident Brad was asleep before opening her eyes. She'd been lying beside him, listening to the sound of his breathing, for hours now, waiting for his breath to regulate, to even out, to convince her beyond any shadow of a doubt that he was, in fact, asleep and not just testing her. He'd tested her once already tonight, and she'd come perilously close to failing.

Jamie glanced at the red numbers of the digital clock beside the bed without moving her head, shuddering at the memory of her narrow escape. It had come just before one o'clock, two hours after he'd kissed her good night and told her to take off her clothes and turn over so that he could hold her while they slept. Mercifully, he hadn't pressed her for sex, sensing perhaps that she was too fragile. Or maybe he was just tired after driving all day. Whatever the reason, he'd seemed content just to lie there beside her, and he'd drifted off to sleep with remarkable ease, his arm draped heavily across her naked body, like an iron chain, holding her in place. Jamie had lain there for what felt like an eternity before somehow working her body free of his arm and carefully sliding out from underneath his weight. He hadn't moved. It was only when she was at the foot of the bed and reaching for her jeans that his voice stretched across the darkness, like a hand, to grip her shoulder and stop her cold.

"What do you think you're doing?" he'd asked, the question a coiled reptile, striking at her soul.

Jamie struggled to keep her own voice as flat as possible, despite the mad fluctuations of her heartbeat. "I have to go to the bathroom."

"Since when do you put your jeans **on** to go to the bathroom?"

"I wasn't putting them on."

"What were you doing?"

"I have a headache. I thought I had some Excedrin in my pocket."

"And do you?" He flipped on the light beside the bed, watched her intently.

Jamie rifled through her pockets. "No," she said, the dejection in her voice real. "Maybe there's some in my purse."

"You better check." He pointed toward her purse on the dresser.

Jamie shuffled toward the dresser, conscious of Brad's eyes following her naked body. She grabbed her purse, her fingers searching for anything that might give credence to her story. "Here they are," she said, relief washing over her like a giant wave, bathing her in perspiration as she lifted a tiny bottle of Excedrin into the air.

"Better take them then," he said.

Jamie nodded, continuing into the bathroom and swallowing two pills with a glass of water.

"Might as well pee while you're in there," he advised. "I don't feel like getting up again tonight. Big day tomorrow," he added chillingly.

When Jamie returned to the bedroom, both her purse and her clothes were gone. She thought of asking where they were, then thought better of it. Clearly Brad had put them somewhere beyond her easy reach, his way of telling her he wasn't taking any more chances. She climbed back into bed, resumed her former position.

"Hey, Jamie," he whispered, kissing the side of her neck. "I hear that sex is really good at getting rid of headaches."

"Please, Brad . . ."

"Relax, Jamie," he said, his arm reaching across her, like an anchor, weighing her down, securing her position. "I was just teasing."

Jamie closed her eyes, swallowed back tears.

"Sweet dreams, Jamie-girl."

Sweet dreams, Jamie-girl, Jamie repeated now to herself, wondering if she dared risk a second attempt at escape. It was almost four o'clock in the morning, and while they were only half an hour outside of Dayton, they were still in the middle of nowhere. Even if she somehow managed to get out of the room and away from the motel, where was she going to go? There'd be no one at the desk at this hour, no phone she could use without proper change or a calling card, no doors she could go pounding on without running the risk of discovery. She had no money, no shoes, no clothes, for God's sake. Could she really run barefoot and naked into the night, hoping to reach the highway and salvation?

If Brad were to wake up and discover her gone, there was no doubt he'd come after her. And if he found her? Then what? **Trust me—nobody's ever gonna find old Gracie-girl,** she heard him say.

And yet, what choice did she have? He'd already murdered at least one woman—probably two—and was about to murder another. It was only a matter of time before he decided she was as expendable as the others. She had to at least try to get away. Now might be her only chance.

And so, Jamie shifted her body just slightly, as if she were turning over in her sleep. Brad stirred slightly but didn't wake, his arm still draped across her hip. Again, Jamie altered her position, slowly flipping onto her back. Brad moved with her, his arm now sliding across her stomach. She felt his breath warm on the side of her face. He sighed, as if in the middle of a pleasant dream. Was he dreaming of his former wife? Was he thinking about what he planned to do to her?

Jamie tried picturing Brad's wife, but all she could see was a woman cowering in a corner, her bruised arms covering her face, shielding her head from the blows she knew were inevitable. Somehow she'd found the courage to escape her tormentor, to gather up her son and run away. And yet, even after a year, even after obtaining a divorce and moving halfway across the country, finding what she thought was a secure haven in Ohio, creating a new identity, a new life for her son and herself, she still wasn't safe. He'd found out where she was, and he was coming to kill her. Just as Jamie knew he would come after her should she make good on her escape.

In that instant, Jamie understood that she would never be safe again, as long as Brad Fisher was alive.

She waited a full five minutes before turning back on her side, Brad's arm sliding off her hip as she moved. Now was her chance, she recognized, although her legs still refused to move. Where are you going? they seemed to be asking. Where can you run?

It didn't matter, she decided. It didn't matter that she didn't know where she was going, or that she was naked and had no money, no shoes, no identification. Nothing mattered except that she get the hell out of there. She'd worry about everything else later.

Slowly, she inched her torso up in bed until she was sitting. The sheet fell from her breasts. Brad stirred, his lips twitching as his body moved slightly to the left. Jamie held her breath, debating whether to lie back down and abandon her plan. Several more minutes passed before her mind filled with fresh resolve, and she brought her feet to the side of the bed, another minute before she lowered them to the floor. The feel of the worn carpet beneath her bare toes sent shock waves through her legs, as if she'd stepped on a live wire. She'd made it this far before, she was thinking, feeling his eyes on her back, his smirk on her skin. She heard movement behind her and braced herself for his touch. What could she tell him this time? Would she even have a chance to speak before he silenced her once and for all?

Jamie spun around.

There was no one behind her. And when she looked down at the bed, Brad was still underneath the covers, sleeping soundly. Oh, God, she said silently, covering her mouth with her hand to mute the sound of her ragged breathing. She had to be careful. She couldn't afford to make any mistakes. Not when she was so close.

She pushed one foot in front of the other, gradually increasing the size of her steps. Part of her wanted to make a mad dash for it, but she knew that if she did, it would only increase the chance of his waking up. Although her eyes had long since adjusted to the dark, the room was still unfamiliar. She couldn't risk knocking against a piece of furniture or tripping over his shoes on her way to the door.

She had to proceed slowly and with great caution.

She was halfway to the door when she saw Brad's clothes draped over the side of the chair he'd occupied earlier. Slowly, she reached over, carefully dragging his black T-shirt from the top of the pile and quickly pulling it on, her head popping through its round neck, like a wary turtle emerging from its shell. If he's awake, I'll just tell him I got cold, Jamie thought, but when she looked toward the bed, she saw he hadn't moved.

Her fingers grazed the side of Brad's jeans. Were the keys to her car still nestled in his pocket? Was the switchblade knife still secreted inside? Could she get them out without making any noise? Could she take that chance? And if she managed to retrieve the knife, what then? Could she use it if she had to? Was she capable of killing another human being?

Suddenly Brad stirred, as if her thoughts had jostled him awake. Jamie froze, the palm of her hand resting on the leg of Brad's jeans, holding her breath as Brad yawned and flopped onto his other side. From this distance, she couldn't make out whether or not his eyes were open, whether or not he was watching her, waiting to see what she would do next. So she did nothing, simply stood trembling in the middle of the room until, once again, she heard the regular rhythm of his breathing resume.

Slowly, her fingers extended toward the pocket of his jeans, and she carefully wiggled them down inside the heavy denim. The pocket was empty, she realized, almost bursting into tears, which meant that she'd have to turn the pants over, try the pocket on the other side. Could she do that without causing the keys to jangle? Brad's heavy leather belt was looped through the waist of the jeans, and maneuvering them wasn't going to be easy. Still, if her car keys were inside, if she could only recover them, then she stood a real chance of getting out of here, of going to the police, of preventing tomorrow's horrors.

She turned the jeans over, careful to keep the metal buckle from slapping against the wood of the chair, then slid her hand into the second pocket. Neither the car keys nor the knife were there. She tried the rear pockets, knowing in advance she'd find nothing. Dammit, she thought, returning the jeans to the back of the chair and biting down on her lower lip to keep from screaming. Dammit, dammit, dammit.

It was in that moment she sensed something had changed. A subtle shift in the air currents had occurred, a change in the light. Whatever. She didn't have to turn around to know Brad's eyes were open, that his cruel smile was now stretching across his face.

"Are you ready to die, Jamie?" he asked as the sound of a switchblade being released from its sheath stabbed at the stillness.

Jamie didn't waste time turning around. Instead she flung herself at the door, tearing at the safety chain and pulling the door toward her, screaming into the small sliver of night she was able to see before the door slammed shut again, and she was picked up and thrown across the room, as if she were an inanimate object, weightless and of no consequence whatsoever. She struggled to her feet as he came at her again, his fist connecting with her stomach as she was almost upright. The air rushed from her body in one giant whoosh and she crumpled to the floor, gagging and gasping for breath. Hands grabbed at her hair, pulling her head up and exposing the whiteness of her neck against the black of his shirt. She saw the blade of the knife as it swooped toward her throat.

Then she saw nothing at all.

CHAPTER TWENTY-SEVEN

Emma saw the car as soon as she opened her front door. It was parked halfway down the street, in front of old Mrs. Discala's house, and Emma wondered idly if Mrs. Discala's son, the doctor she was always bragging about, had gotten himself another new car. Although this one looked as if it had seen better days. Oh, well, Emma thought. Haven't we all? She'd always loved Thunderbirds for their stylish bravura, and this one was baby blue, which gave it a certain added mystique, although she wasn't sure why. Emma had never owned a car, didn't even have a driver's license, but she decided right then and there that if she ever did get a car, it would be a baby blue Thunderbird just like this one.

"All right, Dylan. Let's get a move-on in there."

"I'm coming," her son called from upstairs, although almost a minute later, there was still no sign of him.

Emma stepped back inside her front foyer. "Dylan, come on. You're going to be late for school."

Still nothing.

"Dylan, please don't make me come up there."

Suddenly Dylan materialized at the top of the stairs. In his hands was a shiny, round, brass object. "What's this?" He extended Jan's trophy dish above his head, as if he himself had just come in second in the Women's Bodybuilding Competition in Cincinnati, Ohio, for 2002.

"What are you doing with that?" Emma was already halfway up the stairs before Dylan had the chance to take a step.

Immediately he hid the brass bowl behind his back, out of her reach. "I'm taking it for show-and-tell."

"Who said you could go sneaking around in my things?"

The omnipresent threat of tears brought a familiar quiver to Dylan's voice. "I wasn't sneaking around. It was in the bathroom. I found it when I was looking for my animal soaps."

"You used the last of your animal soaps last week. Remember?"

"Why can't I take this to show instead?"

"Because it's not yours." It's not even mine, she almost added, then thought better of it. There was no telling what Dylan was liable to burst out with in class.

"But it's pretty."

"Yes, it is. But you can't take it to school, Dylan. I'm sorry. Now, can I have it, please?"

Reluctantly Dylan brought the brass bowl around the front of his body, and Emma pried it from his stubborn fingers. "I never have anything good for show-and-tell," he said, his lips forming an exaggerated pout.

"Well, if you would give me a little notice and not wait until the last minute," Emma said with exasperation, “I might be able to find you something interesting to take.”

“Like what?”

“Like I don’t know what,” she said, taking his hand and leading him down the stairs, hearing him whimper. “All right. Look. We’ll find something.” She walked into the living room, tossed the bowl on the sofa, and looked helplessly around the room. She had to return the damn thing to Jan. But when? And how? What could she say to the woman? How much truth could she afford to tell?

“There’s nothing,” Dylan wailed.

“Yes, there is,” Emma realized, running into the kitchen. “I have the perfect thing.”

Dylan was right behind her as she rifled through the kitchen cabinets. Where had she put it anyway? “What is it?” Dylan asked.

“A mug,” Emma announced, her fingers closing around its cumbersome handle. She spun around, offered the big, ugly mug to her son. “It’s from Scully’s gym. See the logo written along its side?”

Dylan looked unimpressed. “What’s a logo?”

"It's the name," Emma amended, too impatient to explain. "Just show it to the class, and tell everyone that you get one of these free when you join Scully's, along with a free T-shirt." Hell, she might actually drum up a little extra business for Jan, which should help atone for her sins.

"Can I show them the T-shirt too?"

"I don't have a T-shirt."

"How come?"

"Because I didn't join."

"Then how come you got the free mug?"

"Dylan, do you want it or not?"

Dylan clasped the mug tightly to his chest, as if afraid she was about to snatch it away. "I want it," he said.

"Okay. Now, let's get going, or you'll be late." She opened the front door and stepped outside, holding the door open for her son, only to realize he'd vanished yet again. "Dylan, for God's sake . . ."

"I have to go to the bathroom," he called, his little body disappearing around the top of the stairs.

"Unbelievable," Emma muttered, letting the door snap closed behind her as she stared absently down the street. The blue Thunderbird was still parked in front of Mrs. Discala's house, and there seemed to be someone inside it, although from this distance it was hard to tell if it was a person or just the shadow of an overhanging tree branch. What kind of tree? she wondered, watching Lily and her son, Michael, emerge from their house, and thinking Lily would probably know what kind of trees grew on Mad River Road. Lily was the kind of person who knew stuff like that. Maybe she'd ask her. Providing, of course, Lily was still speaking to her. She didn't know if Lily had talked to Jeff Dawson, and if she had, how much he'd told her of the unfortunate incident at Marshalls. How was she going to explain that one? she wondered again, her resolve of last night weakening. Could she really trust Lily with the truth? Did she have any choice?

"Mom," Dylan was saying, tugging at the sleeve of her denim jacket. "Mom, we're going to be late."

"What? Oh. Oh, sorry. I didn't hear you come down. Are you ready now?"

Dylan lifted the mug above his head. "Nobody's ever shown a mug before," he said proudly. "Hey, there's Michael. Hey, Michael!" he called out, already running down the street to where Lily and her son stood waiting. "I've got a mug for show-and-tell."

"Hey, we have some of those," Michael was saying as Emma approached.

"Hi," Emma greeted Lily.

"Hi," Lily said in return, looking toward the sidewalk.

She knows, Emma thought, falling in step beside her. "Hey, do you know what kind of trees these are?" She made an encompassing gesture with her hands that took in all the trees in the neighborhood.

"Well, these are maples, of course," Lily said, managing to avoid looking at Emma as she glanced at her front lawn.

"Of course," Emma agreed.

"And those are oaks." She pointed in the direction of the blue Thunderbird.

"I guess I should know those things," Emma said.

"Why?" Lily asked, still not looking at her as they turned the corner onto South Patterson.

"I don't know." Emma shrugged, wondering if she was just imagining Lily's coolness. Maybe she was projecting the stiffness into Lily's shoulders, exaggerating the natural reserve in her voice. Maybe Jeff hadn't said anything to her at all. Emma wondered if there was any way to find out how much Lily knew, without revealing more than she had to. "So, did you do anything interesting last night?" she heard herself ask.

"Not really."

Emma took a deep breath as the two boys raced on ahead.

"Jeff dropped by," Lily said.

The breath caught in Emma's throat, and she fought the urge to gag.

"He said he saw you yesterday."

Emma waited, said nothing.

"In Marshalls," Lily continued.

"Yes," Emma agreed.

"He said—"

"Mommy," Michael called back. "Hurry up. You're walking too slow."

"Yeah, too slow," Dylan mimicked, laughing. He lifted his hands into the air, then dropped them to his sides, mimicking Emma's earlier exasperation.

"Careful with the mug," Emma warned. But it was already too late. The mug shot from Dylan's hand, crashed to the sidewalk at his feet, and broke into dozens of pieces. "Shoot," Emma muttered as her son began to wail.

Lily was immediately at his side, scooping up the broken pieces of cheap ceramic. "It's okay, sweetheart. I know where we can get you another one just like it."

"But I need it this morning."

"We'll get it right away. Okay?" Lily ran a motherly finger beneath Dylan's watery eyes, wiping away his tears. "Now, you go to school, your mother will take the bus with me to Scully's, she'll get you another mug and bring it to your room in ten minutes. How's that?"

"Ten minutes?"

"Maybe less."

Dylan nodded, dislodging several more tears. Emma knew the tears wouldn't stop until the new mug was safely in his hands.

"Okay, Dylan. Go with Michael now, and I'll be back as soon as I can."

"Ten minutes," Dylan emphasized.

"Go," Emma urged, giving her son a gentle pat on his backside as she pushed him toward the school yard at the end of the street. She shook her head. "Never a dull moment."

"There's the bus." Lily indicated a bus that was fast approaching on the other side of the road.

As Emma ran after her, she saw the blue Thunderbird round the corner and come to a stop at the end of the street. She wondered only briefly what it was doing there as she followed Lily onto the bus, then took the seat beside her in the empty back row.

Lily didn't waste any time. "Jeff told me what happened yesterday," she began. "In Marshalls."

"It's not the way it sounds," Emma said quickly.

"How is it?"

Emma bristled at the question. Did she really owe this woman an explanation?

Suddenly, the bus lurched to a stop, admitting two exuberant, teenage girls, who plopped themselves down in the seats on the other side of Emma, their books sliding off their laps and scattering on the bus floor.

"Oops," one girl said, laughing, as she stretched across Emma's legs to retrieve them.

"You're so clumsy," her friend giggled, lunging after the rest.

"This is so your fault," said the first girl, whereupon both girls doubled over laughing.

"This probably isn't the best time to be getting into all this," Lily acknowledged.

"I agree."

"But we need to talk about some things. Maybe when I finish work?"

"Fine," Emma agreed, glancing out the back window. The blue Thunderbird was no longer visible. Such a pretty color, she thought again.

"You are in so much trouble," the teenager beside her giggled to her friend as Emma turned back toward the front of the bus, staring straight ahead and trying not to think about anything.

"Where's the bitch going now?" Brad asked, keeping the blue Thunderbird hidden behind a white Lexus SUV as he followed the bus past the school yard. He turned to the woman cowering in the seat beside him, as if he expected an answer to his question.

Jamie said nothing. Brad had told her this morning that he didn't want to hear another word from her until they were safely out of Ohio or he'd kill her, the way he should have killed her last night, he'd added, and **would** have killed her, had she not fainted at the sight of the knife coming toward her throat. For some reason, he'd found that amusing, even endearing, as he did her spunk, he'd told her after reviving her with a cold glass of water tossed in her face. "You got a lot of spunk there, Jamie-girl," he'd said. "Not a lot of smarts," he'd added with a laugh. "But a lot of spunk."

Her mother couldn't have said it any better, Jamie thought now, wondering what the poor woman would say if she could see her daughter now, her eyes swollen and bloodshot, underlined in scaly crescents of dark purple, her pale skin splotchy, her lips cut and caked with streaks of dried blood, her arms covered with bruises, her stomach still aching from where he'd punched her, her neck still sore from being wrenched up and away from her shoulders. Why hadn't he killed her? she wondered. What awful role did he intend for her to play in the hours ahead?

"It won't be long now," he answered, as if she'd asked the question out loud. "Soon as I can get the bitch alone . . ."

What happens then? Jamie asked silently.

"That's when I'm gonna need your help," he said.

And after he killed her? Was it to be Jamie's turn next?

He'd known all along she was going to try to get away, he'd informed her last night, after barricading the door with enough furniture to ensure that even should he doze off—"Which I just might," he'd teased, "since I haven't slept a wink all night"—the noise of a table and two chairs, along with whatever else he'd added to the pile, being lifted or shoved aside would surely be enough to rouse him.

"You were awake the whole time?" she'd asked.

"The whole time," he concurred. "Who could get any sleep with you getting up, down, up, down? I figured you were testing me, and I guess I was right, but let me tell you, I was getting a little impatient there, waiting for you to finally make up your mind and do something. You'd sit up, and I'd think, okay, this time she's gonna really do it, and I'd kind of brace myself, although I had to make sure I kept my breathing nice and steady, so you'd think I was in la-la land. Prison teaches you things like that. You see, you can't ever really let your guard down in prison, so you kind of learn to sleep with one eye open." He'd shaken his head at the memory. "Anyway, I thought you did a pretty good job there, even though you never stood a chance. I thought it was kind of clever, the way you put on my T-shirt, so you wouldn't have to go running out the door buck naked, although I'd almost have paid to see that, I tell you. Pretty clever of me too, wouldn't you say, leaving my jeans hanging over the chair like that? Figured you couldn't resist looking for those keys. It might have been smarter to head straight for the door, although I gotta tell you, you'd have been dead before you'd even gotten the chain off. So it's probably a good thing for you, in **retrospect**," he said, putting the last word in invisible italics, "that you **did** choose to go through my pockets. Probably saved your life. That, and fainting, of course. You're awfully cute when you're unconscious." He'd tucked the covers around her chin, cuddled up beside her, allowed the blade of the knife to rest just behind her left ear. "Now I don't want to hear another word outta you until we're safely out of Ohio, or I'm gonna have to kill you." And then he'd smiled. As he was smiling now. "Okay," he was saying. "I can see you got a million questions, so I'm gonna be a nice guy and let you ask a couple. Go ahead—fire away."

He was wrong, Jamie thought. She didn't have a million questions. She had only one. "What is it you expect me to do?"

"Well, now, that's pretty much gonna depend on what Beth does. And right now, it looks like she's getting off this big old bus here."

Jamie watched as the two women from Mad River Road stepped onto the pavement in front of a relatively nondescript strip mall and made their way through the parking lot, Brad keeping her car a suitable distance behind. "What about your son?" she ventured.

"He's gotten so big, hasn't he?" Brad asked proudly, as if she would know. "Amazing how fast they grow, isn't it?" He pulled the car into a spot that afforded him a clear view of his former wife without being seen himself. "We're not gonna do anything about my son just yet," came his belated response. "Not until we take care of his mother."

"And then?" Jamie watched the two women as they paraded past the various storefronts, barely aware she'd asked another question until it was out of her mouth.

"And then—nothing. We get out of Dodge, wait for the authorities to contact me with the terrible news about my ex-wife's untimely death. And then Corey gets returned to his daddy. All nice and legal."

"But surely they'll suspect—"

"Hey, hey, hey. That's enough questions for one morning. You let me worry about the rest, okay?"

Jamie nodded. Did he really think the authorities were just going to hand a young boy over to a violent felon, regardless of the fact they were father and son?

"'Course it wouldn't hurt my case if I were married and settled down," Brad said with a wink. "You said you'd always wanted to see Texas, didn't you, Jamie-girl?"

Jamie sank down in her seat, beginning to suspect she was dead after all. Was it really possible she was receiving a proposal of marriage from a man who only hours before had come inches away from slitting her throat?

"Something to think about," Brad said, leaning against the steering wheel and watching as the two women disappeared inside Scully's gym.

"You're here awfully early," Jan exclaimed as Lily preceded Emma through the door.

Emma caught the look of uncertainty in Jan's heavily blue-shadowed eyes, as if the older woman was considering asking her name and whether she might be interested in taking out a membership. "It's Emma," she said before Jan had a chance to embarrass them both again.

"Of course you are," Jan said. "How are you? Did Jeff give you the mug?"

"He did." Had Jan noticed her trophy was missing? Did she suspect Emma might have taken it? Maybe she should confess right here and now, apologize profusely, beg Jan's forgiveness, try to explain. Except how did one explain the unexplainable? "Unfortunately, the mug is why I'm here," she said instead. "We had a slight accident."

"Her son thought the mug was so special," Lily took over, "he decided to take it to show-and-tell this morning, and on the way to school, he dropped it."

"Of course he did," Jan said, as if this were an inevitable fact of nature. "So you'd like another one?"

"I can bring it back later," Emma offered.

"Don't be silly." Jan reached behind the counter, handed Emma another mug. "Tell him to be more careful with this one."

"He'll guard it with his life."

"You'd better get going," Lily advised her.

"You're not coming?"

"I start work in an hour. No point going back and forth all morning. We'll talk later," she said as Emma reached for the door.

"Sure thing." Emma stepped outside, waving good-bye as she cut through the parking lot to the bus stop, relieved to be on her way. Was that another blue Thunderbird in the corner of the lot? she wondered as a bus pulled to a stop in front of her. She mounted the bus's steps, fumbling in her purse for the correct change. When she looked back, the blue car was no longer there and probably hadn't been there at all, she decided. She obviously had blue Thunderbirds on the brain.

"You're late," Dylan said when she located him in his classroom several minutes later. "You said ten minutes."

Emma apologized and handed her son the mug. He immediately disappeared inside his classroom without so much as a thank-you hug. She was almost halfway down the hall when a woman's voice stopped her.

"Excuse me," the voice called after her, a level of urgency echoing down the corridor. "Excuse me. Mrs. Frost?"

Emma turned around just as Dylan's alarmingly earnest teacher, Ms. Kensit, reached her side. Annabel Kensit was one of those people who always seemed to be moving. She had short, dark hair and small, dark eyes, and spending more than a few seconds in her company always made Emma nervous.

"I've been hoping for an opportunity to speak to you," the young woman was saying, shifting her weight from one foot to the other. She was approximately Emma's age but looked barely out of her teens. Emma wondered why everyone was suddenly so anxious to speak to her. Had Dylan's teacher been in Marshalls yesterday too? Was she here to demand an explanation?

"Is everything all right?" Emma asked warily.

"Everything's fine. It's just that we haven't talked in a while, and I'd been hoping to see you at the last parent-teacher meeting."

"Yes, I'm sorry about that. I wasn't feeling very well."

"I'm sorry to hear that." Ms. Kensit's small eyes flickered momentary concern. "I trust everything's all right now."

"Yes. Everything's fine."

"Good."

"Is there a problem?" Please don't let there be a problem, Emma prayed silently.

"Not really. I just thought there were some things we should discuss."

"Such as?"

"Well, Dylan's such a sweet little boy, but he gets himself so worked up about every little thing. Like this morning. He was so anxious when you were late."

She couldn't have this conversation now. She didn't have the time or the stamina. And while she was tired of all the lies, the sad reality was that she was even more terrified of the truth. The truth would do nothing but complicate things further, make matters that much worse. The prospect of confronting her demons and confessing her sins was simply too daunting. It was better, and certainly easier, to keeping running, keep hiding, keep pretending. The truth held too many consequences. And Emma had never been very good at consequences. Maybe, eventually, she'd find the courage to stop running, to be the woman she'd been chasing all these years, a woman who was unashamed of her past and confident of her future, a woman whose present was alive with possibilities, who didn't need exaggeration and embellishment to be proud of who she was. But for now she had to go home and pack her suitcase, finish what she should have finished last night. "I'm sorry, Ms. Kensit. This isn't a great time for me."

"Oh, dear. I'm sorry. Do you think you could spare a few minutes when you pick Dylan up this afternoon?"

"Absolutely. I'll see you then." Why not? Emma thought. She might as well book all the appointments she didn't intend to keep for the same time.

She saw the old blue Thunderbird as soon as she turned the corner onto Mad River Road. It was back in its former spot in front of Mrs. Discala's house, and as Emma drew closer she saw that there were two people sitting in the front seat. What were they doing here? Was it possible they'd been following her? Had they returned to stake out her house? Maybe they were undercover police officers, here at Jeff Dawson's request. Or worse. Maybe they were here because her whereabouts had been discovered. Maybe whoever was sitting in that car was here to take her son away.

Emma's antennae were on full alert as she

crossed the street, determined to distance herself from the people in that car as quickly as possible. But something about the way the woman in the passenger seat was sitting, slightly hunched over, her back pressed against the car door, as if she didn't want to be there, as if she wanted to be anywhere but there, made Emma pause and turn around, her curiosity getting the better of her. She approached the blue Thunderbird, knocked on the side window. "Excuse me," she began testily as the car window lowered. **Have you been following me? Is there some reason you're watching my house? Did my ex-husband send you?** "Is there something I can do for you?" she asked instead.

The woman passenger lifted blackened, swollen eyes toward Emma as the man in the driver's seat spun slowly around. "Yes," the man said, his cold smile freezing the breath in Emma's lungs. "I believe there is."

CHAPTER TWENTY-EIGHT

That's right," Lily was saying. "Only two hundred and fifty dollars to join, plus thirty dollars a month." She waited for Jan to chirp in with her reminder about the free mug and T-shirt, but Jan was strangely silent. Lily glanced toward the trophy cabinet, where Jan had been polishing her trophies for the better part of the last forty minutes. "Yes, well, we hope to see you soon. Don't forget this special offer expires at the end of the month, and includes a free T-shirt and mug." She replaced the receiver and smiled at Jan, waiting for a visual pat on the back, but none was forthcoming. "Something wrong?"

Jan said nothing. She was staring at the cabinet, as if something terrible had just happened. Or was about to.

"Jan?"

Jan stared at her with blank eyes. "Huh?"

"Something wrong? Jan?" Lily asked again when once again Jan failed to respond. "Is there a problem?"

"I'm not sure."

"I'm not following."

Jan looked from Lily to her trophy case and back. "One of my trophies is missing."

"Are you sure?"

"I've counted them ten times. There should be thirty here. There are only twenty-nine."

Lily strolled around the front of the desk, joined Jan at the cabinet, did a quick count of her own. "You're sure there were thirty?" Jan regularly told people she had so many she'd lost count.

"Very sure. Ten per shelf."

"Is it possible you took one home?"

"Why would I take one home?" Jan snapped, then quickly apologized. "Sorry. I know you're just trying to help."

"Which one is missing, do you know?"

"That's what I've been trying to figure out."

Lily scanned the three shelves laden with lovingly polished awards in various sizes and shapes. She could look at them all day and not know which one was missing, but she had no doubt that Jan would soon figure it out. Jan's trophies were her children, and she was obviously as protective of them as she was proud.

"It's not one of the bigger ones," Jan was saying. "I would have noticed one of the big ones missing right away. So, it has to be a smaller one, not a first-place finish, probably a dish or a bowl." Heavily shadowed eyes swept across the bottom shelf. "It's the brass bowl from my second-place finish at the Women's Bodybuilding Competition in Cincinnati, 2002!" she pronounced, pointing to the small bowl's former place of honor. "It always sat right here. Dammit. Where is it?"

"You're sure you didn't move it to another spot?" Lily asked the question, even though she already knew the answer. Jan hadn't moved the bowl anywhere. She was as obsessive about her trophies as she was about her daily exercise routine.

"It was right here. It's always right here. Do you think someone might have broken in last night and taken it?"

"Were there any signs of forced entry?" Lily asked, hearing Jeff's voice reflected in her question. She decided against asking the more obvious question: If somebody were going to go to all the effort and risk of breaking in, why would they take only a relatively worthless, second-place trophy?

"No. No signs of forced entry," Jan admitted. "And I had to unlock the cabinet, which means whoever took my trophy had to have a key. God, you don't think it was Art, do you?"

"What would your ex-husband want with one of your old trophies?"

"I don't know. Maybe he's trying to pull a **Gaslight** on me. You remember that old movie where Ingrid Bergman's husband is trying to make her think she's crazy."

Lily shook her head. "'Fraid not."

"You never saw **Gaslight**?" Jan looked almost as horrified as when she'd realized one of her trophies was missing.

"When was the last time you opened that cabinet?" Lily asked.

"The last time I was polishing. Last Monday, I guess."

"And you're positive all the trophies were there then?"

"Absolutely."

The phone rang. Lily returned to the counter and answered it. "Scully's gym. No, I'm sorry. You have the wrong number." Lily hung up the phone, deciding not to tell Jan the caller had asked for **Art** Scully's.

"Wait a minute," Jan said suddenly, long, orange fingernails piercing the air. "The phone."

"The phone?"

"My nephew called me. Your friend, Emma, was here. I was showing her my trophies when the phone rang."

Lily's stomach fell into her toes. "When was this?"

"Yesterday. I think she came in looking for you. I said you weren't here, and we talked for a few minutes, she asked me about my trophies, and I opened the cabinet so she could have a better look. And then Noah called, and I excused myself to talk to him, and she left."

"And you locked the cabinet after she was gone?"

"As soon as I got off the phone."

Lily looked toward the floor. Was it possible that Emma had stolen Jan's trophy in addition to the items she'd taken from Marshalls? But why? Why would she do something like that?

"You think your friend could have done this?" Jan asked, posing the first of Lily's questions out loud.

Lily no longer knew what to think. But she was damn well going to find out before three o'clock this afternoon. "Look, do you think you can manage for a little while without me?" she asked Jan.

"Where are you going?"

Lily pulled open the front door. "To get your trophy back."

What the hell was going on? Lily wondered as she raced for the bus stop, arriving just as a bus was pulling away from the curb. She ran after it for half a block but gave up when it became obvious the driver had no intention of either stopping or slowing down. She checked her watch, knowing there wouldn't be another bus for fifteen minutes, then deciding she could probably walk home faster than that. It was probably better this way anyway, she thought, taking a deep breath and deliberately slowing her pace. Walking would give her time to cool down, get her thoughts in order. It wouldn't do anybody any good if she were to go charging into Emma's in a fit of temper, accusations flying, explanations demanded. Hadn't she learned from bitter experience that confrontations were largely ineffective ways of blowing off steam, that they rarely benefited anyone? If she wanted answers, she was going to have to ask the right questions. If she wanted to understand those answers, she was going to have to phrase those questions very carefully indeed.

Lily tried imagining the scene she was about to walk into, as if she were constructing a story: Two young women meet and become friends. They visit each other's houses, babysit each other's children, share wine and confidences. And then one discovers the other has been lying to her about almost everything. In short, her friend is not what she seems. But what makes the story really interesting is that the same thing is true of herself.

Lily waited for the light at Stewart to change from red to green, then crossed, wondering how the story would play out.

"You're here early," Emma says, panic flashing through her huge, blue eyes. "I wasn't expecting you until later."

"This couldn't wait."

No, way too melodramatic. Try again.

"You're here early," Emma says, clearly flustered by her friend's unexpected appearance. "I wasn't expecting you till later."

"Something's happened."

Emma says nothing. She appears to be holding her breath. The two women stand facing each other in the middle of Emma's meagerly furnished living room.

"One of Jan's trophies is missing," Lily says, getting straight to the point.

"I don't understand."

"I think you do."

A long silence, then, "You think I took it?"

"Did you?"

"Of course not. How could you think such a thing?"

"Because you were there yesterday. You were admiring Jan's trophies. And now one of them is gone."

"You don't think it's possible Jan misplaced it?"

Lily shakes her head. "I might have, if it weren't for what happened at Marshalls. . . ."

"I told you that was all a big misunderstanding."

"Really? What is it I don't understand?"

"I'm not answering any more of these questions."

"I think you should."

"Yeah? Well, I thought we were friends."

"We are friends."

"It doesn't sound like it to me."

"Emma . . ."

"No. This conversation is over. I want you out of my house."

Oh, that's good, Lily thought. Really good. Start again. Different answers this time.

"One of Jan's trophies is missing," Lily says, getting straight to the point.

A long silence, then, "You think I took it?"

"Did you?"

"Yes," Emma says simply.

Much better.

"Why?"

Another silence. Clearly the answer to this question is not as simple as the first.

"Why did you take Jan's trophy?" Lily asked out loud. The clothes Emma had stolen from Marshalls, Lily could almost understand, if not justify. Emma had no money, no prospects. She was poor, she was depressed, she'd given in to temptation in a moment of weakness. But Jan's bodybuilding trophy?

What could she possibly want with that? Even were she to pawn it, it was doubtful she'd get more than a few dollars. So why bother? Especially when she knew Jan, knew she was Lily's employer as well as her friend. It was such a betrayal.

Was Emma's betrayal any worse than her own?

Lily stepped off the curb, into the path of a red Chrysler Sebring. The driver honked angrily, then threw his hands into the air. "Sorry," Lily mouthed, although the scowl on the man's face told her he was far from placated. Sorry about a lot of things, she thought.

If she was ever going to stop feeling sorry, she had to start telling the truth.

How could she expect people to be honest with her if she wasn't honest with them?

Lily's thoughts returned to the story unfolding in her head.

"You're here early," Emma says, standing aside to let Lily enter. "I wasn't expecting you until later."

"This couldn't wait."

"Look, if this is about what happened at Marshalls . . ."

"It isn't."

Emma regards her quizzically as Lily shakes her head no.

Could she do it? Could she really tell Emma everything?

"Do you think we could sit down?"

Emma leads Lily into her living room. She motions toward her brown sofa, waiting until Lily gets comfortable before occupying the seat beside her. "Are you going to tell me what this is all about?"

"I know you've been lying to me," Lily begins, trying to ease into her confession gradually. "I know you never modeled for Maybelline cosmetics. I know you never sold a story to *Cosmopolitan* magazine. I'm not even sure your name is Emma Frost."

"Hold on a second here," Emma interrupts, jumping to her feet. "Where do you come off—?"

"What you don't know is that I've been lying too."

"What? What are you talking about?"

"I'm not who you think I am."

No. Stop. Way too trite. You can do better than that.

"What? What are you talking about?" Emma demands.

Lily pats the seat beside her. "If you'll just sit back down. . . ."

"I don't want to sit down. What are you telling me here? That your name isn't Lily?"

"No, my name is Lily. That part's true."

"What part isn't?" Emma demands, her own duplicity temporarily on hold.

"Pretty much all of it."

"What!"

"Let me start at the beginning."

Dear God, Lily thought. Did she even know where the beginning was anymore?

Should she start with her happy childhood, temporarily shaken by her father's death from prostate cancer when she was twelve years old? Or with the brother who'd stepped in to fill his shoes, assuming the role of guardian and protector, although he was barely a year her senior? What about the normal rebellion of her teenage years, the girlfriends she'd made, the boys she'd dated? Was any of that relevant? Or should she start with her first encounter with the man who would change her life forever, their subsequent marriage, and Kenny's horrible death? Was there any way to condense the last five years, anything she could say that would make them more palatable, easier to comprehend?

"For starters, my marriage wasn't what you think it was," Lily begins.

"What was it?"

"A disaster. Like yours."

Was it possible? Lily wondered, continuing down the street, oblivious to her surroundings. Could both she and Emma have chosen the same kind of man? Was that what had drawn them to each other?

"What are you talking about? You were married to the perfect man."

"I was married to a monster."

"Tell me," Emma directs.

Except how could she explain?

It was too easy to say that everybody makes mistakes, although that simple statement was probably as close to the truth as anything. There was nothing in her background, nothing in the way she'd been raised, to predict disaster looming. She had wonderful parents, an older brother she worshipped, friends she adored. And then she'd met a man at a party and fallen head over heels in love. They dated; she got pregnant; they got married. And while her parents and friends had their misgivings, initially everyone had been willing to put those concerns aside, to give Lily's new husband the benefit of every doubt. Only her brother had remained steadfast in his distrust of the man behind the disarming smile.

Ultimately distrust had given way to disdain.

It was that disdain that had led inexorably to his death.

On the back of a motorcycle.

"You're losing me," Emma says impatiently, pacing back and forth across her

small expanse of living room. "I thought it was your husband who was killed in a motorcycle accident."

Lily shakes her head. "I lied. It wasn't my husband. It was my brother."

Her brother, Lily repeated to herself, wiping several involuntary tears from her eyes. Kenny had been less than a year older than she was, her twin in so many ways, closer to her than anyone on earth. And in a blind rage that could no longer be contained, he'd gone charging off on a misguided mission to avenge the latest batch of bruises covering his sister's arms and face, bruises she no longer had the strength or desire to dismiss with a reassuring wave of her hand: "Clumsy me, I slipped; I walked into a door; I tripped over one of Michael's toys." Not after a day filled with arguments and threats, a day where she'd finally worked up the courage to tell her husband she wanted a divorce, and his response had been to tell her he'd see her rot in hell first. And when day had turned into night, and his threats had turned into fists, and even those fists had failed to quash her newfound resolve to take her son and flee this travesty of a marriage, he'd thrown her to the floor and raped her, savagely and repeatedly, their son screaming all the while from the next room. And when he was through, he'd left her there, curled up in a fetal position on the cold tile, crying and bleeding. "You're not going anywhere," he'd said.

She'd waited until he was asleep before grabbing Michael and running to her mother's house. Kenny was there, and one look at her told him everything he needed to know. "Please, Kenny. Don't do anything crazy. He's not worth it," she'd begged. But Kenny was already storming out the door and climbing onto his motorcycle, racing into the rain-filled night.

Even now Lily could hear the sound of his squealing tires as they weaved through the Miami downpour. She felt the vibrations of the large bike as Kenny lost control on a slippery turn, and the motorcycle careened off the road into a giant palm tree. She heard her mother sobbing quietly beside her in the hospital room, her distraught voice reassuring her, over and over again, that the accident hadn't been her fault.

Lily knew her mother was right. Technically, she wasn't to blame for Kenny's rash decision to take off after her husband; she wasn't responsible for his decision not to wear a helmet, to speed through rain-slicked streets. Still, she'd been unwilling to let go of her guilt, because letting go of her guilt meant letting go of Kenny, and she hadn't been ready to give him up.

But it was time to stop allowing her past to control her present and dictate her future. It was time for a new beginning, Lily understood now, turning the corner onto Mad River Road.

She saw the blue Thunderbird almost immediately and thought she recalled seeing it there earlier. Somebody has a visitor, she thought, watching Carole McGowan exit her house with her two overweight schnauzers. Carole waved as the dogs pulled her toward Lily. "Hi," Lily greeted her neighbor, watching each dog stop to lift his leg at the side of the curb. "What are you doing home at this hour?"

"Mortimer was acting peculiar all weekend," Carole said. "So I took him to the vet's."

"Is he all right?"

"Perfect." She reached down to stroke Mortimer's back. "Turns out it's Casper here who has the problem." It was Casper's turn to have his ears scratched.

"What's the matter with Casper?" Lily asked absently, looking toward Emma's house.

"Turns out he swallowed a chicken bone. He's such a pig. Aren't you, Casper? You'll eat anything, won't you?" As if to illustrate her point, Casper began chomping on a few blades of nearby grass. "Honestly. You'd think we didn't feed him. Anyway, the vet said we were lucky the bone hadn't torn his stomach all to shreds. But he seems to be okay, and all's well that ends well. Isn't that what they say?"

"That's what they say," Lily agreed, sensing movement behind Emma's living room curtains.

"That Emma's really something, isn't she?"

Carole remarked, following the direction of Lily's gaze.

What was Carole talking about? Had Jan already phoned her, told her about her missing trophy? "What do you mean?"

"I mean she's a great addition to our club. She's smart, and she sure knows her stuff."

And what she doesn't know, Lily added silently, she makes up.

The dogs began straining on their leashes. "I guess I should let these guys finish their walk before I go to work."

Lily watched the woman until she and the dogs were out of sight. "All's well that ends well," she repeated under her breath, crossing the street and walking toward Emma's house.

Of course, not everything ended well. Certainly her marriage hadn't. Instead, her husband had made good on his threats to make her life a living hell if she left him, harassing her at work and calling her friends at all hours of the day and night. After several months, Lily's mother had suffered all she could take and moved to California to be closer to her sister. Lily had been all set to go with her, when a judge served her with an order forbidding her to remove Michael from the state until his custody had been determined by the courts. "Why are you doing this?" she'd demanded of her husband.

"Because he's my son." That was when he'd boasted about what happened to people who crossed him, told her about a certain appliance salesman in Miami he'd slaughtered with his bare hands.

"You have to go to the police with this," her friend Grace had urged.

"They won't believe me. I'm not even sure it really happened."

"You're sure."

"It's my word against his."

It turned out her word had been enough to get the ball rolling. In fairly short order, Ralph Fisher had been arrested and, because he was considered a flight risk, denied bail. Lily consulted a lawyer and had him served with divorce papers almost immediately. Then she'd resumed her maiden name, packed up her son, and headed north. Ralph was currently sitting in a Florida prison, awaiting trial. When the trial was over and Ralph had been safely put away for what Lily could only hope was the rest of his natural life, she'd join her mother in California. In the meantime, she'd decided it was better to keep a safe distance from those she loved. Just in case something went wrong, and he made good on some of his earlier threats. Her friend Grace had promised to keep her updated with regular e-mails, although Lily hadn't heard from her in several weeks. Maybe later she'd go over to the Internet Café and drop her a line.

But first things first, she decided, ringing Emma's doorbell and listening for the sound of approaching footsteps. For several seconds, there was no response, and Lily was about to ring again when she heard the familiar voice.

"Come on in," Emma called from the interior of the house.

Lily glanced over her shoulder at the empty blue Thunderbird, took a deep breath, pushed open the door, and stepped inside.

CHAPTER TWENTY-NINE

Jamie sat on the armrest of a beige-and-green chair, unable to move. She heard the front door open and close. In a matter of minutes, at least one woman would be dead, and more likely two. If I'm lucky, Jamie was thinking, he'll kill me too.

"Emma?" a woman called from the front hall. The house felt unnaturally still, as if it were holding its breath.

"I'm in the living room," Emma called back. Her voice sounded distant and strained, as if she were in another part of the house, and not sitting in the seat right beside Jamie.

"I'm sorry to barge in on you like this. I know I said I'd come by later." A pretty young woman with blond hair and anxious eyes appeared in the entranceway to the room. Brad had said his ex-wife's name was Beth, but Emma insisted her friend's name was Lily. "I hope I'm not catching you at a bad time."

Jamie saw the look of confusion settle quickly onto Lily's face as she scanned the room. She wondered if she had any sense of the danger lurking and tried to crawl inside Lily's head, to absorb the scene from her perspective: her friend, Emma, was sitting, ashen-faced and ramrod straight, in the chair at right angles to her sofa. A stranger was perched on the chair's armrest, her eyes blackened and her chin bruised, the bruises in sharp contrast to the beautiful gold-and-pearl earrings she was wearing.

"I'm sorry," Lily stammered. "I didn't realize you had company."

"That's all right," Emma said, although clearly, it was not.

"I'll come back later."

"No, don't go," Emma said, her voice a plea. "Please, come in."

"You're sure I'm not interrupting anything?"

"You aren't."

Jamie wondered if Emma was going to introduce them.

"I'm Lily," the woman said before Emma had a chance, offering her hand as she approached. "I live down the street."

"It's nice to meet you," Jamie responded, keeping her hands at her sides. "Lily, you said?"

"Well, actually, it's Lily-Beth," Lily elaborated. "I dropped the 'Beth' about a year ago. But in the interest of full disclosure—" She broke off, her cheeks blushing bright pink as she glanced toward Emma. "We can talk about that later. You are . . . ?" she asked, looking back at Jamie.

"Jamie. Jamie Kellogg."

"Kellogg?" Lily repeated, obviously more to fill the awkward silence than from any real interest. "Any relation to the cereal people?"

"No," Jamie responded, without shaking her head. It hurt too much to move.

"Sorry. You probably get asked that all the time."

"Not so much anymore," Jamie said. Were they really having this conversation?

Again Lily glanced at her friend.

Did she not notice how stiffly Emma was sitting? Jamie wondered. Did she not realize that her hands had remained motionless behind her back throughout their entire exchange? That a tight rope bound her hands together, digging into the soft flesh at her wrists?

If she did, Lily gave no such indication. "What about you guys?" she was asking. "Are you two related?"

Emma said nothing.

Lily slowly lowered herself to the edge of the brown sofa, her eyes falling on a small brass bowl lying carelessly on its side on the center cushion. "You **did** take it!" she exclaimed, spinning around suddenly toward Emma. "I don't believe you. How could you do this?"

"I'm so sorry," Emma stammered as tears filled her eyes.

"I don't understand. Why would you . . . ?" Her gaze shifted from Emma to Jamie. "What's going on here?"

Jamie held her breath. She felt a slight stir in the air, saw Brad push himself out of his hiding place in a corner of the dining room. He raised his fingers to his lips, warning her to be silent. Was there any way she could warn Lily? Was there any way she could atone, at least in part, for what had happened in Atlanta?

"Okay, clearly I'm interrupting something here," Lily was saying. "And I have to be back at work in a few minutes anyway, so"—she pushed herself to her feet as Brad ducked back into his hiding place—"I'll take this back to Jan, and we can talk later."

Neither Emma nor Jamie moved.

Lily walked to the entrance of the living room, hesitated, then stopped.

Don't stop, Jamie tried to warn her with her eyes. Run. Run as fast as you can.

Run for your life.

"Look, is something wrong?" Lily asked, unaware that Brad was now creeping toward her, that he was only inches from her back.

She had to do something, Jamie thought frantically. She had to warn her. She couldn't just sit here and let him murder another human being in cold blood. The way he'd murdered Laura Dennison. The way he'd murdered Grace Hastings. The way he'd murdered that appliance salesman from Philadelphia. The way he'd murdered God only knew who else.

"Going somewhere, Lily-Beth?" he asked.

Jamie watched the color drain from Lily's face. She understood that Lily didn't have to turn around to know who was there, that she didn't have to see Brad to know he was smiling. She watched Lily's eyes close, as if accepting her sad fate. Perhaps she'd known all along that someday he would find her. Perhaps she was relieved that day had finally come.

And then suddenly, Lily was spinning around, slamming the brass trophy into the side of Brad's head and using the confusion of the moment to throw herself toward the front door. Jamie tried to follow suit, but her legs refused to move. She watched helplessly as Brad, blood pouring from the fresh wound to his head, wrapped his arms around Lily's rib cage, like a deadly python, squeezing the breath from her lungs as he lifted her, kicking and gasping for air, and carried her back into the living room, where he tossed her to the floor at Jamie's feet.

"Okay, Emma-girl," he directed the whimpering young woman in the seat beside her, "you come over here to me while Jamie ties Beth's hands behind her back. And her feet too," he said, grabbing Emma's arm as she staggered toward him, and pressing the knife against her throat. "I'll gut her like a pig if you don't do exactly what I tell you," he warned Jamie.

Emma's complexion went from pale to ashen. A small cry escaped her lips. Lily didn't move as Jamie retrieved the rope hidden beneath the white stacking tables. She offered no resistance as Jamie tied her hands behind her, listening to Emma whimper as the blade danced across the veins in her neck.

"Make sure that's nice and secure," Brad warned.

Jamie finished tying Lily's wrists behind her back, then began securing her feet. Could she really be doing this? Could she be rendering another woman as helpless as she was? Two nights ago she'd waited in the car as Brad slaughtered a defenseless old woman. Today she'd graduated to the role of full-fledged accomplice. And it didn't matter that she had no real choice, that he would kill her if she didn't comply. The chances were good he'd kill her anyway. If not today, then tomorrow. Or the day after that.

Besides, there was always a choice.

And there were three of them, she reminded herself. Three of them and only one of him. Although even with those odds, Jamie knew it wouldn't be a fair fight. Three battered and terrified women were no match for one knife-wielding lunatic.

"Tie her feet too." Brad pushed Emma to the floor beside Lily. With her hands tied behind her back, Emma had nothing to break her fall, and she landed on her right shoulder, crying out in pain.

Jamie quickly began wrapping the rope around Emma's ankles.

"Ralph, please," Lily started.

"Name's Brad now," he corrected her.

"What?"

"You dropped the 'Beth,' " he said. "I added a 'Brad.' "

"This doesn't concern anyone but you and me," Lily told him. "There's no reason to involve anyone else."

"Looks to me like they're already involved."

"Ralph—"

"Brad," he corrected testily. "Don't make me have to tell you again." He kicked at her legs with his heavy black boots.

"Brad," Lily whispered, fighting back tears. "Please, let them go."

"Well, now, Lily-Beth. How am I supposed to do that?" He bent down, checked the tightness of the ropes binding the two women. "Jamie's here because she's my girlfriend. Sit down, Jamie-girl," he directed with a wink, and she promptly obeyed, balancing on the arm of the beige-and-green chair, where she'd perched earlier. "And your friend, Emma, well, she's here because she's a big old snoop who butted her nose in where it didn't belong, so I guess it's true what they say about curiosity killing the cat."

"Oh, God," Emma cried.

"You don't have to hurt her, Brad. I'm the one you want."

"That's true, I guess." For a few seconds, he seemed to be mulling it over. "But how can I let her go when you know as well as I do that she's gonna run straight to the cops?"

"No," Emma protested. "I won't. I swear."

"Swear all you like, sweetheart. I can't let you leave."

"Please, Ralph . . . Brad," Lily corrected immediately, although it was too late to stop the pointed toe of his boot from connecting with her shin. "She has a son."

"Yeah, I saw him this morning." Brad knelt down beside Emma, his knees cracking inside the denim of his jeans. "Cute kid. Not as cute as Corey, of course. Corey's **my** son. 'Course you probably call him Michael. That was Lily-Beth's name for him. Insisted we name him after her father. Very important to her. So, nice guy that I am, I said okay. Michael Corey Fisher, we called him, although I always preferred Corey myself. Just like I always preferred Beth. But then, we never agreed on much, did we, darlin'?" he asked Lily.

"Please," Emma whimpered. "I don't know who you are or what you're talking about."

"No? She didn't tell you about me?"

Emma shook her head.

"Well, that wasn't very nice," Brad said. "Not to tell anybody about the love of your life, the father of your son. I'm feeling kind of hurt." He stood back up, paced back and forth, as if deeply upset.

Jamie knew what he was doing. He was playing with them, the way a cat plays with a mouse before going in for the kill. Tormenting them was almost as much fun as killing them, Jamie understood. She glanced at Lily, knowing she was thinking exactly the same thing. If only she had a little of that woman's courage. If only she had the strength to fight back.

But he'd robbed her of that strength when he raped her, then pummeled her spirit into submission the next night with his fists. Not so fearless now, was she? Even without ropes, she was as bound and shackled as the women on the floor beside her.

"So, what's **your** story?" Brad asked Emma. "We didn't get much of a chance to talk before Beth here came calling. What's your son's name?"

"Dylan," Emma whispered.

"And Dylan's father? What's he do?"

Emma paused a split second too long. "He's a policeman."

"A policeman?" Brad repeated, with a mischievous grin.

"You should go. He comes home around this time every day for coffee."

"Really? Well, I guess, in that case, I better hurry up and slit your throat." Brad instantly dropped to his knees, grabbing a fistful of Emma's hair as Emma began to scream. Jamie closed her eyes and buried her face in her hands. "Shut up," he barked at Emma. "And don't lie to me. I hate it when women lie. Although I guess I should be used to it by now."

"I won't lie," Emma whimpered.

"I mean, you think I'm stupid here? Is that it? You don't remember me checking this place out when I first got here? I've been upstairs, Emma-girl. I've seen your closets. I know there's no man living here. Shit, what kind of moron do you think I am?"

"I don't think you're a moron."

"Well, now, that's good to hear. You keep talking nice like that, and I might not kill you after all."

"Please don't kill me," Emma begged.

"Jamie," Brad barked. "Get your hands away from your face."

Immediately Jamie lowered her hands to her sides.

"See what a good girl she is?" Brad crowed as a wave of shame flushed over Jamie. "Now suppose you tell me where Dylan's father really is," he instructed Emma. "And don't lie to me, because I'll know the minute you start, even if it's only a tiny little white one, and I'll stick this knife in your heart without so much as a 'tsk-tsk.' Are we very clear about that?"

Emma nodded, although his hand in her hair afforded her little room for movement. “I won’t lie,” she promised a second time.

Jamie saw Lily lean forward, almost in spite of herself.

“So, where’s your old man?”

“He’s in San Diego.”

“How long you been divorced?”

Emma hesitated.

“You’re not thinking of lying now, are you?” Brad poked the blade of the knife against her Adam’s apple.

“Almost two years,” Emma said quickly.

“And what’s this guy’s name?”

“Peter,” Emma replied. “Peter Rice.”

“And what’s Peter Rice do for a living? I know for sure he ain’t no cop.”

“He’s a salesman. Computers, software, that kind of thing.”

“No kidding.” Brad laughed out loud. “I had a computer business once. Didn’t I, Jamie?”

Jamie stared at the floor, said nothing.

“So what made you leave San Diego and Mr. Peter Rice?”

"I had no choice."

"And why is that?"

"Because he was going to take my son away from me."

"That would be Dylan?"

Again Emma hesitated. "Martin," she whispered after a pause. "His name is Martin."

Brad laughed. "Well, what do you know? You think there's anybody on Mad River Road who goes by their real name?" He lowered himself to the floor beside Jamie, leaned his back against the beige-and-green chair. "Come on down here, Jamie-girl," he directed, pulling on her arm and dragging her down. "Join the party. We're gonna learn everybody's secrets here."

Jamie knew Brad didn't have the slightest interest in Emma or her secrets. She knew he was only playing with all of them, prolonging his enjoyment by prolonging their suffering. Brad would keep them alive only as long as they continued to amuse him. Then he would slaughter them one by one.

"So, what you're saying is that instead of letting him take your son away from you, **you** took his son away from **him,**" Brad said. "That doesn't sound too fair to me. Tell me, Emma. Was Peter Rice a bad father?"

Emma shook her head. "He was a good father," she acknowledged. "That wasn't the point."

"Really? What was?"

"The point was I thought my son was better off with me."

"Is that what the courts thought?"

"No. They sided with Peter."

"They awarded him custody? That's kind of unusual, isn't it? The courts granting the father custody? Why'd they do that?"

Emma closed her eyes. When she opened them again seconds later, they were filled with tears.

"Tell the truth now, Emma. Were you an unfit mother?"

"I'm a very good mother," Emma insisted, looking to Lily for confirmation. "But I've done things, things I'm not proud of . . ."

"What kind of things?"

"Please . . ."

"Don't get coy on us now," Brad warned. "This is just starting to get interesting. What kind of things?" Brad let go of Emma's hair. Her head snapped toward her chest in defeat.

"I've stolen, and I've lied."

"Well, well, well. So you're a thief and a liar, are you?"

"Yes," Emma said clearly. "I'm a liar." She turned toward Lily. "I lied to you. About my past. About my ex-husband . . ."

"You don't owe me any explanations."

"Yes, I do. I owe you. And I owe Peter. And most of all, I owe my son."

"Hey, don't forget about me," Brad said with a laugh.

"Peter wasn't the monster I've made him out to be," Emma continued, unprompted. "He didn't cheat on me. He wasn't a pervert. He's a good man, and I'm so sorry I inflicted all this pain on him. He was just this basically decent guy who got in way over his head. He tried to understand why I did the things I did, why I lied when it was just as easy to tell the truth. I didn't have any answers for him. What could I say? Why would he believe anything I said? After a while, he just gave up, said he couldn't take the drama anymore, that he wanted a divorce, and that he thought Martin would be better off with him. I knew he was right. I knew I didn't stand a chance in court, but I just couldn't let him have my son. He's the only decent thing I've ever done with my life." She took a deep breath, released it slowly. "I love my son so much. You know that, don't you?"

"I know that," Lily whispered.

"You sure pick some peculiar friends, Lily-Beth," Brad said. "Although I gotta admit, I like this one better than old Gracie-girl."

Lily's mouth fell open. Her eyes grew wide. "Grace?"

"Yeah. Did I forget to mention I paid her a little visit last week?"

"What did you do to her?" Tears immediately filled Lily's eyes.

"Well, I wouldn't waste a lot of tears on old Gracie-girl. She's the one who gave you up, told me where to find you."

"What did you do to her, Ralph?"

"Brad," he reminded her.

"You killed her, didn't you?"

"Well, I have to admit the last time I saw her, she **did** look pretty dead." Brad laughed as if he'd just told the funniest joke in the world. "God, I'm having a good time. How about you, ladies?"

"Please," Emma pleaded. "Just let me go. I swear I won't tell anyone."

Instantly Brad's hand shot from his side. Without even looking in her direction, he plunged the knife deep into Emma's chest. Emma's eyes widened as a cry of disbelief escaped her lips. "Tsk-tsk," Brad said as he pulled out the knife. "Didn't I warn you about lying to me?"

Jamie stared in disbelief at the blood that rushed from Emma's chest, soaking the front of her pretty yellow blouse. The slaughter was starting, she realized. First Emma, then Lily, then herself. And if Brad didn't kill her, if he chose to kill the others and let her live, would she be able to live with herself?

When are you going to start accepting responsibility for your actions? she heard her mother and sister demand in unison.

Had they been right about her all along?

And suddenly the room filled with the sound of screaming as Jamie threw herself at Brad, jumping on his back and ripping at his eyes with her furious fingers. Brad spun around in an effort to dislodge her, but she held firm, even when he began blindly slashing at her arms with the already bloodied knife.

"Goddamn it," he shouted, stumbling over Emma's legs as Lily's bound feet shot toward him, catching him around the ankles and sending him sprawling across the room, the knife flying from his fist into the foyer. Jamie leapfrogged over him, lunging for the knife. But even now Brad moved with alarming speed, his hands latching onto the slightly flared bottoms of Jamie's jeans just as her fingers found the switchblade's carved wooden handle.

"No!" Jamie screamed as he reeled her along

the floor toward him, her fingers losing contact with the knife.

"You really are a feisty little thing, aren't you?" He laughed as he flipped her onto her back, his fingers lacing around her throat. "I'm sure gonna miss you, Jamie-girl."

Jamie felt a rush of air, saw Lily throw herself at Brad, landing on his back with a thud strong enough to knock the wind from his lungs. In the second it took for him to regroup and shrug Lily off his shoulders, Jamie was sliding out from under him, her eyes frantically searching the floor for the knife. She found it just as Brad was reaching for her again, and she clambered to her feet, Brad right behind her. Before she could get to the door, he was spinning her around, his hands once again reaching for her throat. "You ready to die, Jamie-girl?" he was asking.

There was a flicker of movement, a sudden flash of metal. Jamie didn't see the knife as it slid between Brad's ribs; she saw only the surprised look on his face as he crumpled to his knees in front of her. She watched as, seconds later, his eyes rolled back in his head, and he fell backward to the floor, the handle of the knife protruding from the vicinity of his heart.

She raced to the phone, punched in 9-1-1, hollered for an ambulance. Then she untied Lily's arms and legs. Both women rushed to Emma's side, Lily cradling the semiconscious woman in her arms.

"You're going to be all right," Jamie assured her, trying to stanch the flow of blood with her fist. "Do you hear me, Emma? You hang on. You're gonna be all right."

Emma stretched her head toward Lily's, strained to speak. "Tell my son I love him," she said.

Emma's ashen face and transferring her limp and bloodied body onto a stretcher.

"Can't say the same for this one," a second paramedic said, looking down at Brad.

The echo of the siren's wail still filled Jamie's ears, although it had been at least an hour since the ambulance left Mad River Road.

The police had arrived within minutes of her frantic call to 9-1-1. Almost immediately after that, another officer had rushed into the room, followed by a woman in a belly-baring, gray sweat suit. "Where's Lily?" the woman was shouting as an officer quickly dragged her from the house. "Lily, are you all right? Jeff, do something."

The officer named Jeff had assured her he'd call her later and that Lily was indeed okay. Jamie looked over to where Lily sat now, on the brown sofa, crying softly in Jeff's arms. Clearly, this was more than a professional relationship. It was a small room. Jamie didn't have to strain very hard to overhear their conversation.

"We located Peter Rice," she heard Jeff say.

CHAPTER THIRTY

Jamie sat on the beige-and-green chair, tears streaming down her cheeks. She made no effort to wipe them away or push them aside, although occasionally the woman officer standing beside her reached down to dab at her cheeks with a tissue, and someone always seemed to be inquiring if she was all right. How can I be all right? she asked them without speaking. I killed a man. A woman in Atlanta is dead because of me. Another woman might not survive her injuries, although the paramedics seemed hopeful that Emma would recover from her wound.

"She's still breathing," Jamie recalled someone shouting as the ambulance crew jumped into action, securing an oxygen mask around

"He confirmed that his ex-wife kidnapped their son almost two years ago when the court granted him custody, says he's been searching for them ever since. Her real name is Susan, by the way."

Lily shook her head. "She doesn't seem like a Susan."

Jamie smiled sadly. People are so rarely what they seem, she thought.

"Anyway, he's flying out here on the next plane."

"That's good." Lily rubbed the wrist of one hand with the fingers of the other. There were still red lines on her skin where the ropes had been. "You know that Emma isn't the only person who's been lying," she told Jeff. "There's so much I have to tell you."

"You don't have to tell me now."

Lily's smile was full of gratitude. "Can I tell you later?"

"I'm not going anywhere."

Lily reached over to stroke his hand. "How did you know to come over?"

"I went by the gym for my workout. Jan

told me about that stupid trophy, and how you'd taken off and hadn't come back. She was worried, and frankly so was I, so we decided to drop by, see what was up. We saw the police cars and the ambulance as soon as we turned the corner. My heart just about fell to my knees," he confessed.

Jamie smiled as Lily lay her head against Jeff's shoulder. She was thinking that Jeff Dawson was a nice man. Lily had found herself a good one.

"So, how're you doing?" the woman officer asked Jamie. Jamie wasn't sure, but she thought the ebony-skinned woman had introduced herself earlier as Angela Pauley. Officer Pauley looked to be about ten years Jamie's senior and was maybe twenty pounds heavier.

Jamie shrugged. What could she say? She had no idea how she was doing. One minute, she'd been sitting on the floor, quietly preparing to accept whatever sad fate awaited her, and the next minute, she was on her feet and fighting for her life. "You ready to die, Jamie-